"Iriset," Her Glory says. "Come."

If not for the null wires, Iriset would feel a draw of falling force, a pull to Her Glory, but she continues to hesitate. There's a trap here, and if she doesn't find its edges she'll walk straight into its heart. She sifts through her memory for anything she's heard about Her Glory, but only comes up with a few tidbits: barely a year younger than her brother, known to be grand in generosity and all manner of appetite, a tastemaker since she was a child, fond of wearing her hair down and as little jewelry as possible in favor of skin paint and intricate, loose robes. She's said to be a fitting mistress for the Moon-Eater, being as extravagant as the goddess Aharté is simple.

Imagine what Her Glory would want if she realizes Iriset is Silk. Can Iriset use that? Can she accept this as the Little Cat's daughter, but enter the palace as his pet apostate? Is it worth the risk?

Iriset knows what her father would say.

This is a chance out of here, this prison wherein she can do nothing. In the palace, though there will be great danger, there also will be great opportunity.

"Yes," Iriset says to the most powerful woman in the empire.

The Moon Heresies: Book One

TESSA GRATTON

orbitbooks.net

This book is a work of fiction. Names, characters, places, and incidents are the product of the author's imagination or are used fictitiously. Any resemblance to actual events, locales, or persons, living or dead, is coincidental.

Copyright © 2025 by Tessa Gratton
Excerpt from *Six Wild Crowns* copyright © 2025 by Holly Race

Cover design by Stephanie A. Hess
Cover illustration by Eleonor Piteira
Cover copyright © 2025 by Hachette Book Group, Inc.
Map by Tim Paul
Author photograph by Natalie C. Parker

Hachette Book Group supports the right to free expression and the value of copyright. The purpose of copyright is to encourage writers and artists to produce the creative works that enrich our culture.

The scanning, uploading, and distribution of this book without permission is a theft of the author's intellectual property. If you would like permission to use material from the book (other than for review purposes), please contact permissions@hbgusa.com. Thank you for your support of the author's rights.

Orbit
Hachette Book Group
1290 Avenue of the Americas
New York, NY 10104
orbitbooks.net

First Edition: June 2025

Orbit is an imprint of Hachette Book Group.
The Orbit name and logo are registered trademarks of Little, Brown Book Group Limited.

The publisher is not responsible for websites (or their content) that are not owned by the publisher.

The Hachette Speakers Bureau provides a wide range of authors for speaking events. To find out more, go to hachettespeakersbureau.com or email HachetteSpeakers@hbgusa.com.

Orbit books may be purchased in bulk for business, educational, or promotional use. For information, please contact your local bookseller or the Hachette Book Group Special Markets Department at special.markets@hbgusa.com.

Library of Congress Control Number: 2025932663

ISBNs: 9780316578790 (trade paperback), 9780316578806 (ebook)

Printed in the United States of America

LSC-C

Printing 1, 2025

To everyone who remembers what radicalized them

FALLING

Without Silence, there is nothing to break.
—Word of Aharté

Strand of silk

High above the sharp-edged palace of the Vertex Seal, the moon hangs motionless.

And far beneath it, a young god struggles.

———— • ♦ • ————

There is a line in the sister works *Word of Aharté* and *Writings of the Holy Syr* that has been debated for nearly all the centuries since the two pamphlets were published. In *Word of Aharté*, the line reads: "My empire will fall on a strand of spider silk." In *Writings*, the line is: "Can an empire trip and fall on a mere strand of silk?" The prophetic tone of the former stands out in the otherwise practical *Word*, while the irreverent humor of the latter is typical of *Writings*. What strikes scholar-priests most deeply is that both Aharté and the Holy Syr would comment so specifically on the same thing, but as if they disagreed on those very specifics.

It is not a translation issue, for both works were composed in pure mirané—the first known examples, in fact. Perhaps it is a conversation between the goddess and her wife that they continued in the pages. Though the Holy Syr explained so many of Aharté's laws to us in her *Writings*, we are supposed to put faith in the goddess's word over that of her wife, given that she is a goddess. But you know it is not spider silk that brings down the Vertex Seal.

An alarum trembles through the glazed-brick walls of the hidden fortress of Isidor the Little Cat, but his daughter, Iriset mé Isidor, does not hear it.

Tucked down against the geometric tiles in her workshop, she carefully lifts her crystal stylus, drawing a line of force up from her planning vellum into the air. She holds her breath as she completes the connection of this corner line to the seventh squinch supporting the dome of the spell.

A prodigy at architectural design, she discovered by the age of thirteen how to disrupt the threads of force humming through the walls without the use of null wires, creating a workspace devoid of interference. It is convenient when building an intricate scale diagram for a new invention—much less so when under attack from soldiers of the Vertex Seal.

The delicate dome she's building vibrates with ecstatic force, signaling she's completed the internal structure correctly. Iriset releases her breath and smiles smugly, leaning back onto her bare heels. Sweat drips down her spine to the loincloth she wears to work; she prefers as much of her skin open to the air as possible, in order to feel the slightest change in the forces around her. The nape of her neck, inner wrists, and small of her back are particularly sensitive, and so, she's recently discovered, are her lips. Her mask is folded beside her knee, along with her red robe, jacket wrap, and pantaloons.

The design diagram is beautiful.

Exquisite lines of shimmering silver architecture display the plan for a low, wide dome built of all four forces—rising, falling, ecstatic, and flow—that are the basic elements of her craft. The dome is meant to be settled over a small-scale model of Moonshadow City, and when connected to the Holy Design via illegal interface, it will reveal the places where architecture has shifted or changed since last the dome was applied, and therefore reveal where new security measures are set to capture her father.

Just in time for his birthday.

The door to her study jerks open. Hard alarum threads sweep inside, buzzing along the tile floor. Iriset shrieks and reaches out, trying to capture the alarm before it hits the first edge of the diagram, but her bare hands can't grasp the threads. "Bittor!" she snaps as the structure collapses in upon itself, dome wavering first, then unraveling. "You always knock when I'm working! You know that! You…"

Her gaze meets the dilated cat-eyes of the man panting in the arched doorframe. There is blood on his face, and blood on his unsheathed sword.

The hairs on Iriset's arms and neck and small of her back rise: the alarum! Now that the study is breached, she hears pounding chaos from the stairway beyond Bittor. A shock of fear freezes her in place on hands and knees.

Bittor charges inside. "Give me your silk glove," he orders. In his left hand is a burning candle.

Iriset grabs her red robe and throws it over her head, then shoves her arms through the tight sleeves. Bittor never commands her! He has no right. "Why? What's happened?"

Instead of answering, he stalks directly to the north curve of her study wall and puts the candle flame to the lowest of the layered orb webs.

The spiderwebs catch in a flash, curling in on themselves and drifting suddenly unattached from the white tile walls. She sees the fat-bottomed spiders scurrying for safety, but Bittor is faster, smashing them with the butt of his sword.

"What are you doing? Leave them alone!" Iriset yells.

"Your silk glove, now," Bittor says, sparing her a fast glance before putting the flame to a cluster of scrolls and half-sketched diagrams piled upon a kneeler. "And put on the rest of your clothes! Get two floors up to the blue landing. The army has taken your father, and you cannot be found in here with the designs. Is your spider mask here?"

"Father..." she says, slowed down by the crisp smell of her work turning to ashes. Rising force fills the air, stifled by tarnishing smoke. A scream sounds outside the room, and a huge tremor shakes the tower. Iriset leaps for her low desk and grabs up the glove woven of spiderwebs and the finest worm silk. She clutches it to her chest, nails digging too roughly into the delicate material. It's her greatest invention, and Bittor is setting her work on fire. Grief grabs at her when she looks at the smears on the wall: everything left of her poor spiders. They had *names*.

Bittor says, "Give it to me and go, Iriset." He sweeps everything off her desk, kicks a floor pillow and raggedy braided rug into the pile, and drops the candle into it all. A smolder begins immediately.

Iriset stares at the disaster blossoming around her. There in the pile, knocked off her desk, is the glinting black spider mask. Fire reflects wildly the facets of the lower eyes. It won't get hot enough to crack the chips of smoky quartz, but the glue will melt.

"Isidor said I should tell you, 'Sign Amakis,'" Bittor says.

The code is a slap across her mouth. It's her mother's name, and by invoking it, Isidor invokes the bond Iriset swore when she turned seventeen, in order to remain in his court as an adult. She swore to protect herself above all else.

Bittor steps close and takes the silk glove. Then he kisses her. Surprise opens her mouth under his, and she gasps at his lips. Bittor rarely instigates. Quickly she puts her hands to his jaw and kisses back. It might be the last time, if the day doesn't go well for them.

Though in the Little Cat's court it is known they are friends, if not that they are lovers, outside Iriset and Bittor could easily be mistaken for born family: Both are colored like dark desert peaches, with pink lips and the square jaw of the Lapis Osahar dynasties. While her eyes are sandglass brown, Bittor has rare cat-eyes, with slit pupils and vivid sea-green-blue irises filling most of the space between his lids. Hundreds of years ago apostatical human architects designed the eyes for one of Bittor's ancestors, and unlike most apostasy, this manipulation bred true through generations, popping up here and there. The Silent priests determined the children are at no fault for the apostasy of their ancestors and are thus allowed to live. But Bittor's gaze is disconcerting to say the least. He doesn't mind, as his eyes give him a boost as a night-thief and escape artist. Iriset has tried to examine them with her stylus when he is most relaxed, postcoital. Bittor says it's one thing for her to seduce him in order to study his masculine-presenting body and how the four forces interplay within him during sex; it's quite another for her to act like she's eager to dissect him.

Bittor pushes away. He stares at her, pupils narrowing to slits as the fire grows behind her. "When they take you," he orders, "make sure everyone knows you are the daughter of Isidor the Little Cat, and you won't be harmed. Not by the Vertex Seal, not by your fellow prisoners."

Iriset sets her teeth. Bittor is the Little Cat's escape artist: He'll have a way out. "Why can't I go with you?"

"That isn't his command," Bittor says simply.

Nobody will go against her father except her. She says, "They have my father already?"

Bittor nods, and frowns beneath his thin beard. His voice is low as he says, "There is nothing you can do, and you can't get down to the street. They are below us, on nearly every level, surrounding the whole Saltbath precinct, and brought with them investigator-designers who drove hard falling forces down through the streets in case we had tunnels. They *knew*, Iriset." Darkness colors his cheeks and he bares his teeth helplessly.

"Someone betrayed us," she says calmly. Too calmly.

Bittor ignores it. "Do not let them think you know what you know of design."

"I know what I am bound to protect," Iriset says. Herself. She's not allowed to protect her father or Bittor, nor any of the cousins of the court. She must prioritize her own life, not claim her mask-name. She must allow fire to strip away all the evidence of her discoveries. Rising force inside Iriset lifts painfully, a yearning pressure.

Bittor kisses her again, and then pushes her toward the door. "Go, Iriset."

Iriset snatches her clothes and red silk mask off the floor and obeys.

The air outside the study is cool with morning breezes from the windcatchers carved into every level of the tower, but that wind brings sounds of battle and desperation: steel clashing and cries of pain, the shaking of stone and ecstatic force. Iriset dashes to the wide spiral stairs up and up along the outer edge of the tower. Her bare toes hardly touch the limestone bricks, and her fingers skim along the smooth white stucco walls, until she spills up into the blue landing.

Untouched yet with violence, the landing is a small sitting area with two levels: one of perfect mosaic tiles in the shapes of blue gentians, the second layered with rugs and pillows in every shade of blue beside a huge lattice window spanning nearly half the entire curved wall. The glittering lattice snakes that usually wind through the cutouts, soaking in sunlight, are nowhere to be seen. Hiding, she hopes, sparing another brief thought for her poor dead spiders.

Iriset sits hard on the second level and pulls on her pantaloons, knotting them around her waist under her robe, and adjusts the laces at her ankles. She shoves her arms into the short jacket and ties it under her breasts, but loosely in case she needs to run or scream or fight. Finally, she pins the red silk mask to her hair, tucking it up so that a quick tug will let it fall over her eyes.

By now Iriset hears voices just below, methodical and ordered: soldiers searching the levels of the tower.

She stands. Through the soles of her feet she feels the tower's architecture trip and startle. Fear disrupts her body's design, an influx of ecstatic energy. She's unused to being afraid under either name she's used: Safe as Isidor's daughter, coddled by murderers and thieves. Safe as Silk, too, thanks to her own skills and the Little Cat's favor. Now Iriset needs to balance her inner design for calm. Fear serves nothing once its warning is made.

Hard boots clomp up the stairs to the landing.

She is Iriset mé Isidor, and even in his absence she will make her father proud.

Her father, so tough and sly he rules the Moonshadow City undermarket. He is slight and wiry, hardly larger than her, yet he commands respect through his reputation and deeds. He would not give Iriset sympathy, were he here, but snap at her to lift her chin and face the consequences of their choices with eyes clear. Wear her mask demurely, be what he needs her to be in that moment—a daughter sheltered and no threat to the empire. Keep her criminal identity secret. Survive what comes next so that she can make better, slyer choices in the future.

Just as the first soldier's head appears in the well, Iriset jerks the red edge of her mask down. It brushes her nose and falls just to her lips.

The world turns hazy red as she peers through the thin silk.

The soldier's own cloth mask wraps tight around their hair and face, leaving only a slit for their eyes, a blatant white that continues down in a uniform of lacquered armor over a short white robe and pants and thick boots: all clearly displaying the crimson splatter of their work. Their short sword is dark with smears of it. Behind them come more soldiers, identical in uniform and size, who stop around Iriset in a half ring. One says, in an impatient fem-forward voice, "Who are you, girl?" The speaker's eyes are black, the slit of skin visible a darker brown than her companions'. None are the mirané brown of Moonshadow's ruling ethnicity.

"Iriset mé Isidor," she says boldly.

"The Little Cat has a *daughter*?" one of the other soldiers says. Iriset doesn't move.

The woman soldier darts a hand out and Iriset recoils, expecting a slap, but the woman only rips the mask off her face.

Anger flushes rising force up her spine, and Iriset struggles not to show it. If this woman will not give her the little respect of the mask, what else might be taken from her?

"Get her out of here," the commanding soldier says, and her soldiers obey with grabbing, hard hands, dragging Iriset down the spiral stairs.

———— • ♦ • ————

This is what Iriset does not know about the attack on the Little Cat's tower: The city army of the Vertex Seal has been targeting her specifically for over a year. Or rather, targeting *Silk*.

Rumors of Silk's existence have filtered through the gossip of the small kings of the Holy City for nearly seven years now. She is said to be a prodigy at design who invented a wondrous—and proprietary—material called craftsilk that every architect in Moonshadow would like to get their hands on. But Silk doesn't share. She works exclusively for the Little Cat, and rumors accuse her of everything from creating design nets for cheating at cards to illegal human architecture that can disguise the features of Isidor's thieves and spies so they can slip into the halls of power or infiltrate a rival's bank. Some say Silk can cause a heart attack with a kiss of ecstatic force, others that she merely helps the Little Cat toy with his prey, using tricks of flow to keep a rival awake for questioning or wearing a mask of a Seal attendant's face to whisper here and there, shifting the tides of scandal. Perhaps she is a rumor only, or an amalgam of several talented designers in the Little Cat's employ. The latter opinion held the most favor for a while, until Silk herself began publishing brief, passionate papers that edged extremely near a pro-human-architecture stance. In the third paper she directly refuted the rumors she was several people.

But the city army has little evidence of anything other than that Silk is a woman. All they *know* is that since her appearance, the Little Cat has grown bolder in sending out his disciples. They scale towers like rock skinks and paint his graffiti for all to see, smuggle goods through blockades held by the city army, and hijack force-ribbons in order to stop traffic, jamming the schedules of the richest folk in Moonshadow for whatever no-doubt nefarious reason. And they never get caught. They leave only evidence they intend to leave.

Under the leadership of the Little Cat and his pet apostate, the undermarket has thrived.

While the Little Cat keeps his people to thieving, gambling, and smuggling, the occasional venture into fixing scandals or tugging small kings' political strings—oh, and a few memorable murders—the recent growth has made many in the army concerned about how easy it would be for Isidor's organization to turn to outright rebellion. And the Vertex Seal is always deeply concerned with rebellion.

Two years ago, apprehending Silk and her benefactor, Isidor the Little Cat, was declared a priority by the mirané council, with the backing of the Vertex Seal, Lyric méra Esmail His Glory. But for internecine mirané council reasons, the army has been denied their request for access to investigator-designers from the Great Schools of Architecture. Then some enterprising commander suggested they stop arguing for access based upon the crimes the Little Cat had been accused of—for what are such atrocities as murder and thieving to the Vertex Seal, which expands its imperial grip in ever-increasing waves through much the same? Lyric, however, is known for his piety and devotion to She Who Loves Silence, and so might not apostasy be an easier argument to make? Surely Lyric could be convinced of the likelihood that Silk had broken the goddess's proscription against engaging in human architecture, not merely written of it. Apostasy, not atrocity, would spur him to action.

It worked. The zealous can be quite predictable.

No offense.

So the city army, the small kings who rule the various precincts of the city, and the Great Schools of Architecture bound themselves together in the chase. (The Great Schools argued for Silk to be taken alive, for their magisters are desperate with envy that an unknown, anonymous designer had learned to fashion the forces of architectural design into spells as fine as spider gossamer, when they themselves could not even *replicate* such workings. Ha!) This was an unheard-of alliance hunting Silk and the Little Cat, but an initially unsuccessful one, for the criminals slipped again and again through the army's fingers.

Until a young designer with just the right combination of curiosity and ambition set ans mind to tracing Silk through less obvious means. Raia mér Omorose is just twenty-two and from a Pir-pale family of little means to buy ans way into a Great School or bribe any of the ranking designers to apprentice an directly. So Raia relied on ans wits and determination and no small skills at design to find other ways of promotion.

An charmed ans way into the possession of a scrap of a thin scarf Silk had created apparently to wrap around a thief's face and work as a half-mask that would add a birthmark or beard to their jaw. It was, as suspected, dangerously close to human architecture. But it only hid the face of the person wearing it; no alteration took place. Carefully dissecting the threads of force—mostly flow for flexibility and ecstatic for the amazing adhesive qualities—Raia realized Silk was not imbuing her designs into actual spiderwebs alone any longer, if she ever had been so exclusive (she had), but strands of pure silk. Though an hardly could afford silk anself, ans brother had been recently married, and for the seed necklaces, Raia's mother had purchased a small skein of raw silk from the Ceres Remnants. The silk had come already twisted into stronger threads of seven or ten strands, and cut shorter than this single long, nearly invisible strand woven through the designed scarf.

This led Raia to a startling epiphany: Silk was unspooling her own strands of silk from the cocoons of the worms. She—or someone on her behalf—was importing cocoons so that she could control every aspect of her material.

Although ans admiration for this mysterious woman's ingenuity was veering toward a dangerously romantic swell in ans heart, Raia revealed the discovery to the investigator-designer in charge, since Raia anself did not have the resources to trace imports from the Remnants into the empire.

Thus, on day two of the Blossoming Contemplation quad—today—the army of the Vertex Seal surrounded a six-story tower in the Saltbath precinct. As the sun rose into a dawning sky the same purple of winter cacti, soldiers blasted through a beautiful arch of design security and attacked.

The Little Cat's daughter

When Iriset was seven years old, her father brought her a three-legged bobcat kitten. How she'd adored the black tufts at its ears and its round green eyes, the large pads of its feet and long, fluffy tail. Its fur was colored like sand in the shadow of a drooping juniper, just like her father's hair. She'd watched it learn to leap without stumbling, to play awkwardly with only three legs, and she'd designed it a pair of wings made of linen, her own hair, and long twigs of rolled vellum. In a slick work of genius, she married the wings to the kitten's musculature so that it could control them, inventing a new sort of creature. The wings did not give flight to the desert cat, but helped it glide, helped it balance. They beat gently in the slightest breeze.

Her father was furious but did not yell, instead only took the bobcat kitten away and explained in plain terms that such design reeked of forbidden human architecture: No designer could attempt to create life of any sort, for life was the purview of the goddess alone. "Do you understand why the time before Aharté is called the Apostate Age?" he asked.

"Because architects could do whatever they wanted," she complained.

Instead of laughing at her sass as he often did, Isidor's mouth hardened. "I will have a collar of null wire fashioned for you if you do not appreciate the dangers of apostasy. Architects created wonders *and* they created monsters before the Glorious Vow. Not only the fragments that remain now—the skull sirens and micro-vultures—but chimeras, half-men, undead, unicorns, and flying whales capable of devouring entire families." The Little Cat stopped talking, for he saw the thrill blossom in her gaze.

"Unicorns?" Iriset whispered.

He crouched and put his warm hands to her cheeks, staring into her eyes, and she stared right back. Her father's eyes were gray and flecked brown, just like a Cloud King, and even then Iriset was wondering if she could design a window that looked exactly like them. She'd seen a dead man's eyes once, when she snuck out of her bedroom in their old petal apartment. Her father had been conducting business he expected to be nonviolent, or it wouldn't have happened where his wife and child slept. Iriset hadn't witnessed the kill, but she'd stared at the blank eyes of the dead man, his head tilted toward her and blood all over the floor.

Though at seven she'd not yet designed her first craftmask, or even conceptualized it, she made the intuitive leap that it was not accuracy nor detail that would create the perfect illusion of life in a craftmask, but motion and reflection. Death was still. Life trembled with force.

"Iriset," her father said gently, seeing her curiosity regarding the unicorn. "I was wrong. You do not have to understand. You simply have to obey. Do not turn your attention to human architecture, or anything that glances against it. If you do, I will collar you. That is my vow. Now it is your turn."

She put her small peach-brown hands against his white cheeks so that they mirrored each other's poses. "Did you kill the kitten?" Iriset asked.

"Yes."

Ecstatic force crackled down her spine, a tremor she automatically breathed into balance with the flow of her heartbeat. It was fear, but not only fear: excitement, too. This topic mattered so much, it could kill. How could anything less dangerous signify? Iriset said carefully, "I will do as you command; that is my vow."

Thus went her first bond, carefully worded to be bendable. She only ever blatantly broke it once, and never regretted the choice.

———— • ♦ • ————

When Iriset was eleven and her mother recently gone, her father pulled her onto his lap on the slender throne in the basement of his first gambling den. Her lanky limbs sprawled everywhere, limp in her grief, and Isidor held her tightly, haggard in his own. He buried his nose in her knotted hair, holding her back-to-chest, and together they breathed.

"I understand what you are now," Isidor said to his little daughter. Awe and fear tangled in his voice, but Iriset couldn't read such things then. She only turned her face toward his neck to cry.

But Isidor caught her jaw in hand. He looked at her sticky lashes, the splotched peach of her cheeks, and saw her mother in the turn of her lips. "But, Iriset," he said, "the Little Cat's daughter cannot—must not—think or perform or even smell like human architecture."

She blinked at him, and unlike the tone of his voice, she could read the tension in the tiny muscles around his eyes, the fear and concern and love set like a scaffold against the architecture of his face.

"Do you hear me, Iriset?" the Little Cat demanded.

"Yes," she whispered. "I can't be your daughter."

Isidor's mouth pressed down in displeasure. "No."

He waited. He knew she'd get there without further hints.

Iriset tucked her head under his jaw. He allowed it. She tried again. "Iriset has to be innocent. I need someone to blame."

"That's better. Do you know why?"

"Even the Little Cat is afraid of apostasy," she said dully, accurate and scathing in the way of children.

———— • ♦ • ————

When Iriset was seventeen, the Little Cat held a winter feast. Iriset did not attend.

It was the third night after the Night of Deep Hunger, when the tilt of the world makes the moon go dark, and the people of Moonshadow City celebrate the Moon-Eater, that old red god whose hunger for She Who Loves Silence was so great he ate his own moon like an apple. Bitten to the core, it fell from the sky.

The Little Cat's court had grown over the years, thanks to money from roving gambling dens, favors paid and favors owed, and not to mention the occasional murder-for-hire or excellent score. He smuggled already, too, but before Silk he only could use the methods used by every other ambitious undermarket cat. On this third night after the Night of Deep Hunger, the Little Cat offered a feast to his most loyal, to his associates and helpers and their husbands and cousins. This year it took place in a catacomb disguised to look deserted by all but the dead. Disguised with design, of course.

But just before midnight someone put one delicate crystal stylus to the design net and tore it down.

This person walked through the low stone hallways, following the shade-torches and graffiti, past crouching thieves and revelers in full-face masks. None stopped them, for everyone was invited if they could find the door.

The Little Cat held court at a table of polished geode, with less impressive tables scattered about the largest of this catacomb's chambers. Force-lights clung to the carved red-rock ceiling, illuminating people in apple masks and cactus masks, masks like the starry sky and masks of feathers and alliraptor skin and plain canvas masks painted with the favored foods of the old red god. They ate, they drank, and they moved in subtle patterns around the Little Cat, who sat alone in his dark blue robes and a mask with yellow rays like the sun.

The stranger slid along the red stone, dragging streaks of black silk and purple muslin. This person had taken pains to disguise any form, hiding in the comfort of androgyny, dark hair knotted at the nape and a terrifying mask covering their features from crown of the head and dripping over the chin.

Shaped of black-glazed ceramic, the mask gleamed with shards of smoky quartz glued into six faceted eyes arrayed around the actual eyeholes, which were covered by sheer black silk.

The spider walked into the Little Cat's feast, and the room fell quiet.

"What do you want?" the Little Cat asked, flicking a hand to clear the space.

The spider knelt. When she spoke it was in a feminine-forward voice, enticing and plain. "I have come to bargain my design skills with the Little Cat."

"I already have designers."

"Not like me," she said, and snapped her fingers. A surge of woven ecstatic and flow forces lifted the strips of silk and muslin, and her outer robe flared out around her in eight long lines, like a spider's legs. Like a black sun.

The Little Cat leaned forward. "What do you want in return?"

"A workshop." Her voice behind the spider mask hooked up in amusement. "The best tools and supplies a small king's money can buy."

"Your costume is cute, but not enough."

The woman stood and raised her hands slowly to remove the eight-eyed mask.

Gasps stuck in throats, and the Little Cat's court shied away.

Under the mask was the face of the Little Cat himself.

He removed his own sun mask, tossing it away.

Upon comparison, the spider looked a little more like his baby brother, or little sister. The jaw was not quite correct, the wrinkles too smooth, the nose a little too short. But it was close. Close enough.

Whispers of fear slithered through the catacomb. Whispers—and awe.

The Little Cat laughed, then reined in his knowing stare.

The spider grinned. "Imagine what I could do if I'd had a chance to be really close to you, study your structures, your expressions."

"I'd rather not," the Little Cat drawled. "Tell me your name, and I'll give you a trial run."

"Silk," she said, and covered her eyes—her eyes that looked just like the Little Cat's—to bow.

Even in the palace of the Vertex Seal, they heard the story of how the Little Cat found his apostate.

Meanwhile, the Little Cat's daughter grew up to be gentle and pretty, with a quick wit when she chose to engage with her father's people, and a wry smile when she did not. She wore simple cloth masks like the workers in her local Saltbath precinct and occasionally appeared at the undermarket court to serve her father coffee or rice wine imported (smuggled) from the southeastern territories of the empire. Iriset mé Isidor spent most of her time studying and running her father's household, visiting her grandparents on her mother's side, and sometimes wandering the Saltbath markets. She was quiet and rarely seen, and her grandmother hoped she would take an interest in mechanics, but Iriset tended toward more scholarly pursuits. She always brought her grandmother trinkets and her grandfather the night-blooming hothouse flowers her mother had adored. She knew the names of every shopkeeper on their street, and several for many petals in every direction. At least, that's what people said about her.

They knew her mother had married a smuggler—a trader when people felt generous—and that Iriset remained at his side when Amakis died. As Isidor's reputation grew, Iriset was seen less frequently on the streets, and she only visited her grandparents every few weeks. There was gossip she was being courted by a charming young Osahar boy but that he worked for the Little Cat and surely couldn't provide a stable home. Sometimes a baker or mechanic on her grandmother's row tried to tempt Iriset away from her father's life of crime, but she always smiled and said her father was good, and the life she had was good. Besides, if her father was a criminal, wouldn't he have been arrested already?

If people thought her naive, all the better. Though if they found her too innocent, that was bad, for the last thing she wanted was anyone trying to rescue her. The delicate tension kept a mind like Iriset's engaged in the game.

At seventeen she began arranging flowers in her grand-uncle's flower shop once a week, and let people know she was no criminal, but if they needed the Little Cat, perhaps she could pass a message. Iriset has always loved flowers, and loves the art of arranging them into bouquets. The balance of asymmetry and beauty might seem plain and innocent, but it feeds her unruly imagination.

If she wonders at the shape of leaves that turn toward the sun, or the exact number of petals on a mum and the curve of a thorn, if those thoughts lead her down long spirals of theory and potential, who is to know? All to be seen is the elegant arrangement of ghost lily and weeping spine fig and burst of scarlet moonflower.

See?

Sure, there is an apostate working for Isidor the Little Cat. A friend, lover, sister, bond... Who knows? But not his daughter.

The daughter of the Little Cat is no threat to anyone.

Prison

The soldiers of the Vertex Seal take Iriset to the apostate's prison at the edge of the Crystal Desert in the center of Moonshadow City. She knows, because even trapped inside a ribbon skiff with null wires circling her neck and wrists to bar her from manipulating external forces, she can trace their path through the streets using her other senses and extensive memorization of the map of the city. Her father used to make a game of it every morning over breakfast. The better to avoid authorities and locate safe houses, the Little Cat said. The better to understand the security habits of the royal architects, Iriset answered. Both were true, of course.

In these days, Moonshadow City is the heart of the empire, literally and metaphorically. Moonshadow, the Holy City, glimmers inside a massive red-rock crater eight miles across. From the central palace complex built like succulents with sharp-edged leaves, the city unfurls with exacting Design: Sixteen precincts divide it into four quadrants, each ruled by the four forces of rising, flow, falling, and ecstatic. Brilliant white towers with star crowns and needle roofs poke up among vivid blue and green domes. Petal-style housing complexes spiral and curve like stucco roses in which people live and work. Peristyle halls frame green space to create temples to Silence, and there are gardens of lush rainforest plants, gardens of sand and glass, and water gardens filled with mirror fish and black lotus. Elegant force-bridges sweep across avenues and canals, humming with the hollow song of skull sirens, those tiny birdlike creatures from the Apostate Age that feed on the layers of rising and falling forces woven together to keep the bridges active. Dominating the skyline are the four Great Steeples in the north, south, east, and west that anchor the forces of the city, rising tall enough to cast thick shadows across multiple precincts.

The edge of the crater in the south glints with glass from the windows of pocket apartments cut into the red rocks, and the western cliffs are taken up by barracks shared between armies. The eastern crater face is terraced with gardens and walking paths and chapels, while the north is reserved for catacombs piercing deep into the earth.

The Lapis River passes into the crater via underground caverns, bursting up near the Rising Steeple to pour south and cup the city with its flow. Two sprawling canyons slice through the city, mirroring each other though they are on opposite sides of the crater: They are left over from experiments during the Apostate Age to draw water up from deep in the earth. People carved homes into the sides of the canyons, which flood in the rains and dry to dust during the Days of Mercy.

It is the most beautiful city in the world.

And above it, Aharté's silver-pink moon hangs like a pearl affixed to the brocade of the sky.

———————— • ♦ • ————————

Iriset's cell consists of design-resistant walls and floor, empty but for a sleeping shelf and a clay bowl for relief. Once a day she's fed soda bread and nutty cheese with a shallow bowl of water. The soldiers do not remove the null wires around her wrists and neck.

She paces the dirt floor, walking the lines of a four-point star, then eight-, then sixteen-point. The room is too small for thirty-two points so of course she convinces herself that nothing will relax her *but* thirty-two points. How is she to calm down without being able to sense forces thanks to the fucking null wires? Only walking patterns, only the repetition, and she needs the complexity of thirty-two. Her heart won't stop pounding, she feels feverish and lightheaded, working herself into an intense state of anxiety until she finally falls asleep.

Iriset is unused to idleness.

The best she can do to distract herself is mentally indulging in wild theories of flight, which she's never forgotten as she's never forgotten the bobcat kitten. It's her favorite architectural problem to chew on, and her theories have moved away from wings over the years: Some spiders, when young, build delicate gossamer webs with which to catch the wind, ballooning up into the air to travel miles and miles to new lands, new homes. She thinks perhaps that is a key to flight that doesn't smack of creating new life. But the mathematics are impossibly complex, to heft a human woman's weight on a thread of force, considering wind vectors and tensile strength and how to combat—or use, or use!—the falling force always dragging downward to the earth.

She wishes she had writing materials, or even just the company of her poor darling spinners, burned and smashed in her study. She misses the shiver of their tiny feet on her forearm, each step a shock of ecstatic force. She wants Bittor to crouch beside her, tell her he didn't kill them, then wrap arms around her to ground her in her body. They spent hours testing force-reactions on each other: a bite here, a lick there, tickling the elbow or under the wrist, finding ways to draw out the rising force of desire. Iriset took notes comparing their bodies' reactions, how Bittor's masculine-forward design conveyed physical reactions to ecstatic force differently from hers. They made so many innuendos about rising force and flow.

(That was the essay that revealed Silk was a woman, when she included personal observations about pleasure in a feminine-forward body and theories about using the forces generated during sex to trigger delay-releasing medicines or poisons. Her father read it, as he read all her work, and told her to stop experimenting on his best escape artist. Raia mér Omorose read it in secret, and thought about Silk touching an tenderly, transforming ans body to a better gender. Bittor read it, too, and was so embarrassed he didn't speak to Iriset for days and never read one of her pamphlets again.)

By the fourth day in prison Iriset's robe is filthy, her mask balled up with her jacket like a pillow upon the shelf. Pale stucco dust sticks in the creases of her skin, and her fingernails are cracked to the quick from scrabbling to sketch equations upon the floor.

Halfway through the day, the cell door unlocks, surprising her onto her feet: She only has time to smooth hair off her face and wish she'd spent the moment grabbing her mask before two soldiers grasp her elbows and haul her from the cell. The stucco-smooth hallways wind upward, and they shove her into a room flooded with sunlight. Iriset winces away.

Her bare toes warm against a plain black-and-white geometric rug. There's a long table at the center of the room, and a lattice window allows in blue sky, fractured sunlight. Beside it stands a young person in the simple tight robe of a palace architect. She assumes an is a man, which is the point of ans carriage and masc-forward clothes.

It is Raia mér Omorose, who earned a place with the palace designers for locating Silk. An makes a noise of distress and points to a bowl and pitcher at the corner of the table, and a pile of folded blue cloth. "Take a moment, please, to steady and drink, and change if you would," an says, and leaves her alone.

Iriset tears out of her dirty clothes. Instead of using the bowl for gentle washing, she pours water straight from the pitcher onto her chest, swiping under arms and breasts, between her legs and then down her back. She tips her head upside down and does what little she can to scrub at her scalp. She needs a pick for the tangles, or to chop it all off.

When the pitcher is empty of every drop, she pulls apart the pile of clothes to find the mask first, which is a cloth mask, typical of the lower classes and first-generation citizens. With it, Iriset twists up her heavy hair, winding the plain linen across her forehead and under her chin, securing it all firmly, with a fluttering edge by her ear to hide her eyes if she needs it. Only then does she find the robe and loincloth and vest. Having her hair wrapped again is such a relief she almost laughs, longing for the luxury of a few moments to stand nude atop the table, free of null wires, to feel for errant threads of ecstatic or rising force.

The gentle knock and long pause before the door opens again are an unexpected kindness that relaxes her slightly as she positions herself beside the lattice window where she can feel a breeze on her cheek, if not the omnipresent hum of force-ribbons outside.

Raia immediately touches ans fingers to ans eyelids. It's polite, a gesture of respect for the goddess Aharté, who prefers her children not to share the intimacy of long eye contact unless they're family or otherwise bound—it is also an old tradition against human architecture. If you show your eyes to none, none can design a mask of your face. That's why the masks, too. An old tradition—or superstition, Iriset might say—born with the mirané people.

Iriset touches her eyelids briefly in return. She does not draw the mask across her sight.

"I am named Raia mér Omorose," an says.

Before she can help it, Iriset smiles at the descent indicator Raia uses in ans name, which reveals ans preferred gender. Alternative genders are not forbidden under Silence, but they are certainly discouraged. Raia smiles back tentatively. Ans mask is only face paint, as is typical of architects and also in fashion with the miran these days. Architects dislike masks of cloth, leather, or particular ceramics for how they might interfere with intricate design. But most body paint is mixed to be architecturally neutral. Raia wears jagged stripes of black—the color of flow—painted down over ans eyelids and narrow cheeks. Ans hair is straight brown-black and skin Pir-pale. There is little mirané blood in the shape of ans nose and brow, though ans cheek- and jawbones are very symmetrical and therefore more difficult to draw, but easier to create a craftmask for. An wears no beard (of course an *could* not without the aid of apostasy), further marking an apart from the miran, for whom it is in fashion to cut their beards in patterns to match their masks and face paint. An is young to be interrogating Iriset.

She realizes, as she catalogs information, that she's staring with Silk's eyes, practiced in memorizing bone patterns and gender-design details, not with the gaze of the modest daughter of a famous thief. She immediately draws the cloth mask across her face.

"Are you Iriset mé Isidor?" Raia mér Omorose continues, as behind an two more people arrive. The man—judging by his masculine-forward design—has a tightly curled beard and a military mask of white leather flat across his forehead that curves like scythes down over his cheeks, cupping his eyes but not at all obscuring his vision. His heavy brow lowers into a glare at Iriset. His skin is mirané brown, lined with fine wrinkles, and he wears the white robe, leather vest, and weapon sash of the city army. The woman hurries in, cloth-masked and robed in plain linens. She puts a box on the table and leaves, dragging the door closed behind her.

Raia doesn't introduce the glowering soldier, but opens the long box and begins laying out items from it.

A design stylus.

A pair of delicate forceps.

One-half of wire moth wings.

Iriset's own white silk glove, with a dot of dry blood atop the thumb. The one she gave to Bittor.

He would have planted it on Paser or Dalal, Isidor's other designers, to help one of them take the fall as Silk. Iriset hates the thought of another getting credit for her work nearly as much as she hates the idea of another dying for her.

"Do you know the glove?" Raia asks.

"Where did you get it?" Iriset asks in return. "Where is my father? I want to see him."

The older soldier snorts. "We got it off Silk, of course."

"Alive?"

"For now."

Iriset stares at the spot of blood, wishing she knew who had taken her mask-name and is probably taking her punishment. She can't ask without giving away the game. "And my father?"

"He's still alive, too, Iriset," the architect says, "and if you cooperate it's more likely you'll be granted a few moments with him before his trial."

She inhales with a hiss. "Yes, I know the glove. So?"

"Do you know how she made it?"

Suddenly Iriset thinks of a way to claim some of her design without ruining the sacrifices her father's people had made for her, without disobeying his command. "She allowed me to assist sometimes," she says, leaning toward the glove. "I spooled the silk for her, and held it because my fingers are small, and that helped her."

"So you aided in the illegal activities. In apostasy," the older soldier says, with a satisfied but angry press of his lips.

Raia interrupts, "I'm not interested in that, Iriset. You have not been named as a criminal, nor shall you be if I can stop it. We need your help, though, to understand how Silk did what she did and in order to bring in any of her remaining designs and find ways to work against them."

"No."

"I only wish to understand," Raia says eagerly. "I've studied what I can of Silk's work, and it is genius. What she's done could help so many people if it was turned away from thieving and illegal practices, and toward the greater purposes of architecture."

Iriset holds herself still, angry pride in her heart because she knows what her craft could do; she longs for it.

Raia continues, "Imagine the more flexible building materials Silk's research could help us develop, or security nets. Alarms and fiber glassworks, stronger ropes and suspension architecture for better bridges."

"Oh." Surprised into meeting ans excited gaze through the

shimmer of her borrowed mask, Iriset realizes an isn't lying about what an wants. Raia mér Omorose is a designer like Iriset, who sees possibilities. How can she use it? Can she trade it for a chance at saving her father's life, or Bittor's, or any or all of them? Pretend the Little Cat's daughter is Silk's innocent apprentice, and get what she needs?

The older soldier says, "And you'll tell us what you know of Isidor Little Cat's business, names, meetings, everything you remember."

Iriset snaps her mouth closed. She dislikes her father's name in his mouth. *Little Cat* is a sweet diminutive to hide the vicious truth, a palatable euphemism, but when the old soldier says it, the words flow with disgust.

"That's the deal, child," the soldier says. "Raia mér Omorose and I come together. He wants your magical knowledge, but I require practical information first."

Raia flattens ans mouth but does not naysay the soldier.

Iriset forces her eyes to lower and lies, "I do not know any details about my father's business."

The soldier, who so rudely has not named himself, comes around the table and she backs away, knocking her heels into the stucco and her shoulder into the lattice window. He stops himself a breath away, overwhelming Iriset with his size and steely silver smell. His eyes are half-circles and hold flecks of green among the mirané brown; his long, tightly curled beard nearly brushes her chin. "If you do not agree, you will remain in prison and be sent to a work camp eventually, do you understand? Your sheltered daughter's life will not stand up to the camps, and will not help you break limestone or plow the delta."

"He is my father," Iriset says.

"Do you think even a man like the Little Cat would see his

daughter so abused for his own sake? Violent criminals and prisoners of war and the petty thieves or innocent who end up there are not separated, child. The Seal laws do not hold well in the camps, where wardens and guards have too much else to do than to make sure no young girls or skinny boys are being raped."

"Bey!" Raia cries, aghast and hurrying to put anself between them.

The old soldier—Bey—remains expressionless. "She is the Little Cat's daughter, Raia, and surely cannot be shocked by the mere mention of murder or assault."

Iriset says, "You do not make me want to betray my father with this theater."

"Good." Raia touches her shoulder. "Fear only pushes us to act irrationally," an says more to Bey.

"The name of the Little Cat will protect me wherever you put me, except from animals like yourself," she says.

Bey the soldier smiles grimly. "I told you, Raia mér Omorose, that she was one of them."

The architect ignores him, turning fully to Iriset. "I know you love the design; I saw it shine even through your mask, Iriset. That is what I am interested in: architecture and its secrets. What would we design for love of the work? If you agree, I will find a way to speak with you again."

Iriset looks past Raia to where Bey shakes his head once for her. She understands: The architect is not in command here, though perhaps an naively believes an holds the power. But Iriset understands something else, too, about Bey's inner design: He will be brutal with the truth, but he will not lie. If he were willing to lie, he'd have agreed with Raia to manipulate her.

"I agree," she says to Raia, though she doubts it matters.

Iriset does love the work of design. But the only time she ever designed *for* love, it was the worst kind of apostasy: She cut into a human body to redesign malignancy. To heal. To save. Imagine the widespread application of that discovery—twelve years gone! How many dead might live today had she been allowed to breathe a word of her success? Given the chance, she could cure apostatical cancer. Start by pulling apart a miran to compare their design with that of any other of the empire's ethnicities more susceptible to the mutation. It might be that miran do not know such diseases because they were designed by the hand of Aharté herself, from her flesh, but Iriset thinks it safer to study and be sure. Next she might discover the stoppage of flow that causes squared arteries in the older architects, or invent a night-vision applicator based on the design of Bittor's eyes, or dig into a brain and root out the source of nightmares. Retro-design the skull sirens to determine how and why their skulls push out through their faces as they mature, and how they survive it. Interrogate the design-root of consciousness! Pinpoint the triggers for aging or miscarriage!

She understands why chimeras and certain kinds of human architecture and chemistry are dangerous, but not healing and refinement. Humans are intricate design and is it not our right to understand ourselves?

When someone suggested to her once that merely thinking such thoughts went against Silence, Silk said, "Wasn't I, after all, designed by the goddess? If Aharté did not wish me to seek transformation, why design me with this desire?"

You see, Iriset was always destined to break the world.

4

The Little Cat's apostate

In a different cell of the same apostate prison, a young woman grits bloody teeth. Her lips peel back into a grimacing smile, and she peers through pain-narrowed brown eyes at General Bey méra Matsimet. Behind the city army general, Raia mér Omorose claps hands over ans mouth and backs up.

The young woman throws her head back, and any designer worth their silicate would perceive the sharp staccato of ecstatic force tearing up her throat—they might even catch it in time to stop it, had they the proper tools. Or, any designer worth their silicate and not distracted by horror the way Raia is. It takes an too long to feel the pop, and by the time an throws anself forward, it's too late.

The young woman laughs, a choking raven call, devoid of voice.

"Do you think this will save you?" Bey asks, bored and disgusted.

The young woman—*Silk, she said, is only my mask-name,*

right before snapping her jaw shut and activating whatever hidden design just burned her voice out—slumps suddenly, the design taking its toll on her internal forces. She tilts on her stool, and Bey keeps Raia back from catching her. She hits the dirt floor with a bony thud, one arm bent awkwardly under her. Black hair splays in oily twists.

Raia's hands drop to ans sides. An hates this. Silk is a genius, and ought to be treated as such. Invited to the palace with appropriate precautions, null manacles, and offered good food and the benefits of state-sanctioned design. The Vertex Seal has kept the numen alive and imprisoned for a hundred years; they could certainly manage a young human genius.

"Let's go, Raia," General Bey says, dismissing the passed-out apostate. "You architects will have to figure out a way to undo her scorch."

But Raia knows they will not. It's human architecture to alter, affect, or transform life, and the Vertex Seal won't allow such design, not for any reason. He would say justice gained through apostasy is no justice at all.

When the Little Cat asked Silk to create a design to destroy a voice and hide the design in a pill or button or lace rosette or something tiny and easily activated, she barely gave a thought as to why. She simply muttered that destroying was so much easier than creating, and couldn't he give her a real challenge instead? Then she did it.

She put it in a prickly pear candy, because the sugar crystal could maintain the structure of the design almost as well as quartz. Candy was better than a button, she told her father, because candy would deliver the design directly to its target in predictable slippery streaks. Isidor was skeptical, but Silk shrugged in nonchalant confidence. She still never asked why.

When it matters, the candy functions exactly as designed, even with a null collar against the user's neck, for the null collar only affects what it touches, and it does not touch the candy or the larynx.

———•◆•———

Three days later, the door to Iriset's cell clangs loudly as the lock is inexpertly undone, and she blinks from the shelf, exhausted and hungry and lulled into a dull, meditative slump.

Instead of her usual guard, two soldiers march in, slamming the cell door shut behind them. They stare at her: The weaponless one is so obviously feminine-forward, for the rust-red uniform jacket of the Vertex Seal's guard does not hide her large breasts and hips, or her languid pose. The other is a woman, too, by appearance, roughly the same height, but a woman who knows how to stand like a soldier and wear a Seal guard uniform fit to her hard body.

The first woman reaches up and with a relieved sigh unwinds the full-faced Seal guard mask from her face and hair, letting massive amounts of black curls fall. "Oh," she groans, "that weight was giving me a neck-ache." Her voice is light but sounds like a purr.

Iriset presses back into the wall, digging her fingers hard against the stucco.

The second woman doesn't remove her mask, which covers her head and face but for a slit over her dark brown eyes. She says, the sneer quite audible, "It will have to go back up when we leave this pit."

"You're the Little Cat's daughter," the first woman says, brushing curls away from her handsome face. Her bright eyes are rimmed with black that spreads in thick lines to her temples, obscuring the shape of her cheeks, and black glints on her ripe-looking mouth. When she smiles, her white teeth gleam. Her mirané-brown skin glows with youth and health. This is a noble woman, soft and generously built. She does not belong here.

Her companion tugs her Seal guard mask down off her face then, revealing a long nose and oval lips of Bow ancestry, but mirané-brown skin. A thick stripe of red paint masks across her eyes like blood. "We're not here to play, Iriset mé Isidor."

Iriset swallows, to find her voice after days of silence. When she speaks, it scratches like a sandstorm. "Who are you?"

The first woman—the soft, luscious miran—laughs. "I am your deliverer, daughter of thieves."

"And I am her body-twin," the other says. "Sidoné mé Dalir. Cover your eyes for the Moon-Eater's Mistress, Amaranth mé Esmail Her Glory."

Immediately Iriset slips onto her knees and presses her hands to the floor, lowering her head as she reins in shock. For all that her father is the Little Cat, and she prides herself her Osahar and Cloud King ancestors, she comes from no holy bloodline, while this, *this* is the most holy. Amaranth is the sister of the Vertex Seal himself. And the lover of the Moon-Eater. She congresses with a god.

"Your Glory," Iriset says, desperate to be free of the null wires so she can sense force again. With her complete faculties she's good at reading motivation, but so hampered how will she figure out what Her Glory wants in time to negotiate in her favor?

"Yes, hiha," Her Glory says, and Iriset hears the rustle of

cloth as Amaranth kneels and touches Iriset's head. "I have come to make you an offer."

Sidoné mé Dalir scoffs, but otherwise the prison cell falls silent again as Iriset thinks furiously what to say. Her Glory patiently strokes Iriset's tangled brown hair, and Iriset is appalled at how dirty she is, how disadvantaged by her borrowed mask uselessly folded on the shelf, her bare feet and her stink.

"What offer, Your Glory?" she asks finally, when it becomes apparent she must.

"You are the daughter of the great thief known as the Little Cat, yes?"

Nodding scrapes the tip of Iriset's nose lightly against the rough floor.

"I would have you come to the palace and be one of my handmaidens."

A crackle of ecstatic force pops in Iriset's ears. She blows it out in a balancing flow.

Amaranth mé Esmail laughs, throaty and slow, then leans away. "I would not, I think, have a handmaiden who refuses to look at me."

Iriset pushes up from the floor, carefully, until she sits on her heels and folds her hands in a lying semblance of peace in her lap. She drags her gaze up Her Glory's body, then meets Amaranth's bright mirané-brown eyes. The spark in them belies the lazy way Her Glory carries her weight, belies the laconically lifted thick black eyebrow. It's a spark of challenge, and Iriset likes it.

"Why me?" She expects a lying response, but it must be asked.

Behind Her Glory, Sidoné mé Dalir shifts from one hip to the other and clenches the hilt of her curved sword as if to echo the question.

Amaranth smiles over her shoulder at her body-twin, then turns the smile upon Iriset once more. "You are a novelty, daughter of thieves. And as pretty as was reported to us, though that is a bit shadowed by your time here in our least hospitable of rooms. Too bad you are no miran, but I like to surround myself with beautiful novelties, and my Moon-Eater appreciates my taste."

It's disconcerting—bordering on rude—how intently Her Glory studies Iriset. But Her Glory can stare if she wishes to stare, and never be accused of impoliteness. Iriset stares back, but makes herself blink timidly, for she's not Silk, she's only her father's sheltered daughter. "I'm only my father's sheltered daughter," she says softly. "Hardly a novelty."

The Moon-Eater's Mistress scoffs. "You underestimate yourself. The Little Cat and his pet apostate are the talk of the Holy City. Even the highest princes of the mirané council are interested in all their associates. And wouldn't it be interesting if you can be tamed? The child of a villain and associate of the great apostate Silk?"

Iriset hums. She lets her gaze flicker over Amaranth's gorgeous visage.

"My dearest friend on the mirané council doesn't think you'll agree," Amaranth says enticingly. "Prove her wrong. Even if you won't like to be tamed, think of the luxury, the potential futures in store for you at my side. You could...well. Do anything eventually. When you've proved yourself at my side. Come with me, hiha."

"You could command me," Iriset says.

"I am not looking for a slave. My handmaidens are my companions. My friends. They have power." Amaranth raises her lush eyebrows. "I am strong enough to offer trust first."

Behind the Moon-Eater's Mistress, Sidoné clenches her jaw.

Iriset glances low, hiding her stare, as is polite. "The old soldier, Bey, he said I would have to give him something in return if I was ever to be free. But I won't betray my father."

"I will not ask you to."

"Where is he?" Iriset clutches her hands together. "What is his sentence?"

"In the apostate tower, alone. He has not been sentenced yet, though he will almost certainly be killed during the Days of Mercy."

Iriset shudders, not with fear, but because she thinks, *I will save him first.*

"Iriset," Her Glory says. "Come."

If not for the null wires, Iriset would feel a draw of falling force, a pull to Her Glory, but she continues to hesitate. There's a trap here, and if she doesn't find its edges she'll walk straight into its heart. She sifts through her memory for anything she's heard about Her Glory, but only comes up with a few tidbits: barely a year younger than her brother, known to be grand in generosity and all manner of appetite, a tastemaker since she was a child, fond of wearing her hair down and as little jewelry as possible in favor of skin paint and intricate, loose robes. She's said to be a fitting mistress for the Moon-Eater, being as extravagant as the goddess Aharté is simple.

Imagine what Her Glory would want if she realizes Iriset is Silk. Can Iriset use that? Can she accept this as the Little Cat's daughter, but enter the palace as his pet apostate? Is it worth the risk?

Iriset knows what her father would say.

This is a chance out of here, this prison wherein she can do nothing. In the palace, though there will be great danger, there also will be great opportunity.

"Yes," Iriset says to the most powerful woman in the empire.

5

Hypotheticals make the world go round

Iriset is brought to the palace a day later, cloaked and alone but for a pair of real Seal guards wearing the Moon-Eater's band, and most importantly, free of the null wires.

Forces press, cling, and spark around her again, and she barely resists the temptation to reach out and touch the errant threads of rising and ecstatic magic that pull free from the palace design like wisps of hair that refuse to settle into a braid.

Her room—and the women who bathe her insist it is hers—is tucked in a curve of a complicated suite of the women's petal of the palace. A rug woven like a sunrise in pinks and reds and gold spreads thinly across the floor and the walls are lined in flat pillows and long bolsters. One large lattice window overlooks the palace complex and the shimmering quartz field of the Crystal Desert from at least a hundred feet up. The walls are pale curving meltwood, lifting to a low arched ceiling, where at the tip a tiny eight-point star cuts into the roof. Directly below it is a matching cutout in the floor. Too tiny for anything but breeze and spiders to pass. Iriset has heard rumors the palace was built so that there is no chamber the steady moon—the silver-pink Eye of Aharté—cannot see. Even into the lowest levels, the heart of the palace, an arrow could be threaded directly through moonlight.

Certainly it's a better prison than her last.

One corner holds a hive of cubbies for belongings, and there's a trunk full of robes and slippers and masks of several sorts: cloth masks in a rainbow of sheer silks, thin molded leather masks, and even a single ceramic mask with inlaid silver filigree. Iriset is directed to dress in an orange silk robe over trousers encrusted with tiny moon-pink silk flowers. The jacket that ties over her breasts leaves her arms bare and is decorated with strings of white horn beads. Never in her life has she worn such finery. It suited neither of her identities.

She has not seen Amaranth mé Esmail Her Glory or Sidoné mé Dalir since they left her in the cell, but was promised a meal with Her Glory later, once she's rested and bathed and once Sidoné clears her presence with the Seal guard. Presumably that old soldier Bey will not be happy. But what can he do in the face of Her Glory's preference? The thought makes Iriset feel rather smug.

Iriset kneels upon one of the flat cushions, analyzing plans of action.

There's nothing immediate she can do for her father, but several long-term options:

—Befriend Her Glory as a means to reach the Vertex Seal himself and convince him to grant mercy to Isidor, as it *will* be the Days of Mercy only four quads in the future. She'll have to quickly make herself a perfect friend, indispensable even.

—Weave her way into the confidence of royal architects in order to access materials she needs to fashion tools to rescue Isidor herself. A craftmask, weapons, wall-slicers, anything.

—Discover every means in and out of the apostate tower.

—Contact Bittor (if he's alive) to align her plans with his. If she can't get her father out, they should coordinate a rescue for the execution itself, when the soldiers will be forced to bring Isidor to them.

To achieve any of these things, Iriset will have to be like her spinners. A spider in a web, careful, beautiful, skilled. Always wary and always ready.

She worries her bottom lip between her teeth, longing for stylus and vellum, or chalk or charcoal for drawing. If not magical designs to soothe herself, then at least she could sketch the shape of Amaranth's mouth or Sidoné's nose, which curves like the sharp sword at her hip. It's frowned upon to draw human faces, for that leads to studies of human symmetry and structure, which leads in turn to human architecture—exactly the reason everyone covers their faces with masks, and no portraits are made of the miran or small kings or anyone whose facade might be copied for nefarious reasons. It's all ridiculous, for although the basics of design could be learned by any, and the most rudimentary understanding of architecture might allow a designer to create adequate foundations, the design of a recognizable human face that mirrors life, shifts with emotions, laughs and frowns and cries, is extremely difficult.

Iriset has come close to doing it, of course. The hardest part is the eyes, especially without the intimacy of individual study. The only eyes she currently has sufficient access to are her own, but maybe if she plays the good handmaiden she can study Amaranth's eyes well enough to make a craftmask of Her Glory. With that she could command near any prize. The only better option would be a craftmask of the Vertex Seal himself.

Iriset's body goes entirely still at the reckless apostasy of even thinking such a thing.

Her pulse races, rising force drawing blood to her cheeks and nearly making her hair stand on end.

Iriset's thoughts are interrupted by commotion outside, just before the thin lacquered wood door to the chamber sweeps open.

A man stands there, glaring.

Wary of playing her role, Iriset touches her fingertips to her eyelids politely, but otherwise doesn't move, knowing from a lifetime in the Little Cat's court to let a mystery present itself before she overplays her best guess.

"You are the daughter of the Little Cat?"

Lowering her hands, Iriset studies him in quick glances. The man presents extremely masculine-forward, stereotypically so, and is several years her elder, with curly black hair falling around his face to his chin, his short beard shaved into a repeating star pattern, and eyes glittering mirané brown. He has the sharp, symmetrical bones and wide-planed cheeks of the miran, but his rich tan skin is likely to come from Sarenpet blood. Red paint stripes across his temples and eyes, just like Sidoné's, and he wears a plain black robe and trousers, flexible boots, and two curving force-blades at his hips. Those swords hum with contained force and it's all Iriset can do not to reach for one to inspect it—she's never held a living blade before! But she stops at the way his teeth bare in distaste.

She answers, "Yes. Iriset mé Isidor."

"I am Garnet méra Bež," he says, confirming his gender, "and I will study your face before you are allowed from this room."

It's rude and intimate of him to demand such a thing. "Do you serve Her Glory as Sidoné does?"

"No." He crouches before Iriset with the controlled power of a griffon. "I serve His Glory, the Vertex Seal."

She doesn't drop her gaze, meeting Garnet's with all the insult she feels. She senses she ought to show no weakness to this man.

Garnet examines her, flicking his eyes across the planes of her face, takes in her heavy knotted hair, her modestly tied vest, her cold hands clutched together upon her thighs. She guesses he memorizes her features and hands, everything he can use to identify her if she ever nears him or Lyric méra Esmail His Glory. Iriset has no paint to shift her cheekbones, nor kohl to change the shape of her eyes, no lip stain, and has not decorated herself at all, for she's not been given the opportunity; besides, she wouldn't have. Better to present herself like a plain spider, eager to please but knowing herself. A maskless face, open and honest. Spiders don't pretend to be other than what they are. Let Her Glory choose the form Iriset will take. That will tell Iriset plenty.

Finally, and with simple formality, Garnet says, "While Amaranth's handmaiden you will go every morning to Her Glory's side and there be masked in the paint or cloth or ceramic of the day, to Amaranth's will, and in line with her other handmaidens. If you are not with her, you are allowed a plain attendant's cloth mask, in palace orange, red, or white."

Iriset pinches her left thumb to her left forefinger, creating a circuit for the ecstatic force rushing through her blood.

"You will agree," Garnet says, "or you will return to the prison."

"I do not think you can take me back without Her Glory allowing it," she argues gently.

"But her brother can, and he will if I insist."

Her position is tenuous already. If Garnet méra Bež holds so tight to the ear of the Vertex Seal, it will do Iriset better to win him to her side. Though she hasn't the least idea how to accomplish it: Within his inner design she senses a determined flow. He knows exactly who he is, and his loyalty never wavers. His choice whether to trust Iriset or not will come from her actions. From her own balance and proof of loyalty. And so she nods.

"Good." Garnet stands, and Iriset does, too, as smoothly as possible. Her eyes are near level with his nose, and he doesn't step away. Instead of lowering her gaze, Iriset boldly tilts her chin up to continue meeting his. He smells like most men she's known: hair oil, sweat, leather, but something extra tickles her nose and reminds her of the stuffed eagle in Isidor's office.

Burned and ruined now.

Iriset closes her eyes suddenly, aggrieved, and turns away, upset with guilt that she forgot the destruction of her father's tower even for so small a moment. Distracted by the new game, she's forgetting it is *not* a game. It's her father's life. And her own.

"Iriset mé Isidor."

She glances over her shoulder. Garnet stands half out the door, giving her a dangerous, black look. "My mother works with the royal griffons and she has told me that once you are forced to threaten a young griffon, you have already misstepped with the creature, either through its temperament or your own. I would not like to misstep now."

And he sweeps out of the chamber, leaving Iriset with the echo of implied threat heavier than would have been a threat itself. At least, she thinks distantly, his mother's work explains the smell of dead eagles hanging about him like motes of dust.

Iriset waits, breathing flow and rising and falling and ecstatic forces through her body, as she had in that plain prison. Somehow, she feels worse here, antsier so near to power and plotting, so close to opportunities to help her father. She grits her teeth and keeps to her meditations.

Finally a scratching comes at the lacquered door and she straightens her legs to standing. Another girl in palace orange covers her eyes and summons Iriset by name, then leads her to a crescent banquet chamber.

The low, oval table in the banquet chamber is set with ceramic bowls for different drinks—tea, cloud liquor, and rose wine, and the greatest delicacy: chips of flavored ice with sprigs of rosemary and flecked golden saffron frozen in their centers. Succulents in perfect symmetry grace the center of the table, and the cushions for sitting are stitched in patterns that matched those layered, sharp leaves.

Amaranth mé Esmail reclines on a short-footed sofa, and around her several women with different appearances of femininity array themselves. Sidoné kneels near the Moon-Eater's Mistress in a plain black robe and jacket, her mirané-brown arms bare, and her hair roped and free of any mask. She's striking, raised at Amaranth's side as a body-twin, taught the arts of war and defense that she might always be there to either protect Her Glory or die in her place. It is an old mirané tradition, and in the past generations, the insistence upon true similarity of looks has grown lax.

Amaranth presents herself like water. There's nothing of steel in her pose, her clothing, or body. She's the luscious flooding Lapis River, her baked mirané-brown skin sprinkled with shimmering glitter along cheekbones and shoulders, her eyelids blackened, and her hair tumbling in layers of rich black curls. Red moons clip back a few strands of hair at her temples. Sheer silk and the most delicate layers of linen drape her thick, rolling body, hugging breasts and hips and belly as if that cloth were the most blessed thing in all the world for being allowed to drift so near her flesh.

She smiles, and Iriset struggles to contain the flush of desire suddenly blossoming as if from a seed that's always been inside her. Waiting to meet Her Glory.

Iriset wonders a bit breathlessly if this happens to everyone who encounters the Moon-Eater's Mistress. Is it her morning ritual with the Moon-Eater that imbues her with such thick eroticism? Iriset murmurs, "Your Glory," lifting her hands to shade her eyes.

"Iriset mé Isidor," drawls Amaranth. When Iriset looks, Her Glory waves a hand to indicate she should join them upon one of the cushions. She does, folding her legs carefully. Now that she's free of the null wires, she senses a rush of ecstatic force sparking from Amaranth's direction. It's tempered by a dominant core of falling, and these five other women add their own fluctuating designs to the room.

Quickly the others are introduced: Ziyan mé Tal, the mirané-brown daughter of the small king of the Ribbonwork precinct, who sings like a siren and narrows suspicious eyes at Iriset; square-jawed miran Anis mé Ario, who moves with careful elegance and keeps her eyes lowered; Istof Nefru, who traces her line back to Old Sarenpet and speaks seven languages. Istof keeps glancing at Ziyan, as if to let Iriset know the two of them are united in their suspicion of the Little Cat's daughter. Beside Istof is Nielle mé Dari, a surprisingly ugly girl with vivid mirané-brown eyes too large for her narrow face and a tiny nose. Her body is too shapeless to be called lithe and not fat enough to be plump or perfectly round as a polished apple. Nielle grins at Iriset and says, "Ignore them until they come around."

Amaranth snorts. "She'll win them over herself, or she won't."

Each of Her Glory's favorites wears a slender crescent mask across their foreheads that doesn't hide their faces, but merely suggests a fashionable mask.

Iriset touches her eyelids to all of them, and murmurs, "I am here to be tamed by the Moon-Eater's Mistress, not to win."

A moment of shocked silence follows her words, then Anis mé Ario, with the shy elegance, laughs. Iriset allows herself a smile.

Amaranth instructs the handmaidens to woo Iriset's good behavior by discussing their lives in the palace, and to share their favorite memories of Amaranth. Her Glory speaks of meeting each of them, picking them from a crowd at a Days of Mercy feast, or accepting an invitation to a family concert, or in Sidoné's case the silly tale of the first time Amaranth realized that Sidoné was not, in fact, her twin sister. In the story, Garnet, that somber, threatening man, had teased Amaranth for quads at not understanding the differences between them. Iriset cannot imagine him as a child.

Alcohol is poured repeatedly, as is a sweet mint tea, and Iriset sips but doesn't indulge, too aware of her precarious position to allow her tongue to slur. They eat amazing food: flatbread as thin as a blade of grass and sprinkled with cinnamon, candied almonds and glazed salmon, a salad of cold sliced cactus pears and crisp persimmons, scattered with brilliant red and violet flowers she doesn't know, and their feathered leaves. The main course is cave crab, and as Iriset carefully learns to use the pick to dig free the meat, she realizes the pick is made of crystal. When the crab is whisked away she uses a moment of laughter to tuck the pick into the tight bodice of her jacket.

Crystal makes the best design stylus.

Once, they're interrupted by a tall woman in architect's sleek robes.

Amaranth claps once. "Welcome, Menna. You have it?"

The architect bows, briefly touches thumb and forefinger to her eyes, and says, "I do, Your Glory."

"This, Iriset, is Menna mé Garai, the Architect of the Seal. Stand."

Iriset obeys, lowering her eyes cautiously. This royal architect is the highest ranked of designers, for she personally serves the Vertex Seal and his sister.

Menna drifts nearer, feeling dominantly of rising force, and Iriset realizes with a spike of anxiety that she doesn't know how the daughter of the Little Cat should feel with regards to the forces. She habitually, naturally balances her inner design, but would a girl who is *not* Silk? Iriset touches her eyelids and waits, willing some ecstatic force to unbalance the rest. Perhaps she should claim to be extremely devoted to Silence, as such worshippers are practiced at meditation. But it would be a difficult lie to keep up.

"Iriset mé Isidor," Menna says, "I have heard much of you from my associate Raia méra Omorose. He was determined to put you into our grasp, had Her Glory not succeeded first."

"Raia was very polite," Iriset murmurs, glancing up. Menna

is twice Iriset's age, and wears a mask of paint in simple white stripes, eight of them, vertical down her mirané face. She wonders if misgendering Raia is on purpose or unintentional.

"I made this for you." Menna holds out a small black box.

Iriset lifts the lid. Inside, upon a cushion of white, rests a jade cuff, inlaid with a golden seal of the Moon-Eater.

Amaranth says, "Put it on, Iriset."

Swallowing, afraid of null wires, she obeys. The cuff is cool to the touch, but when she clasps it around her left wrist, the center of it, just below the inlaid seal, is warm. Iriset shivers as threads of force slip through her skin, seeking her inner design.

"Sensitive," Menna comments.

Iriset's gaze flies to Her Glory, who watches her with knowing eyes. Iriset protests, "I was only being taught. A little."

The Architect of the Seal shrugs. "You will be tracked now. Through locks and barriers throughout the palace complex. Do not remove it."

"All my girls wear one," Amaranth says, unconcerned. "You'll become used to it, and with it comes the privilege of my retinue."

Iriset should have expected such a thing. If she doesn't trick the design mechanisms of this cuff, she'll never be free. However, when she looks, she sees similar cuffs about each of the handmaidens' wrists.

They ask her, when she sits back down, to speak about her father.

"First, if you allow," Iriset says, without meekness, "tell me what has become of his court."

"Broken up by the city army," says Istof the linguist.

Amaranth says, "The Little Cat's court will be tried individually, for what crimes can be proved. I suspect all will be found guilty. Some will be killed, some freed for mercy's sake, and some sent to labor camps."

Iriset nods jaggedly and swallows more wine. She knows little of the camps, beyond rumors and the threats made against her by Bey méra Matsimet. Prisons in the empire are only for holding people until their trial. If not executed or released, the only third option is such a camp. They are said to be everywhere in the empire, filled with all sorts of criminals punished to build roads and lay ribbon or blast the bedrock for steeple foundations or mine toxic minerals in eastern quarries. All of which might very well kill them anyway if they're under a worse warden. A slow death, of exposure or starvation, or a quick one from a gang's knife.

(Sometimes escapes are made, but there are no rumors about it, as witnesses are put out of their misery. Once, a successful camp rebellion was later put down by the army and called a boil plague in the news graffiti.)

"And my father? Has he been sentenced?"

"The Little Cat will die on the Day of Final Mercy."

It's exactly as Her Glory said before, but nevertheless blood drains from Iriset's skull, the drag of falling force, and she reaches out to grasp the shallow bowl of rose wine. Tasteless as it is in her mouth, it scours her tongue with its sharp delicacy. Now she knows her timeline, at least.

"Tell us about him," Nielle demands. "Why shouldn't he be killed?"

Iriset bites the tip of her tongue. Any stories might reveal her own true nature, so she must be cautious. She tells them about her father by telling them about her mother.

Amakis was her name, a solid Lapis Osahar name, though Isidor had only called her Kiss.

The handmaidens swoon, and Amaranth smiles. Sidoné presses her lips in a line that might be stifled amusement or disapproval.

Their courtship was smooth and lingering, Iriset says, for Isidor busied himself with building his court and Amakis was the daughter of a mechanic in the Saltbath precinct: dark, lovely, and in no hurry to leave her mother's house. Nothing dramatic occurred, there were no enemies nor rivals. The two people simply wove their lives together. A perfect pattern. Eventually they'd braided so fully into each other's lives there was nothing to do but tie it off with a marriage knot. And so they did. Iriset had been the second knot in their shared life.

"Did she not care that her husband was a criminal?" asks Ziyan, the singer.

"What was there to care about? He was good at it."

Sidoné laughs once, without humor. "Being good at something is not justification itself."

Nielle says, "If he was good enough, he wouldn't have been caught."

Iriset stops feeling bad about thinking of Nielle as the ugly one.

"It wasn't the Little Cat's mistake that caught him," Amaranth says before Iriset can snap back. "Silk left tracks."

A spark of ecstatic force bursts coldly in Iriset's vision and she breathes too deeply, shoving air at her unbalanced stomach. "Silk had no tracks."

"Ask the architect who found her," Sidoné says, a dare in her cool tone. "The one Menna mentioned, Raia mér Omorose."

"We were betrayed," Iriset says. "And not by Silk." She tries to remain calm, to smooth over the raw falling force.

At her side, Anis mé Ario has been quiet for most of the

conversation. Now she reaches with sympathy, putting her fingers against Iriset's wrist bone. Iriset meets Anis's dark brown gaze. To distract herself, she stares at the handmaiden with Silk's practiced eyes. Short lashes, thin lips, a pleasing symmetry between eyes and mouth and chin, her shoulders broader than the narrow rectangle of her mirané-brown face would suggest. White and black interlocking squares painted her jaw, tiny and delicate, but beneath it... she needs to shave. Iriset lets her eyes slide down Anis's arm to the hand that touches her: heavy knuckles, but with a grace in fingers. Those fingers freeze in their comforting stroke, and Anis pulls away.

She's hiding something, too. A discord presents itself to Silk: two patterns overlaid not quite in alignment.

Anis's design is masculine-forward. She's not like Raia mér Omorose, who claims an old gender from before Aharté's reign, unsettled between masculine and feminine. Anis hides her design under all the trappings of femininity she can because while the goddess of Silence merely discourages the older genders, to claim her Holy Design is wrong is heresy. Iriset has met such people before, done work for them through the undermarket—wonderful, apostatical human architecture to give them bodies that better reflect their gender—but she had not expected anyone like this in the palace itself.

"What happened to your mother, Iriset?" Anis asks by way of distraction.

"Apostatical cancer."

"I'm sorry."

Amaranth says, "Iriset, did you witness Silk perform human architecture?"

Shocked at the change in direction of the inquiry, Iriset tears her eyes off Anis and to Her Glory.

"Allow me to pose a hypothetical," Amaranth continues.

"Your Glory." Iriset touches her eyelids.

"When a friend of mine was born, their body's external design by all appearances was that of a man, yet this person's inner design, that none may know but the person themself and She Who Loves Silence, was that of a woman. What do you think that would be like?"

"It would be difficult," Iriset says, not glancing at Anis. "A difficult way to live. Trapped with only two options."

"But are they a man or a woman? Which is more important, outer design or inner design?"

Iriset feels trapped herself. What does Amaranth want?

This is the test. Not leaving her alone all those hours this afternoon, but this.

She *should* say Aharté does not make mistakes. The external design of men and women is perfect, balanced. She *should* say, in teaching with the empire's laws, that only Aharté can know which is more important, outer or inner design. That they must trust Silence, trust Aharté's designs, and if there is such disagreement between a person's outer and inner design, then She Who Loves Silence intended that disagreement to exist, and so the person must live with the disagreement. But Iriset doesn't believe it is so simple. She has examined human bodies in great detail, and the more details she explored, the more certain she became that dividing everyone into merely two was one of the stupider things the miran had done. No stool with but two legs can stand. The most stable designs require four points, four forces. Rising, falling, ecstatic, flow. In the mirané calendar there are four days in a quarter, four quarters in a quad, four great forces. With that in mind, how odd it is that Aharté's Holy Design and her mirané language do not account for at least four genders.

The empire sometimes acts against its own internal design in order to oppress what it cannot control.

But that is not what Iriset was asked.

"Aharté does not make mistakes," Iriset says slowly, maneuvering through respect for the laws and what she knows to be true. Without referencing Silk's heretical writings. Amaranth said she collects exceptional handmaidens, and so Iriset ought to behave exceptionally. "But *we* make mistakes. Life, and the Holy Design, are immensely more complex than we understand, Your Glory. Perhaps what we expect when we ask either-or is our mistake, not a mistake in her Design. There are more than two forces in the world, and maybe more than two options for a person's design."

"Apostasy," Amaranth says, rather blithely.

"To be expected from the daughter of the Little Cat," Istof says dismissively.

"No." Iriset's hands curl into fists. "It is not apostasy to say we are less skilled architects than Aharté herself, it is only apostasy if we consider the alternative."

The smile that breaks across Her Glory's mouth melts Iriset's anxiety and confusion into rising relief.

"Aharté designed you as she intended to, *of course*," Iriset says to Anis, suddenly ferocious. "There is only one conflict, and that is who you are versus what you are allowed to do about it."

Anis studies Iriset for a moment. Then murmurs, "Very well, Amaranth. We can keep her."

Amaranth laughs—as do Nielle and Ziyan, in delight and relief, respectively—and takes back the reins. "It is apostasy, though, Iriset: Once, before Aharté, there were at least four genders we lived with in our crater city, and the Sarians named them ahz, ahzran, friahz, and frian. You likely have not studied the language, but that prefix, *fri*, can only be translated rather complicatedly as *weighted toward balance*. Is that not charming? You might say *friahz* means *weighted toward woman* or *toward woman* and that if we were apostates or spoke Sarenpet, perhaps someone like my hypothetical friend could be called such a person. Friahz. But that is my hypothetical friend. *Anis* is a woman. Do you understand?"

Iriset nods, thinking that she does. "Anything balanced serves Aharté."

Her Glory snorts. "Your mistress Silk, who you claim taught you design, is a proven apostate. We have heard of her terrible work. Would she have been able to redesign my hypothetical friend a face and body that better mirrored their inner design?"

Suddenly angry, Iriset says, "If that is what your friend actually wanted, and if the Little Cat was paid well enough for it."

Silence cuts through the chamber. None of the handmaidens move or even breathe. Then Sidoné turns her head to Amaranth as if to claim the winnings of a bet.

But Amaranth only says, "Careful, kitten."

Iriset freezes. Her father called her that. What is Amaranth trying to say?

She lets Her Glory stare at her for a moment before rising, shaky with the adrenaline of fear and anger. She moves around the oval table to kneel at the foot of Her Glory's low sofa.

"I am your servant," she says, and hides her eyes against the floor lest she give herself away.

6

The red moon

It is said that if Moonshadow City is the heart of the empire, then the Vertex Seal is the heart of Moonshadow City. It's true, though not because his palace is the location from which flow moral and legal proclamations, nor only that it's the geographical center of the city. It is true because the palace of the Vertex Seal marks—no, the throne itself marks—the focal point of all the Design of the empire.

Moonshadow City glimmers in a red-rock crater, a wound gashed into the center of the continent millennia ago. To the north, red-rock mountains grow slowly from the arid forests that used to be Ilmar and Saria, the earth filled with minerals and gems ready to be mined, and beyond them rise the drastic peaks of the Cloud Ranges.

Fertile rolling fields and gentle forests spread to the west through the former Land of God, then give way to kinder mountains of Ur-Syel dividing the empire from the martial Bow queendoms with their canopy cities and volcanic magic.

Plains push east, flat and dry and perfect for cattle and sheep, toward the prairie with its troubled clans and states that once had been an empire of their own. But our empire drove countless Pir refugees and broken Reskik peoples across those plains into Huvar, a pleasant enough oligarchy that only survives because the empire, when it expands, must expand in all directions equally thanks to the necessary balance of the four forces.

The Lapis River pours out of the northern red mountains and dives toward the city in a rush, curving east to cup the south of the crater before widening into a glorious channel slow and steady enough for barges and ships to enjoy. Then it dives into the deserts of the south, carving canyons and caves for miles, before it becomes a snaking jungle river that spills into the sea. That is where the Ceres Remnants maintain themselves, islands that once were a continent of their own, with a grand empire of their own, but some other young god struggled there long ago and destroyed that world. The islands are rich, and safe from the empire because Aharté's Design does not do well on the open sea.

The empire flourishes. Within its boundaries Design works wonders. Within it, power is in the hands of architects and therefore in the hands of the Vertex Seal.

But once there was nothing in the center of the continent except a river, broad and bright as a line of the sky, slipping south where it widened into a great coursing waterway. Floodplains flushed green in the spring, nurturing rainbows of flora and thriving tiers of animals: insects, fish, birds, alliraptors and desert lions and pack dogs, and the soaring griffon.

And there used to be a second moon in the sky. Some suggest it orbited the Eye of Aharté, not the world. A moon for a moon. Tiny, and red as a drop of dried blood. Then it fell through our atmosphere and slammed here, cracking in four pieces. The crater is eight miles wide.

A god climbed out of the cracked moon, beautiful and oh so hungry. He summoned people to him, and they came curiously, sensing the trembling forces. This god gave names to those architectural forces, taught his people how to manipulate them, and there in the center of the crater, a cult was born. A cult of young designers and holy people, worshippers of the god of the red moon. First they carved homes deep into the flattened earth and rim of the crater, then they fashioned stucco warrens, and finally they lifted above the ground with primitive windcatchers and force-supported steeples. The river bowed around the crater and the god taught the people to blast through the spiking walls and allow water in, to draw it with underground canals and falling force and locks. Crops grew in the circle of devastation, then flowers and hardwood trees, and animals returned, creeping toward sustenance. They had food, they had families, and they had a god of design. The crater city was a paradise.

Those first architects embraced every wild hope their craft promised. They invented force-ribbons to draw vehicles, they built needle towers that swayed with the wind, they manipulated children still in the womb, making angels and monsters. They spliced creatures together in glorious and dreadful ways, melding flesh and earth, tree and sky, anything they could imagine—some healing, some unsustainable. Never had so much pain and misunderstanding stained the world with its effects; never had such beauty reigned. Living rainbows, men with cat-eyes, women with four arms, friahz with skin of feathers, flying fish, small-smaller-smallest eagles, and iridescent beetles the size of a cloud. They tested theories to make lives better: Could a child be born with unbreakable bones? Could a woman be made never to age? They acted on whims: What if a bird's skull was on the outside of its face? What if instead of a tower flexible as a tree, they grew a tree as hollow as a tower? Could flesh be blue as the sky, or sparkling as diamonds? Where was the infinitesimal line between conscious, living being and growing crystal? Imagine! Go wild! Do not hold back.

Well, the god of the red moon gave his knowledge to humanity, and humanity made a mess.

Rival factions attacked their enemies with monsters, with force-poisoned food and tainted air. They butchered one another with mutations, with ecstatic death and hot rising death, with the slow yearning death of hopelessness. All while winged serpents dragged across the sunset and the river sang with the voices of changed alliraptors. Beautiful. Terrible. The architects did not understand the patterns of life intimately enough to create it perfectly, and thus rebellious cancers appeared with no summoning, the consequences of our dreams.

Some people fought toward peace, toward the betterment of their neighbors. Some were called to service, to drag their fellows along a path that did not allow harm. They were good, they had hope, and they knew relationships of empathy were what made people stronger, not better bones or better swords or better poisons.

The problem was, the god of the red moon was not on *their* side.

Maybe he lacked empathy. Maybe nobody ever told him a good story. Maybe because he'd fallen from the sky, he was always sore. Maybe he was hangry. Maybe he missed Aharté.

Oh yes. Aharté. Watching from her own moon, that larger silver-pink moon still hanging in our sky. And she missed him, too, didn't she?

Meanwhile, outside the crater of paradise and hell, desert kings of Bes had united under Sarenpet the Great. Sarenpet and his kings conquered the lands around the Ilmar and into Saria. They came to the red god's crater, and because Sarenpet was as hungry as the red god, the god invited the king to remain. Thus was founded the dynasty of Bes and Sarenpet, under the red moon banner.

For three hundred years the Bes and Sarenpet forced purpose onto their folk, and the crater's influence grew. What once was a cult of architects became an empire. But it lacked balance. Was volatile.

It was too loud.

A boy was born, Maimeri Sarenpet, with a whisper of Silence in his heart. As he grew, he abjured architecture, though he sensed the forces against his skin and within his bones. He listened, quietly. He recognized patterns, and one day followed one such thread outside the crater. That day a star appeared in the sky and it fell. It fell hot and hard, and when Maimeri Sarenpet reached its much smaller crater, he found a woman sitting with an alliraptor's smiling head in her lap. She told Maimeri she was Syr, wife of Aharté, She Who Loves Silence, and together they would save the world.

(There is another version of the story that says the alliraptor stood up and turned into another woman, this one as red-brown as the crater, as red-brown as the god of the red moon, and said her name was Aharté. Then Aharté turned and walked away from the city, away from her wife. Maimeri Sarenpet begged her to remain, but she said her wife was better at magic anyway. Then Aharté vanished into the trees.)

Anyway, the Holy Syr taught Maimeri the true gospels of Aharté that they together might balance the forces of architecture and destroy the red moon god—whom she named the Moon-Eater, as if the god, in his hunger, had so devoured his own red moon it had weakened and fallen from the sky. If he was not stopped, this whole planet would weaken as well.

Together, in perfect architectural balance, they unraveled the Moon-Eater until nothing remained but his teeth.

With epic power, under the always-watching eye of this silver-pink moon, they leveled the apostatical inventions, from towers to giant bugs, unraveling the patterns of all those creatures and structures (and people) that struggled to live. If it could not survive without constant design intervention, it did not survive.

(Why did the skull sirens live? Why the micro-vultures? Is it something about birds? Can you tell me? And every once in a while a child like Bittor is born with cat-eyes, as if that recessive trait refuses to be eradicated. There are rainbow bees bobbing in every garden, rep-cats and lattice snakes, and rumors Iriset has heard of people with feathers in their hair or scales in the dry skin at the smalls of their backs.)

In the ruins of the Moon-Eater's city, Maimeri and the Holy Syr founded the Vertex Seal.

Before anything else, they laid the foundation stones for the palace, and the matching stones for the Moon-Eater's Temple so that humanity would always remember his devastation. Those structures will exist as long as the empire itself does, the palace complex in the very center of the crater and surrounded by the quartz yards. The yards gleam under the sun, a flat expanse of quartz and shells, symmetrical half-moon pools, a quarter mile in every direction so that nothing and no one might approach the palace without being seen.

The Holy Syr said, "Here is my daughter, the daughter of Aharté. She is the Vertex Seal, Her Glory, prince of my flesh. My second daughter is the Moon-Eater's Mistress, Her Glory, prince of my flesh. Balance to bind, always. One must be claimed with blood, satisfied and silent, paired to the other in hunger and sacrifice."

So it was etched onto the throne of the Vertex Seal: *one claimed with blood and paired with hunger, always binding.*

The Holy Syr's daughter was born with red-brown skin (moon-red, it might be said, mirané it would soon be called), just like the Moon-Eater's had been. (Just like Aharté's.)

Over time, the children and grandchildren of Maimeri and the Holy Syr learned the balance of Silence, and with Aharté's proscriptions firmly in place, they once again harnessed the four forces to push the city out, so that it spilled toward every edge of the crater, in elegant rising levels like the ruffled petals of a mountain rose. Design steeples spiked up, white as bone, in spiral and cross-diamond patterns, binding the Holy Design of the city. It was that web of craft that allowed Moonshadow its arching tension bridges, stepped-marble squares and fire gardens, impossibly high gilded domes and domes glazed turquoise and blue like the sea and sky. The web-powered force-ribbons looped, streaking throughout the city, pulling skiffs along with the slightest tug of craft. In each of the cardinal directions a massive force-steeple was built, each with an elegant, glowing Design to lure and funnel one of the four forces: falling, rising, flow, and ecstatic.

Moonshadow was perfect, a paradise of bound design.

And the children of Aharté's flesh, the miran, ruled.

7

Establishment

Iriset has sixty days to save her father.

Of her four-point plan, the first—befriend Amaranth and her brother, the Vertex Seal, in order to make herself indispensable—is the easiest to begin with, for as Her Glory's handmaiden, she's expected to be at Amaranth's side most of the time.

The familiarity the handmaidens share with one another strikes Iriset, for always they're touching: to redirect conversation, to comfort, to flirt. Iriset is bad at joining in, forcing herself to reach out and brush her hand to Anis's elbow or pat Ziyan when she's sad to miss a canceled concert. It never becomes second nature to her. Even with her grandparents Iriset was unlikely to initiate casual contact. (And oh merciful Silence, her grandparents! Could she get a message to them?) Never one to shy away from critical self-analysis, Iriset suspects her distaste for casual intimacy has to do with how carefully she worked to hold Silk and Iriset separate, despite Silk being her more true self.

Iriset can hardly bring herself to touch Amaranth at all, given the strength of her attraction, though the handmaidens do so, frequently, causing Iriset to wonder if they're all her lovers. The

Moon-Eater's Mistress is not supposed to take pleasure outside of the god's temple, but who would deny Amaranth? And nothing in the mirané laws forbid women from each other. It's congress between men and women that is closely regulated, for a man and a woman might weave the pattern for a child in their lust. Giving life belongs only to Aharté and should not be done without her approval.

(Once Iriset said to Bittor, "If Aharté did not approve of a man's desire outside of her marriage knot, she'd not have designed your unmarried parts to harden so nicely for me." "My *parts* do not know the difference between married and not married, or between masculine- and feminine-forward," he responded, exasperated. Iriset thought he liked her academic seduction. "I want to know all there is to know about design, and you will let me study you," she said the first time. Bittor laughed at that, and distracted her so well she forgot to catalog the patterns of force his body wove as he came. Oh well, they had to try again.)

Her Glory encourages her handmaidens to educate themselves, and the options are plenty: lectures on government, philosophy, history, and religion offered by various tutors through the palace libraries, attended mostly by the children of miran and palace workers, though some soldiers join, too; one might simply drift into the library shelves and read any book or scroll or comic pamphlet in the unrestricted sections of the libraries; physical arts are practiced in the broad gymnasium, in groups separated by gender as the miran prefer; and four small galleries provide different sorts of fine arts both for viewing and pursuit.

The Little Cat gave Iriset a basic education, but once she displayed her proficiency in design and disinterest in, well, everything else, Isidor narrowed her tutors to a variety of well-bribed architects. The options available to Iriset now are nearly overwhelming.

So Iriset chooses based on that which she thinks will suit her cause best. First of all she doesn't wish to be separate from Her Glory too often; not only does that defeat the purpose of befriending Amaranth, but it would be suspicious to seem reluctant. So when Amaranth daily dances in the gymnasium with silk ropes, spinning and stretching, so does Iriset. When Amaranth joins a lecture on the conquest of Saria, so does Iriset. At a point every day the handmaidens are dismissed while Amaranth attends the Hall of Princes for Seal business, or if she has private luncheons with various mirané ladies or goes into the city for an afternoon garden party with a small king. During those hours, Iriset finds a regular art class in the Gallery of Shades, for if Iriset practices drawing and sculpture, it's not suspicious for her to have vellum, charcoal, and even graphite knives in her chamber. The crab pick she stole needs to be shattered into a finer point if she's to use it on the jade cuff, and for that she'll need some clay to fashion a finger handle at the end or risk slicing her skin. Where better to acquire it than an art class?

When she doesn't have a class but can't be with Amaranth, Iriset spends time in her chamber, ostensibly napping, but in truth carefully peeling back the palace architecture one strand at a time in order to read the security. With no more than the crab pick and a thread pulled from the hem of a silk robe, she sets an alarm across the hall beyond her door to alert her if a servant comes so she'll have just enough time to hide her business.

It takes a square of days to feel she's got a strong grasp of the basic security, and she sets off alone to explore between lectures and dinner with Her Glory, in order to mentally map everything.

The palace complex is designed like a garden. In the center the palace itself consists of eight bright domes lifting higher and higher, surrounded by curving petal-wings and sleek spiral towers like it's a living, crawling bramble of flowering lowland cacti. Four force-steeples surround it in exactly the cardinal directions, their shapes fitting the force associated, and direct threads of power connect them to the city's Great Steeples, giving Moonshadow its anchoring spokes. The Moon-Eater's Temple is a dark blue, squat dome between the Flow and Falling Steeples, and the Silent Chapel a gleaming white four-point star of columns between the Ecstatic and Rising Steeples. Around the palace, outer corridors slip toward and around various amphitheaters and courtyards, tiled in every shade of blue and green, white and pink, giving them names such as the Blue Between Sea and Sky Courtyard or the Winter Sunset Courtyard. Fountains trickle in most corners, between rows of pillars that snake with gold-inlaid script describing the Silence and Aharté's promises for design and the spiraling patterns of the world. Clear, quiet pools mark meditation gardens tucked in every corner of free space.

The tall, airy gazebos are capped with honeycomb arches so perfectly made, Iriset finds herself standing with her face tilted worshipfully up until her neck aches. Inner walls burst with geometric mosaics, and outer walls of stucco are painted like the skies and oceans, or encrusted with quartz shards—or opals or saltrock especially suited to Design.

Most archways mark her jade bracelet as she passes beneath them, though Iriset suspects the other handmaidens can't feel it. The effect is nearly instantaneous, and Iriset confuses two palace servants by walking in and out of one doorway again and again to see if any delay accumulates.

At first, Iriset doesn't visit many of the inner chambers, where the miran live, nor the men's petal hall. She doesn't see the Hall of Princes where the Vertex Seal rules from a chair settled over a square of blood-red moon rock.

But in the Color Can Be Loud Garden, Iriset discovers flowers that turn their delicate faces to the strongest thread of design, and to her that is more beautiful and awful than any famous throne or the words carved there by the hand of a god.

———— • ♦ • ————

There are three people besides Amaranth and her women who Iriset sees every day: The first is Shahd, a sixteen-year-old mirané girl who works in Her Glory's women's petal. On the fourth day of Iriset's life at the palace, she asks Shahd's name and recognizes it as an old Sarian god name. It surprises her, because most assimilated tribes and families, especially those as prominent as Sarians, refuse to name their children with given names from outside of Silence.

Shahd is clearly mirané, and nothing but her name suggests otherwise. Iriset stares so long, searching for bone markers or stance or the shape of an ear or how her eyes fold at the corners, that Shahd not only lowers her gaze, but kneels upon the floor in submission.

"Oh," Iriset says, falling to her knees as well. She takes Shahd's hands—as dry as her own, though ministrations with oils here in the women's hall are slowly recovering Iriset's skin from her prison days—and tries to smile. "I mean no offense, Shahd. I only know your name is a marker of the holy pilgrimage site at the center of Saria's old city, and did not expect it in such a perfect miran." Then Iriset adds, in a whisper of an old Sarian war dialect she grew up with in the Saltbath precinct, that sometimes is an undermarket code: "We live and we die."

The girl nods, and her fingers curl harder around Iriset's. She whispers the rest of the message, "We weave vital threads to their knots."

Iriset immediately makes her first request of Amaranth, that Shahd be assigned to her permanently. Her Glory agrees with an air of disinterest so bland it must be a facade. So Iriset waits a few days before giving Shahd a note to hide in one of the Little Cat's city drops, in hopes that someone is checking them. She asks if Shahd will visit her grandparents, and when the girl hesitates, Iriset asks simply that she look. Iriset only needs to know they're all right.

The second person is the Architect of the Seal. Every morning, she shows up in Amaranth's rooms to paint Amaranth's and Sidoné's faces in matching geometry. She brings, along with her box of paint and styli and brushes, entertaining gossip. As she paints, she teases apart the tangles of mirané relationships, and updates Amaranth on any changes to the current politics among the design schools—who jockeys for which position, and where any rumors have arisen about human architecture, or non-Silent cults.

From distant observation only, Iriset finds Menna to be extremely competent, if unimaginative in her design. Such makes sense for an architect in her high position, especially under a Vertex Seal known for his strict faith. Iriset expects no help will come from that arena. Especially as Menna treats Iriset with cool distance, as if she smells ever so slightly of something distasteful.

It's a strange sensation to allow someone who clearly dislikes her near enough to paint thin lines of complex patterns against Iriset's cheek or forehead. Iriset offers to paint herself, and does it so flawlessly in a mirror, Anis (the elegant one) and Nielle (the ugly one) applaud. Menna sniffs, eyeing Iriset's work. The Architect of the Seal says, "It's too bad," with a little shrug of indifference.

"Too bad I'm the daughter of the Little Cat?" Iriset asks with every thread of gentleness she can dredge up.

But Menna scoffs and gathers her things to leave without further comment.

Amaranth tugs at Sidoné's wrist and the two of them go with Anis to dress Her Glory for the day. Nielle leans toward Iriset and pops a slice of cactus pear into Iriset's surprised mouth. "It's nothing personal," the handmaiden says. "She doesn't like Istof, either."

Iriset crunches the pear and thinks it through. Honestly, it takes her longer than it should to get it: "Because we're not miran?" she says incredulously.

"Several of the princes on the mirané council feel the same way."

"An *architect* should be beyond such things."

"Some will always be miran before they're anything else," Nielle says, as if that justifies anything at all.

Nielle is also the one who explains to Iriset about Garnet—the third person Iriset sees every day.

His full name is, rather dramatically, The Garnet That Blooms in the Broken Heart. Every son born to mirané parents the year of his birth was given an elaborate line of prayer for a name, and Garnet's is such a sad one because his father died just beforehand, and his mother, Bež, was truly heartbroken. But her son had his father's will and his father's way of making Bež laugh like none other but her griffons could do. Garnet was raised in a nest of griffons, nursed while his mother cradled him in one arm and flung chunks of meat with the other. Critics suggested Bež unnecessarily risked her son's life, but she ignored them except to say it was a testament to her relationship with the queens of the sky that her son survived.

While under usual circumstances, Garnet could never have been made the body-twin to A Lyric to Bridge the Silence—also born that year—because Garnet's skin color obviously distinguished him from His Glory, the two young boys met as toddlers and became naturally inseparable. Such love was valued more in a prince and his body-twin than an exact physical match, for the point of such a relationship was permanence. Both boys were focused, quiet, and determined to be what they were born. As they grew, Garnet gave in to his martial inclinations, filling out spectacularly, until he was nearly as powerful and quick as one of his mother's griffons.

By the time Lyric méra Esmail ascended, Garnet had thwarted three assassination attempts and befriended or impressed everyone important. He is everywhere in a way the Vertex Seal cannot be. If you want an invitation to speak with Lyric, the most direct route is through Garnet, not the palace steward nor the mirané council. Despite his official role as elite bodyguard, he acts more like the Vertex Seal's chief ancillary. As such, he consults often with the Moon-Eater's Mistress, or rather, with his mirror in her service, Sidoné. No other man spends more time in Amaranth's women's hall than Garnet méra Bež.

He finds Iriset, twice, when she's mapping the palace grounds early in the mornings. The first time, she feigns slight confusion and asks him to escort her back to Amaranth's petal as if she so easily became lost. Her gentle flirtation hits his jaw like thin falling force against magnetic cobalt, sliding right off. That's fine, though, as he never flirts back with any of the handmaidens. She hides her eyes behind her fingers. When he drops her off after a silent walk, he merely nods and goes about his day, presumably.

The second time he comes across her, six days into her new life as Her Glory's handmaiden, Garnet asks directly what she's doing out and about. Iriset, ready with a lie, suddenly remembers what Garnet said to her about the griffons, and Amaranth insisting she only takes on exceptional handmaidens.

So Iriset tilts her face away but does not cover her eyes. "You know who my father is. He taught me to know where I am."

She can feel the long look Garnet gives her pressing against the palace-orange cloth mask wrapping her hair. It's impressive that he's so good at balancing his inner forces. Even Iriset can barely detect the dominant flow. "Be careful alone," Garnet finally says. "Your father is not popular here."

"When I'm alone, like this"—Iriset gestures vaguely at her whole self—"nobody knows I'm anything other than a new attendant they've never met."

"That won't last."

Iriset lets her chin fall as if in defeat. Garnet carefully cups her elbow in escort, and she determines not to do her mapping in his vicinity anymore if she can help it. She needs to take her time getting to know Garnet méra Bež, without arousing his suspicion. He is closest to the Vertex Seal, after all.

Strangely enough (or perhaps a thread of perfect Silence), as if her choice to be a little bit more overtly exceptional marks the way, Iriset makes a new friend all on her own that very day.

The drawing class Iriset takes in the Gallery of Shades is less concerned with precision, and more with organic recreation. They sketch clouds and wavering pools of water, concentrating on the shadows rippling again and again. They draw the repeating patterns of a butterfly's wing, then compare it to the layered feathers upon an owl's. Everything has a pattern, if you can only discover it.

Iriset relaxes in the peaceful tension between allowing her lines to wander amateurishly and familiarity with the craft. Drawing beneath her level is difficult. And frustrating! She wants to sketch the corner of her instructor's mouth, or that square hand working beside her on the bench, or the fluttering shade from that sculpted cedar as it changes the color of the man's eyes to her left. Iriset longs to draw faces—she needs to. When she struggles, the urgency of her father's situation rears itself, and she feels sharp guilt at every second of enjoyment or relaxation. But this *is* part of her plan. Become a beloved handmaiden. Trusted within the palace. Gather art supplies that double for design. It all serves her purpose. She has fifty-eight days.

"Are you speaking Old Sarenpet?" the man to her left asks.

Iriset blinks, realizing that as she drew tiny petals, she murmured one of the counting songs her mother used to sing. "Yes, sir," she says, glancing over.

The man is older, and by his accent, the blessed tongue of miran is not his first language. She lowers her lashes respectfully.

"I have heard Sarenpet shares some grammatical structure with the ghost tongue—unlike this slinking mirané." He says it with a merry wink, proving no offense. His square face is plain, subtly wrinkled, unpainted, a cool tan, and beardless, but there are white tattoos delicately placed along his hairline that vanish into his hair. If he hadn't mentioned the ghost tongue, Iriset would know he was from the Ceres Remnants by those alone. The tattoos list out his ancestors in ghost writing the Remnants will not teach to outsiders. Iriset guesses him to be early in his sixth decade. Six small copper hoops pierce his right eyebrow, and six more curl around his right ear. All his hair is bound in thick silk ropes that create a large pink, silver, and red flower at the nape of his neck. It matches his long embroidered coat and his billowing skirts.

"I am Iriset mé Isidor," Iriset says, wondering if he's heard of her father and how he'll react. Yesterday a guest instructor stopped speaking to her when Iriset said her name, until another classmate hissed that she served Her Glory now. Iriset struggles to act like their scrutiny bothers her. (In reality, it is easy to ignore the feelings of those around her. If someone isn't in her way, why should she care what they think? She hasn't realized yet that caring about what everyone around you thinks and wants is the core of politics.)

The Ceres man doesn't hesitate to answer: "I am Erxan, Ceres ambassador to your Vertex Seal. That blossom looks like an eye," he adds, pointing with his charcoal stick at her detailed rose.

She glances down at her art. Iriset has been drawing the facets of an iris surrounding the dark pupil. These roses with their hundreds of layered, tiny petals are very like a living eye.

Erxan says, "In my home, we paint magnificent portraits of our gods and kings, though I know it is anathema here. You would be an honored artist, young woman. Handmaiden, I see, by your pretty green bracelet." Ease and humor coat his tone, and Iriset looks up as shyly as she can.

With her chin she indicates the blurry, shapeless flowers on his vellum. "You are not very good at this."

"No." Erxan laughs deep in his chest. "But I like it, and learning your art, learning to appreciate it and enjoy its essence, is more important than being good at it."

"Can you truly understand it if you are not good at it?" she asks openly. This is the sort of argument her father would invite, over a nightcap, or after a successful operation. Asking the question makes her feel closer to Isidor, though he suffers alone in the apostate tower.

Erxan hums thoughtfully, and says, "When you see my Singix at midsummer, you will understand that it is possible to understand beauty without creating it."

"Singix?" Iriset pronounces the name carefully. For all the ambassador's claims of links between Ceres and Sarenpet, Iriset is not well versed in the tonality.

"Singix Es Sun," Erxan says, voice lifting in admiration.

"Wait until you see her, handmaiden. You have seen none so lovely as she—designed, as you would say, by the demon of beauty herself."

"I look forward to such architecture," Iriset murmurs. "When does she arrive? Is she your daughter?"

Ambassador Erxan pauses now, then laughs with a merry surge of ecstatic force. "You haven't heard of her? She's to be your own king's wife."

Iriset frowns, generally unconcerned with the small kings, and certainly not having one of her own. The small king of Saltbath has been married for ages.

Erxan's laughter calms, flowing more peacefully. He has a strong dominant force of flow, Iriset thinks: Those good at persuasion and diplomacy often do. "The Vertex Seal," he encourages.

And oh, Iriset's lips part in astonishment. She had no idea the Vertex Seal is engaged. It's quite the thing to miss.

"You really are an artist," Erxan says. "Unaware of anything that isn't your work." Somehow, he doesn't sound patronizing in the least. And it's certainly accurate. Silk has always drowned herself in design. "Singix will like you."

Desperate to rally, having found herself dropped in the lap of another potential resource for getting close to the Vertex Seal, Iriset smiles back and leans in to whisper, "Perhaps if she is as gorgeous as you claim, I'll paint her after all, and give up my Silent ways."

Erxan winks. "I'll spirit you to safety in the islands if it comes to that."

Iriset's smile grows. That's a promise she might hold him to one day.

8

Engagement

Although people from every conquered land live and work in Moonshadow—people of Bes and Sarenpet, of the old Pir tribes, Sarians, Urs, descendants of the Bow, Mirithian, Reskik, various migrant peoples from the coast, merchant cult-clans pressed into Silence, even rare earthbound Cloud Kings and ruby-cheeked northerners—although so many call Moonshadow home, can rise to lead their neighborhoods by democratic or draconic methods, can become small kings, it is the mirané council who are the true rulers of Moonshadow, and the empire at large.

These sixty-four princes of mirané descent compose the body of folk who advise the Vertex Seal, debate policy, philosophy, and law, and oversee slices of land or business or both. One must be born into the council, through direct family lines, and visibly mirané in every way.

The leader of the mirané council rotates, theoretically, but for most of Moonshadow's recent history the position has been traded among three families. At the time of Iriset's tenure in the palace, the seat is held by Beremé mé Adora, a forty-year-old woman whose father and grandmother both had spent nearly as much time as she at the mirané pulpit. Beremé is overly thin, but uses it to her advantage with harsh paint slashing her cheekbones and darkening her eyes into vivid pools. Her smile doesn't soften her face but brings her features into a predatory alignment. Iriset finds her fascinating, an ideal example of unique architecture used with purpose.

Amaranth clearly agrees, allowing Beremé to flirt openly, and even share a kiss when no others but her handmaidens might witness.

Amaranth doesn't take lovers publicly, for she's devoted to the Moon-Eater, but Iriset is certain the two women have done more than kiss. She wonders sometimes which of the women takes more advantage of the other in their political games.

This is the only of Amaranth's connections wherein Iriset is aware of Sidoné's deep disapproval. At first she imagines jealousy, but learns eventually that it's the popular grudge of assimilation cutting between her and Beremé: Sidoné, though mirané, has the bone structure and obvious nose of the Bow, Iriset noted upon first meeting, and is the granddaughter of the last famously defeated Bow warlord. The one Amaranth's grandfather stripped and lashed to the nose of his river barge to die of exposure and thirst on the return home from conquest.

Beremé had liked, in the early days of Sidoné's work as Amaranth's body-twin, to point to her as the ideal outcome for conquest and the laws of assimilation. When followed to the letter, a conquered people could, within merely a single generation, achieve not only Aharté's favor but that of the Vertex Seal. See! Sidoné mé Dalir is living proof. Once, Beremé attempted to parade Sidoné through the Flow Steeple Shadow precinct in the wake of a violent rebellion by the Reskik in that neighborhood, as a sort of mascot.

That had been quashed by Amaranth herself, newly the Moon-Eater's Mistress at the tender age of fifteen, with the support of her brother, Lyric, whose distaste for flagrant displays of power already was well known, despite his not rising to the Vertex Seal for several more years. (When his hand is forced, Lyric prefers a precise, sudden violence with little in the way of collateral damage, but very much in the way of terror.)

Sidoné never forgave the mirané prince for the attempt.

It's Sidoné's face this morning that gives Iriset her only warning that Beremé is already with Amaranth when Iriset is ushered inside Her Glory's personal chamber.

This octagonal room rules the women's petal like the pistil of a flower. It's larger than the petal rooms and thrice as tall so that where its honeycomb dome lifts high, there's space for massive windows latticed with delicate star shapes. Its star-eye hole is immediately at the pinnacle of the dome, and paned with thin crystal tinted slightly blue. Beneath it is a glorious blue mosaic star, caulked with real gold. The rest of the floor repeats blue-green-white patterns of waves pushing away from the star toward the pure white stucco walls. Amaranth's raised bed sways on a trundle, her bed's veil spilling in white and pale blue and peacock green like a voluptuous skirt.

Amaranth herself lounges on a low sofa, a bowl of soup cradled in her hands halfway to her mouth, as she teases Beremé mé Adora about Beremé's lack of interest in marriage alliance. "—and can't imagine giving yourself to the romance of the design seed."

"I like my inner design the way it is," Beremé sniffs, flicking invisible motes at Her Glory.

Sidoné turns away from the whole room.

"You like stringing everyone along that maybe someday they'll be able to have you."

"Yes," Beremé drawls. "I'm so very desirable."

Amaranth touches the rim of her bowl to her lips and drinks, eyes on the mirané prince. She's wearing loose morning robes barely tied over her body, and has yet to spend her daily allotment with the Moon-Eater. Iriset is learning this makes her volatile the longer she puts it off, as if it takes her communion to settle her forces into place after a long night of dreams.

"Ah, here's the little criminal."

Iriset blinks at the brusque charge and finds herself the center of Beremé's skull siren gaze. She touches her eyelids and holds herself in a shallow bow.

Amaranth says, "Kitten."

It should be condescending, but Iriset only feels quiet arousal at Amaranth's slow tone. She shouldn't—it's her own father's pet name for her. But there's nothing Iriset can do against the sensual flow of the Moon-Eater's Mistress.

"Your Glory," she murmurs.

"Tonight is Nielle's engagement dinner, and Beremé thinks you should attend at my side."

Amaranth has been working toward the engagement for months, according to Nielle herself. It's not the inevitable ending for one of Her Glory's handmaidens to marry out of Amaranth's petal, but for the ones who desire it, Amaranth is happy to oblige as long as the handmaiden in general doesn't mind being used for political maneuvers. "I'm the way I am, so it's only to my benefit to have someone like Amaranth backing me—I come with power and the ear of the Moon-Eater's Mistress: Who wouldn't overlook a few things?" Nielle had said. At Iriset's expression, she'd laughed. "It's not just my face, Iriset. Plenty of people can look past that, or even like it, but I truly struggle to be less than blunt. I say what I think. Trust me, if it could be beaten out of me, my parents would have."

She'd said it with such joking grace, but Iriset had been offended on Nielle's behalf. Too bad she couldn't do anything about it.

In the end, Amaranth had settled on Sian méra Sayar, the young small king of the Ecstatic Steeple Shadow precinct. He was younger than Nielle by a year, younger than the Vertex Seal by five, and inherited his crown through an archaic system of so-called voting by the merchant guild and holy temple attendants in his mother's precinct. Each small king had their own internal arrangements for inheritance, you see. But Sian was well liked, and had a significant stake in several mines along the southern edge of the crater, as well as some scattered down toward the sea. His cousin ran the Osahar shares of the ribbon network, several of his grand-aunts toe-dipped in everything from public gardens to the Ecstatic School of Architecture. Nielle claimed Sian was sweet, glowed with mirané eagerness, had tried to kiss her almost immediately, and she wasn't worried about getting anything she—or Amaranth—wanted from him.

(Nobody told Iriset that Naira mé Rinore, the seventh prince on the mirané council, had wanted to marry her niece to Sian, but in the wake of the two-years-long grappling to secure the marriage of the Vertex Seal to Singix Es Sun, Amaranth had decided that she would do anything in her power to keep Naira from getting what she wanted ever again. Naira and Amaranth's mother, Diaa of Moonshadow, had been united in their dislike of marrying Lyric to a non-mirané foreigner, but while Diaa argued based on laws of Silence, Naira had allowed her disdain for non-miran to show like roots on an otherwise perfectly dyed head of hair.

Regardless, Naira had built an alliance of several other mirané princes in an attempt to thwart Amaranth, and Amaranth repaid that sort of thing in full.)

In Amaranth's bedroom, Iriset sinks to her knees, eyes lowered. "Whatever Her Glory commands," she says.

The sounds of sweeping robes whisper toward Iriset. She does not glance up at Beremé. "Oh, Amaranth, she does seem tame."

Iriset goes rigid, ecstatic force tightening muscles and spine with little pops. She breathes through flared nostrils as slowly as she can, drawing flow through her blood.

"No need to be rude," Amaranth says lightly.

"I'm impressed. Did we settle on a wager after all?"

It's impossible for Iriset not to grind her teeth. A pointy finger tucks under her chin and lifts her face. Iriset trembles with the effort of lowering her eyes—she is domesticated, isn't she?

"That's mine, Beremé," Amaranth says much less nicely.

Beremé releases Iriset's chin. "Well, I know, Your Glory. And you, Iriset mé Isidor."

Iriset raises her eyes just to Beremé's mouth.

"Can you think of a way you can play a role for Amaranth?"

"Tame," Iriset murmurs.

"Naive. Trusting. Obedient."

"That's hardly what I want." Amaranth's robes swirl in front of Iriset's face as she kneels, nudging Beremé aside. "Get out, Beremé."

With a brief sigh, Beremé sweeps away. "See you tonight, Your Glory."

Amaranth cups Iriset's face in warm hands. Her mirané-brown eyes study Iriset, steady falling force pulling Iriset in. "Beremé said your name to me, before I'd ever known it. It's her fault I claimed you. Her suggestion, even. But that doesn't make you beholden to her in the slightest."

"I wouldn't," Iriset says, allowing herself to enjoy Amaranth's touch. She wants to stay here, under Amaranth's undivided attention. She wants Amaranth to kiss her. Iriset rubs her fingers against her thighs, scratching up some ecstatic friction to help her center herself.

"Good." Amaranth lets go, sitting back on her heels. "But I do want you at the dinner tonight. A handful of the groom's family from the Ecstatic Steeple Shadow precinct will be there, and they might like talking to someone from outside the palace."

"Even the Little Cat's daughter?"

"Especially," snaps Sidoné, prickly as ever in the remains of Beremé's presence.

"Did you wager?" Iriset asks.

Amaranth smiles only on one side of her face. She glances at her body-twin. "I would never give Beremé the satisfaction."

———— • ♦ • ————

Her Glory sends Iriset off to find Nielle in her workshop with a peering sort of expression Iriset can't parse. But even not knowing what Nielle makes, Iriset cannot resist the siren song of a *workshop* and goes eagerly.

The answer is better than Iriset had imagined: Nielle creates masks. In a small section of the handmaiden's bedchamber, walled off by a lacquered screen much like Iriset's, Nielle has a long table and carefully labeled shelves covered in sketches and material, sewing tools, glue, knives and styli and scissors. Every imaginable mask base, from ceramic and silk to leather and glass. It's magnificent.

Ziyan is already there, the two of them bent over the low table as Nielle cuts a strip of black leather with a razor Iriset could use to shave silicate.

"It's you," Ziyan says.

Iriset ignores her and kneels across from them. "Her Glory sent me. I'm joining you all for the dinner tonight," she says, unable to tear her eyes from the various tools.

"Oh, good," Nielle says with satisfaction, leaning up. "We'll find something perfect."

As Iriset listens to Nielle carry on about her favorite sorts of masks—the ones that accentuate something unique about the wearer, or draw out different things upon different faces, which Iriset suspects is the mark of a genius artist—it occurs to Iriset that the peering look of Amaranth's means this is a test, too. Could the Moon-Eater's Mistress suspect how Iriset feels about a workshop like this? The pull to apostasy that isn't relegated to Silk. That Silk...

Amaranth never asks directly when she could scheme instead.

Iriset swallows unease and *accidentally* knocks over a shallow bowl of bone and shell beads. During her protestations that she's just not used to this sort of situation, as Nielle assures her the beads get spilled and lost in cracks in the tiles all the time, Ziyan curls her lip and helps pick up a single bead at a time.

Nielle notices and rolls her eyes. "Ziyan, just tell Iriset why you don't like her."

Iriset laughs once in surprise. She's come to appreciate Nielle. She wishes she could be herself with the other woman. Not hide her laugh behind a demure hand. But even in the Little Cat's court, nobody treated her—either Silk or Isidor's daughter—so freely. Not even Bittor, unless she had her fingers up his ass.

"Nielle," Ziyan chides.

"I don't mind," Iriset says, looking directly at Ziyan. The woman is perfectly mirané colored, reddish-brown skin and matching irises, her black hair undertoned like the red rock of the crater. Her eyes are wide apart over narrow cheeks, and she has a sharp jaw that points toward an elegantly curved mouth and long neck, but without the broader, more handsome bone structure of the oldest mirané families. Iriset watches as Ziyan smiles tiny and sharp, ready to lay it out.

"You act like you deserve everything," she says in her lovely voice. "You're quiet, yes, and pretend to be modest, but you have no shame for your background, for your father's crimes."

"Oh." Iriset taps her lips with her first two fingers.

"Everyone knows what the Little Cat does. He's practically a rebel. Murder, gambling, thievery, *apostasy*. And I know Amaranth forgives you or doesn't believe you're responsible. You could at least act like it."

Iriset lowers her hand. People only think they know her father. He always broke up talk about rebellion, despite Silk's rampant human architecture. It was a tool to the Little Cat, not a belief system. (Once, over ecstatic wine, Dalal idly shared stories she'd heard from her grandmother of a group in the Morning Market precinct who'd rebelled against the Vertex Seal in their great-grandparents' generation, singing verses of glory and hope and longing. Iriset had asked what they were rebelling for, and Bittor said, "You rebel against something, not for something. Their songs are about hope." And Dalal, who was older, told Iriset the rebels had simply wanted to marry who they wished, regardless of Safiyah the Bloody's reformations. The Little Cat had appeared, looking for his escape artist, and instantly dismissed the whole conversation. He said, "All the rebels died in their futile war, and nobody got married to anybody. They should have cheated, lied, or left.")

To Ziyan, Iriset says, "You want me to be grateful."

"You should be."

"Grateful my father will die, my friends and family jailed or fled? My life shattered. And as for shame, what has Dad done that's worse than the last quad of Vertex Seals?" Iriset leans toward Ziyan and keeps her voice low. "I am grateful Her Glory plucked me out of the apostate prison. But I didn't belong there in the first place. Amaranth told me she wants extraordinary handmaidens, so I don't see that I'm doing anything wrong. I embrace who I am. Who are you, Ziyan? Why do you belong at Her Glory's side?"

A dark flush spreads up Ziyan's long mirané neck.

Nielle slaps a hand onto her worktable. Both Iriset and Ziyan startle. "This is why I *do* like Iriset so much! I have an idea." She waits until both the others tear their gazes away from each other. Then Nielle grins so big it pulls her features even more asymmetrical. "I'm going to make Iriset a cat mask."

Ziyan scoffs.

Iriset, though, really wants to wear a little cat mask to the party. Too bad she does know her place and instead says, "I'm not sure that's the kind of attention Amaranth wants tonight."

"I'm the one marrying the small king," Nielle says in a singsong voice. "These are my future relatives. We're doing it. Ziyan, you can be a pretty bird."

"No," Ziyan says slowly. She narrows her eyes at Iriset, then says, "I'll be a cat, too. Then it's not quite so overt."

As Nielle hums, considering, Iriset nods at Ziyan. "I love it."

———— • ♦ • ————

The engagement dinner, Iriset discovers only when they're on their way, is taking place in the private dining room of Diaa of Moonshadow.

Thirty-one years before Silk was captured, Diaa gave up her familial name when she married the Vertex Seal. She declared that her family was all of the empire, and none should think to compel loyalty from her based on who she had been before. The devotion to her husband and her children-to-be had won her many followers, especially those just as devoted to Silence.

She bred that simple devotion into both her son and daughter: one of whom was destined to be the next (last) Vertex Seal; one of whom would be the most infamous Moon-Eater's Mistress ever to serve (aside from Safiyah the Bloody, who had been both Mistress and Seal in her time). Both children were steadfast in their belief in the strength of their thread in the Holy Design of the world, though both preferred the other's thread to their own: Lyric wished to have been born second, and thus the devoted Mistress; Amaranth wished to rule.

Diaa never minded, for their gentle rivalry presents itself only as a slight distance between them. If her son wishes he'd been born a farmer or such so he could swear himself into a Silent monastery, and if her daughter dreams of being an enthroned spider in the center of an empire's web, at least they can push at each other's ambition and strengthen the empire by it.

The lady is fifty-four years old now and drifts throughout the palace complex however she likes. She takes coffee and mint cakes with Amaranth on a whim, asks how the Moon-Eater fared that morning, and offers an amusing verse she learned from her lover's cousin who recites poetry under the shade of the Ecstatic Steeple on market days. Then the next afternoon she appears with candied rose petals for the handmaidens and directs her daughter toward an insightful critique of some mirané prince or other's proposal for stripping an annexed people of one of their rights, so that Amaranth can either use the critique herself or pass it along to Garnet or another, thereby maintaining the illusion that Diaa herself never engages in politics.

That is her pretty secret: Her sharp political mind had tempered her husband Esmail's orthodoxy, for Esmail had been inclined toward warmongering like his great-great-great-grandmother Safiyah. Of course, in Safiyah's time the empire still had lands to conquer, while the constraints of the Holy Design kept Esmail from physically expanding the empire in any direction. His tendencies had to be expunged via tightening his control over the edges of the empire, cracking down occasionally on outer cities that perhaps hadn't done anything quite illegal, but would have—might have—soon. It was under those terrible expectations that Lyric came of age and learned to maneuver. If not for his mother's influence, he might have grown up to be a psychopath.

(One day in the near future, Iriset overhears Sidoné complain she does not understand why Diaa holds so determined to be underestimated, even now, for the appearance of weakness or even nonchalance invites enemies, where obvious strength holds them at bay. Amaranth replies that if an enemy sees your strengths, they can better invent weapons to tear you down, and Sidoné argues back there are always, *always* enemies fashioning weapons for use against the empire and especially the Vertex Seal. But Iriset admires that Diaa finds balance in preserving part of herself only for herself. None of them realize who Diaa's true enemy is.)

If Iriset had a choice, it would not have been to meet the mother of the Vertex Seal wearing a little cat mask as a cheeky slight against the entire mirané council. Technically, Amaranth approved her handmaidens' accoutrement. Sidoné, however, sneered and said their irreverence made it a good thing Lyric himself couldn't seem to approve or disapprove of small king marriages and therefore would not be at the party.

That disappointed Iriset. How had she been living in his palace for thirteen days and not laid eyes on His Glory?

Amaranth and her group of four arrive in her mother's petal early, sweeping in a colorful palette of pinks and red for the Vertex Seal and white for ecstatic force, the force that rules the Great Steeple in Sian méra Sayar's precinct.

Diaa welcomes them with open arms, pink robes falling in long, wide sleeves, and belted around her ribs with glittering silver and mint green. A netting mask woven of copper holds glass flowers—scarlet succulents and moon orchids with their sharp tongues—against her temple and left cheek. Several glass flowers dot her twisted black hair. Her eyes are painted in complementary pink and green swirls, with the light touch of a true artist who can smooth wrinkles without ruining them, turning Diaa's age into part of her beauty. She's shorter than her daughter, but holds herself straighter than Amaranth's constant lounge. Something about the structure of how she leans lets Iriset guess she injured her right leg at some point, or her hip aches. It's good Iriset's cat mask hides her expression entirely, but for her bottom lip and chin. She stares with Silk's attention all she likes.

Except, after kissing her daughter's cheek, Diaa turns unerringly to Iriset. "You're the new one."

"Your Glory," Iriset murmurs, lowering her head. Her mask is made of a stiff leather frame with painted cloth pulled over the skeleton, and sweeps up on either side into pointed ears, tufted with glittering fluff. She covers her eyes with one hand.

"Poor thing," Diaa says, immediately taking hold of Iriset,

looping an arm around her waist. "I'm glad my daughter has been taking care of you. Come have a nip of this mulled rockwine. It's supposedly the favorite of Sayar's, so we're treating the whole family tonight."

Iriset flicks her gaze to Amaranth, who smiles like an alliraptor and shrugs one shoulder. Nielle waves, pushing her mask up over her hair to talk with a striking woman Iriset has never seen but who looks familiar in the way that she's likely related to someone Iriset knows. "Thank you," Iriset says softly. Diaa pats her hip in a motherly fashion. Iriset hasn't had a mother in fourteen years and does not know how to react.

The strange kindness flees her mind when she sees who Diaa is leading her toward. General Bey méra Matsimet poses in a vivid green robe instead of his uniform—bearded, grizzled, as grim as Iriset remembers—at a sideboard stacked with ceramic cups and several steins and decanters of colorful drinks.

"Here is General Bey," Diaa says once they've reached the miran. "I believe you've met under less pleasant circumstances. Now that you're in the palace with Amaranth, here is what you need to know: Bey plays whatever role best serves the security of Moonshadow and the will of the Vertex Seal. If he was cruel to you, it was on my son's behalf, to get what he needed."

Bey tilts his head in a way that might be agreement but might also be ridicule. His eyes are hard to read through the thin gray cloth mask.

Diaa says, "We trust him because he loves my son as one loves a nephew or the child of a dear friend. They do not belong to you, and so you are not responsible for their everyday needs or survival."

"It makes room for a different sort of loyalty," Bey says, low and calm. "Like the edge of a knife, simple and never fraught with misunderstanding."

Iriset keeps her eyes lowered. Her pulse is loud in her ears, too much ecstatic and rising force, inviting something akin to panic. The two speak as if they always talk in this layered way, agree this much, and intend something for her that she just cannot quite grasp. Except it feels like a threat from the Vertex Seal himself.

"Little Cat's daughter, indeed," General Bey says, then snorts. "She was like this in prison, too."

Diaa's arm tightens around Iriset. "Don't be obnoxious."

"Brother, who are your terrorizing now?"

Iriset looks toward the bright newcomer: It's the striking woman Amaranth greeted, who's left the Moon-Eater's Mistress behind near the door to usher in new guests.

"Iriset," Diaa says, "this is Lapis mé Matsimet, the other Mirror General. She proved herself decades ago on the western battlefields against the rebellious Bow in Lyric's father's time. There was a crisis, as there always is, and Lapis lifted up the command mantle to reorganize a successful offensive out of a near-certain loss. Her strategies have never failed outright. And so we have the Mirror Generals, you see."

"What an impressive description," Lapis says merrily.

"I don't see," Iriset says. It's even true. Though the siblings look very alike in the shape of their skulls.

Bey knocks back his drink and holds the cup out for his sister to refill it.

Diaa lifts one elegant brow, shifting the colors of flowers painted to her eye. "Bey and Lapis serve the army of the Vertex Seal in opposing capacities. Bey leads the central army, which reigns in the city as you have directly experienced. Lapis directs and oversees the workings of all four external branches. Her job is predominately administrative, while his allows for more hands-on action. His domain is Moonshadow, hers the farthest reaches of the empire. It was Lyric's idea to put them in charge of the city and the empire, respectively. Quite smart, positioning them so that their interests align but do not perfectly match. Slight, constant friction hones their power and their principles."

It occurs to Iriset that Diaa is teaching her. Why, she has little idea. For her own reasons, no doubt. Just like everyone here.

"Sister," Bey says, tapping his refilled cup to hers. "This is the prisoner I told you about. The daughter of Isidor the Little Cat."

"Oh?" Lapis eyes Iriset, not quite rude enough to focus on her face behind the mask. "A handmaiden of Her Glory now? That is the strangest way of holding a prisoner of war I've ever heard."

Bey drawls back, "How would you know? You never send home prisoners, sister, only slaves and orphans."

"Which is Iriset?" Lapis asks, laughing at her own joke.

Neither yet, Iriset knows, feeling their disregard sink into her design. But Diaa squeezes her hand and pushes a cup of mulled rockwine into it. She is so kind, and Iriset can't read ulterior motives into her touch as easily as she can with Amaranth. Whatever Diaa wants or thinks, her pretense is so thorough Iriset has no idea where to even look for a crack.

9

A slip of silk

Iriset makes a charged stylus with the carefully shattered crab pick and clay stolen from her art class. With it she pulls apart the plumbing in the baths of the women's petal to obtain a thread of braided flow and falling to settle around the jade cuff as a stasis ring. Such threads can often be found in flushing mechanisms. She mistakenly opens a pipe she expected to be dry, and ends up exploring the intricate weave style of the mechanism entirely soaked. It's worth it.

The next afternoon, when the sun shines directly through her lattice window, Iriset uses the bright light to examine the jade bracelet. The braid of flow and falling she curls into a circle and sets the cuff into it: The design shivers into delicate stasis. It shouldn't alert anyone that she's meddling like a null wire might.

Once the seal is open, Iriset gently pushes at the elegant layers of threaded architecture to find the knots and braids that work the power. She feels a twinge like nausea in her wrist, but she continues to figure the best way to temporarily shield or quiet the cuff so the royal architect won't be able to trace her paths through the palace.

Iriset triggers a thread of rising force and the entire seal chars almost instantly.

To hide her meddling, she puts all the design back together and snaps the cuff in half, making sure to crush the seal. She grits her teeth and splays her hand, then uses the stylus to drive ecstatic force through the skin of her wrist and tug at the flow of her inner design to break capillaries so that a bruise flushes in exactly the shape of the cuff. It should appear she's hurt herself when she accidentally broke the seal.

Satisfaction curls in her chest as the bruise forms: Such delicate work takes tremendous control.

Menna is not happy with the damage, but within hours has a new seal built for Iriset.

But Iriset knows how to trick it now. She needs only four shards of tourmaline to build a balanced shield cap to mitigate the energy of the seal when she wishes not to be traced by the palace architecture.

There's no way she can source design-grade tourmaline in an art class, and even Nielle's mask making wouldn't be good enough cover to ask for a high-quality force conductor. And once she's free to move around, she'll need specialized design supplies to make a craftmask to disguise her father.

That is what brings Iriset, nearly a quad after Amaranth rescued her from prison, to knock at the door of Raia mér Omorose's office in the branch of the palace reserved for royal architects. (She has forty-five days to save her father.)

"Come in!" Raia calls, voice muffled.

Iriset settles her shoulders and enters, face tilted down in the appearance of politeness. Because she's not at Amaranth's side, she wears a plain attendant's cloth mask, as Garnet commanded that first afternoon. Behind the orange cloth, her eyes scan everything.

Raia's office is octagonally shaped in smooth stucco, as many architectural offices are, to better serve balanced design. A worktable is affixed to the southernmost wall, narrow as a shelf, and the rest of the walls are covered by cabinets. No window opens the room to light, though Iriset spies the star-eye cut into the ceiling with its opposite directly below in Raia's floor.

The designer kneels in the center of the room before a squat square table covered in vellum that curls at each corner but is held down by glass drop weights. A blue cloth mask binds ans brown hair from ans face, though much of it tumbles down ans back along with the tasseled end of the cloth. Raia designs in a long-sleeved robe, full trousers, and slippers. If she were free to be Silk, she'd tell an that ans design would immediately improve by a quarter margin if an learned to sense force resonance with ans lips and spine and the soles of ans feet.

Raia focuses on the diagram before an, using the thickest point of a quad-stylus to pin the corner of three force-lines down. Iriset moves nearer, steps silent in her palace slippers. She cranes to see, and in surprise says, "It's a triangle."

The designer glances up. "Oh, it's you."

She touches her fingers to her eyelids as an sits back on ans heels. "Raia mér Omorose," she says politely.

"Iriset mé Isidor."

Raia set down ans stylus and stands. "I am glad to see you, Iriset. I thought to invite you here, for a conversation, but did not know if you'd be willing. In a few quads, when you've settled... I would have."

"I thank you for the consideration."

They study each other for a moment.

"You look better," an finally says. Ans bottom lip is flushed, and Iriset wonders if an chews it as an works.

Clasping her hands before her, which sends ans eyes to the jade cuff, she says, "It was suggested that I ask you how my father was captured. It must have been betrayal, I thought, but that is not what Sidoné mé Dalir claims."

Raia's shoulders jerk as an takes a fast breath, then an blows it out loudly and turns away from her. An walks across the tiled floor to one of the cabinets. With a ring on ans left forefinger, an keys open an architectural lock and reaches inside to remove something.

It's a scrap of silk.

Her silk. So sheer and delicate ans fingers are visible through it. It frays at the diagonal where it must have been carefully cut free of the mask she'd made.

"You recognize it."

Iriset realizes her lips have parted and she tastes ecstatic force snapping at the tip of her tongue. She closes her mouth and lowers her eyes. "I do."

"I've never seen anything so fine. When it functioned, it must have clung to the face like skin."

Glancing at an, she sees the admiration in ans face, and recalls the eager arguments an made to her in the prison, wanting her to explain what Silk taught her, wanting to work together. "Why show that to me, when I ask about betrayal."

"It was not betrayal," Raia says, sympathy gentling ans excitement. "I thought Silk was making her own material, from raw cocoons, and so we traced the imported worms. That's how the army-investigators found your father's tower."

Iriset's knees weaken. It was her fault.

Instead of fighting it, she lets her body bow, sinking slowly to the floor as despair sours her stomach.

Raia kneels beside her, not touching. "I am sorry, Iriset. I imagine what I would feel were my mother or father facing execution. You do him credit, to seem so strong. You do all the Saltbath credit, and your extended family."

"Don't be kind to me," she murmurs, wondering vaguely if her grandparents are all right. If they're attempting to submit petitions on her behalf. They might, though they should know better. If it went well it would still take quads to work through the overtly complex bureaucracy of the Holy City to free the Little Cat's daughter. If it went poorly, they might be arrested, too. Better if they leave it alone.

Maybe Amaranth will find out for her, or Sidoné, if Shahd can't. Or won't. Iriset looks back at the scrap of sheer silk. It just flops there, still in ans hand and pressed against ans knee. Iriset reaches out and skims her finger against its softness. Would Raia offer it to her, a memento? Unlikely.

"It's so perfect," an says, releasing the silk. "She is such an innovator. I have examined her glove, too, and what little was recovered."

"Is that how you earned your new office?" Iriset asks sharply.

"Discovering the means to locate Silk was how. The rest is my duty."

Iriset slides the silk into her lap, spreading it against the dark green linen of her trousers. The silk takes up a green shade. When she flattens her hand over it, her palm tingles with remembered resonance. She whispers, "Has she given anything to you?"

"I am not participating in her interrogation any longer."

A tremor of discomfort accompanies ans words, and shame makes Iriset vicious: "No stomach for torture?"

"She used a trick to ruin her voice," Raia says. "Something she swallowed."

Iriset stares. The candy. She'd thought it was for some scheme of the Little Cat's. Blackmail or something—no. She hadn't thought at all.

"Will she break her own fingers before she writes anything down?" Raia asks so softly, there's no voice left in an, either.

Iriset shakes her head. But maybe. She, at least, invented no such tool. Dalal or Paser would have to hurt themselves the old-fashioned way. Iriset hates this, hates her torture applied to someone else. Hates the cold, sickening relief to be spared it. There's no way for her to ask if the Vertex Seal ordered the torture of Dalal or Paser without giving away that neither is Silk. As long as the Vertex Seal believes he has the apostate, she's safe enough with Amaranth. "And my father?" she asks instead, though it's hardly better. "Is he being hurt?"

"I do not know, Iriset. But if you consider how many he has hurt in his turn, perhaps you will have some understanding of the army's perspective."

"Do not lecture me about my father from the heart of the Holy City. The empire itself relies on harm, on the suffering of others, Raia mér Omorose. It is the nature of empire to consume."

The designer's eyes widen into circles at her outburst.

Iriset clenches her jaw, pressing her mouth and eyes shut, irate at her loss of control. Isidor the Little Cat had said that to her, more than once. *It is the nature of empire to consume.* To him it was a fact, an excuse to consume in turn. The Moon-Eater, unraveled, is only hunger, and the Moon-Eater's Mistress feeds him. The Little Cat feeds the undermarket. Normal, natural, the Holy Design of things.

But on the floor of a royal architect's study, the words sound to Iriset more like a rallying cry. A rebellion.

It's not illegal to criticize the Vertex Seal, but Iriset's position is too precarious for harsh opinions. She takes a deep, shaking breath. "I'm sorry," she murmurs. "Her Glory said they will execute him during the Days of Mercy."

"So..." Raia pauses and begins again. "So I have heard as well. But, Iriset, there is nothing you can do against the will of Aharté."

She clenches her fist around the silk scrap, crushing it. "You mean this all is the Holy Design," she says, and doesn't hint at the bitterness she feels. The words remind her of her mother: Many people say apostatical cancer is part of Aharté's pattern, too. Iriset hated nothing worse than that excuse when her mother was dying.

Raia says, "You understand design, and the foundations of architecture. The Little Cat eventually would need to be balanced, somehow. And, Iriset, I *am* sorry for your suffering."

It doesn't matter if Iriset believes an—she pretends to. "Teach me," she says, as if it will convince her to forgive an. "You wanted my knowledge, from Silk, in prison. And now I don't need you to free me, but I would work with you as you suggested: give what I know of Silk's methods in return for your instruction."

She glances up. Ans eyes seem darker with concern, or responsibility, as an promises, "I will ask that you be allowed to work with me some days."

"Will you tell me why you're designing a triangle?" She glances at the project an'd pinned down as she arrived.

"I am experimenting with forms of stability that do not require all four forces to hold. It would be a strong grounding form that did not include rising force, but ecstatic kept flow alive, with falling holding it in shape."

Iriset smiles slightly. "You surmised that from the silk. She used ecstatic to create a connection between the mask and the face of the wearer."

Raia nods, and begins to point out the exact weave of ans design.

———— • ♦ • ————

That evening, Shahd brings Iriset a small dish of mint ice, and as she moves around picking up and straightening, she says, "All the notes you have asked me to place remain untouched."

None of the Little Cat's court is checking the drops. If Bittor could, certainly he would. Certainly.

Iriset clutches her spoon, determined to move faster.

"But your grandparents seem well," Shahd continues in her wispy voice. "Or free, at least, when I walked past. There was no graffiti implicating them at their home or your grandmother's mechanics shop."

"Thank you," Iriset manages.

The girl says nothing else, drawing Iriset to the bed, where she unknots Iriset's hair and finger-combs it, rubbing sweet oil into the ends. It feels so familiar, familial. Her grandfather was the first person besides her mother to do this. Iriset clenches her jaw and breathes so carefully. She can't worry about them, but can only focus on her father, and where she is right now.

Once Iriset's hair is combed and oiled, Shahd touches Iriset's wrist briefly. Then she departs without another word.

Get out of here, Iriset wants to say. *Go to your family and don't return. Stop helping me before it's too late. I'll use you if you let me.*

Or she wants to tug Shahd back and return the favor of combing out her hair. Like a big sister. Or like a lover. Undress Shahd, find out what makes her rising force rush or the taste of her clavicle. If Shahd were willing, it would be allowed here. It isn't as though Iriset hasn't heard soft lovemaking through the walls and moon-cut floors.

But if Iriset gave in, her lovemaking wouldn't be soft. Someone would scream. Probably herself.

She watches Shahd leave and flattens out onto her stomach, refusing to touch anything.

———— • ♦ • ————

Permission is granted for Iriset to study with Raia. The arrangement is informal, at both Menna's and Amaranth's insistence. Iriset is not apprentice or design school material, after all: She is the Little Cat's daughter and now Her Glory's handmaiden, thus can be bound to none other for service or learning.

That suits her. When Raia allows, she joins an in ans office during her free hours, though she doesn't give up drawing class. (The Ceres ambassador returned to class, by the way, claiming that he'd considered it and decided that, yes, one might truly understand a thing even if one is not good or skilled at it. Perhaps, he suggested slyly, one who merely studies but does not perform might even understand some things better than those with mastery. Iriset scoffed, and their argument spiraled and meandered throughout their encounters that summer. She firmly intends that if she and her father are forced to flee Moonshadow, she's carving out a refuge in the Ceres Remnants.)

Iriset behaves with Raia, though she struggles to maintain the illusion of apprenticeship and ignorance of the finer details of Silk's work and genius. It's difficult to step herself back from the ease with which she's truly capable of designing in order to go through the process on a basic level. Once, she automatically pinches falling and rising together in a shortcut and has to ruin the entire design they constructed together before Raia notices.

Mostly, instead of beginner lectures or patronizing questions, an shows her the things an is considering, ans theoretical experiments and practical ones. They talk through the ideas, describing potential outcomes and which are more likely than others. An sometimes asks her specific questions about Silk, or one of her recovered tools. Iriset partners an in some delicate balancing structures, when an would need an assistant anyway, and Raia seems relieved to have her—an relaxes with her as an does not if others are present.

Raia asks her one day about the spiders.

"What spiders?" She frowns, eyes wide to hide the dip in her mood. She still misses her spinners and can find none in the palace outside a cool, shadowed corner of the Color Can Be Loud Garden. An old Osahar tradition claims orb spinners are a sign of healthy design, because with their eight legs and eyes and perfect webs, they're avatars of Silence. Clearly, the Vertex Seal disagrees.

"I've been going through one of Silk's sketchbooks"—an pauses and glances wryly at her—"once the investigator-designer blacked out the notes on human design." Raia pauses again but doesn't ask directly about Silk's apostasy, nor does Iriset offer. The architect sighs in small defeat. "She drew huge numbers of webs, and spiders, and there are notes about spiders being inherent architects themselves. She even wonders if they're lost children of Aharté, just like the miran."

Iriset laughs, surprising herself. Her laughter rarely appears these days.

"It isn't quite heresy," Raia says, bending ans lips into a bow as an fights off an answering smile.

"She's interested in flight," Iriset says.

"Flight? Spiders don't fly."

"Some do, when they are tiny, newborn. They throw up strands of their silk and float away. It's flying. It's beautiful, if you've never seen it."

Raia nods slowly, eyes distant. "Why? Why flight? To help thieves easier slip into upper levels of rich houses?"

Iriset presses her hands flat together. "Her patron was the son of Cloud Kings, and my father wanted to know if their ways could be reinterpreted here. But besides that, understanding tensile flight might lead to better bridges, or even raised force-ribbons. What if our carriages and skiffs could fly from here to the edge of the empire instead of dragging along the ribbons? What if we could capture the wind itself to lift us? Find a way to travel as the Cloud Kings do? Could we fly so high as the moon? Visit Aharté, or merely look down upon the glory of our city? Have you never dreamed of flying? It is a worthy—"

She stops suddenly, afraid she's given herself away.

But Raia reaches out to her hands. An puts ans around hers, and curls long fingers around her wrists. "I feel it, Iriset. I hear you. You're his daughter, and you wanted your heritage, too."

In these days the Cloud Kings cannot visit Moonshadow—the Holy Design Steeples disrupt their massive sky castles. The Rising School of Architecture offers a regular prize to any designer who discovers a way to harness the Cloud King design within the constraints of Aharté's Silence. Iriset would have liked to win it. Pulling away, Iriset says, "Silk began studying them for flight, but the spiders gave her the silk."

Raia's brow wrinkles. "But she changed to worm silk."

"Not for everything, though worm silk is easier to source." Iriset barrels on so she doesn't start thinking down those lines again: "Spiderwebs don't seem strong to us because we so easily sweep through them, but the tensile strength of a single strand of spider silk is incredible. Spider silk is flexible, adhesive, with extensibility. Also organic, and sometimes spiders eat their own webs. Silk invented her silk to be all of those things. She had rope of it stronger and thinner than any other, and even suspension wires for moving between windows, and I—once, we spoke of possible application for jewelry. Not to mention the healing potential we've already discussed. Blood patches and casts for broken bones. Neither of which is human architecture."

An stares at her, and Iriset cuts off. She looks away. "I only mean you should not dismiss spiders. Their architecture is perfect."

"You hide a vast faith in Aharté, Iriset," Raia murmurs.

Iriset thinks that is hilarious.

But it's nice having a designer to talk with, though Iriset can't ask the questions she most wishes to ask: about the threshold security in the palace, the rumors she heard all her life that alarms are carved into the rocks of the quartz yards, or about the rhythm of the force hum she only feels when curled upon her sleeping pillows at night—it's no four-mark pulse, but rather with a cadence like breathing. The palace design seems alive. But that, surely, cannot be true.

Ah, well.

When Raia asks her to fetch something, she makes sure to

mistake which cabinet an means each time until an thinks her spatial awareness and memory appallingly slow for such an attentive student. But it allows her to map where an keeps ans tools and notes, the various resonant and disruptive materials, the styli and vellum and miniature bricks.

She finds the tourmaline quickly, and slips some into the tiny pocket she cut into her sleeve when she's briefly alone. More easily she steals a striker, which she hides in her knotted hair, and design-grade vellum. Too bad she can't take her silk.

Before long Iriset has what she needs.

• ♦ •

In her room during the night, Iriset works by the gentle light of a force-lamp, placing chips of tourmaline carefully into tiny pinched wire. It requires perfect balance, and each chip is charged to a different force. Most beginner designers hold their breath for such delicate work, but Iriset knows to slowly, carefully breathe in an eight-count. It keeps her steady.

The Little Cat taught her the breathing. When she was young and prone to anxiety after her mother's illness, Isidor held her in his lap, arms tight around hers, legs wide around hers, effectively cocooning her with his body. He hummed a gentle melody with the eight-count, just hugging and humming, until Iriset hummed, too, and eventually relaxed.

Later, he taught her the methodology behind it, that it was his favorite of the old meditation techniques the first worshippers of Aharté developed to align with her Holy Design. It could be broken down into a force-meditation, balancing flow, falling, rising, and ecstatic into perfect alignment. Perfect Silence. The Cloud Kings had a version, but Isidor liked this better.

He took her out with him beginning when she was twelve. In the night he taught her to scale a wall or find the best shadow, and they kept up the breathing exercises. Iriset did not care for the skills of thieves, and never got very good at such things. But she learned how to feel her way along in the darkness by listening to and tasting the threads of force in the air. She learned to detect certain identities based on their dominant forces and unique rhythms cutting against her own. And eventually Iriset designed slippers and skin-tight hoods that dampened such identifiable patterns of design and allowed her father and the cousins of his court to slide right through a lot of basic security.

Iriset rarely loses herself in panic or mania anymore, other than when she was detained alone in the apostate prison, because the breathing is second nature, a gift from her father.

When she huddles over her shield cap, breathing carefully as she places the final chip of tourmaline that will allow her to move about the palace complex undetected, it feels like she's not alone:

Her father holds her tightly, humming the soothing rhythm in her ear.

10

The Moon-Eater's Mistress

Every morning, the Moon-Eater's Mistress enters his sanctuary to wake him with her love. It's part of the balance of the Vertex Seal, as written upon the throne: *one claimed with blood and paired with hunger, always binding.*

The Vertex Seal himself spills a drop of blood upon the moon-red rock beneath the seat of power every day. Amaranth, as second born, is the one paired with hunger. She belongs to the Moon-Eater, to feed his appetite.

The story that the Holy Syr and Maimeri Sarenpet unraveled the Moon-Eater until there was nothing left but his teeth is the most commonly retold version.

Priests of Silence debate the meaning of *unraveled*. To some it means Aharté blessed the Holy Syr's stylus, allowing her to physically destroy the Moon-Eater, pulling his outer design apart until the energy of his threads joined the four forces. His teeth remained as a reminder. To others it means that Aharté herself reappeared and drew the Moon-Eater's threads up to her silver-pink moon but left his teeth below with us so that he could not eat her as he had eaten himself. Variations of both versions scatter through sects of Silence and apostatical cults.

The Vertex Seal, and the line of miran, follow the tenet that the Holy Syr had unraveled the Moon-Eater literally with her design, and yet he existed still, his inner design spread throughout the forces because he was energy, which ultimately cannot be destroyed. His will remains strong, and he longs to reweave his own design, to become a god again that he might face Aharté—though to love her or destroy her, the priests avoid saying. The Moon-Eater's Mistress exists to distract the apostate god from said goal. To divert his attention from Aharté, to give him a piece of love without serving up She Who Loves Silence whole.

And so every morning, the Moon-Eater's Mistress conciliates her lover.

———— • ♦ • ————

Mistress is a mirané word, with both dominant and possessive connotations, coded feminine because mirané is a stringently bigendered language. There is only man or woman, which is hardly a stable balance. At least three points are needed for stability, and true design balance requires even numbers, so they ought to have had four genders *at minimum*. There were only two because that had been the simplest solution to rampant apostasy, as well as the easiest to control, and the most reductive with nothing in between. Or else two because it most mirrored Aharté and the Moon-Eater, if one could call the goddess a woman and the young god a man at all.

Regardless, the word they will someday call Amaranth is

savior, but at the time, the word did not yet exist. Or perhaps had been forgotten.

———————— • ♦ • ————————

Iriset sleeps upon a pile of silk and linen cushions, beneath a curtain of sheer green that hangs from one corner of the ceiling and can be rolled up or tied aside. Most of her life she's woken up naturally in the mornings, and it's no different at first in the palace. Iriset's body is so attuned to pulses of force that once Her Glory is up, and her handmaidens, subtle fluctuations in the architecture of Iriset's chamber floor shake her out of dreams. But lately her intense night work has drained her to exhaustion, and she must be dragged awake. This morning an attendant who is not Shahd touches her shoulder and calls her name, saying she's needed in Her Glory's bedchamber immediately.

"Fashion emergency," the girl says without a hint of teasing.

Iriset frowns. What does she have to do with Her Glory's wardrobe? But she readies herself anyway and follows the attendant to Amaranth's chamber.

In the center of the room Amaranth stands, arms raised, expression demanding with a smile. Sidoné lounges upon the low sofa to the right, beside a stack of thin books and a table loaded with breakfast cheeses, smoked fish, and cranberry corn muffins. The third and fourth feminine-forward miran in the room are both royal tailors. One, fifty and intimidating, holds a length of deep violet silk. The other, perhaps twenty-five and grinding her teeth impatiently, tugs at the end of another scarf partly wound around Amaranth's waist.

"It will not stay without glue, Your Glory," the young one says, in a tone of one repeating herself.

"Iriset," Amaranth says with intense satisfaction. "The rest of you are dismissed."

Iriset holds her fingers to her eyelids despite her concealing mask and waits as the tailors depart.

"Come help me with this," Amaranth says.

Sidoné appears at Iriset's side to hand her a slab of cheese and sliced cactus pear. "You need fortitude."

Iriset drags off her cloth mask, tucking one edge along her waist, and accepts.

The Moon-Eater's Mistress sighs and waves for Sidoné to bring her some food, too.

"How can I assist?" Iriset asks, then nibbles on her breakfast. Her coffee cools, cupped in the palm of her left hand.

Amaranth holds out her arms again; the veils and scarves and robe she wears shift to reveal quite a bit of her mirané-brown flesh. "I need this all to stay where I want it."

Iriset frowns. She wants to help—in the time she's been here, Amaranth has yet to ask her for anything, or offer any particular sign of favor. How can she ingratiate herself if Her Glory wants nothing from her? She says, "I know nothing of clothing but how to tie my own. Those seem like scarves, not...not a tunic. Or even a skirt."

"This is eight wide scarves and two veils. I would like them to drape over me as if they might fall away at any moment, as if the slightest motion on my part will reveal a breast or my belly or the long line of this thigh." She strokes her left thigh. The nipple of her right breast glances out as one of the scarves slides.

"I..." Iriset stops.

Amaranth smiles a little smile of satisfaction. "Only as if, Iriset. I do not actually wish to flash my brother or his mirané council. I only want to very firmly remind them what I am."

"What you are?"

"The person who fucks a god every morning to keep the empire safe."

Iriset stares at Amaranth, pear forgotten in her fingers. Her inward attention slips lower, much lower, than her stomach, and she hears that delicious, harsh word echo in her ears. Carefully, Iriset licks her lips and swallows. It isn't her mouth where she wants to put something.

Amaranth reaches out and takes the pear from Iriset's loose fingers, popping it into her own mouth. She chews slowly, leaning on one hip in languorous glory, half naked, her dense black curls spilling over her shoulders and down her back. No paint mars the curved planes of her face yet, no eyeliner nor lipstick, and even unadorned she's spectacular: smooth mirané-brown skin, wide cheeks, luscious mouth, surprisingly plain red-brown irises surrounded by unimpressive lashes. Thick eyebrows, and a perfectly straight nose. Her shoulders slump from a long neck, and though Iriset has seen Her Glory lift weights and her own body off the ground in class, her arms are soft, as is her round belly. Over yet rounder hips her waist cuts in sharply, making a fold in the flesh, and her breasts hang heavily enough to balance those hips and the muscles of her thighs.

Iriset thinks that anyone with eyes could never forget what Amaranth is: power.

"Finished staring, hiha?" Her Glory drawls.

Her face is already hot, but Iriset ignores it to say (rather breathily), "I still don't know how I can help."

"Make it stick."

Sidoné laughs. "Do you see her face, Amaranth?"

"I do. Iriset, your *mentor* used design to create a mask that can stick to a person's face like second skin. I want this"—Her

Glory holds up the end of a creamy scarf—"to cup my breast and not let go, then curve around my hip. And this"—she touches violet silk—"to fall from my center and modestly down between my legs. The rest can slither, fall, curl however. But the illusion must be of delicate, careful design. Can you do it?"

Though the answer waits behind Iriset's teeth that she was merely an apprentice, that such skill is beyond hers and belongs to Silk alone, the look in Amaranth's eyes stills her reply.

Her Glory is looking at her with challenge. With assumption.

Iriset's arousal vanishes in a cold flash.

If Amaranth already knows the truth, or guesses, she must have a plan for Silk. For bringing an apostate here. Seducing her with promises and indifference and potential. In that case, what could Iriset gain from lying to the Moon-Eater's Mistress, the one who plucked her from prison and set her here in the heart of the empire? Amaranth wants her, wants something from her, maybe many somethings, whether Iriset and Silk are the same or not. Amaranth already admitted she likes uncommon girls. Is Silk not the rarest of all?

Wasn't Iriset just complaining that Amaranth never asked anything of her?

Fine. But not for free. She sets the coffee bowl upon the tiled floor and says, "I can do it. But not fast. I need embroidery thread or silk—ten-strand is fine. I need a stylus and an octagonal frame. Do you know what that is?"

Amaranth nods. "Anything else?"

"A pound of fine clay powder. Clear water. A brazier and dragon bone resin. A few afternoons left alone." This is more than she needs for Her Glory's project, and as much extra as she thinks she'll get away with requesting.

"It will be done."

"And a few days to infuse the thread and another, with those tailors to weave it. Oh, and all those scarves, of course. Three mornings from now, you for modeling and building it."

Her Glory grins. "Oh, I am glad to hear it, hiha."

"And—"

"More?" Sidoné puts in.

Iriset ignores the body-twin. "My grandparents. They have nothing to do with any of this, right?"

The grin waiting on Amaranth's face slides into something knowing. "Right."

"Then I am yours to command," she says, lowering her eyes again.

"Good. Now eat, and then go with me this morning to the Moon-Eater."

Iriset bows and touches her eyelids—in respect, yes, but more to hide her shock at being invited along. Anticipation flares in rising force, heating her cheeks again, and flow pushes faster at her pulse. She can't wait to witness Her Glory's morning conciliation, however it's allowed. This is a rare honor.

Amaranth tells Sidoné to invite the tailors back to dress her in something else, and Iriset moves to the breakfast table with her coffee and kneels, eating a little and attempting to balance her forces without letting on she's nervous at the prospect of visiting the temple. Her Glory strips, tossing the scarves to Sidoné, and apologizes to the tailors. They demur and quickly remove clothes from a chest. Shades of purple and red and orange soon cover Her Glory's body: sheer sleeves, a vest laced to cup her breasts, and strange trousers that are more like a skirt for each leg, wrapped ingeniously and low around her hips, falling in folds all the way to her ankles. But when she walks, a slight flash of inner thigh appears, and Iriset realizes with a flush that if Amaranth spreads her legs, she'll be fully exposed.

The tailors finish, and a jeweler replaces them. First this new woman brushes gleaming red dust down Her Glory's neck and collar and shoulders to burnish her skin even redder than mirané brown, then adds more along the lines and folds of her exposed belly. She wraps Amaranth's waist with a thin chain of bronze, clipping the jeweled end to a ring pierced through her navel. Complementary rings cuff her ears and wrists, and another girl plaits Her Glory's hair at the temples and slides a bronze band with an attached cloth mask over the top, covered in tiny embroidered crescents.

Finally, Menna, the royal architect, arrives to paint Amaranth's lips and eyes, and she stripes black and purple down her left cheek, slashing across it all with a thin arc of white.

Sidoné stripes her own eyes and bridge of her nose with the thick red line of a body-twin, and wraps a wide red sash over her black robe to hold her force-blade. Her hair an attendant braids simply and winds into a crown, then tucks a short black cloth mask over the whole of it with combs that can be removed to draw the mask over her face.

Menna somehow paints Iriset's cheek to match Amaranth's while also ignoring her completely, chattering at Amaranth about mirané politics. An attendant fits a ceramic crescent mask over Iriset's forehead, with the tips aimed down. From those tips, tiny red beads fall against her cheeks. It echoes the crescents in Amaranth's cloth mask. Beside Her Glory and her body-twin, Iriset is a less elaborate doll, a little sister.

Then, nearly an hour after Iriset arrived, Her Glory is ready to depart.

They leave the women's petal for the palace proper, there joined by Seal guards for the walk to the Moon-Eater's Temple.

Iriset has seen the temple from the palace, of course, from the windows and the Sunset Garden, and has heard and read descriptions of it, but has never been inside.

A plain building, it's merely a huge square of stucco carved with the entire *Word of Aharté* in gilded sigils. A single column stands at the gaping entrance (a black oval like a mouth), painted with bright red shapes: crescents, half-circles, full circles. They are phases of the old red moon.

Beside the red-moon column, a Silent priest is always posted, wearing a black cloth mask that covers them crown to toes and is opaque enough no face nor outline of shape can be seen. Impossible to know their gender, or sometimes if they even breathe.

Amaranth strides through the door, and Sidoné nudges Iriset to be certain she follows. The guards remain outside.

Inside, the morning sunlight cools immediately, and Iriset smells water. A basin of it waits in the alcove. Amaranth touches her fingers to it and flicks them before her to bless and cleanse the path ahead. The alcove is plain stucco, though two tall candelabras frame the archway, which is shut off by a lattice of wood. "Go with me, Iriset," she says.

What can the young apostate do but follow? Surely the god of apostasy will welcome her.

Overhead the ceiling vaults on a foundation of blue-white honeycomb into a broad, shallow dome mosaicked with the darkest blue that ceramic fire can produce. No windows offer light, but four forever lamps burning with fire and rising force create deep shadows. In the center of the mottled marble floor rises a granite altar, upon which nestle seventeen tarnished ivory-cream teeth: ribbed molars and curved, sharp fangs as long as Iriset's hand.

"Come," Amaranth says softly, holding her hand out for Iriset.

Iriset obeys, sliding her hand into Her Glory's. Amaranth squeezes it and draws her to the altar. Though until this moment the lines of power between them have always been too sharp to cross, Iriset feels something turn: shared respect and awe for the place in which they have arrived together. It feels so right, Iriset doesn't even think of how to use it for advantage.

Every advantage is Amaranth's here, exactly as she intended.

Her Glory says, "You may touch, if you like."

Pressing her hip to the altar, Iriset reaches out, but hesitates. Does she wish to know the weight of that massive molar? She's seen diagrams of mammoth skulls with teeth this resembles, though much older than the art, and... Iriset touches its surface with the tip of a finger. Dull, cold, dead. Rock. It's a fossil. Ancient monsters dropped these teeth, not a god. What to say? She bites her lip and looks to Amaranth guardedly.

Her Glory watches her, clearly amused. "My uncle, who was the Mistress before me, told me once he believed they were not from the mouth of the Moon-Eater, but a great apostatical creature designed by the Moon-Eater."

Iriset is shocked. Not at the idea—though it *is* wrong, these teeth are older than even the age of apostasy—but at the Moon-Eater's Mistress voicing it. She tries to look politely surprised.

Rolling laughter answers her look, and Amaranth's face bends with merriment, almost ugly, but very human. "Oh, Iriset. You are so bad at lying."

"I didn't say anything, Your Glory!" Iriset insists. It isn't *true*: She can lie. Oh red god, she hopes she can lie.

"You didn't have to. But listen." Still chuckling, Amaranth puts her arm around Iriset's shoulders. "It doesn't matter about the teeth. What they are or where, or what mouth dropped them—probably different kinds of mouths, really, unless it *was* a monster of the Apostate Age, to have such tearing fangs and such grass-eater teeth, too. What matters is that when I perform my conciliation, I feel him. This place and my role, they matter. They pin the power of the empire in place. Maybe he is not a dead god, maybe he is only energy, a spark of design chaos, but he is real."

And that makes my power real, Her Glory means. Iriset understands clearly. Amaranth never says directly what she can say from an angle. Just like her hypothetical on Iriset's first night in the palace. Just like the costume of scarves she's commissioned and letting Iriset see Nielle's workshop.

Playing her demure role, not the apostate, Iriset ventures, "And so must Aharté be real?"

Amaranth shrugs. "My brother believes it—balance, after all. The answer I meant, though, is that the empire is real. Our mission, our purpose. Whether any Holy Design dictates our paths or histories or choices, the empire is a knot that has lasted and is meant to last. I know it, because every day I feel evidence of it."

Iriset nods slowly. It's not worth fighting against the Vertex Seal, Amaranth means. The empire is all, the dominant balance of the world. What is Iriset, or any undermarket king? Amaranth wants Iriset to belong to her. "Your Glory," she asks slowly, "why did you bring me here?"

"I like you, and want you to feel it, and to trust me. Someday you will give me the truths of your inner design, kitten."

It feels to Iriset as though Amaranth is the Vertex Seal in that moment, not her mysterious brother: Amaranth is the center of the Holy City. This room, this woman. The falling force that dominates Her Glory's inner design is a drawing, lilting energy that tugs toward her center—even Iriset, who knows it's happening, is pulled to trust Amaranth.

But the Little Cat's design is dominated by falling force, too. Iriset has to keep her mind clear. Hold her own. She swallows and touches her fingertips to her eyelids.

"Now leave me as I wake the Moon-Eater."

As Iriset darts away, relieved to be outside Her Glory's attention, she glances back to see Amaranth slide free the lace tying her robe closed over her breasts.

Sidoné leads her to a dark wooden screen that Iriset hasn't noticed, it blends so well into the wall. Behind it wait stools and a pitcher of water with several plain clay cups. "Here," Sidoné murmurs. "When she wishes to be alone, I return to the alcove, but she wants you here, to share."

Iriset sinks onto a stool, her body melting a little after the strain of resisting Amaranth. Sidoné remains standing, shoulder leaned against the wall in a relaxed pose, and her eyes drift closed. She seems to go immediately to sleep.

Relaxing is impossible for Iriset, though no matter how intently Iriset strains to hear, nothing echoes from the chamber.

Then comes a long sigh, and Iriset parts her lips to set the tip of her tongue in the air to taste it, and the forces.

In the sanctuary, at the altar, Amaranth mé Esmail Her Glory touches herself, sliding her hands along her skin, pinching and caressing as she knows her body likes. She slowly, attentively, raises herself to pleasure.

Iriset knows this to be happening—that is the duty of the Moon-Eater's Mistress, that is how to awaken the dead god, to draw him here. But it's not the only thing happening: Force pulls from every direction in thin lines as Amaranth draws force toward her own center. Iriset's head falls back as she gives in to the sensation, as she listens and feels with tongue and lips, as she turns open her palms to feel the tingling there. If she were alone, she'd follow Her Glory's lead and touch herself, too. If she had the time, she'd invent a force-net for self-pleasure that cycles through the forces and wakes the body the way the Moon-Eater is woken. She'd call it the little eater.

The threads of force draw together, slithering and sparking past Iriset, toward the center of the temple—always toward the center. They twist around one another, looping, braiding, tighter, tighter, then loosening like a sigh before winding up again, and finally, finally, finally they knot into a whole.

That knot traps the breath in Iriset's throat, and she shudders. Her whole body is on the edge, only from listening, tasting the forces, from letting her mind imagine touch and heat. Sweat tingles her spine, under her breasts, and she's wet enough to feel it.

Amaranth sighs, an airy moan.

Iriset sighs so softly, wanting to be in there, wanting hands on her, a pull at her scalp, teeth on her neck. Anything.

The forces tangled around her tighten, and Iriset's hands curl into fists, low over her belly. She breathes rapidly.

The central knot unravels.

What *releases* are not balanced forces, not falling and flow and ecstatic and rising but something parallel to them, from within them... like a fifth force.

It feels different, whole unto itself, and passes through the air, through lattice and flesh and bone, out into the rest of the world. Then it is gone.

Silence—true Silence, the tension of perfect balance—hangs in the Moon-Eater's sanctuary, and deep, deep within herself, Iriset feels a thump-thump like a heartbeat.

Maybe it's her own heartbeat. She feels gladness, satisfaction, belonging, and—

"Iriset."

Her name drifts low from the altar.

She opens her eyes, unmoving. Iriset is unsure she wishes to emerge, but Sidoné shoves her. She stumbles past the screen.

Her Glory is slumped on the floor, around the far side of the altar. Her mask covers her face, spilling over hair and chest. Its scalloped edges flutter against the sunset colors of her wrapped trousers.

"I'm here." Iriset kneels, shaky.

"Did you feel him?"

"I felt something." She doesn't have words for what it had been. Maybe a god. Maybe only Amaranth. But it was intense, unlike anything she's felt before. "Then it was gone."

"He doesn't remain awake," Her Glory murmurs.

Iriset makes a questioning sound. The most she can manage. As she recovers herself, she grows somehow more dazed, more awed. The details of what she experienced fade, like a dream, but leave behind a wavering understanding of something impossible to know.

Amaranth says, "It isn't that I wake him for the day—I only wake him for a moment. A moment of unity, and Aharté is with us, too. Or maybe they're the same. Aharté and the Moon-Eater. I cannot say." Her voice lifts, falls, drifts with rolling languor.

"All the forces moved," Iriset says. "I have heard that Aharté unraveled him, but every time you do this, you put him back together. Only for a moment. You are an architect."

Amaranth's shoulders shake and she says in a deeply irreverent voice, "An architect of *love*," as if love is nothing but a dirty joke.

"But, oh, I've never thought of love that way," Iriset says, awe-drunk and undeterred. "As a force. Or a knot. But falling draws things together—that is love. Flow is always changing—that is love. Ecstatic flares, brightens, brings us genius, makes us better! Rising makes us yearn and grow. What is love but that?" With each word her voice pitches higher, thinning with thrills. Iriset's heart pounds, and she feels it—something—just past her eyes, just beyond hearing, barely out of reach. And in that moment, despite all the reasons not to, Iriset begins to love Amaranth mé Esmail. Just a little bit, a seed, but it is there.

Her Glory laughs lightly, joyfully. "I knew I should bring you here, little designer."

───── • ♦ • ─────

It is fitting what happens next, that very afternoon.

Iriset sits on a narrow bench in the Garden for Four Winds, lazily sketching details of a briar rose growing around a small obelisk marked with gilded lines of *Writings of the Holy Syr* ("This life is ours: your gift, my design"). The top edge of the sun passes just behind the bottom edge of Aharté's moon overhead, signaling the beginning of summer, and so Amaranth and her handmaidens spread throughout the garden, enjoying one of the last lovely days before the true heat settles in. Iriset suspects it is for her, as the languid sense of understanding has stuck to her like honey, like bobbing rainbow bees buzzing in her skull. She'd not be good for anything more strenuous than drawing in the garden. Maybe Amaranth is taking care of her. Maybe she does like Iriset, and can learn to trust her in time to save the Little Cat.

Maybe it's all manipulation, and Iriset should resist. But her inner design is too strange with her morning experiences to scheme.

Tucked beneath the royal residential petals of the palace and beside the mirané dome, this garden is small and perfectly square, cornered by tall windcatcher steeples painted white for ecstatic force, blue for rising, black for flow, and green for falling. From the four-point star-shaped fountain in the center, four long streams were dug into the earth, tiled in the deep red of the Vertex Seal like channels of blood reaching toward the towers. The streams are narrow enough to step across and stocked with tiny blue-green minnows. Hardy flowers like desert rose, fleshy succulents, violet-eye creepers, and needle sage are planted in perfect four-count patterns. A gardener feeds the minnows a few paces from where Amaranth lounges in the sunlight while Anis mé Ario draws white geometry upon her hands and arms in extremely delicate lines. Sidoné has stripped to her sleeveless shift and rolled up her trousers to her knees in order to show Istof Nefru a few grappling moves, and Ziyan mé Tal sings softly where she perches on the edge of the fountain, a harp cradled in her lap. A Seal guard stands at each of the two arched entrances cut into the garden wall. Occasionally a couple of miran enter, greeting Sidoné before approaching Amaranth.

Iriset focuses on her sketching, or her mind will drift higher and higher into airy philosophy or gloomy futures, and she'll crash hard into anxiety: She recognizes the symptoms and cannot afford the results here in the palace.

The roses are her favorite to draw because they embody all the forces: rising in how they climb, reaching for the sun; flow in their creeping vines, with which they embrace the small obelisk; falling in the layered, spiraling pattern of their petals, clinging toward the central stamen; ecstatic in the sudden thorns for sticking, gripping, defense. She wonders if she can design tiny thornlike hooks in the filaments of silk thread to make the ecstatic connection between skin and mask even better. Or to hook the air itself perhaps? Did she have time to experiment? She has thirty-two days to save her father.

Her hand trembles and Iriset breathes her eight-count balance.

Leaning over her bound book of vellum, she begins a new detail: the petals of this unfurling deep red rose. Their scent, delicate and airy, surrounds her, filling her nostrils until it's a thin layer of taste at the back of her throat. Her eyes drift closed and she uses one hand to lift the rose head nearer her cheek, brushing it to her skin. It is softer than silk, cool and erotic. She touches it to her bottom lip. If she'd had this with her in the Moon-Eater's Temple, just this slight brush of living silk on her lip might have made her come. Could she bring herself right here, with subtle tugs of rising force, the rose petal a focus on her lip? She has all afternoon to play. Amaranth is just as close right now as she was in the temple, undone. Surely Her Glory would notice…

A quiet sound beside Iriset startles her; she gasps and crushes her hand around the narrow stem. Tiny thorns sting her fingers.

"I am sorry," says a man, voice low. He sits down beside her on the bench. "May I?"

He holds out a mirané-brown hand, paler on the palm. Iriset stares at his forearm, slender with muscle, the knob of his wrist she wants to dig her teeth into. (It will haunt her, someday, that first glimpse of him. She was already thinking about sex.)

Her lips part, instinctively tasting his rising force, as she lifts her gaze.

A priest of Aharté, she thinks, for he wears a simple sleeveless wrapped robe in contemplative style, in burnt red like the Silent priests and guards of the Vertex Seal. Lean, and shapely as a dancer. His face is clean-shaven, as Silent priests prefer, his black hair loose, thick, and slightly waved around his ears and neck. His eyes are a dark brown with a flare of perfect mirané-brown flecks around the iris, and tilted up at the outer corners as they balance evenly over wide cheekbones. Beneath a straight nose his lips rest in a gentle frown. A scatter of black freckles spreads from his left cheek out over his temple, marring the easy symmetry of his face. Concentric four-point stars have been painted in mesmerizing green and blue along his same cheek, to distract from the iconic freckles. He's magnificent. Iriset wants to touch him. With her open mouth. She wants to do more than that.

He calmly allows her to stare, and Iriset only late remembers she's *not supposed to*, and hides her eyes with her fingers.

The man asks again, "May I?"

Iriset nods, forgetting what he wants, and he takes her stinging hand away from her face, cupping it in his own. All Iriset's willpower is required not to moan. A slight frown bends his mouth as he studies her flesh. She forces herself to look, too, at the tiny dots of blood on the underside of her knuckles.

"Garnet, do you have . . . ?" He glances out at the garden and Iriset's eyes follow to where the large Garnet méra Bež stands beside Sidoné with his hands on his hips. The priest at Iriset's side trails off, shrugs. "She's bleeding."

"Glorious Silence!" cries Amaranth. "What are you doing to my handmaiden?"

Iriset opens her mouth to speak, but her hand is still cupped in his, and she can't breathe very well as understanding batters against her lust.

"I startled her," the man says, abashed.

Garnet strides to the fountain, tearing off a section of the red cloth mask that flutters at the side of his head. Iriset stares at him, the better to avoid glancing anywhere else. He rinses it, wets it again, and brings it over, scowl carefully modulated.

"Thank you," says Lyric méra Esmail His Glory. Then the Vertex Seal gently dabs blood from Iriset's skin.

Lyric presses the cloth to her palm, holding it there. Iriset clutches at her vellum, her charcoal stick trapped against the material, likely smudging her roses. When he raises his eyes to hers, Iriset immediately drops her gaze. She can't tug the end of her mask across her face because both her hands are extremely occupied.

"You're Iriset mé Isidor," the Vertex Seal says. "I'm very glad to meet you finally. My sister and Ambassador Erxan, and even my mother, speak well of you."

"Oh." It's all she can manage. And breathy at that.

Rising force dominates his inner design. It lifts the design around him, lightening her thoughts: She's dizzy, dazed.

"What are you drawing?"

Iriset gently frees her hand from his and offers him the vellum book. "Flowers," she says, eyes safely on his hands as he accepts the book and smooths two graceful fingers along the edge of the vellum.

"You're very detailed," he says.

"Details are where the design appears." Thank Silence she can finally complete a sentence.

"Do you see knots or hints of the larger patterns of Holy Design when you study these smallest creatures?"

"I haven't looked for larger patterns, Your Glory," she says softly. Lying. Demure. She is not Silk. She cannot have this man.

The silence stretches between them, and Iriset draws careful breaths both to balance herself—to pull inward and away from his strong rising force—and to hide the depth of her uncertainty. It is too easy to sit beside him. He held her hand and holds still much worse within his purview. Her father's future. The entire empire's future! She's too off-balance from her morning with the Moon-Eater. How could she have let this happen today of all days? She's unprepared to coax him, to be sweet or even figure out the best approach to his sympathy.

"You draw with Erxan," Lyric says.

"That is how I met the ambassador, yes. I get along well with him."

"And he with you. He believes Singix will like you."

Iriset wants to cheer, *Yes, yes, bring me closer to you,* but she only lowers her eyes. This man, this Vertex Seal, will marry Singix of the Beautiful Twilight. "Erxan speaks highly of her. I hope I can have the chance to be liked by someone like her."

In the quiet following, Iriset glances up. He's watching her with a tiny frown. She couldn't have said anything wrong.

Finally, the Vertex Seal says, "May I ask a favor of you, Iriset?"

"You do not need to ask, but only command, Your Glory." She struggles to keep the words from biting. To remain soothing and soft.

Lyric pauses. He turns a page in her vellum book, revealing an elaborate drawing of butterfly wings. Next, the repeating patterns of stars in the lattice of her bedchamber window. Next, a study of a coiled stem of needle sage. Next, repeating curves of flow force, like waves, with tiny numbers counting off the rhythm of that strange almost-breath Iriset hears humming through the palace architecture at night.

There the Vertex Seal stops. His posture is so very straight, as if even in repose he can't relax his design. "I would prefer to ask, as my question is of a personal rather than princely design."

A thrill of ecstatic sparks in her, helping her resettle herself like a rock tossed into a still pool. He wants a favor from her. "Ask, then, Your Glory," she murmurs.

"My sister has always judged people well. Though your provenance is obviously questionable, I have yet to be wrong when I trust Amaranth's opinion."

He pauses to look at her.

Iriset quickly looks down. "Her Glory saved me. I can only balance her trust with trustworthiness."

"Yes." The Vertex Seal adds no more.

"You... have a favor to ask, Your Glory?"

He makes a light sound that in anyone else Iriset would think was a tucked-away laugh. "Will you allow Erxan to teach you some Ceres? I would like for my wife-to-be to have folk to speak with in her home tongue when she arrives."

Surprised, Iriset barely stops herself from agreeing immediately. She'd say yes to anything to make him indebted to her, but this has several possible advantages. New language skills, drawing her closer to the ambassador, and setting her up to befriend the future consort of the Vertex Seal. "I want to do that, Your Glory. And I will. But..."

Lyric waits as if he has all the time in the world.

Iriset asks with all the hope she can conjure, "May I see my father?"

There's a pause, and she stares at the knob in his wrist. His hands are so relaxed. "Very well," he finally says. "Briefly. Tell Sidoné to arrange it."

"Thank you," she breathes out, shoulders sinking. Permission to see her father will make disguising him with a craftmask so much easier. A smile grows on her lips.

"Thank you."

There is so obviously an answering smile in his voice that Iriset looks up, meets his mirané-brown eyes for a flash, then skews her gaze to the black freckles at his cheek and temple. No shape aligns the dots, no pattern she can discern.

His hand lifts and he touches the freckles with two fingers. "Garnet wants me to cover them up completely, as they're an obvious signal of who I am, my external design. Easily re-created."

"No," Iriset answers before she can stop herself. "They're asymmetrical, which makes them very difficult to design—for an architect. Symmetry is a human necessity, differentiating our designs from those of She Who Loves Silence. A mask of your face would be a challenge, unless there were freckles on both sides, in even numbers." She leans nearer than she needs to, counting swiftly. "Thirteen. A terrible number for architecture."

With a teasing smile, Iriset flicks a glance at his eyes, then realizes she's flirting with the Vertex Seal. Over apostasy, of all things.

But Lyric studies her thoughtfully. "I will tell Garnet he should stop pressing Menna to cover my flaws up, then."

"Only..." Iriset swallows to regain her voice. "Only Aharté is master of asymmetrical design. Rather than a flaw, it is her blessing."

Something shifts in the gaze of Lyric méra Esmail as she rudely stares, but he says no more.

That night, Iriset begins to draw the eyes of the Vertex Seal.

FLOW

My Aharté is not the world's Aharté.
—*Writings of the Holy Syr*

11

The little cat

The afternoon before Iriset is to visit her father, Raia tells her that Silk is dead.

"Silk," an begins, and Iriset startles hard enough to stumble.

Raia reaches for her elbow and she jerks away. How did an know? What gave her away? She draws her shoulders back and tilts her chin up, pulling a cool smile across her face.

But the architect's gaze is angled down. "I'm sorry," an murmurs. "She's been poisoned. General Bey believes the Little Cat instructed it be done so that she gives no more secrets of his away—not that she was." Raia grimaces.

"Oh. That…" Iriset struggles for the appropriate grief response amid waves of extreme relief. "Is…to be expected," she finishes in a whisper.

Raia's mouth pulls into a disapproving line. "It ought not be. It's terrible. She served him, he shouldn't—it's a betrayal."

Iriset grasps her hands together against her chest. Her identity has not been uncovered, and it makes her furiously glad.

It hadn't been her, she isn't dead. She's alive and can still save her father.

The sheer relief makes her cold enough to shudder.

A woman is dead because of her, a friend, and she's *glad*.

The cold flashes hot as unruly ecstatic charges take over.

Nausea like strings of rising force climbs sticky up her throat. She's selfish in her relief, and depraved for being glad. Iriset swallows again and again, then manages, "She expected it. She knew it would come. It was part of her bargain with my father."

"That's monstrous," Raia says.

It is.

But Iriset shakes her head. "Everyone—everyone bargains with him."

"Iriset," the architect begins, reaching to brush ans knuckles against her shoulder.

"May I go?" she whispers. She has to get control of herself.

An gives her leave and she flees back to her chambers. Once there, she pulls the door closed and stumbles to the lattice window to press her forehead against it. She stares through star-shaped cutouts and whispers a balancing count prayer, an invocation of the four forces. Her breath catches a wisp of her hair, ruffling it against her chin. A tear spills from one eye, then the other, asymmetrical.

She doesn't even know still if it was Paser or Dalal who took her place. Paser had a lover, and Dalal had a son. That child could get the news Iriset dreads: His mother is dead. To keep Iriset safe. Because Iriset is more important.

The reality of it scoops out a hunk of the pride she's always embraced, splattering it onto the floor like viscera.

She aches to curl down against the cool mosaic of the floor. To melt. She's no mastermind. She's not supposed to be the one plotting, just making tools to enact her father's will. Inventing, experimenting. Scheming isn't her job! Or her purpose. Design is her only purpose. All she's ever wanted. Her only ambition.

Iriset grinds her teeth to maintain control before she falls to pieces.

If she doesn't maintain her poise, her father *will* die next.

She purses her lips and blows a long, quiet sigh. When she's pushed out every ounce of air, she pauses, deprived, not drawing any new breath.

In this moment Iriset feels it, with one teary cheek pressed to the window lattice: the slow rhythm of the palace's design. Like someone else's careful breathing. In her fog of panic she imagines a sleeping lion beneath the foundations, a hibernating tortoise from the Apostate Age, its shell the stones of the world itself.

Iriset matches her breathing to the rhythm of the palace's design. Her thoughts meander along curious, distracting paths: Could the rhythm maintain foundational integrity? Did designing in a repeating pulse hold the complicated threads of alarms, plumbing, wind, shieldwork, art, ovens, and a hundred other systems knotted together without degradation? Push back against entropy?

Impossible. All design deteriorates, she knows. Either maintenance or demolition is necessary eventually. Someday even Aharté's moon will fall.

Isidor the Little Cat is incarcerated in the apostate tower, the highest, most isolated of the prison towers. To reach him, Iriset is forced to pass through one of the three branches of the main prison building—three to keep it off-balance and always rippling with a tension between the foundational forces. The missing force is ecstatic. While some doors hum with ready rising force and threads of alarm, others are nulled and no architecture can pass through. It's a design built to disrupt rather than reject.

As Iriset follows behind a Seal guard, she marks every variation and its effect upon her jade cuff. She's theorized that the design of the cuff itself, its link to her inner design, will allow it to hold its spark of force even when she slips through the null doors. Luckily, the jade cuff functions as she posited. Which means the craftmask she spent the night perfecting will, too.

At the base of the apostate tower, a soldier and an army combat-designer work in tandem to unlock a small wooden door. Iriset steps first into the dim glow of force-lanterns, then up into the narrow, spiraling staircase. The Seal guard follows, turning his shoulders so the heavy padded armor fits. The narrowness and tight curve, the steepness and depth of the steps, are meant to further impede escape or rescue. The only quick way out of the apostate tower is to leap from the mortally high window.

A thin crescent landing tops the staircase, and at the center of its inner curve is a waist-high door. "You must crawl," says the soldier who came up behind the Seal guard, and shoves herself between them to crouch and unlock the short door.

"You have an hour," adds the Seal guard.

Iriset nods and gets to her hands and knees.

Nervous sweat drips down Iriset's temple as she emerges into the cell. Plain, dull tiles cover the floor, and the wall is curved stucco. A pallet and thin pillow are rolled up beneath a small, tightly latticed window; there's a slightly thicker sitting pillow, a relief bucket, a pitcher and bowl for water, and a stack of three books.

Her father stands at the window, his back to her, and Iriset knows he does it to prove his lack of fear, lack of concern over whoever enters.

She quietly gets to her feet, scrubbing dust from the knees of her trousers, and uses the end of her mask to discreetly wipe sweat from her temple. She bites her lip, staring at Isidor. A threadbare brown robe hangs from his narrow shoulders; his feet are bare and dirty beneath the ankle ties of his trousers. His hair has been razed close to his skull, and in the bare light that pierces the quad-scythe pattern of the lattice, it shines silver.

Isidor the Little Cat doesn't turn. His patience, when hunting, is legendary.

"Dad," Iriset says, and in a spark of ecstatic movement, he spins.

"Iriset," he breathes. His gray eyes dart over her, taking everything in. Iriset does the same, noting the lines at his eyes, the paleness of his lips, the ragged brown-and-silver beard the same length as his shorn hair. The suntan that used to darken his ruddy Cloud King skin to a tone more like that of his daughter's has faded. There are hollows under his narrow cheekbones, and the knot he's never let her fix in his proud nose stands out angrily. As she stares, his hands twitch into fists.

"I'm all right," Iriset says. Her heart pounds, for she doesn't know if he'll approve of her game.

With the grace of the cat for which he was named, he strides to her, cupping her face. In Old Sarenpet, which has no personal pronouns, he says, "Bags under daughter's eyes. Lost weight."

"Stink," she shoots back in the same, but a whisper. Then she falls against him, arms around his neck. She squeezes, pressing hard, ear to ear. The fuzz of his hair tickles her cheek. It doesn't matter that he smells of sweat and grime—it might've been worse. The cell is clean, watered. He doesn't reek of urine or blood or infection.

Iriset clings to him. Her heart blasts and she feels like everything inside her flares white as lightning. He's alive—alive!— and they have a chance. *She* has a chance. She tucks her face against his neck and he puts his chin over her head. They breathe together, automatically falling into the eight-count meditation.

Like Amaranth, Isidor's dominant inner force is falling, the kind of pull that turns the attention of others toward him and inspires loyalty. Though much of his youth had been spent attempting to avoid that attention, as his undermarket empire grew, Isidor learned to manipulate his charisma to gain friends, allies, followers. His daughter has always relied upon it, loved best to reach for that falling force with the spikes of her dominant ecstatic, allow his energy to calm hers. To center her in him.

But in the cell, when she opens to him, his falling force drags at her like a whirlpool. He needs so much, and never has before. Iriset clutches tighter. She breathes carefully.

"What is kitten doing here?" her father murmurs into her mask.

A shudder plunges through her body and she pushes back to look at his face again, but leaves her hands on his shoulders, unprepared to let go. "Getting father out. Have a craftmask wrapped in this cloth mask, and extra clothing, and overlarge slippers. A perfect Iriset mé Isidor mask. Dad must drop shoulders and keep hands mostly hidden in the sleeves. There's a flow-net woven into scarf to help."

Isidor's brow lowers. "And daughter?"

"Must wait here. Only one entered, only one can leave."

"And then daughter will be imprisoned. You expect me to agree to this?" His calm voice has fooled many, convincing them he houses no anger, nor disapproval. But Iriset knows the calmer he seems, the more danger he nurses.

"These past quads," she says quickly, following his switch back to mirané, "I've been handmaiden to Amaranth mé Esmail Her Glory."

Isidor studies her again, still frowning. "How did you manage that?"

"Oh, Dad." She smiles only a little, but proudly. "They believed I was not Silk. The trick worked. Her Glory came for me, thinking I would be a fine addition to her menagerie—and I am. I was. I made her my friend, as much as such is possible, and I've spoken personally with the Vertex Seal. He asked a favor of me. I know the ambassador from the Ceres Remnants. And I work with one of the royal designers—that's how I stole the materials I needed for your mask, and Raia trusts me. Dad, even if they punish me, you'll be free. Outside this tower you have the allies and power to free me in return. They won't execute me, as they will you."

The Little Cat sighs, a small, irritated hum. "I will not trade myself for you."

"You must! It's my fault!"

"What is?"

Her pulse roars in her ears and she's dizzied with panic at the thought of confessing. But she must. He has to know. "They traced me. Silk. They traced my silk imports to the tower. If it weren't for my mistake, you wouldn't be here. I can't let you be executed when it's my fault."

"Kitten, I imported those cocoons for you."

"But—"

"No. You worked for me, I am ultimately responsible. Do not take this on your shoulders."

"It's my fault!"

"Stop." He says it hard, and next he'll snap his fingers. If she doesn't stop, he'll slap her.

Iriset bites her tongue.

Her father glances away. It's his scheming face.

She waits, though she hates it. Her fingers go cold, then hot.

It takes very little time before her father turns decisively.

"You cannot give up this new position, Iriset. Power at your fingertips and allied with the strongest of the empire. You could do anything from that place. Take anything, transform anything. I could never have given you so much."

Shock widens her eyes. He is her father. He gave her *everything*. "Dad! It's nothing. I don't need power, or—or riches. We can be safe far away from here. We can flee to the Ceres islands. I don't need them, I need you."

"Iriset. They will convict you of human architecture."

"But—"

"They will know you for Silk. Then Paser's sacrifice will mean nothing."

Iriset closes her mouth on all replies. She lowers her eyes. It had been Paser. Her lover is a widow now. For Iriset.

Her father's hands find her shoulders, then her neck. He cups her face again. "You have done so much, so well."

"Not enough!" she says viciously, spiking with fury. She tears away. "I have to save you."

"You can't save everyone, kitten."

Back turned to him, Iriset hugs herself, gripping her own elbows tightly through the belled sleeves. She cannot look into his eyes now, not when they both think of her mother.

"Can you even imagine what she would say if I allowed you to do this for me?" Isidor asks gruffly.

"She wouldn't want you dead, either," Iriset grinds out through her teeth. This can't be happening. How dare he reject her rescue.

"No. But she would choose you."

"Dad."

"You cannot make me don your mask. You will not win this argument."

Iriset holds herself tighter.

"Make me proud instead, Iriset. Make your mother proud. Do something with this position in which you have found yourself. Make a mark, or change something. Anything. The whole empire. If anyone can, you can. I've seen what you are capable of doing when you decide."

"Dad."

"You challenged Aharté herself, and won, when you were ten years old. What can the Vertex Seal do against that?"

Iriset stares, lips parted, and feels like—nothing. Nulled, as if the wires bind her wrists again, or a thick collar clenches her throat. She's choking on nothingness. She can't accept this. Her knees give out and she sits abruptly on the floor, knocking her tailbone hard.

Her father kneels beside her, pulling her close. "I love you, kitten. Iriset, my Silk. I will die your father, rather than earn the appellation of villain in my own core."

"I'll find another way," she whispers. "Beg for your life on the Days of Mercy. Is Bittor alive, do you know?"

"As far as I know, he was not killed or imprisoned."

"I'll get a message to him." She'll find a way. If the undermarket isn't checking the old drops, she'll find a new one. "Bittor will get cousins to the execution, and we'll rescue you. I will find all the flaws in their security. Be ready."

"As long as you do not show your hand. And if you ever must flee, there is money and a cache of jewels in the Violet Break."

"I know." It's a small crevasse in one of the catacombs where they've hidden things only Iriset (or some similarly skilled designer who happens to know the exact location and engagement sequence) can get to, with a careful application of forces. "I am sorry about Paser," Iriset whispers.

"Her family is well cared for."

Iriset quietly asks after the rest of their cousins and courtiers, and Isidor tells her what he can of who is free, who captured, who killed, who sent to work camps already, and who likely will be executed at his side in twenty-six days. They move to the wall and sit with shoulders pressed, hands together. Iriset listens to her father, to the liquid words, his charm as he tries to give her some comfort, to convince her he's well enough and proud and will go to his death with no regrets. She tries to listen, not letting her thoughts wander to contacting Bittor or asking Shahd or Amaranth for aid. These moments are precious and she has to be in them. A new plan can come later. Tonight.

Her father asks for stories of the palace. "I've never explored it, you know, kitten. I made it to the Silent Chapel once, but never into the palace itself, nor the Moon-Eater's Temple."

And so Iriset describes the temple to him, and the fossil teeth, even tells him what Amaranth said about them not belonging to the Moon-Eater. "But she feels him, or something, Dad. I did, too. A connective knot. And all the palace complex is woven together, architecturally, into a great array. It's like an organism, a massive one—not just like the Holy Design of Moonshadow. The design of the palace is ancient. Apostatical design, though I'll be careful to whom I say such a thing."

She tells him about the star-eye windows in every room, about the feather dragons prowling the gardens like cats for skinks and rats, and the flowers that turn their faces to the strongest force. He asks about the food, and she's extravagant with her report, because he's hungry, and it helps assuage the longing to imagine in extreme detail.

"Now tell me about this favor asked of you by the Vertex Seal himself."

"He asked me to learn as much Ceres as I can, quickly, in order to be a friend to his newly arriving wife. He believes she will be comforted with some handmaidens knowing her home tongue."

"Thoughtful."

"If we needed to, Dad, we could run to the islands. The ambassador might help me—and I already know some of the language. They might not expect that, thinking you would head for the Cloud Kings."

Isidor is silent for a moment, then takes her hand again, weaving their fingers together. "You might run there, then. Do not think of me."

"You can't command such a thing." Tears collect behind her eyes, pressing her voice into a whine.

His hand squeezes, hurting her knuckles as his fingers crush hers. "I do."

"Dad."

"Your willfulness has served you, Iriset, but do not let it get you killed. Do not let it ruin you. You gave me your bond."

Iriset digs her nails into the back of his hand. "How can I live with myself if I don't try? What kind of monster would I be?"

"Ah, girl, do not make me worry constantly my last days!"

Tears burn her eyes, her cheeks are hot, there's a staggering in her pulse. Iriset keeps her eyes on their hurting hands. "Don't make me say goodbye to you!"

Her father's grip loosens. She chokes out a sob and pulls her hand free.

Isidor takes her shoulder instead and pushes her to face him. A haggard frown drags his expression. "Goodbye, Iriset."

"No."

"Iriset."

She climbs to her feet, using the wall for support. She shakes her head, no, no, *no*.

"Where is your pride?" Isidor asks gently.

Spiking ecstatically, twisted in a dreadful fall, a glutted flow, with nowhere to rise, no hope, no prayer to the silver-pink moon in the sky.

"Gather it," orders the Little Cat.

Iriset puts her fists together over her sternum, shoved against her flesh, then pushes down until her fists are a pressed heart of force right over her core, the center of her balance. She breathes. Air flows into her, cooling the spikes of ecstatic fury, the sparks of excitement. Blood pumps to her palms and soles of her feet, pushing out and inward again, a gravity centered within her. Love and longing drift together, lifting toward the lightest cloud of warmth as she sighs it out across her tongue.

Isidor brushes his fingers along her temple, then kisses her lips, her forehead, and touches his forehead to hers.

Hot tears fall in straight lines down her cheeks. Her lips tremble. "I won't say goodbye, Dad."

His sigh crackles with a growl.

"I swear I will see you again. Even if it is at the unraveling pier."

"Do not watch me die," Isidor says.

"Stop commanding me! I will watch if I must. If I cannot free you, I will face the consequences of our life, of my failure. *That* is my pride!" She steps back, holds his gaze. "Like this, and you can find me, find my eyes across the field of curious and death-seekers come to watch the Little Cat perish. If nothing else, promise me you'll look for me, look at me, and let me—let me be the last thing you see."

"Your eyes, kitten, and the clouds in the sky," he whispers, so tense with emotion the words almost disintegrate.

12

Poor fairy

Iriset leaves the apostate tower in a state of alarm so restless it could be felt by anyone sensitive to threads of force. The Seal guard says nothing, only moves after her as she darts back to the palace.

Curses on her father's integrity for refusing her help!

Iriset closes her eyes, pressing tears out, and grits her teeth against a wail. She keeps going.

Sweat itches her scalp, runs down her spine, and she suddenly, halfway across the quartz yards, jerks at the winding cloth mask, tearing at it, pulling it out of its knots and twists. She frees it, and her thick brown hair falls down, knotted in places, braided in others, but messy for how she's undone the mask. Her stylus falls to the path and she grabs it up; it was hidden in the carefully twisted headdress, and the scrap of silk that is her craftmask, too. Her *perfect* craftmask. It's genius! And she made it from scraps and stolen tools! It should be a triumph. But she crumples it angrily and stuffs it into the front of her robe.

Her cloth mask is pale orange, and she snaps it out fully into its broad rectangle, then settles it over her head with the short side over her face, the rest falling over her loose hair. She finds the pinholes sewn in and pins it in place against the braids at her temples. She'll not display her grief, her fury and frustration, for everyone.

From beneath the sheer mask, the world turns various shades of orange and red, shadows of fire.

Watching her is Sidoné mé Dalir.

Iriset stops. Her shoulders heave as she wrestles herself under control.

Sidoné cocks her head and Iriset waits for an *I told you so* or false sympathy. But the body-twin merely says, "Her Glory would like you to help her with the dress and go with us to the mirané hall for its presentation."

Iriset blinks her tear-tacky lashes. She'd forgotten that the scarf-dress she designed is complete. Delivered to Her Glory this morning.

"I can tell her you're ill," Sidoné offers skeptically.

"No."

After dismissing the Seal guard, Sidoné takes a corner of Iriset's mask and wipes it gently against Iriset's cheek. She steps nearer and keeps her eyes on her work until she's dried away every smear of crying. "It's hard, sometimes," she says.

"What is?" Iriset demands, not wanting to share compassion. She's alone, not a member of some sisterhood of handmaidens.

But Sidoné pinches Iriset's chin exactly like a scolding sister. She angles Iriset's face toward her own. "Holding everything together."

Iriset tugs free of Sidoné's grip.

"Being forced to remain calm at Amaranth's side will help you find balance in it. Come with me, and be what you are here to be."

Iriset goes. She has little choice. And Sidoné is correct: She needs focus.

No one in the women's petal inquires after her visit, thankfully. But Iriset is still rather sullen as she helps Her Glory into the ecstatically linked scarves, careful not to touch her skin when possible. Amaranth notices and leans in, or turns unexpectedly, teasing Iriset with physical contact until Iriset huffs herself into smiling, too. It's good. Amaranth acts like her friend, and that will work to Iriset's advantage when she makes her next move. It must.

Anis mé Ario brings out a long, lacquered box of paints and artfully decorates not only Amaranth's face but all the handmaidens', including Sidoné's. Ziyan makes a point of asking Iriset which colors will complement Her Glory's dress best. Iriset pauses just long enough for Ziyan to know Iriset understands the other handmaiden is trying to include her, to make up for previous rejections. They both wish Nielle were here.

When they're finished, thick black lines their eyes, small interlocking blue and white four-point stars dance along their cheekbones, and mirané brown covers their mouths. On Her Glory and the mirané handmaidens, Anis lines the lips with thin black so that their mouths match their skin in perfect mirané tone but stand out just as their eyes do. The same color darkens Iriset's lips, and Istof's, but while the rich color flatters Istof's mouth, turning her cool tan skin coppery, the mirané brown clashes with Iriset's dusky peach cheeks. On her, the color is like a wound.

For Anis's turn, Iriset is voted artist for her skill with drawing. She doesn't bother pretending she can't do it anymore, and lines Anis's eyes and mouth exquisitely. Iriset places the four-point stars perfectly to balance the thickness of Anis's lips with the square shape of her jaw. And she reshapes the shadows of Anis's brow with a curving line of black.

It's then, looking at Anis's painted face, that Iriset feels better.

When Her Glory sweeps into the mirané hall with her handmaidens, the impression they give is of a god and her mirrored avatars.

The Hall of Princes not only houses the throne but is home to the mirané council, any session of justice presided over by the Vertex Seal, royal announcements, and the intermittent social event.

The latter is the occasion for that evening's gathering.

The peristyle court is built of towering dark wood, raising stacked domes in patterns four layers high. The central dome caps directly over the Vertex Seal, its apex pierced by a star-eye window through which the moon always glows. Webs of flow force tied with ecstatic knots spread between the columns, and in their spectrum flower petals hover, along with faceted glass beads reflecting rainbows. At the touch of an architect bearing the proper stylus, the webs rearrange into new patterns: a rose of light, then a few moments later a four-point star, and after that a word of power that could be read in line with the rest of the webs to create a poem honoring the Vertex Seal or Aharté. It's a fancier, more intricate version of city graffiti.

The occasion is to welcome home a frontier ambassador who'd been stationed along the Cloud Ranges. General Bey méra Matsimet appears in glorious uniform, and octagonals of other soldiers from both the city army and the Empire Forces Army scatter throughout the crowd to honor the ambassador.

The miran̄é council attends in full, small kings from various city precincts, prominent architects in the competing colors of their specialty schools, artists, priests, and all the spectacle of the empire.

Amaranth blows through it like lightning, drawing every eye, flirting, arguing, and deigning to bless with her attention, flanked always by her armed body-twin and her handmaidens.

The gown of scarves is perfect, shifting with her movements, threatening to bare every fold and curve of her body but never—quite—doing so. The architects salivate over its delicate design and no few miran applaud delicately. A lanky and unusually gender-ambiguous miran laughs in delight, then chides Amaranth on lack of subtlety. Amaranth quietly replies, "Hardly obvious enough for my target."

It makes several people markedly uncomfortable, Iriset notices with interest. Amaranth is the Moon-Eater's Mistress and everyone knows exactly what she does every morning, for the line of Mistresses have done the same for hundreds of years. Yet here is a thin miran̄é woman whose lashes flutter with distaste when Her Glory passes; there a cloud-pale Ceres man in the ambassador's party whose neck and cheeks spot absolute fuchsia and he cannot speak but to sputter as he stares at the low side curve of her breast bared by a diaphanous blue scarf.

It's a quick way to see who doesn't quite accept the Moon-Eater's Mistress for exactly what she represents. Iriset wonders if Sidoné is keeping a list. Somebody should be.

Iriset does her best to play her role, careful to move with the other handmaidens, copying their light steps, holding her hands loose as they do. Sometimes they achieve an illusion that they're mere extensions of Amaranth's dress. Nobody pays Iriset attention except as part of the Moon-Eater's Mistress's whole. It should have been strange and soothing: Iriset is not inclined to fading into any background, either as her father's daughter or as apostate, but this way, all eyes are on her yet not taking *her* apart. What an intriguing tension!

Her Glory is given a cup of honeyed beer, and nods that her handmaidens can accept, and Iriset does so hurriedly. It's heavy on her tongue but dulls the taste of that humming energy.

She hears Sidoné hiss slightly just before Amaranth slinks toward a Silent priest with wiry white hair stuck out from her mirané skull in tight curls, and deep smiling wrinkles aging her face. Silent priests (and Lyric méra Esmail) wear their faces clean-shaven, and Iriset wonders if the fashion was intended to favor fem-forward bodies.

"Amaranth," the old priest says warmly. She's flanked by two younger mirané men, also in the high-collared sleeveless red robes of Silence. One lets his eyes take Amaranth all in before lowering his gaze politely, the other's mouth tightens in disapproval before he smooths his expression bland again and touches both eyelids.

"Holy Peace," Amaranth says, inclining her head ever so slightly.

Ah, she's not any Silent priest but their most tranquil, the head of the order. Iriset doesn't know her name and recalls that divesting oneself of even a name is considered necessary for achieving true Silence. A name disrupts balance just by existing.

(*There* is a thing the Silent priests and the numena agree upon! To the priests a name is a shackle to break, to the numena an angle for interrogating even the most basic principles of the universe, for when we are the ones to put names to those principles, we simultaneously conjure them.

Do you know who named the fifth force?)

"These are your successors?" Amaranth continues boldly, eyeing both younger priests. Their modest priestly robes fall to their knees, and red trousers and slippers cover the rest of them. Only faces and arms are bare. Each has a hood pulled over their short hair, the sheer cowl hanging to the bridge of their noses in a pretense of hiding their eyes. Beside them, Amaranth is naked. She studies them as if intending to eat them.

The Holy Peace's humor disappears slowly as she watches Amaranth, and Iriset guesses why: Neither the Vertex Seal nor the Mistress is supposed to show preference for who the Silent priests choose to lead them, but somehow Amaranth is making a move.

Now her talk of a target makes more sense. Though Iriset can't read exactly what Amaranth communicates to the priests, they certainly can. None of them approve, but the mirané priest who barely hid his dislike of Amaranth's attire trembles once.

"How very handsome you both are," she says.

"Balance does not require beauty," says the more pleasant of the two. "Only discipline."

"Both please the Moon-Eater."

"And discipline pleases your brother," the less pleasant one says.

"Oh yes." Amaranth skims a painted hand down his bare arm. "The balance between us maintains the whole empire. Seal and Mistress, Silence and Hunger."

The priest manages not to flinch away from her, and Iriset finds a moment to admire his discipline, indeed. Amaranth's touch is a thing to drown in.

"Her Glory understands discipline," the Holy Peace says. "To please the god every day."

"And herself the rest of the time," says Beremé mé Adora, the head of the mirané council, as she joins them.

Amaranth smiles sharply. "Just because I am not always

pleasing you, Beremé, it does not follow that I am always pleased. It is a simple matter"—she flicks her glance at the Holy Peace again—"to displease me."

"Something to take care with, Your Glory," the Holy Peace answers. "Lest your displeasure find its way to the Moon-Eater."

"The Moon-Eater accepts everything I offer him," she says, gaze firmly on the old priest. Bold, daring.

It's like a confrontation between cousins of the Little Cat's court. A dominance challenge. She wonders which Amaranth favors, and why. Iriset takes a drink of her honey beer to cover again the disconcerting hum on her tongue. Her movement draws Beremé's shrewd glance and Iriset instantly regrets it. None of the other handmaidens pulled attention.

"One must be displeased on occasion," says the unpleasant priest, caught up in the conversation, "if one is to be alive."

"Surely there is displeasure in death, Brother," answers the other priest.

"Not for the dead, who return to Aharté's Holy Silence."

Amaranth breaks her challenge-stare with the Holy Peace. "Wisely spoken, Brother," she says, marking *Brother* with an intimacy that's anything but familial.

The poor priest's lips part and he says nothing, lowering his eyes fast. The nicer priest raises his eyebrow, clearly suppressing a smile.

Amaranth has won.

She nods to the Holy Peace and moves away. Beremé follows at her side, maneuvering between Her Glory and Sidoné. "Crass, Amaranth," the sharp-faced mirané prince says, obviously amused. "But somehow still elegant."

"I thought he might hate me a little if I made him hard while standing next to his Holy Peace."

"If he hates you and still is appointed to the council, you won't have done yourself a favor," Sidoné says.

Amaranth glances at her, and Iriset is positioned perfectly to see the tilt of her brow that suggested Her Glory knows Sidoné only speaks up in order to disagree with Beremé. "But the Holy Peace will have to appoint him fully aware that he'll make an enemy of the Moon-Eater. She can't pretend ignorance now. None of them can."

Beremé says to Sidoné, "And if he hates her openly, even Lyric will notice and take less of his counsel."

"Why drive a wedge between Lyric and his council?"

Beremé gives the impression of rolling her eyes without doing so.

Iriset suddenly realizes: It isn't the mirané Amaranth wants her brother to trust less.

Sidoné seems to understand, too, and scowls. Her glance at Amaranth, though, is shocked. Is Sidoné a true believer?

That's—Iriset turns her head toward the throne, feeling a sudden draw of…humming? No, something insubstantial. A tug of forces. Except, this argument is about alliances on Lyric's privilege council. The Holy Peace is ready to appoint someone to replace her. Iriset should be paying avid attention. It's in her best interest. But something near the throne is strange. Everyone in the hall moves around like they don't feel it, like Iriset is the only one *not* wearing a null wire.

"Your handmaiden is bored," Beremé drawls.

Her Glory frowns at Iriset, who directs her attention back to the game.

"Tell me who fashioned this dress for you," the mirané prince continues, asking Amaranth but eyeing Iriset with slight flicks of her gaze and side-eyes—the only polite way to study a face. Iriset stares at Beremé's opal rings instead. Opals welcome design, and the rings are likely functional as well as pretty. "Menna is not capable of such imagination."

"A friend in the Ecstatic School, Beremé. Do you think you know all my friends?" Amaranth teases.

"I should hope so."

Her Glory laughs prettily and dismisses her handmaidens with a broad, elegant wave.

Iriset slips away immediately.

A dark brown man with a flat nose stops her, saying her name a bit too loud. There's a ripple in the nearby people, whisperings of *Little Cat*, but then the man introduces himself as a merchant interested to know if Her Glory has discussed garlic tariffs.

For a moment Iriset can't even think what garlic is. She shakes her head, avoiding him, but is interrupted by another man, older, with a fresh honey beer for her. He's mirané, claims to be related to Bey and Lapis mérs Matsimet, and curious to know her better. Iriset takes the beer and listens just long enough to not seem rude, before excusing herself with a tight smile. But a sudden tug on a trailing scarf from her robe nearly trips her, sloshing her drink. An older miran touches his forehead in apology with the absolute fakest expression of sincerity she's ever seen. Someone else snickers. Iriset clenches her jaw. A mirané woman steps forward and offers to help Iriset tie up that scarf and, as she does so, chatters at Iriset about a garden exhibit during the Days of Mercy that her family is hoping Her Glory might visit. The woman's friend taps a fan against her thin ceramic mask and says they should be asking about the soon-to-arrive Singix's interest in the flowers of Moonshadow.

Iriset murmurs about asking, then darts away. She moves through the party nearer to the throne in a spiraling pattern, as though she seeks to lie to herself about her target. She keeps her eyes down behind her mask, not wishing to be caught again, though it's good—it has to be—that she's being sought out for access to Her Glory. It means she's a known quantity, and some courtiers are beginning to test her. The ones willing to look past her parentage, at least.

Can she use mirané networking to rescue her father? She doesn't have enough time for developing a vast web of conspirators!

"Iriset mé Isidor," says a miran, sidling up beside her. It's the ambiguously gendered person who laughed so delightedly at Amaranth's outfit. "I was sorry to hear you weren't wearing a cat mask again."

Iriset's smile is pinched. "Can't repeat myself."

The miran laughs the same tinkling laugh. "Hehet méra Davith. Allow me to entertain you for a moment."

Iriset hums, looking for a way out. She certainly won't trust anyone who approaches so openly, only after she's separated from Her Glory.

"That dress truly is spectacular. The delicate use of—what is it? Friction-buttons?"

She stops. "I'm sure if I knew I'd be sworn to secrecy. But you could ask Her Glory."

Hehet leans in, all his straight hair shifting across his shoulders. He's got at least thirty-two glittering stars painted with some sort of mica paint shimmering all over his face. It's a very successful mask if the goal is to obscure or confuse features. "Ask directly? My dear, asking requires an answer and I'd never put Her Glory in the position of having to lie to me."

"But it's well and good if I do?"

"Naturally." Hehet's grin is as spectacular as his starry mask, and look, there's glitter in his teeth. "Now, if you ever want someone to lie to *you*, talk with Forez méra Baret over there, leaning on Dove méra Curro, who never lies but always seems to be."

"Sounds like they don't have much to talk about," she murmurs.

"One leads a faction who only believes in undercutting your mistress, the other has no faction at all, which is an impressive feat."

"What do you want from me?" Iriset asks, finally looking directly at Hehet. The dazzle of glitter on his cheeks might actually be made of tiny mirrors.

Hehet puts a scandalized hand over his breast. "Such directness!"

She waits.

With a sighing little pout, he says, "I want to be the friend of Her Glory's friend, of course."

"The Moon-Eater's Mistress and I aren't friends," she snaps, exasperated. Glancing at the throne. Why can't anyone feel that bizarre hum she's feeling?

In the sudden silence Iriset looks back at Hehet. He wears an unbelievably satisfied smile.

"Excuse me," she says, without excuse, and ducks away. She pushes past several people, hoping she remembers to ask Sidoné about this annoying person later.

She approaches the throne itself, cutting behind it to avoid the Vertex Seal where he stands chatting with Ambassador Erxan. Iriset wants to stare at him: Her brief glance told her he isn't wearing paint at all, and a small white mask lies discarded around his neck. He took her thoughts to heart.

But behind the throne is where the tug of threads has its core.

Crouched barefoot on the shallow steps of the dais, leaning its rear against the moon rock forming the throne's base is a man—or a man-shaped thing. Worn gray trousers tie at its ankles and about its whip-thin waist, and a dark sleeveless robe hangs open over its chest. The thing's skin is a washed pink, drained of true color, as if once it had been a glorious, oiled miran, but centuries of shadows have withered its rich skin from that red-brown of the Moon-Eater's moon into this sickly salamander pink. Even its long, lank hair is the same shade, its lips, its fingernails, and what should have been the whites of its eyes. Around a vivid pink pupil its iris is faceted black. Like shards of black diamonds drawn together and glimmering sharp.

A thick steel collar rings its neck. A chain is attached to the collar, its other end bolted to a ring at the base of the Vertex Seal throne. No one else in the room pays it any attention.

Iriset can barely breathe.

She slips nearer, unable to resist, and offers her warm cup of beer.

The creature takes it in both pink hands, and its long fingers brush the back of Iriset's knuckles. She shivers, and the creature's skin flushes silvery for the briefest moment, then falls to its dreary pink again.

Iriset stares. It drinks the beer in one long pour, its diamond-black eyes on Iriset the entire time.

"I'm so sorry," she whispers as she accepts the empty cup again. "I'll bring you more if I can."

She does not know why she makes the promise, except that her inner design thrums with power at its nearness. Its lips part and sharp pink-ivory teeth show: a line of tiny fangs. It says a word she doesn't know, in a rasping voice like tearing bark off a tree.

Shaking her head, Iriset backs away. Suddenly she's terrified. Her eyes widen. Being noticed by such a thing cannot suit her role, her scheme. She can't sympathize with this prisoner when rescuing another prisoner is her goal.

As she leaves, her blood slows to its regular paces, and ecstatic force pops in her ears; rising a tingle at the back of her neck; falling a churn in her gut; and flow flow flow like nausea. She hadn't felt any forces when she was near it, but had somehow thought she felt more! What a mystery, but too dangerous of one.

"Poor fairy," says a voice, catching her. Diaa of Moonshadow, Amaranth and Lyric's mother. Iriset covers her eyes with her fingers and says nothing.

"It's been here longer than I've been alive," Diaa continues softly, putting her arm around Iriset to murmur. "For a hundred years and more, captured trying to murder the Moon-Eater's Mistress during the reign of Ladalir mé Idris Her Glory. There is nothing you can do, hiha, but I always approve of the new courtiers who are affected by its presence."

With that, Diaa squeezes her and floats away to a new encounter.

Iriset doesn't know if she should be impressed or horrified that the mother of the Vertex Seal considers such monstrosity no more than a gauge with which to judge the personality of her children's friends.

13

The numen

Actually the creature chained behind the throne of the Vertex Seal had not come to kill the Moon-Eater's Mistress a hundred years ago. It came for the Moon-Eater.

The creature, a numen, has been called many things—fairy, angel, ghost, she, he, es, xe, ah and an, alushad, they—but among a people like the miran who name the sky *it* and a mountain *it* and the moon *it*, so it wished to be known, too. Its own people have no such words. They hardly have words at all anymore, because words confirm and conform, they create meanings and enforce the patterns of the universe instead of dancing between.

A word enslaves, much like the collar snapped around its neck, binding the numen into a single pattern, an exclusive form.

But no matter: It can hunt from any cage.

Stories of numena pop up around the world, though they're out of fashion in most places with rigid structures of religion or magic. Places children are encouraged to stop believing in fairy tales, societies above all that nonsense of interconnectivity and free spirits and fun. The only reason anybody believes in numena in Moonshadow City these days is because, well, they have one.

It doesn't speak to anybody, though sometimes laughs in a scratchy voice as worn as wind-scoured bones in the high desert. It eats what amuses it to eat: sometimes dust gathered slowly over a week in its underground prison, sometimes flower petals provided by miran who think they know what it is, sometimes meat but only raw because it's funnier that way for how the miran dislike it. Sometimes it doesn't eat for years. Then there are those rare occasions when a guard gets a tad too near and it manages to touch, to soak in those forces that make it.

This numen is patient.

Others, not so much. One had its favorite hat stolen in Ur-Syel and waited no time at all to follow the culprit home, where it slaughtered him through three generations in every direction, teaching the Urs that one should never pick up unclaimed clothing left lying around. In the Bow they're called trick men and tend to untie canopy bindings and spoil milk, unless one can be tricked back into a bargain, in which case they give unending blessings for defeating enemies. Across the prairies and leading into the ancient empire of Res, they were the fickle, strong wind, summoned by snapping pennants and worshipped with every breath. It's unclear whether they ever really lived in Res. Numena are tiny as bumblebees or towering as gods, depending on the convenience to the story. They're excellent lovers unless they decide they're hungry, they carry the souls of the dead to whatever heaven the souls of the dead go, they talk to birds, they soak up sun like flowers, they travel by stepping through shadows and curse through dreams. They've never existed in the Ceres Remnants, though their people have plenty of stories about demons of humanity's own making.

The Vertex Seal Tor méra Ladalir tried for thirteen years to kill the imprisoned numen. He attempted cutting off its head, a reliable method if there ever was one, to no avail. The numen's head fell, unraveled, vanished to nothing, then reappeared on its body. The person serving as the Architect of the Seal at the time suggested that the null collar stopped working on the head the moment the head was detached, and therefore those forces of the numen's body were able to rejoin the Holy Design. The architects attempted a null net, and a system of nulled accoutrement like bracelets and necklace, waist-chains and a cap, but the results were the same. When they put the null cap on its head, the creature laughed.

Tor méra Ladalir tried to have the numen bled, starved, hanged, and even suggested the Vertex Seal's historically preferred method of execution: unraveling. His brother, the Moon-Eater's Mistress, argued that unraveling would free the numen, not kill it, and since the Mistress was the one in the most danger from the creature who (they believed) had come here to kill the Mistress, the Vertex Seal and his mirané council gave extra weight to the man's opinion.

(There is only one way to kill a numen.)

Since they certainly couldn't set it free and had no clue how to destroy it, they spent quite a bit of effort paid in money and hours to secure it in a prison that should last a thousand years.

It was Lyric and Amaranth's grandfather who decided to flaunt the numen sometimes, situating it behind the throne, chained to the red foundation rock broken from the fallen red moon itself. Initially it caused a stir, both curiosity and outcry, but the Seal guards didn't allow anyone too near, and the numen itself reacted to nothing at all—not offers of ecstatic wine in delicate flutes or beer thrown in its face. Eventually it lost its luster, and the miran ignored it, teased one another about it, pointed and told stories to comfort themselves, and drifted away.

When Lyric was fifteen, he came across it already chained to his father's throne, hours before the start of the party that would fill the Hall of Princes. Startled, on his way between the Silent Chapel and the high arch leading to the office of the Vertex Seal, he stopped.

They were alone in the echoing chamber.

He'd seen it before, of course. Lank hair, falling in pieces over pale gray-pink shoulders bared by the long vest it wore. Naked feet with toes splayed inhumanly against the tiles. It crouched so that its legs seemed too long, knees too knobby. And it stared at him with black diamond-shard eyes. Lyric breathed deeply, in a slow four-count as he'd been taught in the temple.

There was nothing he could do, and if he unlocked the null collar and chains, what if it slipped away to murder his uncle? By the time Lyric inherited and could make such a decision to let it go, it would be his sister in danger.

But Lyric always felt it when it was in the mirané hall. Not the hum of forces felt by certain others, no—for Lyric it was the weight of his own expectations and the weight of choice and privilege. Imprisoning it did not fit into his understanding of Silence, of Aharté's Holy Design. It had been captured attempting murder, but hadn't actually hurt anyone. It was a mystery, yes, and dangerous, certainly. It should have received swift and just punishment. Death or a term of sentence, whatever his forebears decided. Not this slow, sick, unending apathy. It was wrong. Torturous. Unbalanced. He wanted his reign to be marked by justice, by the balance and peace of Aharté's Silence. The promise of it.

Then again, the next time Lyric méra Esmail the Vertex

Seal was alone with the numen chained to the throne—which, thanks to the death of his father, was suddenly his—he had already commanded every sixteenth person in the Rising Two refugee camp executed, whether child, adult, elderly, infirm, guilty, or innocent. A handful of refugees coming in from the northwest in the wake of a bad plague—on top of civil war in the great Lakesea—had broken into the army warehouses of animal feed and stolen the grains for rough bread. They'd been protected by the people in the Rising Two camp, of course, because they fed those people. Instead of hunting the specific perpetrators, the army rounded up the whole camp and committed the Vertex Seal's deterrent.

You are welcome here, the Vertex Seal said, *so long as you obey the Holy Design. Harbor criminals or apostates, and this is what you face.*

The number of refugees in the camp was seven hundred and sixty-eight. A perfect number divisible by Aharté's best number. Proof, was it not, that the decimation was part of her Holy Design? Forty-eight died. Also a holy number. Maybe some of the thieves were among them. Maybe not.

After having done such a thing, Lyric looked at the numen as it wasted away behind his throne. He saw the injustice. He saw the slow cruelty of it. But in the face of everything else he had to consider now, the balance of violence and compassion, the numen was nothing.

14

The beautiful twilight

In these days, the moon never moves. It hangs like a massive pearl high over the throne of the Vertex Seal.

Iriset does not know why. Nor do any of the citizens of the empire. For centuries that silver-pink moon has been anchored to Moonshadow City.

The year is marked by how far beneath the moon the sun shines at midday. When the days are shortest, the sun swings three times that of a raised fist below the moon. As summer approaches, the sun's arc lifts closer and closer to the moon, finally slipping behind it at noon, until the day of a total eclipse. For eight days after the initial total eclipse, the sun moves higher and higher, cresting at midsummer in the Vertex Eclipse, when a brilliant white-hot crown of sun caps the moon, the rest obscured behind. Then the sun falls for eight days back into the second total eclipse, before continuing its long path south again to midwinter and its lowest arc.

These sixteen days between two summer eclipses are known

as the Days of Mercy: two octagonals, one rising and one falling, dedicated to balance, faith, and celebration.

Isidor the Little Cat will be executed on the Day of Final Mercy.

The initial eclipse is in ten days, the Vertex Seal's wedding in seventeen, and the execution in twenty. That is exactly how long Iriset has to work out a new rescue plan.

———— • ♦ • ————

"What do you want, Shahd?" Iriset asks the girl as she adjusts the sash around Iriset's robe.

"Honorie?" Shahd pauses, her hands drifting away from Iriset's waist.

"What can I do for you, because you are working for me?"

"I work for Her Glory."

Iriset falls silent for a moment. Trust is impossible, but faith must be found. "You have taken messages for me before, and I need you to do so again."

"To the Little Cat's drop."

"Yes."

"There was no reply."

"But you told me five days ago the drop was empty. Someone took the message."

Shahd inclines her head. "I don't want anything. Now."

An open bargain, then. A favor now for a favor later. Smart, as Iriset doesn't have much of a choice. She can't leave the palace herself. Shahd is quiet behind her, tense lines of flow stretching between them. The young woman hasn't betrayed Iriset. Yet. She seems to like her, well enough. Shahd is descended from an old Sarian tribe, or possibly even a cult. There will be secrets there that Iriset can use if she ever is forced to. Iriset says, "I will help you to the best of my ability, when you do want something. Or my friends will, if I am unable. Use the name Amakis to get what you need from the undermarket."

The only reply is Shahd's hands again at the sash, fixing the tasseled ends in place.

That evening, Iriset gives Shahd a thin chip of vellum with two eyes sketched: one a cat's eye, the other her own. So far she'd only sent probing messages, nothing to implicate anyone. Little hints to the undermarket drops that she's reaching out. For anyone, any word. But now she needs Bittor. He's the only cat-eye in the undermarket. If he lives, if anyone loyal to Isidor sees this message, they'll get it to him. And he'll get a reply to her.

Shahd takes it without comment.

———— • ♦ • ————

Iriset hears that palace security will be entirely recast for the imminent arrival of Singix of the Beautiful Twilight, that the ambassador agreed to let the Vertex Seal arrange everything, and that the needle obelisks appearing in every corridor, hall, and garden are design-anchors for the wedding spectacle. It explains why she's seen Raia so infrequently, as the architect has been pulled into the security redesign. Without permission to join an Iriset can only go for walks around the palace complex at different times of day again, between her activities as Amaranth's handmaiden. When possible, Iriset suggests picnics in various gardens with the others, or taking a circuitous route to her drawing class or lessons with Erxan. She pauses to touch a security knot here, taste the wisp of a tangle where the shield lines of the Crystal Desert hiccup as they enter an arched breezeway there. Building a map in her mind.

She waits for news from Bittor. She draws repeating patterns, the succulents of the palace complex like an elaborate garden, hundreds of roses clustered together. She hides the map in the lines.

She waits.

When she can't settle down to sleep, but nor can she work on the map for how tired she is, Iriset changes to drawing eyes and lips and hands, skeletal systems. She listens to the pulse of the palace, which should relax her, but instead riles her up. She pulls out her own hair to knot into little spiders, sparking them to life with ecstatic force so they dance and skitter across the tiles. She hums against the lattice window in the four rhythms of the four forces, summoning sleepy rainbow bees and a tiny family of skull sirens who eat up her forces like worms. She fucks herself from the inside out, focused on the pull of flow and arousing rising forces in her blood and skin, deep ecstatic in both mouths, tracing those falling connections from teeth to nipple to navel to clitoris, to see if she can bring herself without touching. Or sometimes she does it the old-fashioned way with pinching and penetrating fingers.

And when exhaustion passes her out, Iriset dreams very badly.

Amaranth asks what bothers her, what draws bruises under her eyes, and Iriset doesn't try to hide. "Can you imagine what this is like for me? Waiting? Waiting as my father waits to die?" she asks. "Imagine, and then help me. I want mercy for him. I want to beg mercy."

Her Glory simply says no. And, "This is the end of your old life, hiha, and it is supposed to hurt."

On her way back to her room from an afternoon lesson in personal combat from the grim Sidoné, Iriset is sweaty and feeling some kind of melancholy way, but with hardly any time to bathe before her lesson with Ambassador Erxan. Her mind swarms with the need to get closer to the security designs, and when Iriset sees Garnet méra Bež standing alone near the Silent Chapel, she instantly veers toward him.

The palace's Silent Chapel is across the complex from the Moon-Eater's Temple. Built of sparkling silver-pink marble, it's composed of a spiral of columns that lead to the central altar. A lofted dome of clear quartz and pink amethyst rises above it, four times higher than the columns. Iriset has never been inside it, but assumes it's like the Silent Chapel she visited in Saltbath, meant for walking meditation and dotted with small alcoves and rock gardens for contemplation.

Garnet glances at her, then settles back into his waiting stance. Hands on hips, chin down. His force-blade is sheathed against his back today, the hilt aimed down to be drawn from his right hip.

"Why don't you pray with him?" she asks when she arrives, assuming Lyric méra Esmail is pacing the route of the labyrinth.

"Not feeling quiet enough today," Garnet says. "Can I help you with something? You look in a rush."

Iriset taps her fingers to her eyelids, then looks directly at him. "I've been working with palace architect Raia mér Omorose, but since an was assigned to the princess's security, I've had no chance to practice design. I want to assist an."

He turns incredulous eyes at her. "On security for the Vertex Seal's wedding."

Iriset lowers her gaze, though it chafes more than usual. "Why not?"

Garnet says nothing.

Eyes still down, Iriset shrugs one shoulder. "I know security well."

"And I should give you better access to it," he drawls with deep sarcasm.

"Yes."

Garnet stares at her, and Iriset changes tactics. "Let me see your force-blade."

The body-twin barks a laugh—he sounds genuinely amused. "Do you think I can hurt you with it?" Iriset scoffs, though obviously she could—just not by using it as a sword. She'd strip the force from the metal and fling it at him. Paralyze him maybe, or shock his entire system and stop his heart. But she *won't*.

Garnet presses his rather lush lips together and grasps the hilt. He twists to unlock it, then pulls it free in a smooth motion.

Iriset steps back, focused on the shine of it, on the cleave of forces as the edge slides through the air. It's force-magnetized steel, with lines of design etched into the blade. Iriset has read that a true master can channel any force through it, but that most are inclined to their dominant force and their blade attuned to their personal inner design. "May I?"

The body-twin flips the force-blade, so that the cutting edge lines up along his forearm, and holds it out, hilt-first.

Unable to keep the grin from her face, Iriset takes it. Her fingers stroke along his rough knuckles and she barely even notices. When she holds the smooth hilt—inlaid with opal for silky resonance—he lets go, and the weight of it bends her wrist. But Iriset is lost in the feeling of the forces. Garnet's dominant force is flow, the opposing force to Iriset's ecstatic. He is all heartbeat and breath, the transformation of ice into water into vapor, where nothing is made or destroyed, but everything becomes everything else.

The force-blade warms in her palm, and she draws flow up through her veins, into her chest. She'd intended to slice through a bit of the security at their feet with the blade and then stitch it back together, but with the weapon in hand, the sensations are all she can think about. Iriset closes her eyes and begins to move.

The blade guides her, and she shifts one step, then another, lifting it to slowly swipe down, turning toward the tug of rising force drawn up from the crystal ground by the sun. She reaches, gathering it without cutting, but bending instead, twisting the rising force—it scatters around her, and she frowns just a little. Heat kisses her all over, and she turns with the cutting edge vertical. She lowers it, imagining how it would feel to be barefoot, bare-bodied, dancing through the natural forces with this blade as a guide.

Iriset stumbles a little, her arm already beginning to ache from holding the heavy blade.

Rising force presses to her back, lifting the small hairs of her neck. Two fingers brush her elbow and slide down her skin to her wrist.

"Like this," the Vertex Seal says in her ear. Only his two fingers touch her, but she feels the flush of rising force, like pure light and yearning vines, up and down her body from heel to nape.

Iriset's eyes snap open and she cranes her neck to glance at him. Lyric's attention is on her arm, on his two fingers gently lifting her wrist. He glances briefly at her and she lowers her eyes fast. As if given permission he cups the base of her hand, making a basket of his to cradle her and the hilt. He moves her hand, her arm, and moves with her.

She can't stop her popping ecstatic from spiking out at him.

In the corner of her eye she sees his lips quirk up. "If I wasn't fresh from the temple that pop might be distracting."

Merciful Silence, the Vertex Seal is flirting with her. Iriset fumbles Garnet's force-blade and jerks away, spinning to lower her head and cover her eyes with her fists clenched tight around the hilt. "Your Glory," she says. She knocks the cold pommel to her forehead.

"Give me that," Garnet says. Amusement paints his tone thick.

Iriset relinquishes the blade but keeps her eyes lowered, splaying her fingers like a mask instead. Lyric moves nearer, the priest-red of his robes swishing in her vision, bloody against the bright floor of the Crystal Desert.

"There are classes for wielding the force-blade," the Vertex Seal says, unaffected. He gently lowers her hands from her face. Barely touching her, which is so much worse than if he'd woven their fingers together.

"Ah," she says smartly, tingling all over from crystal dust and sweat and also the absolute burn of how badly she wants to fling herself at him, or almost anyone really, just to relieve this pressure. "I, ah, am learning with Sidoné. How to fight. With my hands. Hand-to-hand, I mean."

Unbelievable.

But Lyric smiles just enough to tilt his eyes. "You didn't learn in the undermarket?"

"Not me." Iriset flicks her glance at Garnet. *I'm harmless*, she tries to project. "I was much more invested in the security-design side of defense."

Garnet snorts, then says, "You have a meeting with Baladin Yadira shortly, Your Glory."

"Yes. Excuse me, Iriset."

"I need to get cleaned up for my last lesson with Ambassador Erxan," she says as if it matters that she's busy, too.

"Oh yes." Lyric looks out to the south, toward the gates through which his intended will walk tomorrow. "Thank you," he murmurs.

Iriset bows lower and waits for them to leave. When their soft footsteps have faded enough, she straightens. She presses her hands against her belly and whispers, "*Fuck.*"

—— • ♦ • ——

But seven days before the initial total eclipse, on the ninth day of the quad of the Smiling Sun, Iriset receives permission to assist Raia in ans security work.

—— • ♦ • ——

The quartz yards surrounding the palace complex are flat planes of crystal boulders, quartz sand, crushed shells, and pools shaped to honor the forms of force in whose quadrant they shine. In the summer, heat lifts in visible waves, reflecting off the surface every hour of the day but for midday, when the sun is partially eclipsed by the moon. Palace architects set knot obelisks low to the ground to anchor threads of design like a web to catch the naturally occurring rising force and direct it into tight channels: The excess energy powers part of the palace wind system to keep the force-fans turning. A century ago, enterprising rebels hijacked the channels and used ecstatic force to trigger a massive fire hot enough to burn flesh. The Vertex Seal's youngest son died in the attack. But summer life in the palace is intolerable without the wind system, and so instead of tearing out the design, the architects assigned to its regular maintenance will all be executed if anything goes wrong.

The work Iriset does with Raia is not the usual reorientation of the security of the quartz yards; it's specialized for the first royal wedding in thirty-one years. As they crouch in the heat, hair tied high and white cloth masks covering their necks, sweat slides down Iriset's temples and her breathing thins. Tiny sheer-moths with fibrous, fluffy wings kiss their tongues to Iriset's skin for the salt, while overhead grass kites soar in perfect squares, soaking heat and lifting on the summer eddies. Their sharp shadows slice occasionally across the sand. Waterskins slump beside Raia's toolbox, warming unpleasantly but still drinkable. Iriset grumbles to herself that this would go quicker without her robe, so she could use every surface of her skin to sense the forces. But they'd both be burnt crisp—anyone would be, this time of year, under this high sun.

They ought to have been working at night, when the sun is no obstacle, but that's when the aesthetic designers swarm the yards to ready the wedding decorations and entertainments.

Raia's careful work impresses her, the intricate way an braids knots within knots so that the security threads weave seamlessly into the anchors already planted, and when an hands two knots off to her it's with an elegant hooked motion, ans stylus transferring force to hers easily. Iriset smiles as they work, at the sheer relief of designing again. She only wishes she could ask for her silk glove: She'd made it for exactly this sort of design, when stretching force-ribbons between multiple hands is necessary, for the glove replaces the stylus in gripping and directing the forces, so one might pinch or pull, and use the multiple fingers for intricate knotting.

But that would certainly give her away.

As she works, a tiny hole gnaws at her heart: falling force dissipated with longing. Even the heat, even the sticky, sweaty discomfort, the cramped ankles, and sore neck she gains by the end of the day remind her of her favorite work. But by Silence, Iriset relishes the focus. This is the closest she's come to feeling like herself in quads, and she won't resent it. It's bliss to participate in this massive design, fixed with various dominant forces, perfectly balanced, perfectly attuned, and meant to web over the whole of the palace complex. It's the largest design she's worked on, and though not the most complex, everything else she'd designed had been intended for solo work. She could not have built this alone.

But she can certainly take advantage of it. She knew this would be the perfect excuse to study the layers of palace security. By the end of these few short days, she'll be an expert. Garnet was right to hesitate. It's worth the wait.

If only she could tag the work with her name. Sign the knots *silk silk silk. Silk was here.*

That last day in the quartz yards, sweating as they break for water, she asks Raia about the creature behind the throne.

"Oh," an says softly, wiping ans forehead with the end of ans cloth mask. Raia glances at the damp spot turning the linen translucent against ans fingers. "The numen."

Iriset frowns. She thought Diaa of Moonshadow was being facetious when she called it a fairy. "Numen are real?"

"Numena, plural." Raia's voice remains distant. "It's from a pre-Sarenpet word that means something like 'those who manifest' because they appear from nothing, supposedly."

(The Moon-Eater's mother gave them that name, when she said they must be a people in order to matter, and people have names. To her it meant *to express*.)

"I thought they were only a story—or all gone from here after the Apostate Age."

What Iriset knows of numena now is only this: They're magic. Not force-crafters, not architects, but magic, because there is no internal logic to their ways, no bearing on nature or science. And Iriset does not believe in magic.

Raia says, "I understand they are rare, and they stay far away from the empire because of our design. They are creatures of change, of chaos, and we put everything into stability and balance."

Iriset stares at Raia's discomfort, at ans refusal to glance toward her or angle ans head in a way to indicate an listened without making rude eye contact. She says, "That numen chained behind the throne is not healthy."

An flips ans hands awkwardly. "What can we do? He tried to kill the Moon-Eater's Mistress."

"Not Amaranth."

"So he should be freed?"

"Or killed."

Raia looks at her eyes then, shocked. "Iriset."

"It is not mercy, or kindness, keeping him this way. I spoke to him, and he is a living creature. Would you chain a dog for a hundred years?"

"You see yourself in his collar."

She holds Raia's gaze, neither agreeing nor denying.

"I will not allow that to happen to you, Iriset," an says with quiet passion.

"Not even if I attempt to murder the—"

Raia's hand flashes out and covers her mouth. "Never say such a thing!"

Ans fingers smell of lilies and quartz dust and sweat, and they tremble against her lips. Iriset lowers her eyes and an lowers ans hand. "I am sorry, Raia," she says, swallowing her anger.

They silently return to their design orientation, and every once in a while Iriset allows her elbow or hand or the end of her mask to drift against ans, so that an will forget she'd been so bold.

The very next day, Singix of the Beautiful Twilight arrives.

• ♦ •

The late morning veils itself with sheer clouds that do nothing to cut the light and heat, but palace architects have prepared for weeks so that force-fans waft gentle breezes up and down the path leading through the quartz yards to the pavilion where His Glory awaits his bride.

Gone is Lyric's simple priest's robe, replaced with an elaborate sleeveless robe in deepest red. He wears gilded sandals and golden earrings, his hair loose. He is just as beautiful as the last time Iriset saw him. She feels the ghost of his fingers against her wrist. It's a problem.

Amaranth wears black and burnished pink, and aside from black eye lines and red lips, her only face paint is a gaping black circle on her forehead, with eight tiny rays also in black added evenly to its circumference: the Moon-Eater's mouth. She's veiled by nothing but her long, waved black hair falling free past her elbows and to the small of her back. Simple, sumptuous, vivid.

The handmaidens wear simpler costumes of cream and pink, all in matching layers and face paint and sheer pink veils for masks. Accessories.

Her Glory grins, bouncing a little on her feet. Iriset glances at Sidoné, and the body-twin leans close. "Ama was instrumental in Lyric's decision to accept this marriage. She's been arguing him around to it for years. It is a triumph for her faction—those who would see the empire expand in new ways."

Expanding the empire through marriage and alliance instead of conquest and death seems preferable on the surface, but Iriset knows by now how Sidoné has struggled with the assimilation laws, how so many of the minor rebellions of the past two hundred years have been because of multiple generations of resentment and oppression, not the immediacy of war. The empire is still the empire, chewing and swallowing. But Amaranth believes it's better to kiss than to chew—funny for the mistress of the hungriest god. It's all the same to Iriset: being claimed and losing.

When word comes by force-ribbon that the Ceres Remnants retinue has arrived at the quartz yards, Lyric méra Esmail His Glory takes his sister's hand briefly, then places himself at the fore, stands calmly, chin up, hands relaxed at his sides.

From the pavilion, the quartz yard spreads, veined with straight-edged paths of blindingly white shells. People of Moonshadow fill the space, miran nearest the center, and line the main road along which Singix Es Sun approaches. Excitement thrills in the air with ecstatic pops and Iriset feels very alive, and entirely part of the world.

Designers trigger rising force arrays that draw hundreds of

flower petals in red, white, fire blue, and sunset orange high to hang in the air, trembling, catching light. They swirl together into shapes over the crowd: massive roses, a burst of fire, a royal griffon that spreads red-petal wings.

In the distance, Iriset sees the first billow of red: Designers line the path with long sheets of thin red cloth. As Singix approaches, exact forces are applied and the cloths lift into the air one at a time, shaped like holy arches with the point at the apex, creating a tunnel of shade for her; after Singix Es Sun passes they fall, wafting a gentle breeze at her back. Singix's arrival is marked by a moon-red, welcoming wave.

Overhead, the floating petals form the Ceres flag: a seven-petaled lily against a deep purple. The flower is odd-numbered on purpose, for in the islands they worship a multiplicity of gods, not all of which require balance. Each petal represents a different value: strength, loyalty, family, hierarchy, obedience, courage, and beauty. As all watch, the center of the lily births a red star with four points: the Vertex Seal. It doesn't consume the lily, but joins with it, both turning together and growing larger and larger against the sky. A perfect symbol of the coming union.

Singix walks in on her own, long skirts dragging behind her. The peacock-blue gown hangs from her shoulders in straight folds, hiding the shape of her body beneath a flattening chest piece that glitters with glass beads, vivid rubies, and aquamarines. Her cape is just as formless, layers of jeweled fuchsia and pink, too many bold colors. In a compromise with the traditions of the miran, she holds a square-shaped mask of stretched silk in front of her face with two delicate white hands. It is sewn with what can only be diamonds, in lines like the sea and clouds. She's a fountain of brilliant color, scattered light.

In two columns behind her march soldiers in molded black leather armor, their swords plain steel, and then Ambassador Erxan with seven men and women bearing gifts.

Lyric shifts his weight to one hip, then almost immediately balances himself again: the only sign of anxiety. He's never met Singix before, though they've exchanged a few brief—chaperoned—letters.

Instead of allowing the princess to step up onto the pavilion, Lyric suddenly walks down to meet her. He doesn't bow but lifts his hands to touch his fingertips to his eyelids in a show of great respect from the Vertex Seal.

Singix's hands, holding the square of silk, are tattooed in intricate ghost writing, like veins of silver fire barely brighter than her skin, and so perfectly rendered the lines seem to lift out from within her, an expression of her lovely inner design. They will be the names of all the royal ancestors of the Remnants. Singix lowers the frame.

Iriset gasps quietly. All the various bold colors of Singix's costume serve only to highlight the princess's bare face. Oval, with balanced high cheekbones and a high forehead, her skin is flawless as far as Iriset can see—a smooth, polished pearl, her lips just as pearly but pink, and her large eyes a bright dark brown. They are flat along the bottom and arched along the lids, with short black lashes and black brows that slice just imperfectly enough to be perfect. Sleek black hair is pinned away from her face and gathered into a large, soft-looking cloud of small braids and smooth lines at her nape. The traces of ghost writing at her hairline tease and promise, and Iriset wants to taste them as if they are lines of rising force.

Then Singix Es Sun smiles. Even her smile spreads perfectly, without one corner lifting higher than the other, and the muscles around her eyes fulfill the promise of that smile, transforming her already immaculate features into something holy.

Ecstatic force pings fast in Iriset's blood; her palms are cold, despite the heat and the sweat beaded along her spine.

"Welcome to Moonshadow," Lyric says in gently accented formal Ceres. Then in mirané, "Welcome, Glorious Singix."

As Singix answers in the mirané tongue, "I am so glad to meet you, Lyric Your Glory," Iriset is relieved to note her voice is as plain as anyone's.

Lyric turns enough to hold out his hand for Amaranth, who descends for introduction. At the same time, Erxan walks up through the column of Ceres soldiers and bows, then gives a more elaborate introductory speech relating the poetical biography of Singix Es Sun, Singix of the Beautiful Twilight. Overhead, the petals draw together to form a fluttering canopy that hardly blocks the heat but creates a dappled shade rather like light through water. A mystical, dreamlike way for a husband and wife to meet.

The Vertex Seal offers his hand, palm up, and the princess places hers against it; the two ascend to the pavilion and face the crowd spread out across the quartz yard. The sun fully emerges from behind the moon, the architects release their petals, and a lovely rain of flowers drifts down.

Then it's over.

The royal party removes themselves from the blasting afternoon, Lyric and Singix bidding temporary farewell to each other so that all might rest and prepare again for the evening celebration with only the miran of the council and the palace.

Before the feast begins, Garnet méra Bež arrives to take Iriset to the chambers where Singix will live until her wedding on the afternoon before the Day of the Crowning Sun. Garnet, too, has changed into his formal uniform, and two force-blades cross over his back in a way designed to accentuate the breadth of his shoulders. He bows to Iriset, says nothing, and turns to lead her. Iriset walks closely behind him, recalling the energy of the blade in her hand. She parts her lips to taste the flavor, but the sheaths are covered in glazed ceramic that dulls—or contains—the force.

Just when they reach the princess's rooms, Garnet pauses. He glances at her, at the jade cuff, and says nothing. Either he's begun to trust her or he chooses to pretend for the sake of His Glory and Amaranth. Surely it's the latter.

"May I attend Her Glory now?" Iriset asks.

Garnet scratches at a line of skin razed clear of beard in a thin repeating star pattern. "You told Lyric not to wear face art."

She noticed the Vertex Seal only rimmed his eyes in black lines today. "That is not exactly what I said."

"The opinion of the royal architects should be given more weight than a disgraced daughter of the undermarket."

Iriset scowls. "It is not my fault he believed me."

"So long as you stand by your claim," he says mildly.

"I do."

Garnet gestures for her to knock. He remains outside as she's greeted by Ambassador Erxan and pulled into the chamber.

"Here she is, darling," Erxan says, hand delicate at Iriset's shoulder blade. His hearty smile shows his teeth, and he smells of sharp rice liqueur.

Iriset catches only a glimpse of diaphanous pale green before touching her eyelids.

"Hello, daughter of Aharté," Singix Es Sun says in mirané.

"Your Glory."

"Ceres, Ceres!" says Erxan. "I've worked too hard this past season to allow you mirané, sweet Iriset."

Her eyes snap up at *sweet*. But the ambassador presses his hand into her shoulder and lets go, pleased and expectant. Iriset looks to Singix's perfect face and is startled to realize they're the same height. Singix seemed taller in her wafting layers of costume. Her current pale green dress still hangs shapelessly, hiding her body, but it suggests the elegance of a poplar. Latched at her collar is a vivid red cape that complements the red glass beads, red embroidery, and jade coating the breast of her gown. Tucked into her hair is a long comb attached to a small square of stretched silk that rises over her head like a square halo, painted with a sky of sunrise clouds.

Singix smiles, and Iriset begins in Ceres, "We are glad to have a partner for our Vertex Seal."

"I am glad, as well. Do you...?" She speaks words Iriset hasn't learned, and Iriset glances to her tutor.

His wince is elaborate, but filled with humor. "If you speak of art, Princess, and the faith of Silence, Iriset's vocabulary will be better."

To Iriset's delight, Singix laughs prettily. "Are we art, Iriset?" she asks, glance flicking between their elaborate costumes, and with a twinkle of irony.

"We are," Iriset agrees. "But the best art, for we are...we are both art and art-maker."

"I would like to be maker of myself," Singix says, or that is how Iriset understands it, and impulsively she reaches for Singix's hand, thinking how important it is to know one's own design.

15

Between the sun and the memory of the sun

Shahd vibrates as she enters Iriset's room, eyes down, cloth mask drawn carefully across her face. Her hands give her away.

Iriset thinks, *Bittor*, and says, "Tell me."

The girl's fingers curl into fists. "Someone came to my family's house. They did not put a message in the drop for me, but came to my family's *house*."

Satisfaction draws through Iriset. "I am sure your family will be well, as long as I am."

Shahd says, "It was not necessary."

Iriset touches Shahd's taut knuckles. "You have my signal, use it if you need to. But the undermarket isn't like the Vertex Seal. Coming to your house could be an invitation. A welcome. Not a threat."

Shahd parts her lips but says nothing. She gives the distinct impression of holding back an eye roll.

"Not *only* a threat," Iriset concedes.

"If you say so."

"I do."

Shahd breathes in and out, staring, then moves behind Iriset and pushes her gently onto her stool and digs fingers into Iriset's hair to start untangling it.

"Now tell me what the message is," Iriset says, leaning her head back into Shahd's hands, pretending to be more relaxed than she is.

"Today. Resin delivery. Third descent."

"Today," Iriset repeats, frowning, eyes closed. "Resin delivery?"

Shahd says nothing.

Iriset nods. It's for her to figure out. She gestures for Shahd to continue their morning routine.

———•◆•———

As it's Singix Es Sun's first full day, the ambassador shows her around the palace. Iriset joins them, splitting her attention between their conversation and mentally drawing her force-map of the complex. She couldn't have thought of a better ruse for moving freely about the areas she has less reason to visit. Thanks to the Vertex Seal's personal favor, she thinks, almost giggling. It's just nerves: Iriset is simply racked with expectation like a million tiny rainbow bees in her veins, because if all goes well she'll see Bittor later today.

Ambassador Erxan walks slowly, sweating in his layered dress as he speaks careful mirané to Singix. The princess listens with a sweet smile, and sometimes asks Iriset a question. Iriset does her best to answer, and Erxan might comment in Ceres, reminding them that Iriset needs to better her vocabulary. (She picked up the grammar easily, probably because she could see its design.) They create a game of naming everything in both Ceres and mirané as they move from the women's petals to the gardens to the libraries, then repeating and looking for rhythm between the languages.

The competition spurs Iriset on, and she becomes caught up in the game, laughing sometimes at the twists she puts her tongue through. Singix always returns her smiles. Those smiles hit like a blessing, and Iriset can't tell if everyone feels this way about Singix, or if Iriset is supremely susceptible because she can see the perfect design in every shifting muscle of Singix's face and neck. Either way, right now the smiles are all for her.

Behind them trail two Seal guards and two Ceres servants holding large stretched-silk fans they use to waft gentle breezes toward the princess, fluttering Singix's loose baby hairs. Her dress is the same style as the one in which she'd arrived: formless and hanging off her shoulders to hide details of her body. The chest piece is not so heavy today, decorated with gold thread and tiny chipped garnets, but stiffened with strips of godgrass sewn across the back (Iriset knows because she asked in slow Ceres, thinking about what perfection the rest of Singix's body must be).

Unlike Amaranth, Singix gives no hint of scheming or layered meaning to what she says—or perhaps Iriset simply can't pick up on the nuance of Ceres, or Singix can't put it into mirané. That's the advantage of their hindered communication, Iriset supposes. An illusion of easy friendship. If not for the anxious excitement fluttering Iriset's pulse with ecstatic sparks at the mere thought of seeing Bittor, she might be able to relax into the day. Drink in Singix's mild and unflappable nature.

They eat lunch with Her Glory, reclined in an expanse of blankets and pillows on the green-grass lawn of the Sunset Visions Garden. Amaranth speaks clear mirané, and Singix holds her own calmly. She demurs rather a lot, but for that Iriset can't blame her. It's possible that instead of managing as a mild consort, Singix will be swallowed whole by the Moon-Eater's Mistress and her brother, consumed and made to assimilate just like anyone the empire chooses. This is supposed to be an alliance, but Iriset wonders if it's more likely a delaying tactic. Eventually the empire will find a way to spread Holy Design over the ocean and take the islands. The Vertex Seal is inexorable. So the Remnants give up their daughter for another generation's worth of time. Iriset believes Amaranth wants something more like peace, or at least a different kind of conquering, but there's no way Her Glory doesn't have multiple reasons for supporting the marriage alliance. Some people are anxious that the Vertex Seal's children might not be born mirané, if their mother is Ceres. Even Iriset has heard gossip calling it risky of Amaranth to assume Lyric's mirané blood will be stronger than Singix's beauty. If their children are not completely mirané, it will be an indictment against Lyric's piety and Aharté's blessing. While Lyric is clearly fanatical enough not to doubt, Iriset would not have thought the same of Amaranth.

It isn't Iriset's problem, though. She's here for one reason: to rescue her father and get out. No matter what the Little Cat himself says about achieving something.

The heat and rolling conversation, cool food, and iced wine melt Iriset from the inside out. She's tired from repeated long nights, and she lays herself down, propped on a thin pillow beside Singix. It's allowed: Anis and Istof do the same, curling together, while Ambassador Erxan excuses himself to take his midafternoon rest in his quarters. Singix murmurs that she prefers to remain with Her Glory and her maidens in the luxurious shade of their white umbrellas.

Iriset practices her eight-count breathing, listening to the hum of the imported grass and hard red rock of the crater just beneath. Architecture keeps the thick wet grass alive despite the brutal heat of the season, flow and ecstatic braided to pull tiny filaments of water against the equally tiny roots. Beside her, Singix's dominant flow force is just as soothing, and Iriset finds herself imagining Singix a piece of the garden itself, a living statue of flowers twined around an elegant frame of river reeds. She falls asleep thinking of how to grow a skin from a craftmask, like these tiny water filaments, as an extension of the sort of crawling design that can change hair color or skin, but in her dream she sees the numen again, smiling with those sharp pink-ivory teeth. Iriset gasps awake.

"Iriset?" Singix says softly, putting a hand to Iriset's shoulder.

Iriset glances up at the sun: She has an hour or so until third descent.

Immediate relief steals her voice and so she nods and smiles at the princess. Amaranth left, along with her other handmaidens. Singix sits calmly in the shade of an umbrella held by a young mirané boy. The princess's chest piece and cape have been removed, leaving her diaphanous layers of loose dress. A small book rests on her lap. A breeze drifts across them from force-fans in the far corner of the garden.

"You may sleep still, if you like," Singix says carefully. Her dark brown eyes are so large, perfectly wide and balanced over her cheeks. Her black lashes curl perfectly, too, and the strands of ghost writing are just like silvery grass roots reaching down her forehead for water.

Stretching as she sits, Iriset says, switching to Ceres, "No, I finished rest. What do you read?"

"What are you reading," Singix corrects, then offers the slender book. It's embossed with the seven-petaled flower of Ceres. "These are devotions."

"Prayers?" Iriset asks, using the mirané word.

"Ah... meditations?" Singix suggests in the same.

The book has seven parts, each including seven small verses, written in careful characters. Twice, as she flips gently through, Iriset sees mistakes crossed out. "Did you... write the book?"

"I copied the devotions from memory, to bring here. I will make a more beautiful book for my husband."

"It is beautiful." Iriset knows that word, and enough of the rest to understand. "Will you read to me?"

Singix takes the book back and opens to a page decorated with many tiny leaves drawn in black ink. "'A Devotion to Courage,'" she says, pointing to the sigils. "'Here courage is small, a smile when the sun sinks into night. Here courage is as wide as the ocean, a smile for the demon of death.'"

First the princess reads in Ceres, then translates as best she can into mirané. It takes some arguing to explain *demon* to Iriset, for there's no equal word in mirané. Monster, perhaps, and it's on the tip of Iriset's tongue to suggest a translation might be *numen* before she stops herself, thinking of the black eyes and sharp teeth.

The final line of the poem is "Here courage is a daily practice, between the sun and the memory of the sun."

Iriset doesn't like a poem with only three parts, for it rests unbalanced in her mind, eager for a fourth. But she likes the riddle of *between the sun and the memory of the sun*. To her, the answer is design. What is design? It is everything between the memory of the sun and the sun in actual.

She tries to explain this to Singix, who listens, and doesn't grow suspicious that Iriset thinks of design with such subtle philosophy. Why should the princess be suspicious of the handmaiden? Even if she knew of Iriset's history, how likely that she cares about the murdered Silk?

If only Iriset could remain by Singix's side, lazily discussing poetry and design. If only she could be herself, dig into the design of the palace and invent again. Show the Vertex Seal what architecture is truly capable of. Singix wouldn't mind, Iriset knows it. Singix likes her, and she likes the princess.

Her heart beats hard as she longs for everything: power, friendship, family, safety, and the truth of her real name.

Apostasy. Impossible.

Someday, Iriset promises herself, this will be nothing but the memory of a hot afternoon with a beautiful princess. She'll think of it when she thinks of the sun.

Iriset hurries to the rising side of the palace complex, where the delivery docks spread in the shade of the quarter tower. Skiffs and small caravans line up to off-load the goods they've brought across the quartz yards, and an intricate system of pulleys and ribbons lets items be dispersed quickly by the dockworkers. She feels like a kite floating over her body: She's never done this sort of thing before. The con-work of her father's undermarket had been for the cousins, not Silk.

She hovers near the timetable, cloth mask drawn and her arms crossed over her chest to display the jade cuff. Everyone in the palace knows it means she belongs to Amaranth, and nobody bothers her.

The resin merchant arrives with three helpers, carrying a permit for delivery as she walks along the thin ribbon dragging her skiff. The skiff is egg-shaped and decorated with rows of unpolished amber and red sacra and smells like maple syrup.

Iriset studies the three helpers as they unload trays of examples, opening the lids to display a variety of resins, in low bowls or hardened enough to be chunks like the sacra and pine copal. She could identify most on sight, but knows little else, for most resins don't hold design well and thus she has no reason to have studied them. Shifting nearer to the table, Iriset doesn't have to feign interest.

One of the helpers says, "Interested, honorie?" Their voice is soft and high, perhaps a woman's and certainly not Bittor.

Iriset says, "My lady is." A safe enough answer.

"This is unusual," says the servant minding the timetable to a young miran who had just arrived in servant's robe with hems indicating a better rank.

"We don't mind showing our wares to a pretty lady," says another of the merchant's helpers.

Bittor.

Thankfully, Iriset's cloth mask hides any expression that might've crossed her face at the strong jab of recognition in her chest. She tried to prepare herself to remain calm, but the shock of his voice—his actual voice—triggers a flood of rising force inside her. "Thank you," she says lightly. "My lady likes to burn resin for her... devotions." She says the Ceres word.

Iriset steps away, and Bittor follows. His cloth mask is white, as with most of the merchants and workers who braved the quartz yards in the summer. Iriset finds a spot of shade amid the bustle of the docks, then kneels.

Bittor crouches, unrolling a canvas purse with tiny pockets

for various resins. He puts it between them on the dusty ground. "Touch whatever you like, and if one appeals, rub it to your wrist. Your body will unlock more of the particular scent."

Iriset can't speak. Her throat is too tight as she struggles to control herself. She wishes she could be a kite above her body again, instead of trapped by her very physical responses to him. Oh, how she missed him, lover and friend and ally. She wants to be touched by someone who knows her.

"Take your time," he says gently, and reaches up to tuck his cloth mask off his eyes.

She's going to grab him and ruin everything. Iriset stares at his ruddy peach-brown cheeks, the curve of them as his mouth pulls into a smile for her. She knows it'll crinkle his eyes, and finally looks to them. The pupils are narrow spikes in this hot light, and the green-gold glint of irises leave no white at all. The most gorgeous thing she's ever seen. "Bittor," she mouths.

"Iriset," he whispers.

A jagged breath whooshes out of her. She tucks up her own cloth mask so he can see her eyes, too. They can't share too much intimacy while surrounded; eye contact like this will give them away. But Iriset needs it.

"Touch the resin," Bittor says, and she obeys, holding his gaze. The muscles around his eyes, especially his brow, shiver and she sees he shares her need, and the effort to conceal it.

"How is the undermarket?" she asks, looking down at what her hand is doing.

"Dispersed and buttoned down tight. Everyone is in deep hiding, or with distant family. Your grandparents offered to relay messages between families, in return for news of you. I didn't have it and said no anyway."

"Thank you. Dalal?"

"With me. Her son is safe. You know about—"

"Yes," Iriset cuts him off. She glances up. "I saw him. He is in the apostate tower, and I tried to break him out, but he refused to endanger me."

"Hardly surprising."

Iriset huffs. "I have been learning the security of the yards, of the palace itself, and will be able to get you a force-map so you can plan a rescue for the day of his execution. They won't bring him out until then. But you have to get word that he's not to be touched before then."

"That won't come from us, if it happens, but from the army. I've tried getting to them, but the general put people in charge we can't find ways to blackmail."

Iriset nods, thinking of General Bey and his uncompromising honesty. Of course he knows which of his men should surround the Little Cat. She pushes her frown back into pleasant interest as she removes a milky-white chunk of resin and smells it. Sharp, spicy, an undertone of wet earth.

"Can you get out?" Bittor asks.

"Yes. But not until after he is. I have to be here, to keep tracking the security threads, and so that if I must, I can beg for mercy."

"You're making friends?"

"As many as I can."

Bittor lets his fingertips, soft because he keeps them oiled for greater sensitivity, brush her knuckles.

Glancing toward the timetable where everyone busily ignores them, Iriset turns her hand over and clasps his. Her fingers slide between his fingers, turning their hands together, and she shivers as their palms connect with a tingle of ecstatic followed by the rush of rising that comes with relief and hope. "Bittor," she says, and this time lets it be more than silent breath. She wants to ask him what he's been doing, how he got in with these merchants. She wants to kiss him, to bite his lip too hard, so that he feels her for days and she can carry the taste of his blood on her tongue. Iriset presses her tongue to her own teeth instead.

"The Day of Final Mercy," Bittor says, bringing her back. "Can you create a distraction?"

"What kind?"

"As big as you can make it. Safely."

Images and ideas flash through her thoughts instantly—most of them related to the very intricate details she's recently gleaned about the palace security webs already in place. "Oh yes," she murmurs with quite a bit of relish.

"Good." Bittor grins.

"What's the best way for me to send you a map?"

Bittor removes his hand from hers and plucks a chunk of sea glass from the pocket of his linen jacket. The hem of it brushes the dust around him. He puts the greenish glass into her hand. It's sun-warmed and glows.

Iriset hides it between both her hands. Sea glass is perfect. She can reorder the internal structure to hide a design map. They'd hypothesized about such spy-craft two winters ago, tossing the idea back and forth, and Iriset designed a web to impress into the foundational design of the glass. Any amorphous stone like this would, theoretically, work, but she thought natural glass best, and Bittor had remembered. She looks up at him. His pupils have widened as the sun dips behind a cloud. She knows he's thinking she shouldn't be here, shouldn't be the one in the field. Silk is meant for the laboratory.

"I don't want to be doing this, either," she says. "But I must."

"I know. I miss you at my back."

"I miss you," Iriset says, then tilts her smile wickedly. "Under me."

It startles him into a bark of laughter. Bittor glares but for a moment, happily. Then he starts to roll up the resin. "I have to go. Make your map and send that through Shahd mé Sahar."

"Don't hurt her family unless you must." Iriset tucks the sea glass into the bodice of her sleeveless vest. She draws her mask across her eyes, sending the world back into a glaze of orange.

Bittor nods. "I want your escape as part of the plan for your father. I'm getting both of you out that day."

"Yes. I'll be ready."

"Here." He stands with his rolled pack of resin and offers his hand to assist her. Iriset takes it, and he squeezes, putting something into her palm. He withdraws, and Iriset opens her mouth to speak, to call him back, but doesn't.

She watches him return to the others, ignoring her. She doesn't look at what he gave her.

Longing paints streaks down her skin, cold and hot and cold. Iriset counts to eight with her breath. In-one-two, hold-three-four, out-five-six, hold-seven-eight. In-one-two, hold-three-four, out-five-six, hold-seven-eight. She's so torn today, isn't she? Longing to run back into her shadow home; longing to remain with Singix in the sun.

Before the resin merchants pack up, Iriset leaves, walking slow to counter the urge to run.

———— • ♦ • ————

Late that night, after fucking herself as best she can, followed by hours of careful notations on the security and force-threads she's encountered, Iriset sets down her stylus and vellum, the sea glass and scrap of silk that is the craftmask of her own face. Bittor had put three tiny crystal shards into her palm, coated in resin that can be easily removed with the proper vibration. They're from her prototype glove, and part of the fabric that made it useful for manipulating force. With them, she can make another silk glove with which to dig her way through gates and security, or tear down craft and force art.

She can't stop thinking of another use, though.

It's past the nadir hour when she slips out of her room, disengaging the field of the jade cuff with her tourmaline cap. She hurries silently through the curving corridors of the palace, toward the mirané hall.

Under the stark black-and-white domes, the throne of the Vertex Seal gleams solemnly and alone, lit only by low forcelights, and beneath it is the chunk of red moon rock like dried old blood.

She slips through the vast room, too quiet for any echoes, then behind the throne, and finds the ring of iron through which the numen's chain would be bound.

If she leaves the shards here, tucked against the iron base, the numen will find them. Or perhaps somebody else will, servant, attendant, designer. But will they extrapolate the purpose?

It isn't enough to leave crumbs for the numen. Iriset has to do something more. She can't explain it, and is grateful nobody is asking her to. But its imprisonment makes her so uncomfortable. For herself, for her father. For it, though she understands nothing about it or why it had come.

Keeping the shards in her hand, she goes to the wall and touches it. She closes her eyes and parts her lips to sense and taste the argument of forces filling the mirané hall. There's so much empty space that the Hall of Princes roars with tension.

Iriset follows the most basic threads woven into the walls. Ties and anchors for security and decoration, for amplifying and dousing sound, knots for occasionally charging a cool breeze, and nets of rising force for something she can't identify. Toward the back of the hall, she finds an archway almost invisible for the clever way it was built—without design, but only basic building techniques. It opens into a shadowed corridor she suspects will take her to the Vertex Seal's private office.

Across the hall from that archway is another. Iriset dashes to it on silk slippers and follows the shallow steps down and down to a dead end.

There's a hidden door. This one disguised by design to appear like nothing more than wall, but covered with alarum-net. She leans close and breathes on the filaments of force without quite touching. They tremble, and Iriset freezes. If she fiddles with it in the slightest, the alarm will sound. She can't afford that, yet.

It must be where the numen is kept.

The wall is seamless. It looks like a mistake, not a prison or false door.

As Iriset climbs back up to the Hall of Princes and makes her way back to her room, she wonders how many hidden doorways are scattered around the palace.

16

The cult of Silence

Two hundred years ago, perhaps the most famous Vertex Seal lived: Safiyah mé Idris, better known as Safiyah the Bloody. Second born, she spent her early years as the Moon-Eater's Mistress before her brother was assassinated and she ascended as the Vertex Seal. Perhaps due to her bloodthirsty nature and the violent loss of her brother, Safiyah grasped the reins of power with war-gauntleted hands, drove enemies from Moonshadow, and expanded the empire by four times in her forty-year rule.

It was she who took the army northeast through the Reskik to the upper prairies to conquer Erbus, erecting force-steeples to drive the Cloud Kings north to the mountains. Safiyah then pushed southwest through the deserts and into dark forests to encircle Mirithia and consume it all the way to the coast and the Ceres Remnants. Safiyah the Bloody continued her grandfather's campaign against the canopy cities of the Bow in the far western volcanic ranges. She brought back riches as well as an endless stream of captives. She instituted the first assimilation laws to join the strength of her prisoners of war to that of the empire, creating a new working class that paid taxes and prayed to Aharté. Safiyah's sweeping legal reform regulated marriage, worship, cohabitation, pleasure, servitude, art, and fashion, bringing it all into line with the Holy Design of She Who Loves Silence.

The old marriage laws of Safiyah's are the most frequently protested across the seven major cities of the empire, because first-generation citizens are not legally allowed to marry within their ethnic groups, and the law is widely considered to be archaic. It should be an easy law to overturn, as these days there are hardly any first-generations to begin with anymore. The small kings of the various precincts of Moonshadow often bring deregulation proposals to the mirané council, but the miran are too invested in their own superiority to allow any to pass. You see, the marriage laws are foundational to other laws, such as the one stating that children born outside of Aharté-permitted marriages receive a secondary citizenship that refuses them access to many public institutions, such as the Great Schools or tax-free apprenticeship programs. Changing the first-generation assimilation laws would require reformation of the whole marriage legal system and the miran can't have that.

This is all to say that everyone has an opinion about marriage laws, and during these days leading up to the Vertex Seal's wedding, a few caricatures of the Vertex Seal's non-miran intended show up as design graffiti in several market districts. In some she's depicted in all her Ceres beauty until the graffiti ghost writing crawls down her skin to reveal burnt-brown mirané beneath. In others, she births what are intended to be several demons of the Ceres religion. If Iriset saw the work, she'd be very impressed by the artisan-designer who created it. The graffiti is destroyed almost as soon as it's unleashed, but there's only so much the city army and investigator-designers can do to trace it until somebody invents a method for tracking design signatures.

The unrest would have likely stuck with such minor protestations and entertaining satire except for an incident with one of the Silent cults.

The nice way to describe the cults is to call them belief systems or small organizations that do not comply perfectly with the strictures of the Vertex Seal's Silence. They range from secretive philosophy clubs that like to debate predestination to hidden chapels worshipping Old Sarenpet local spirits to Sarians waking up in the pitch of night to light candles for certain constellations. This particular cult is a very old cult of Aharté, in fact, sublimated into the empire with the colonization of the Osahar during the Apostate Age. They are devoted to She Who Loves Silence in every way, but they claim that while creating new human design is, of course, apostatical, healing what design already exists cannot possibly offend Aharté. Too bad that under Lyric méra Esmail His Glory, the only orthodox uses of design for healing are external applications like bandages or warmth-patches. Even ecstatic stitches are considered too invasive.

It happens that the unborn child of a woman in this cult falls into distress, and her priest designs a belt that balances all the woman's forces, holding her inner design in perfect alignment to regulate the child's health. Both the woman and her priest are arrested, for though the belt is external, such a powerful tool certainly affects the growing inner and outer design of the baby. Were the child meant to live as a part of the Holy Design, Aharté would save it. Therefore, to keep it falsely well goes against the Silent pattern.

Someone begins a (true) rumor that the Vertex Seal will grant mercy to the pregnant woman during the Days of Mercy, but until then the woman is imprisoned and doesn't have access to her belt. She's ill, her child might die.

Amaranth has complete sympathy for the woman's actions, but not for her being found out. "If you know the risk, understand the consequences, and believe you must act against the law for the good of your family, I admire that. Family is all. But once you are caught, you are caught."

At that, Sidoné glances askew at Iriset, who lowers her eyes and chooses not to argue with Her Glory today. There's no way for her to win such an argument without examples of forbidden architecture she herself has performed. And in a certain way she agrees with Amaranth, and her father certainly would. Being caught means you aren't quite good enough.

"But the consequences are harsh," Sidoné says. "Without mercy, she—if she survives birth—will be put in a work camp for years, and her child adopted into a devoted family away from her."

Amaranth shrugs and pops a strawberry into her mouth. "With so many pieces of the empire always in motion, any disruption or flaw must be destroyed before it can spread."

"You did not destroy Iriset," Sidoné says, to Iriset's chagrin.

"How can you imply our hiha is a flaw?" Her Glory asks with innocent eyelid-fluttering.

Fortunately for Iriset, whose jaw clenches so hard she thinks her teeth will crack—and *that* she'd have to fix with apostasy—she's summoned then to the side of Singix for the princess's afternoon visitations.

Singix continues to be easy to get along with, maintaining a low-key sense of humor about all the graffiti and gossip, and if she knows—which surely she does by now—of Iriset's criminal background, she doesn't appear to care. She treats Iriset as a companion, not a servant, and continues to teach her more vocabulary and more intricate, poetical patterns of formal grammar.

Iriset would like to ask what Singix thinks of her future husband's likelihood of granting mercy to this apostate mother, as Singix isn't devoted to Silence, nor expected to be as long as she breaks no tenets. But first of all, Singix has barely spent any time with Lyric yet, and second of all, Iriset doesn't know why she suddenly cares about religious philosophy. It's just the bullshit maneuverings of the complex imperial laws, and has nothing to do with her. Silk's apostasy is blatant and she wouldn't even ask mercy for herself.

(Little does Iriset know there are already the first threads of a cult developing devoted to Silk and her outrageous, but fascinating, theories published in that brief series of pamphlets. Oops.)

The day before the first eclipse, Iriset and Ambassador Erxan are to escort Singix of the Beautiful Twilight to a concert on the rising side of the crater, where river caves link together to create an echo the musicians have learned to harness. Iriset is thrilled, as it will be the first time she's out of the palace complex since she arrived. She's nearly buzzing with ecstatic energy up and down her spine, to the point that Singix feels it and grips Iriset's hand to steady her.

Singix's skin is cool and so smooth, Iriset thinks abstractly about applications for flow and falling force in a cream to smooth pores or beads of ecstatic to pop and tighten skin. Not that Singix needs it. Iriset rubs her thumb over Singix's first knuckle and Singix gasps gently as a gentle peach-blossom-pink blush tints under her eyes. *Oh.*

Unfortunately, they're interrupted where they wait outside Ambassador Erxan's quarters with the news that a protest in the

Rivermouth precinct just south of the concert location convinced the Seal guard to cancel the royal appearance. Disappointment drips in syrupy falling force down Iriset's digestive system. Singix asks her to wander the palace grounds with her for the afternoon. They can practice mirané vocabulary, and perhaps Lyric will be able to join them for a time between meetings. Singix squeezes Iriset's hand, and how can Iriset remain dispirited?

(Wandering with Singix is an excellent time to mark hidden spots to set the anchors for the great array she's designing to distract everyone from her father's rescue.)

As they walk, trailed by several Seal guards, Singix asks about the situation that snagged up their plans. Iriset does her best to explain what she can of the philosophical differences between the Osahar cult responsible for this unrest and official Silent doctrine without getting too bitchy about it, or snide about how religion and architecture don't *have* to have anything to do with each other. She wants to say that design is pure, is already perfectly balanced, but introducing orthodoxy just muddles the rules.

Luckily, Iriset knows not to say such things out loud, besides which, she hasn't learned the Ceres word for *orthodoxy* yet.

The sun slips behind the moon, nearly all of its brightness obscured, dimming the afternoon heat enough that the women take the opportunity to traipse through the Little River corridor with its crisp, cool breeze to the Heaven's Clock Courtyard where Seal guards and soldiers of the Vertex Seal exercise together.

Iriset has only attended such practice sessions once, having little excuse to do so. But that once left an indelible mark in her memory because of the complex patterns the soldiers created with their offensive and defensive dancing. This is something she suspects Singix will enjoy watching, and it might help her understand how Silence is woven into everything in the Holy City.

There's a bit of a scuffle when she and Singix arrive and take their place upon cushioned benches reserved for audience. A few of the lines of soldiers rearrange themselves to continue, and the master-of-arms stamps his staff to the marble slab ground to create a new rhythm. The soldiers—in rust-red trousers and nothing else unless they require a breastband—punch, block, and sweep their short, curved swords in an elaborate line dance. Every thirty-two beats the lines change, shifting into star patterns, popping four out at a time to face one another in fast battles.

Allowing herself to relax into the sexy pattern of it all, Iriset's eyes drift, nearly unfocused. She parts her lips to taste the beats of ecstatic force, even as flow vibrates through the stone ground to her slippered feet, and she feels her own falling force pulsing in her core. Her ears ring with the staccato cries of the soldiers, the hum of their efforts. The sky glows bright blue, intensely hot but clear. Iriset wonders if she could use some sort of structure to mimic the formations of the soldiers to amplify her own work in disrupting security fields. A rearranging net, or pulse-anchored crystals, perhaps. If the anchors can pulse in rhythm, or even sequence, then—

Singix's hand finds hers, and the princess slides their fingers together. "Iriset," she whispers, leaning her ghost-tattooed face nearer. "Is that Lyric?"

Startled, Iriset looks straight at him, as if his name alone attracts her gaze.

It is. The Vertex Seal in line with other soldiers, his mirané-brown skin glistening and his hair pulled back with a few braids. He's slenderer than most of the soldiers, tight with muscles but not large with them. As he moves, those muscles work under his skin, and the underlying connective architecture shifts in perfect design.

Iriset remembers what her hand felt like cradled in his, and she experiences a moment where all else falls away but the image of him naked, and his careful power focused on her. Rising force heats her entire body in a sudden flush. She's especially hot in the mouth of her hips.

Beside her, Singix's breathing grows shallow. Her fingers twitch against Iriset's, and Iriset instantly adds the princess to her fantasy, complete with that peach-blossom flush slipping down her neck to her breasts. Iriset doesn't even know which one of them she'd want first.

"We must go," Singix whispers, pulling away, then turns her back.

Standing, Iriset touches Singix's elbow. "Are you well, Princess?"

Under the curlicues of ghost writing at Singix's hairline, the princess's skin gleams with a sheen of sweat. Iriset blithely wonders what it tastes like. "I am," Singix whispers. "I should not see him...so...before we are—we are married."

"Oh." Iriset smiles a little, hunting up simple words in Ceres to convey her meaning. "No people here will be angry. You do nothing bad."

Singix nods quickly. Her long lashes flutter. From her arm, Iriset feels sparks of ecstatic energy and knows the princess is as turned on as she herself. She tucks her fingers into the crook of Singix's arm and squeezes. Because they're of a height, Iriset can easily murmur into the other woman's ear, "It is good for marriage, to have lust."

"Iriset!" Widened, round eyes turn to her, and Singix scolds, "Erxan should not teach you a word like that."

"Lust? It is needed for art."

"Say *desire*. It means more. And is more proper."

Iriset grins, bites her bottom lip, and drags it through her teeth. "It sounds too beautiful for what I wanted to say."

Distress wars with humor, and maybe just a touch of scandalized yearning, in the scrunched expression Singix wears. Then the Vertex Seal calls the princess's name and Singix stiffens under Iriset's touch.

Together they turn.

Lyric méra Esmail His Glory walks toward them from the practice field, sun shining on bare shoulders. He tosses his short sword to an attending soldier, accepts a linen robe from another, and shrugs quickly into it. His bright mirané eyes are smiling, and he picks up his pace for the final few steps. The robe flaps open over his chest and stomach. "Welcome, Princess," he says to Singix in heavily accented Ceres. "I can order you a canopy if you'd like to stay."

"Your Glory," she replies. "It is—it is over-warm as the sun emerges again, too much even for shade."

"It is." Lyric nods and glances around: There's Garnet bringing water, as undressed as His Glory had been, only Garnet has a shoulder harness strapped across his chest and his hair twisted back in furrows against his skull. Sweat drips down his rich tan sternum, glinting off finely curled black hairs just over the belt of his pants.

Iriset fights a slightly hysterical giggle and touches her fingers to her eyelids as the royal people share greetings. For once she's grateful for the tradition: If she can't see them, she might survive this afternoon with her dignity intact.

"We practice before the worst heat of the day," Lyric says, as if he can think of no better opening.

"I did not know you were a warrior," Singix replies, switching to mirané as she demurely takes water from Lyric's own hand.

Lyric obliges the language change. "Hardly that. But I must hold my body to the same standard I hold my mind and any Holy Design of Aharté."

Garnet says in his deep voice, "He is modest. I would not tolerate my Vertex Seal unable to keep up with me physically."

Oh Silence, Iriset wishes she had never heard that.

The princess, though, seems not to follow Iriset's lustful imagination. She hums understanding. Quiet falls, but for the echoing pulse of the lined soldiers who continue their practice.

To speed up their escape, Iriset says, gaze on Lyric's chin, "We were going to order rose ice to the Bright Star tower to cool ourselves and spend the hottest hours in its breeze. If you would like to join the princess, Your Glory."

"I—"

Before he can answer, Garnet tenses, puts a hand on His Glory's shoulder in warning.

"Beremé," Garnet says.

Striding urgently toward them is the sharp, thin Beremé mé Adora, followed by a handful of other mirané secretaries, with General Bey méra Matsimet on her heels.

"Your Glory," Beremé says, hardly brushing her fingers to her eyelids and ignoring both Singix and Iriset entirely. "There's been an incident with the cultists. Ongoing, the army-investigators are there, and Bey's precinct forces, but we need emergency restrictions."

Lyric says, "Convene the privilege council, I'll be there. General, do what you must to stop any immediate violence. You have my authority." The Vertex Seal turns to Singix and continues in Ceres. "My pardon, Princess."

Singix lowers herself into a Ceres curtsy, hands folded in respect. She remains bent as Lyric leaves with Beremé; Garnet shoots Iriset a meaningful look, and she realizes he trusts her to manage the princess.

It feels strange to be trusted even for an instant, for something so small.

Skull sirens nest at the pinnacle of the Bright Star tower.

Up the round sides of the tower, windcatchers gape wide to gather all the breezes, channeling the air down into the palace corridors. But the platform at the top is a lovely lookout, covered in a honeycomb dome painted cloud-blue and the rail is a star-lattice carved from thin white marble. In the center flows a circular pool and its lip forms a bench atop which plush blue pillows wait. The top of the dome is cut out with an eight-point star as wide as Iriset's head, and through it the silver-pink moon overhead can be seen.

The skull sirens built their silk-scrap-and-rose-petal nests into the bases of three arches on the east side. The delicate, strange birds sing to one another from bony beaks, and the glint of their hooded eyes can hardly be seen. Singix Es Sun steps carefully onto the lip of the pool to study them, her lovely face pulled with interest and vague distaste.

"What tiny nightmare creatures," Singix murmurs.

Surprised, Iriset says, "I find them lovely."

"Are they not... apostatical?"

"Yes, but their design must have pleased Aharté, or the Holy Syr would have destroyed them."

"Ah, yes. Therefore some apostatical designs can be... forgiven?"

Iriset leans against the rail, facing Singix, her back to the whole of the palace complex. "I don't know that the designer of the skull sirens pleased Aharté, only the design itself."

"Apostasy itself is innocent, but the apostatical are guilty of betraying your god."

Impressed by the princess's sharp wit and vocabulary, Iriset answers, "If a design is successful, I suppose it earns its innocence."

"What makes design successful?"

"Stability and balance. And self-sustaining design is beautiful in Aharté's Silence, because Silence is tensile strength, perpetual motion, not mere stillness. Um. The pause between breaths. And so if a design falters it will do so in that moment, by not breathing again." Iriset is unsure she conveys her meaning properly. But it's nice to try with Singix, who has no stake in apostasy or Silk or the Little Cat's daughter. "The skull sirens, the sheer moths, the rep-cats, none of them require an architect to survive, to thrive. A successful design is balanced, it does not take force from others without giving back in turn. That is the ultimate goal of design. To create something that thrums with balance, the... tension of perfection."

"You would strive toward apostasy, then, if only to prove that it is not so by making it perfectly." Singix's soft voice doesn't suggest she seeks to entrap Iriset, but only tease with smart curiosity.

Iriset lowers her gaze modestly. Here she cannot be Silk, after all. "I only am still learning to be a designer, Princess. But I believe because we have the power to affect the design that we should. We must. Aharté wants us to, or would have stripped the ability from us."

Singix nods. "If you are successful with a design, Aharté approves of it, or you could not do it."

"Oh, I am not a philosopher. You should ask your husband-to-be, for by all accounts, he is."

"My brother," declares Amaranth as she emerges from the mouth of stairs cut into the tiled floor, "would have rather been born second to my first, and have been a priest."

Behind her, Sidoné says, "And you, then, would be the Vertex Seal."

"And engaged to beautiful Singix." Her Glory smiles flirtatiously at the princess.

Singix's lashes flutter, but she says calmly, "But Aharté made you both as you are, and thus we must all be satisfied."

Amaranth laughs. "I always seek new ways of satisfying myself, for that is how I best serve my Moon-Eater. Iriset there does not settle, either, does she?"

Iriset touches her fingers to her eyelids in acknowledgment, then turns to lean over the rail. She sticks one hand out; the wind strings through her fingers. She revels in the feel of her cloth mask rippling on her cheeks and nose, at the wind strong enough she could almost—almost—grasp it. They fly in the castles of the Cloud Kings, but such architecture doesn't function within the bounds of the empire. The answer to flight within the empire is in the ribbons, in threads of spider silk, in rising and ecstatic force, Iriset is certain. She needs more time.

No, she doesn't settle.

If she were going to do so anywhere, she wishes it could be here. But there is a whole world outside this crater, and people leave Moonshadow all the time. She'll go soon, and take her father with her.

First she needs to get her distraction array in place. From the Bright Star tower Iriset can clearly see enough of the palace and grounds to create a map in her mind's eye. It matches the security map she's begun sketching in order to embed it into the sea glass. When she finishes that, she'll draw a copy and mark up the four quarters of the palace complex to choose anchor locations for their balance, convenience, and the overlay of the security net. She'll need to slip out of her room tonight to begin tying little open-loop knots in the net, starting in the center probably, and spool outward over the next few nights. If she can't steal enough silicate chips, the whole design will need to be streamlined, though Iriset would rather not sacrifice grandiosity for lack of materials.

"It is a stunning view," Amaranth says. "But look who I found wandering the gardens."

"Hello, darlings!"

Iriset spins, nearly braining herself on the pillar. It's Nielle mé Dari, wrapped in vivid yellow with an orange crescent mask spiked with what are almost certainly cactus needles in a sharp halo.

Behind Nielle on the stairway, Ziyan mé Tal and Anis mé Ario nudge out, carrying a tray of rose ice and plates of finger food refreshments, including a subtle honey wine. "I thought," Amaranth says, "we can all camp out here since it's so brutally hot."

Ziyan and Anis set out the trays along the southern edge of the circular pool, and Iriset hops to Singix's side to run interference with Nielle. The former handmaiden is staring at the princess, mirané fingers covering parted lips. Iriset introduces them and Nielle says, "Forgive me, Your Glory, but you are unbelievably gorgeous. I'm so glad they aren't making you wear a mask."

"Nielle," Amaranth chides, but laughing.

Nielle shrugs and touches her eyelids respectfully.

Singix sinks onto a pillow. "My thanks. I am feeling rather wilted, and happy it does not show."

"A wilted orchid is still an orchid," Nielle says, plopping down.

"How is your marriage?" Iriset asks, giving in to her own natural bluntness with Nielle, who will appreciate it. She wishes she could touch Nielle's wrist or throat or mouth and push in little pops of ecstatic force to trace the new lines born in Nielle's inner design thanks to the exchange of design eggs. Iriset has not known many people before and after their Silent Marriage ritual, certainly not well enough to investigate the design-effect.

Nielle grins. It brightens her expression, rearranging her face into something at least interesting. "I've only been able to leave for a day—that marriage knot is no joke!"

"Marriage knot?" Singix murmurs.

"It's the most intense part of the ritual," Nielle dismisses, then her eyes widen. "Oh, but nothing to worry about."

"Nothing to worry about," Iriset agrees softly, touching Singix's wrist.

Anis comes over with cups of honey wine and the bowl of rose ice. She kneels and shares it all out. Then she pulls a lacquered box from her pocket and offers to teach Singix a variation on shuffling shells.

As they listen to the basic rules, Ziyan tunes her lap harp, and then softly plays. She adds in a murmured melody, delightedly attempting to harmonize with the skull sirens.

After some time of gentle play and relaxing rose ice, Singix asks after the crisis in the city. "The Vertex Seal was taken away rather abruptly. I hope all is well."

"I've just left the privilege council, and we've sent in the city army," Amaranth says, lounging upon a frothy silk pillow with a shallow bowl of wine in hand. "And no one is dead."

"Yet," Sidoné adds quietly, tapping her teeth.

Ziyan says, "I am glad it is not my father's precinct this time."

"It often is?" Singix frowns.

"There is always unrest somewhere."

Iriset curls her fingers around three thin shell coins. Perhaps the unrest is woven into Moonshadow's design. Perhaps it's necessary spikes of ecstatic force to balance the flow of expansion.

Amaranth adds, as if thinking along the same lines, "The empire is home to very many people and communities. It's natural for there to be tension. We only must keep the tensions balanced. For the good of all."

"Ah, striving toward perfect design," Singix says, glancing at Iriset.

"If the miran press that tension too firmly, in the same place, it will snap," Iriset says, eyes on the coins in her hand.

Her Glory laughs once. "So our Little Cat's daughter still has her teeth."

"The more complex a design grows, the more flexibility it needs, that's all. And miran are not known for flexibility." Iriset tosses the shell coins and Anis's long-fingered hand snatches the two spinning, and flips the third up her sleeve.

"And your father provided such flexibility?"

"Like a honeycomb arch. In our city's Holy Design, the Vertex Seal is an anchor, as is the Moon-Eater. The mirané council. Everything that creates law, that provides structure is an anchor. The Great Steeples anchor the four forces in Moonshadow, as these four small pillars around us anchor the design of this dome overhead. The laws themselves, the beliefs and actions of the people are the lines between anchors. The threads of force. The connective joints, and the web itself. But honeycomb arches"—Iriset points up—"make this structure possible. You cannot put a circular or octagonal dome upon a four-post anchor with balance or stability unless you have something that flexes between the rigid shapes. Squinches transition from square to circle. That is what my father does: makes stability possible by providing a possibility of communication between anchors and lines, between the system and its people."

It's an inelegant metaphor, but in that moment Iriset believes it with all her core.

Amaranth says, "So by removing the Little Cat, we've put Moonshadow at risk."

Iriset bites her lip, then says, "Yes."

"There was unrest such as this when your father ruled his undermarket empire. He had little influence over cultist activity."

"Yes," Iriset says again. "But in a design so complex as Moonshadow—as the empire—removal of one thread or honeycomb arch or anchor ripples outward, and while it might not cause the entire structure to collapse, the shifting balance will be unpredictable, knots will form. If one of the Great Steeples suddenly fell, most of the city would fall. Or if you took one steeple and stuck it elsewhere, hidden, unable to do what it…" She stops.

Amaranth laughs again, this time as if she's caught Iriset in a perfect cage. "All the more reason for the army to put down this little rebellion hard and fast, before those ripples expand. And better, then, to not allow men such as your father to grow so powerful in the first place that their downfall will ripple dramatically. That must be the best way to maintain stability, and in stability, progress and momentum."

"Of course, keep the miran firmly in power," Iriset says as sweetly as she can. "That is the way of the empire. Crush disruptions, cut out knots in the design. Any break in the gears must be destroyed."

There's something of an alliraptor in Amaranth's eyes as she stares at Iriset. "Seditious, kitten."

Iriset shuts up. She doesn't even care about the mirané stranglehold on the city. She cares about her father, and the freedom to do her work. The ways of the miran create the space for apostasy in the first place. Sure, a different system might mean her work wasn't heretical, but a different system might not provide so much easy access to theory and tools and need for what she does in the first place. Her father didn't want to rebel, and neither does she. She just can't keep herself from arguing.

(She thinks about those old rebel songs Dalal and Bittor sang, though. The ones about hope. Until now she only needed hope once before, and it did make her stronger, smarter, better.)

"You like it, Your Glory," Nielle says with a laugh. It breaks the tension, and Iriset meets Amaranth's gaze for a moment, then looks away.

"Maybe I do," Amaranth admits. "But we're making Singix uncomfortable."

The princess demurs. "I cannot follow the shades of your argument, Your Glory... That is all."

Anis says, "We hear you watched His Glory in line with the army. Was he all you hoped for?"

Singix's eyes widen at the bold talk.

"Garnet," Iriset puts in, her turn to distract, "is extremely masculine in his form and beauty."

"Isn't he," Anis says with a groan. Sidoné laughs again.

Her Glory reaches for her body-twin and pokes her in the ribs. Ziyan says, "He is not so lovely as our glorious Ama."

"That's right," Amaranth says slowly and seductively. The pull of Her Glory's falling force curls around Iriset's lower spine.

"I am pleased with the beauty of the Vertex Seal," Singix

says suddenly, and quickly, as if having gathered her courage, it needed to express itself hard and fast.

Amaranth looks directly at Singix. "He has never been with anyone, so you must be gentle with him when the time comes."

"Never?" Iriset can't help the outburst.

"His is a taxing job, and any favor he bestowed would mean more than a kiss, so he must be overcautious. Besides," Her Glory snorts lightly, "my brother's body is a temple for Aharté, and denial is *apparently* a form of Silence."

"Discipline," Iriset murmurs, thinking back to the confrontation between Amaranth and the Holy Peace.

Amaranth nods meaningfully. She wants a priest more like *her* on the privilege council.

Sidoné says, "Tragic, that both children of the great lover Diaa of Moonshadow are celibate. Until marriage, at least."

Iriset lifts her eyebrows; she doesn't believe it of Amaranth. She's seen the way Her Glory touches Beremé mé Adora, and Sidoné.

"If I took lovers…" Her Glory's voice smooths out, lulling and drawing of its own accord, without the encouragement of falling force. "I could use those favors for the good of the empire and manipulate in ways my brother does not have the core to do. And I would take all the pleasure shared and regift it to the Moon-Eater. Like a harvest."

"A harvest from which all the empire would benefit." Anis sighs.

Amaranth reaches across the shaded tiles and brushes her finger along Anis's jaw, not quite chiding nor quite a promise.

17

Shades of brutality

That night, late, Iriset curls upon a low bench in the Color Can Be Loud Garden, where the ruffled lilies turn their splayed faces toward the strongest threads of design.

For hours she's been moving throughout the inner parts of the palace in her plain attendant robes, masked and invisible to the security net thanks to the cap on her bracelet. Except the hall of miran itself, the whole main complex is set with anchor knots: seven of them. In the next few days, she'll need an excuse to visit the hall, and likely have to make the central anchor while surrounded by people. But this is a good start. She hasn't decided if she can risk setting the trigger point in a permanent location, for stability, or if it's better to have a looser overall design but be able to trigger the distraction from anywhere.

She's weary, tense, and can't quite get rid of the desire thrumming through her. Alone here, Iriset gives in to the temptation to remove her mask and outer robe and slippers, to feel the eddies of the garden's forces slide along her arms and neck and ankles. She wants lips on all those places, hands on her, thinking of the stubborn elegance of Singix's beauty, raw hunger for Amaranth, the casual nature of the handmaidens' familiar touching. Nielle with her broad satisfaction in her marriage. The pull of motion when Lyric and the Seal guards moved in tandem with their dance. They all make Iriset want more. Not just a good fuck but someone to take care of her, to work with her design, her pleasure, to strip away her worries and endless spiraling plans until she's focused on only connection. Someone just to touch her with mutual affection. Not for a favor or prestige or advantage. Just pleasure, and a little bit of love.

She could find a lover in the women's petal. But it's probably harder to lie with your tongue in somebody else's holes.

She misses Bittor. He would do exactly what she commands but sometimes surprise her. She misses her workshop, her spinners, the hum of Moonshadow City's ribbon skiffs, the dirt and sun smell of the wind in the Saltbath precinct. She misses wandering the corridors of their tower, murmuring calculations to herself, being herself. Whichever self that was. She misses her father.

It's terrible to know she'll never get any of it back. Even if they save her father, they'll be forced to flee.

When they save him.

Iriset breathes, reaching for balance as she did in prison. It doesn't take long to calm herself, to find the strokes of equilibrium and tension of stillness and waiting. Silence turns gently inside her, a planet of life on a perfect axis.

In the dim glow of starlight, Iriset's potency draws the hungry lilies. They face her, ruffled petals spilling in four directions. They're vivid, deep orange, but night saturates all into shadows. Iriset ponders the name of this garden: Color Can Be Loud. Only under the sun, she supposes.

A sound startles her. Someone has entered through the open

archway and strides across the entire garden to the far eastern deck. He's shadowy, a glint of black hair, the flicker of robe.

The man grips the elaborate rail with one hand and leans his head back to stare up at the sky.

It's Lyric méra Esmail His Glory.

Iriset freezes. If she doesn't move, if she doesn't let any spark of ecstatic force poke out, maybe he won't notice her.

The Vertex Seal sighs heavily enough Iriset hears the heartache, and his hand clenches around the rail. Rising force flies off him so strongly, threads of it speed away from the lilies and they shift their faces toward him. His ache is longing, the need of rising force to grow, to be better, to reach always higher toward the sky. To burn.

Slowly, as if every muscle and bone in his body hurts, Lyric turns back to the garden. Behind him a glow resonates from the palace complex and the city. Iriset can't see his face, but she feels the deep anxiety in his core.

She's not supposed to witness this.

"Your Glory," she whispers.

His eyes snap open; she sees them glint. Lyric doesn't move, nor does Iriset.

After a tense moment, his shoulders straighten and he walks toward her, smooth and easy. "I did not see you, you're so much a part of Silence."

Carefully letting out a breath of unease, Iriset says, "I am sorry to interrupt you."

"This is no private garden, I could not expect to be alone. May I join you?"

Iriset inclines her head and touches one hand across her eyelids. The Vertex Seal sits beside her on the low bench and she remembers she wears only a thin linen shift and trousers untied at her ankles. Her head and face are bare! Though she knotted back her hair in places, it messily tumbles around her shoulders. This is too intimate for the Vertex Seal, especially when she's been feeling so vulnerable and desirous.

"You also wanted to be alone," Lyric murmurs. He holds a thin book in his mirané hands, turning it over and over. His hair is unbound, too, loose waves gently puffed around his head.

How can Iriset tell him she wishes for the exact opposite of being alone? She envisions grabbing his face and kissing him, wonders if he would let her take them together here in this dark garden. She bites the inside of her lip very hard and breathes thinly through her nose, barely maintaining her balanced alignment.

After a moment, Lyric offers her the book. Cloth-bound, with gilded lettering on its face and spine: *The Seven Hundred Declarations of Safiyah the Bloody.*

"'There are no shades to brutality,'" Lyric says softly. "She wrote that. 'Brutality is only itself, never too much nor too little.' I remind myself of that when I do something terrible. When I want to excuse myself, to say my choice is the lesser of evils, is necessary. When I remember her words, I cannot mollify my horror with excuses. Brutal is brutal, no matter what it balances."

Iriset loses her own balance for a moment, in a surge of ecstatic force. She presses the book flat to her lap. "I've read it," she says. Everyone in Moonshadow reads Safiyah's declarations. "What did you do?"

He doesn't glance at her but continues watching his hands. "The Osahar cultists—they call themselves Singers of Silence, did you know?—I sent them a message. So many here in Moonshadow escaped into the undermarket, into the tunnels and secret alleys tucked inside the city design, the army could not take enough of them. We would have to devastate the entire precinct to root them all out, with much collateral damage. But there is an enclave of them across the river, one day on horse northeast. My army will raze it. If the Moonshadow Singers do not turn over their leaders, every eighth person in their enclave will be killed, by lottery, with no exceptions for age."

"During the Days of Mercy," she breathes. Horror liquefies in her stomach. She can barely feel the book of declarations in her suddenly cold hands.

"I hope they give me the chance to be merciful." Lyric's voice is so thin, taut with despair.

Iriset doesn't know if he deserves to feel so much.

"Why?" she asks, still whispering, as if to speak any of this aloud will make it real. "Why do something that you know will hurt so badly? When it hurts you? You know it's wrong."

"No matter what I do, some will be hurt. I exist to ensure the empire thrives. I must make my choice based on the good of most, the survival of our ways that have served for centuries."

"The mirané ways."

"No," Lyric says vehemently. It echoes in her chest and the lilies shudder away. Then his volume falls again to a murmur: "Aharté's way is for all the empire. That Rising Steeple Shadow precinct has very few miran living there, and my council knew it; some argued for wider devastation. Dig out the Singers, never mind collateral damage. Use it—teach everyone this lesson, not only the cultists. But there are better ways to teach lessons—I won't murder for a lesson. Only to stop a greater massacre."

Iriset has no idea what to say. She doesn't know what's better or worse. Strategic, harsh, targeted action, or broader violence that might take a turn for more damage, more death. In architecture, she would target any flaw, excise it for the good of the whole, rather than pull down an entire design. But people aren't flaws.

She remembers her metaphor earlier, when she said to Amaranth that in a design so complex as the empire, removal of any aspect causes ripples to the full design that cannot always be predicted. And Her Glory said, all the better reason to destroy rebellion before it grows.

Thinking of Amaranth, Iriset says, "Are you certain those two were the only options? Targeted cruelty or extensive violence?"

Lyric says, "There are even worse options."

"Safiyah would have razed the precinct *and* the settlement."

The Vertex Seal nods, and even in profile Iriset reads the weariness in his brief smile. "But there is no shade to brutality."

She swallows, grips the book, and then lightly brushes her fingers against the knuckles of his left hand.

They say no more for a while again, and Iriset tries not to think, tries not to elaborate on this insight into His Glory's core. How can a man like this grant mercy to her father?

As Iriset pulls her horror back into balance, she quietly offers to show Lyric the balancing technique. "It is a simple principle, but many do not think of Silence as balanced design."

He agrees, and she faces him on the bench, straddling it. He mirrors her.

"You are strongest in rising force," Iriset says. "I am naturally ecstatic, but we all know all, and so in this hand"—she points at his left hand, his core hand—"think of rising, of growing, of convection, transformation to a better self. I will match it with falling force." Iriset flexes her right hand, holding it palm up. Lyric holds his over hers, their palms apart by a breath. "I will charge ecstatic in my left hand, and in your right you will hold flow, or rather, let it channel through you."

Lyric nods, and they hold their hands in balance, breathing slowly as Iriset leads him through a straightforward meditation.

"Once you feel balanced, you can let go of me and find ecstatic and falling inside yourself. Hold it all in balance."

In the darkness, with the lilies straining for them, the two breathe and find a design that shares equally between their hands. When he has it a little, Iriset whispers, "Now on your own."

Lyric's hands find hers instead and he presses their palms together. "Can we just remain like this? One step at a time. I feel peace and would rather it not waver for a while longer."

Though her palms tingle, though she feels the gentle touch of his knees against hers, and the bench between her thighs, though she wants to flee, Iriset nods. She closes her eyes and concentrates on the circle of their design. He smells of anise oil, warm and thick.

Their breath aligns. So do their pulses. Slow, steady, fluttering heartbeat with slow, steady, fluttering heartbeat.

"Did you know the moon used to move?" Lyric asks.

Iriset looks. His head tilts back again, as it had when he first arrived in the Color Can Be Loud Garden, expression awash in grief. He looks up at the fixed moon, but Iriset can't tear her gaze from his face. This angle shows her new planes: the exact line of his chin and jaw, the curve of his cheekbones, his dark nostrils, and a fringe of black lashes. She thought once to make a craftmask of his face, but gave up for the lack of opportunity to study him closely.

He says, "In writings from the Apostate Age, they mention the motion of the moon, and its regular cycle of darkness to fullness, and writings from outside the empire write of great calamities and changes in seasons when the moon froze over our city. When the moon is a bright full coin, this garden is colored in silver-pink light. Aharté's kiss, they called it then."

As his lips move, Iriset imagines them against her neck.

Her emotions pepper and spike, knocking their peaceful circle off-center.

Lyric glances down, concern obvious. "Iriset."

Her name whispered, their hands together, this shiver in her loins.

Oh no, she thinks.

"What's wrong?" Lyric asks. His thumbs brush hers.

Iriset flashes her gaze to his, then down again to his neck. His robe is open over a long shirt, and the shirt's collar laced just to the hollow of his throat. She lies, "It surprises me to hear you speak of the Apostate Age. To take seriously anything written then."

"History is something to learn from, not fear," he says. "Even terrible history. Especially terrible history."

"Surely not everything from that age was terrible."

"People were people, some good and some bad, and some in between. But their ways were unnatural, against the will of Aharté. They allowed too much mutation and corruption. The laws were terrible. People are their laws. Their society."

Iriset bites her lip, wanting to argue.

Lyric says, "You don't like our laws."

"Some of them," she admits softly. "Some do not seem to serve people as well as they might."

"The Little Cat—"

"I do not mean my father. He broke laws regardless of how they served the empire. I love him, I understand what he is. I want you to—" She stops, slipping her hands free of his grip.

The Vertex Seal lets his hands fall to his thighs. "No. Isidor the Little Cat is too dangerous. I'm sorry."

Iriset lifts her knee over the bench and turns away. "He cannot hurt you. He never threatened the Holy Design. There are many other murderers and smugglers in the undermarket, giving plenty of miran what they want."

"But none that so thoroughly promote apostasy."

He means human architecture. He means Silk. Her fault, again.

"She is dead," Iriset snaps quietly. She stares at the ruffled lilies.

"Paser mé Ferrin," Lyric murmurs. "Her core unraveled and reworked by Aharté's hand."

Iriset cannot believe he knows Paser's whole name. As if he cares. And prays for her, too!

"I did not kill her, Iriset. She was killed in prison, by someone paid to do it. Most likely by your father before she could reveal his secrets. I wanted her alive. I wanted her to recant and take the Glorious Vow." Frustration tinges his words. "Better for the infamous Silk to forswear human architecture than die a martyr to it."

She scoffs, but there's little power behind it.

Lyric touches the tips of his fingers to her back, between her shoulder blades. Iriset presses her tongue to the roof of her mouth, squeezes her eyes closed. He removes his touch and says, "Have you taken the Vow? Amaranth told me you were apprenticed with Silk and are talented enough to impress the palace architects."

"I have not." What she means is *I will not*.

"Do you believe in it? The mandate against human architecture is the most sacred of Aharté's laws."

Something in his voice makes her look at him. It's too dark

to read his expression well, but if she didn't know better, Iriset might think Lyric méra Esmail His Glory is desperate for her to agree. Invested in her opinion.

The safe response is *Of course*. But after tonight the Days of Mercy begin, and knowing now her father can expect no pardon from Lyric, her plot with Bittor is the only way. This game is ending; she'll never have a chance to speak with the Vertex Seal again, to affect his thinking. As much as she might like to.

Iriset bends to pick up *The Seven Hundred Declarations of Safiyah the Bloody*. She offers it back to His Glory, gaze lowered. "She ascended because an assassin used architecture to murder her brother. But not human architecture. Any designer might use the forces as tools for good or evil. Might the same not be said of human architecture? There is good it can do."

"Healing? I know the arguments, but Aharté cannot trust us with the temptation. I cannot risk my city or empire on wagering that people will choose good."

"That is so sad, Your Glory."

"Yes."

"If you assume the worst in other people, how can you choose to do good yourself?"

He lets go his breath in a soft stream, a release of tension.

Iriset pushes. "Does Aharté's Holy Design merely maintain this world as it is, as if this is the best we can be, or are we supposed to strive for more? To change ourselves and the world in the direction of peace and thriving?"

"That is the thinking that made the Moon-Eater's apostates destroy their bodies with experimenting and mangled the threads of Aharté's web. Pushing too far, too fast—with so much ambition in their sights they forgot what *already* is good in humanity."

"And so we must not even try, because it has gone badly before, because it so easily could again? Never even try, for fear of failure."

Lyric smiles at her. "Catastrophic failure. The end of civilization."

She smiles back, only a little. "At least your name would be remembered, if you ended the empire in a blaze of glory."

"I don't seek to be remembered. I am no Safiyah. I only seek to hold as many of my people safe as possible. To pass on wisdom to my children and give them a future. A home."

"No ambition in a Vertex Seal!" Iriset pretends at shock, that smile still pinning up the corners of her mouth.

"Or is it overly ambitious to think I can keep anyone safe?" he replies.

"Hmm."

They fall into quiet again. Iriset notices that Lyric's design shifts gently within the confines of balance. He's maintained it without her, through this strange conversation.

"I like you, Iriset mé Isidor," the last Vertex Seal says gently. "Take the Glorious Vow, remain in our service. I will give you a title: the Royal Arguer. In honoring you, I will honor your father's design and make certain you are allowed to mourn him in accordance with Aharté's Silence."

Pain grips her: a terrible mingling of gladness, grief, anger, and desire.

"I would rather he live," she whispers.

Lyric stands, taking Safiyah's book with him. Iriset shoots to her feet, ending up too near him. She still feels the warmth of his rising force. He's not so much taller than her.

"That I will not do," he says, specific in his words. *Will*, not *can*.

A brutal distinction.

The cult does turn over their leadership within Moonshadow, and their enclave is spared decimation, though the town itself is burned to the hard earth. Those who fight are captured and sent to work camps, their children given to families who practice perfect Silence. So the cycle of rebellion and assimilation continues.

The woman whose pregnancy began it all lives, and so does her baby. On the first Day of Mercy, her name is called by Lyric méra Esmail His Glory, whose name will be well remembered, indeed, for being the last Vertex Seal, and she is granted pardon.

18

Girls' night

Twice a year in the summer, the path of the sun takes it directly behind the pink-silver of the moon. The sky does not go dark, but the quality of light shifts into twilit purple, an eerie, shadeless existence that fades colors into equality.

If you've never seen an eclipse, then can you even imagine the strange twist of shadows that occurs as the sun slips behind the moon? The shadow of a leaf, a pointed oval quite exactly the shape of its actual form, will tighten and bend into a crescent: the shape of the distant sun. Dagger-edged cuts of light and shadow, crescent on crescent on crescent.

In Moonshadow, the hour of eclipse is marked with an elaborate ritual of balance honoring the four forces.

The Vertex Seal leads the rites himself from the Heavenly Courtyard. The ritual weaves color, breathing exercises, a variety of singing prayers, and rhythmic drumming and soothing physicality designed to bring every participant from Lyric himself to the edge of the audience into energetic alignment. Lyric leads with a simple strength, it is said, calm and certain of his purpose—of his position as the highest point in the arc of society.

Iriset sleeps through it.

She was so alive and awake with hurt and rage following her conversation with Lyric in the Color Can Be Loud Garden, she went back to her room and drew his face furiously, again and again.

Iriset drew the angle of his jaw, the sparkling brown-red of his irises, the fold at the outer edges of his uptilted eyes, and those uneven black freckles. So what if only Aharté can design asymmetrical perfection? So what if Iriset has said again and again architects rely on symmetry? She is Silk, a prodigy and genius, and if anyone can design a perfect craftmask of the most important man in the empire, it's her.

Anger fueled her wild sketching, broke the tip of two pencils, and tore through the vellum once before she paused to compel her breath and inner forces into balance. Suddenly exhausted, she put it all down.

The apostasy torn and wrinkled in front of her was worthless.

Instead, Iriset picked out the sea glass and wove a delicate force-net to restructure the glass in preparation for inserting the security map. The dawn sun streaked pink patterns across the floor of her room and she pushed harder, intensely focused. She would finish it and send it to be delivered to Bittor today.

The sun stretched toward the moon, folk gathered in the Heavenly Courtyard, readying themselves for the eclipse ritual, and Iriset's hand slowed, her mind spiraling; she finally fell asleep.

Iriset wakes when Sidoné thrusts open the door, calling her name. Iriset startles, sprawled upon the cold floor beside her bed with her cheek on her hand. Her hair tangles around her neck and shoulders; she remains in the thin shift she wore to visit the garden.

Thankfully, her vellum is tucked away. Gone. The silk craftmask, too, and the sea glass.

"Iriset, have you been asleep? You're required, you lazy thing. What have you been doing?"

Before Sidoné nudges her with a booted foot, Iriset sits up. She doesn't remember putting any of it away. There—her vellum is folded precisely against the wall of cubbies where she keeps it. Iriset licks her lips. "I will dress," she rasps. Her head aches; she's thirsty.

"Hmm." Sidoné crouches and lifts Iriset's chin. "Shahd said you felt poorly. What have you been doing instead of sleeping, hiha?"

"Thinking of my father's doom," she says, pulling her chin gently away. Her lashes flutter with true anxiety.

"Singix has asked for you. Dress; I'll send in one of the girls."

When Iriset is alone, she scrambles to the loose tile and pries it up. The craftmask is there. It must have been replaced by Shahd when she came in this morning. Iriset doesn't know whether to be relieved or angry.

A different girl comes to help her bathe and dress, so she can't ask.

———— • ♦ • ————

The first few Days of Mercy are overshadowed by the troubles in the Rivermouth and Rising Steeple precincts, until the cultists are turned over and the razing of their settlement completed. Iriset spends those days with Singix, and so misses the first day's sharing of bread, the second day's gifting of smiles, and the third day's unmasking. Each symbolizes different sorts of mercy, and in the Holy City each comes with layers of complicated rituals different people enact differently and with different senses of obligation. But everyone who follows Silence performs them somehow. The cult activity keeps the miran who live in the palace complex inside its boundaries, especially Her Glory and her handmaidens, and the Ceres princess. But each noontime Iriset stands beside Singix to watch the partial eclipse from one of the gardens, despite the oppressive heat. It's nice to be alone, with a Seal guard or two, unbothered by people wishing to gawk at the Little Cat's daughter or the marvelous beauty of Singix. They are gossip-free, and stare-free, and able to drift and speak of poetry and history, of Singix's childhood, and Iriset's. Iriset almost tells the princess what happened to her mother. She almost confesses her double life. The only thing holding her back is her father, alive, waiting to be rescued.

Each evening they go in simple masks of fragile ceramic to witness the calling of names, when the Vertex Seal gives out his selected pardons. Petty criminals, prisoners of war, gentle trespasses, and bureaucratic crimes are covered, and at the pinnacle of the ritual a more infamous name is called, from the ranks of miran, followed by a final name offered posthumous forgiveness.

By the fourth day, Singix seems to lose interest in the unfolding ritualistic dramas and instead is growing remarkably anxious about her wedding, which will take place in three days, just before the Day of the Crowning Sun. Iriset reads her nerves in the tightness of her eyes, the flutter of her hands, and in Singix's hesitation before she steps into any place her husband-to-be might attend.

Iriset sent her finished map of the palace complex's vast security array tucked into the inner structure of the sea glass to Bittor via Shahd yesterday morning, and last night placed her final anchor just behind the Moon-Eater's Temple. Her distraction array is as ready as it can be until the night before the execution, when she'll overlay the final cascade design into the force-threads. Having nothing urgent to occupy herself with, except maybe a nap, Iriset whispers to Sidoné that the princess needs an evening of relaxation, of drinks and laughter and perhaps a bath or massage. Something quiet, intimate, with only one or two friends. Honestly, it's what Iriset needs, and her opportunities to appreciate what the palace has to offer are vanishing with every hour. Luckily, Amaranth thinks this suggestion delightful, and arranges it.

That is how Iriset finds herself naked in a steaming bath inside Singix Es Sun's suite, beside Amaranth, Sidoné, and Singix herself, each in a similar state within their own baths. They've all been massaged and now soak in perfumed water, their hair combed and oiled, sipping thin juniper spirits from delicate amethyst finger-cups. Iriset feels so loose and melting, she wonders if there's any spark of ecstatic force left inside her body. It's all turned to flow: hot, easy flow.

In her father's tower, she never took the time for luxury. Her attention and funds went to her studies, to her obsessions and inventions. While Iriset hardly regrets anything she's designed or created, she wonders if sinking into relaxation or moments of slow heat like this might have unlocked inspiration. Food has been fuel, bathing a necessity, silk a practical requirement. Her father sometimes offered various luxuries, things he claimed were all the rage—hence why they made such good smuggling opportunities. She never asked if he used them himself, or why he'd begun building his network with such dedication after her mother was gone, gathering wealth and associates, agreeing to her apostasy. Not for rebellion, certainly, as so many conjectured. Safety for her, maybe, because he couldn't keep her mother safe, or a luxury retirement somewhere, or a triumphant return to his Cloud King family? Iriset wonders if he did it simply because he realized how good at it he was. That's at least half of why she's obsessed with design. Perhaps she inherited the trait from him.

As her body slumps and drifts in the soft, steaming water, Iriset ponders his ambition, and squeezes her eyes shut against tears of frustration that she can't ask him now. She hates waiting.

No ambition in the Vertex Seal... She teased Lyric about it, and wishes she'd said something scathing instead. About her father, about the Holy Design.

A ripple of water suggests someone shifts in their bath, and Singix says, "Amaranth, will you marry one day?"

Iriset opens her eyes and turns her head against the pillowed rim of her tub. The princess sits, hugging her knees, absolutely gorgeous. Her shoulders press up from the shimmering surface of the water, trailing a glitter of minerals and fine pink petals. Her hair is bound messily up, but thin black snakes of it curl down her lovely neck. The ghost writing shines. But Singix blinks wide eyes at Amaranth, her mouth drawn tight.

It isn't working: The princess is not relaxed.

Perhaps they left her to her own thoughts too long.

Amaranth doesn't open her eyes; her volume of black curls falls loose over the tub, both into the water and dripping down the outside nearly to the tiled floor. Her hands rest on the rim. "No, it is unlikely I will marry. I am the Moon-Eater's Mistress. Perhaps your second child will take my place in fifteen or twenty years, and then I might, if I wish."

"I might marry," Sidoné says reassuringly. A book hangs from one of her hands; she's marking her place with a finger.

"But to a woman," Amaranth adds. "Sidoné would never deign to marry a man."

The body-twin shrugs as if it were obvious.

"And you, Iriset?" Singix asks gently.

"If Her Glory wills it," Iriset murmurs sourly.

Amaranth laughs, low and luscious. "You're so skilled at sounding shitty even as you say exactly what you ought. When did you learn that? You certainly made a great effort to be gentle and submissive when I plucked you out of that prison."

Iriset sinks deeper into the water, wishing to duck her head and hide away. She allowed her true self too near the surface because of her upset. "I am anxious, too, Your Glory. For my father."

"Oh, kitten," Amaranth says, truly sympathetic. "But you, Singix, your life will hardly change, except you will gain power, and my brother will care for you. He does nothing thoughtlessly and has prepared to accept a wife into his heart for years. It is as Silence commands, and he will meet the challenge."

Gritting her teeth, Iriset thinks of the ease with which Lyric balanced his internal forces. She thinks of his wrist, the line of his jaw in the starlight, and the low heat of his hushed voice when he said her name.

She's not exactly jealous; she just wants him.

"I like him," Singix says. "He is attentive, and—pleasing."

Iriset sits up. "His dominant force is rising, and yours is flow." She reaches across the space between their tubs, dripping water loudly. "When you come together, his force will reach for you like this, and meet yours inside you. The Vertex Seal yearns, and lifts his expectations with his inner design. If you are open, if you let yourself relax and welcome flow, all will be well."

Though Iriset hardly thinks that last part is entirely true, being so angry with Lyric, she puts firmness into her words, for the princess's sake. She deserves to be happy.

Singix reaches back to her. Their fingers glance together, then Singix grips Iriset's hand hard. "I am so nervous, Iriset. He is very attractive, but I know nothing. And you all say he knows nothing. None of you can tell me—you're all lovers of women here, or gods." The princess's gaze slides to Amaranth. "How can it help me? I am not allowed to express such worries to the ambassador, nor my women—they would refuse to answer, it is not appropriate. I have heard the empire treats...sex...as architecture, forms and..." Singix swallows and bravely continues, "Pleasure constructed between people. But we do not understand your distinctions on the islands. That men and women are not supposed to do this together here, unless married, but men and men, or women and women can? It is nonsense to me. I've never even seen a man naked! Except in very old art I wasn't supposed to see, either! But I'm expected to have a—to be with him, to have at least two children, and I *do* know what that requires!"

Iriset holds on to Singix's hand, realizing she should have used some of their afternoons alone to offer Singix some practical sex education.

Amaranth says, "I can tell you what I know of men and pleasure, if you like, Singix, though would rather frame it as education, not centered upon my brother specifically, for my own sake. We'll send for wine and some illustrations!"

"Please," Singix answers, fear tightening her voice into a whisper.

"Perhaps," Iriset says, "we should summon a man here now, and be more practical about it."

"Iriset!" snaps Sidoné.

Standing, so that water streams down her naked body, Iriset brags, "Talking about sex is not nearly as good as doing it."

They all three stare at her. Iriset squirms slightly as she's slammed with the full strength of wanting to get off as violently as she had in the Color Can Be Loud Garden with Singix's soon-to-be-husband. She touches her mouth, letting her whole body feel the desire, and looks directly at Singix. Iriset slides her fingers down her chin and throat, dragging against her collarbone and rests her hand on her sternum. "I've been with a man," she tells Singix slowly. "I've done everything I know to do with one. I like it very much, and it's very easy to keep oneself safe, clean, and unimpregnated if you know what—"

"Stop!" commands Amaranth. "Do not speak of apostasy before me. I can ignore what I do not *know*."

Iriset snaps her mouth closed, glances to Amaranth, and after a deep breath says, with all the false sweetness she can, "There are non-design ways to stop pregnancy. Less accurate perhaps, but legal, Your Glory."

Of course, human architecture is the best. Iriset always relied upon it, even when Bittor insisted on prophylactics he acquired himself as well.

"Barely legal," Amaranth says with a long-suffering sigh.

From her tub, Singix stares up at Iriset with wide dark eyes, holding her knees tightly. She's flushed from the heat of the bath, hair sticking to forehead and cheeks. Iriset gives in and trails her gaze down that pale, pretty neck, to the slope of trapezius and smooth round of her shoulder above the water. She looks along the graceful line of Singix's clavicle, following it to the watery shape of her breasts where they press against her drawn-up knees. As Iriset watches, Singix's breathing grows quicker.

Iriset steps out of her tub, water sluicing off her. She walks across the smooth tiled floor, eyes on Singix. No one makes a sound. When Iriset reaches the princess's tub, she bends over her, hands on the rim. Singix doesn't lean away, eyes flicking from Iriset's eyes to mouth, to her hanging breasts, even as Iriset puts her mouth near Singix's ear. "Have you ever had an orgasm, Singix?" she whispers.

Singix whimpers a little as she lets out a shaky breath. It brushes Iriset's jaw. "In—in my dreams, I think."

"Oh, Princess, let me show you."

Water splashes as Singix jerks back. "Iriset," she gasps.

"You'll make me blush, hiha," Amaranth suddenly says. "Or make an impromptu visit to my god."

Iriset wants to sneer at the Moon-Eater's Mistress to get out, then. She stands again, turning. "I don't mind if you watch, Your Glory. I've listened to you, after all."

Sidoné gets up from her tub abruptly. "I'm going to dry off and get started on that promised wine. I need it."

Amaranth laughs once. "Very well. We'll snuggle up near the fire bowl and drink and Iriset will tell us all about her lover." With that, she stretches onto her feet, sensual and fleshy and so unbelievably sexy Iriset realizes she's not ready to give up.

"Singix and I will be out in a little bit," she says with a teasing smile.

As Amaranth snorts, she's hit in the shoulder with her robe, thrown by a fed-up Sidoné.

Iriset returns her full attention to Singix, finding that the Ceres woman has been staring at her this whole time with parted lips. Iriset reaches to cup her jaw, skimming her smooth, dewy skin with a thumb. "Let me, Princess."

"I—I'm getting married in three days."

"You're getting married in *three days*." Iriset smiles. "Until then, your love is your own to give."

Singix hesitates still, but she leans her jaw against Iriset's palm. Iriset slides her hand back, tickling Singix's earlobe, scratching gently at her hairline. "I want to taste that ghost writing," Iriset says softly. "You're so elegant, and I like you, Singix Es Sun. You're funny, and brave, and you deserve to be happy, to know a little of what your body likes beforehand. You know about the exchange of design eggs, don't you?"

"Yes." Singix's eyes are closed. The peach-petal flush on her cheeks blossoms across her collarbone like a necklace of kisses. "But I don't understand how it works."

"Oh, I am a thorough teacher," Iriset murmurs, composing her lecture as she speaks. "Listen to this, beautiful: While there are several kinds of marriage rites recognized in the empire, the Silent Marriage is considered to be the most intimate and important. Any two people—and occasionally four people—may go through the rite, so long as each fully consents." Iriset brushes her thumb along Singix's temple. "The mutual consent is important, for any dissolution of the bond requires mutual consent as well. This is because the rite literally takes two—or four—inner designs and joins them into a singular bound design." She lowers her voice to a whisper. "Only death and unraveling can destroy the bond."

Singix shivers, lashes fluttering. She does not open her eyes.

"To prepare, each individual undergoes purification rituals to display their inner design's most singular elements so the priests can create what is known as a design egg. Each individual brings their egg to the marriage rite, and...well, honestly, Princess, the only important part is placing one's egg within the body of the other." Iriset draws her hand from Singix's hair and touches her thumb to the corner of Singix's mouth. "All humans have some projectile anatomy—finger, tongue, genitalia, elbows or toes or thumbs." She smiles and presses her thumb just a little harder, parting Singix's lips. "And all humans have multiple orifices."

The princess's lips open wider with a quiet gasp. Iriset leaves her thumb where it is and watches Singix open her lovely dark eyes. They're bright and nearly unfocused, but she stares at Iriset like Iriset is the silver-pink moon of Aharté.

Iriset keeps her voice gentle and hot. "It's entirely possible to share the eggs through any, though I've never heard of anyone inserting an egg into, say, a nostril. However, theoretically, it should work, and if it were my rite, I would argue to try the nostril approach. For science," she says with a little smirk.

Singix huffs, tilting her face into Iriset's hand. "Ah. Ah... how can you make it sound so...clinical, and at the same time so..."

"Erotic?"

The princess shakes her head slowly. "I don't know that word, but it must be the right one."

"Erotic. Sensually arousing. Titillating. Explicit. Carnal."

Singix presses her hands to her mouth, and then surges to her feet. Iriset scrambles to back up from the sloshing water, though there's nothing to splash except her bare skin. She catches Singix's elbows and the princess kisses her. Tries to. It's a little like being gently punched in the mouth.

Before Iriset functionally returns it, Singix backs off. Her eyes are huge and she breathes quickly. "I understand your meaning, Iriset. No—no penetration. That is for the marriage rite. The seeds. None of your—your projectiles or mine, in... side...our..."

"Orifices?" Iriset smiles slowly and Singix giggles, squeezing her eyes shut. Iriset says, "Very well. I won't go inside you and you won't go inside me. No penetration. And you'll see how much fun it can still be."

Singix shivers and Iriset squeezes her elbows. "And I'll know how it's different for my body with a changed inner design, once I'm married."

"That's right. And you'll describe it to me in detail, yes? Let me trace the new pattern of forces?"

"I can be *your* teacher then," Singix says so breathily and brave that Iriset is impressed she managed all the words.

Then the princess kisses her again.

It's just lips at first, gentle, shy. Singix clasps her own hands together against her own throat, and Iriset holds her elbows. Though they're the same height, Singix stands in the tub, and it gives her a little advantage. Only their lips brush together, and Iriset opens her mouth, getting a first taste of Singix's bottom lip. She kisses the corner of that pretty mouth, then kisses one high cheek, and right next to her ear. As she leans in, Singix's nipples skim against the top of Iriset's breasts and Singix gasps, fingers clenching together.

Iriset kisses her neck and puts her hands around Singix, pressing them together. They're soft and wet and warm, with the rim of the tub between their legs. Iriset gently scratches her nails along Singix's spine, tasting the floral oils and perfumed water dripping down her neck. Her hair smells like citrusy Ceres incense. When Iriset's hands reach Singix's bottom, she grips the muscles, pulling Singix closer, and dips her fingers to the fold where ass meets thigh. "Out," she murmurs, and Singix nods. Iriset hauls her up.

Singix squeaks and throws her arms around Iriset's neck. It's messy, but when Singix's feet are on the tiles, Iriset kisses her mouth again, and it is so very hard not to push her tongue in, widen the kiss, make it deep and sucking and delicious—but she promised. Instead she nibbles at Singix's lips, licks just a little under her chin, and Singix obligingly lifts it. Iriset kisses down her throat and Singix trembles, hugging Iriset with her head thrown back. Singix exhales a quiet whimper, and Iriset kisses her collarbone, bites the swooping edge of clavicle, then sucks lightly. If only she could give over completely, shove Singix down and do whatever she liked, whatever she needed. Lose herself in this princess.

Finding Singix's hands, she brings them to her ribs, pressing, asking Singix to touch. Iriset nudges one up, putting her right breast in Singix's palm. Her nipple is pebbled already, and Iriset hisses a little in pleasure. She draws Singix's palm away, putting her fingers against the nipple instead. She rolls it on Singix's finger, then arches her back, offering. Singix takes the nipple and pinches. "Yes," Iriset murmurs, pinching her own left nipple, tugging. She wants to be fucked, but this is good, too.

The princess takes both of Iriset's breasts, staring at her own hands like they don't belong to her, and plays gently, too gently, but Iriset can already feel wet heat gathering at one particular orifice, the ache in her pelvic floor begging for friction and pressure. Iriset watches the play of wonder and thrill across Singix's face, the spark in her eyes and damp lower lip. Singix runs her hands all over Iriset's front, exploring. This slow, gentle teasing isn't Iriset's style unless she's taking notes, and she's going to start squirming any moment.

Abruptly, Iriset bends and puts her mouth right over one of Singix's breasts and sucks the nipple in. "Ah!" Singix says, grabbing Iriset's head. Iriset flicks her tongue and sucks harder, and Singix's fingers dig into Iriset's half-knotted hair.

The damp skin is overwhelmingly nice in her mouth, filling her nose with bathwater scent. She fits her lips around as much of the flesh as she can, gently, the flat of her tongue to the hard nipple. She holds on to Singix's soft waist. Singix is pressing her hips toward her in little thrusts.

Iriset grins around Singix's nipple and moves down farther, mouth tracing the center of her stomach to her navel. Singix is shaking.

Leaning away, Iriset detangles the princess's hands from her hair. "Sit on the edge of the tub," she instructs, and Singix does it instantly, like her knees stopped working. "Hold on," Iriset says, putting Singix's hands to the rim next to her hips.

Then Iriset kneels down and pushes Singix's legs apart.

"Oh Leq'ina," Singix curses—the name of the Ceres demon of obedience, Iriset recognizes with a little laugh. But her attention is on Singix's thighs, the pale skin, and the dark hair curling lower than Iriset would have guessed, growing from the nest around her labia down the insides of her thighs like rain. Iriset puts her face to it, on the left, and breathes deeply. Singix whispers her name, and Iriset noses at the soft skin, smelling so much of the lovely bathwater and a sweet musky smell of arousal. It's nothing like Bittor's smell, and despite all Iriset's big talk, she's never been with anyone with a feminine-forward design before. Everything she learned about such bodies she learned on her own.

Iriset is almost dizzy with how excited she is.

Kissing her way toward the center, she holds Singix's legs open. Glancing up once, she sees Singix watching her in a daze, mouth open, panting lightly.

Iriset slides her hands up the princess's thighs and when her fingers brush the outer lips, Singix jerks—but forward, nearly slipping off the edge of the bath. "S-sorry," Singix gasps, and lets her head fall back again. The tips of her long black hair fall into the bathwater. Iriset takes it for the permission it is, and parts the labia with her fingers, staring at the inner layers, vivid pink and slick looking. She leans in and presses her mouth to the folds, and Singix moans.

Iriset kisses Singix for all she's worth, licking and sucking, and only avoids the hot hole, though she longs to dip her tongue inside, reach in with a finger or two, stroke the soft inner walls. She keeps her hands on Singix's thighs to avoid the temptation, and when she sucks lightly on Singix's clitoris, the princess squeaks again and again, turning the little desperate noises into a chant.

Oh Holy Silence, Iriset is so hot, so aching. It tastes wonderful.

"Iriset, Iriset, I . . ." The princess lifts her bottom off the tub's edge and pushes onto Iriset's face. Iriset lifts one of her legs, shoving her shoulder under Singix's knee so the princess has a little leverage to fall apart.

When Singix comes, she does so very quietly, bending over Iriset's head, hugging her, breathing in long, shaking sighs. Iriset holds her, licking her own lips, and tugs Singix to sink forward onto her lap, straddling her. Iriset holds her tight. As Singix melts on her, Iriset lets go with one arm and slips her hand between their bellies. She doesn't expect to need more than a few strokes, to be honest.

She shifts just enough to make a little gap between her legs and gets her finger between her own folds, finding herself hot and rather disastrously wet. Smiling against Singix's neck, she easily presses, only shifting her wrist a little. She slides her first two fingers inside, glad to be free to penetrate herself, she thinks with a private laugh. But Singix blinks at her, then bends away to look down. "Oh," she says, and touches the shallow folds of Iriset's bowed belly. "Can...can I?"

"Please," Iriset begs, and laughs breathily for real at the speed with which Singix slides her fingers down. Then Iriset groans and moves. Singix is using all her fingers, and Iriset doesn't let her explore and tease, not anymore. "There, like that, long and hard," she says, and Singix obeys. It's barely any time at all before Iriset comes with a low moan that's part lust, part relief.

She nearly ruins the post-orgasm pleasure for herself by thinking how glad she is to have tasted Singix before the Vertex Seal gets to.

Once they have cleaned a little—convenient to have the baths right there—and dried off and wrapped up in dressing gowns, they rejoin the Moon-Eater's Mistress and Sidoné in the sitting room. Singix holds Iriset's hand, bashfully, and only nods sleepily when Amaranth demands that Iriset keep her promise to tell them all about fucking a man.

Curled upon pillows and blankets together, and drinking a golden wine that tastes creamy and crisp, the four women discuss sex. Or rather, Iriset and Amaranth and Sidoné do, while Singix listens with her head on Iriset's shoulder, sipping wine and absorbing. Iriset hopes she can stay in the princess's bed tonight. (And she also hopes she is not allowed, or she may fall a little bit more in love with this Ceres beauty.)

It is no hardship for Iriset to describe Bittor, and their first few encounters, their laughter and vicious arguments, what he tastes like and what Iriset enjoyed and did not. Amaranth compares it slyly to women, confessing without confessing that she has been with girls before, very physically, and she speaks quietly of the Moon-Eater's power, the tentative explorations of his presence she had to discover on her own, for the previous Mistress taught her that was the best way to own the god a little bit. Sidoné admits that when she was fourteen, she and Garnet considered each other, for how convenient it would be to love each other that way, when they served so closely. Garnet liked kissing and touching her well enough, she says, but Sidoné had not, and they'd broken no customs of Silence.

They laugh at Iriset as she admits to growing aroused all over again, and Singix cuddles her closer, but only smiles a secret little smile and kisses Iriset's fingers.

It's a wonderful night. Iriset will hold it close in her memory for years, a single night of friendship, where she and Amaranth dance around forbidden topics, Sidoné treats her as an equal, and Singix clings to her with a growing happiness and comfort that plants itself in Iriset until she feels deeply assured they'll always be friends, even if Iriset must beg Singix to send her to the Ceres islands as a traitor. For several moments, Iriset feels like both herself and Silk, beloved together.

Sometime near the peak of darkness, when the moon is half eclipsed by the world's own shadow, Singix wanders to the low table covered with gift boxes and treats. She plucks a narrow plate of tiny caramels striped candy-green and shaped like succulents. Ceres letters of virtue are painted atop them in perfect gold.

Amaranth and Sidoné are arguing in intricate circles around the gossip that two princes of the mirané council are lovers. The women lounge together, eyes half lidded, laughing and shoving each other gently. Iriset nests in a vivid blue silk blanket and studies it with the careful caution of tipsiness, wishing for a stylus to test the stitches for design.

She hears Singix catch her breath, but distantly assumes it must be pleasure at the candies. Then there's a whisper of silk and a heavy bump.

Spinning, Iriset sees Singix sprawled on the floor. Iriset stumbles up, trapped in her blanket, and falls hard on her knees, hands against Singix's perfect cheek. She touches her lips, her neck—there's no design pulse. Ecstatic force pops and bursts inside Iriset, and she tries to touch Singix's flow, or anything. But there's nothing.

Nothing.

Iriset has no stylus nor glove, no tools to press into Singix's body and find the snapped threads of design. "I need—I need a stylus! I need to help her."

"She's already dead," Sidoné says, crouching. She pushes open Singix's mouth. Traces of candy stain her tongue. "Get the Seal guard outside."

Amaranth says softly, "No. Wait."

"Ama," Sidoné begins, but the Moon-Eater's Mistress shakes her head no. She stands like a voluptuous pillar, staring down at the dead foreign princess.

Iriset trembles, desperately holding back a wail of grief—not this, not Singix, not now, tonight. Her princess can't be dead. Iriset folds her hands flat together, struggling to contain her ecstatic panic, struggling for a falling force of calm. She breathes through her mouth, her tongue atingle with design, with the arguing energy of the room.

It was so fast. Singix was only just smiling, only just riding her face! Only just grasping her hair, warm and alive with flow and hope.

Iriset bends over Singix's body, presses her cheek to the silk-covered chest. She gasps tiny little ecstatic puffs. Like Singix's tiny sounds of pleasure.

"This is a disaster," Amaranth says slowly, ramping herself up. "Singix of the Beautiful Twilight assassinated in her own chambers. Three nights before she is to become the wife of the Vertex Seal. Fuck, *fuck*."

The tender passion in her voice turns Iriset's face. She leaves her head against Singix's breast but stares up at Amaranth. Grief begins to flood Iriset's throat, burning her eyes with tears. She wants to cry out. To scream.

"I worked too hard to get to this point for it to be ruined now," Amaranth says to herself.

Sidoné, barely clothed, grips a force-blade in her hand. "I need to get you safe."

"No. We need..." Amaranth's gaze nails Iriset. "This can't happen. I know what we're going to do. Iriset. I need silk."

Iriset sits straight up, suddenly hot. "What?"

"*Silk*. I know what you are," Her Glory says. "If you want to live, you will make a mask of her face and become Singix Es Sun."

ECSTATIC

Destruction is required for vulnerability, my love.
—*Writings of the Holy Syr*

19

The demon of beauty

When she is six years old, Singix goes missing for three nights.

She's a curious child and wanders out of her nursery because a flash of lightning seems to spark greenish, and she's heard that the demon of obedience's favorite color is green. It doesn't occur to her that sneaking out of her rooms in the king's manor is hardly an act of obedience. But the manor is a terraced open-air building of mostly balconies and lanais tripping down the smallest volcano on the first island of the Ceres Remnants, and if they don't want curious children wandering off, they might have built more walls.

Singix climbs a trellis with the help of hearty blue jasmine vines and lands in a cluster of water clover at the edge of a royal spring. Barefoot, she follows the green lightning.

By accident or luck or the blessing of the god of courage, Singix leaves the compound and skips, slides, crawls toward the sea. On the islands, every direction eventually brings one to the sea, but Singix chooses a fast route and ends up on a rocky beach just as the great storm lands. Wind howls and thunder shakes the thick trees. It rains, hot and cold in waves, curtains of water so thick Singix cannot see her hand stretched out at the end of her arm. But she hears the water churning hungrily at the island, so loud Singix claps her hands over her ears and thinks of the legends she's heard, from when the moon was not fixed against the northern horizon, and the ocean breathed in tides.

Through the night she stumbles, shocked, until she kicks the knee of a cloud-eye cypress and crouches in the shelter between its massive roots, face pressed to the knotted bark. It smells of home and moss and the rain that streaks down her scalp, pulling her hair.

Dawn arrives, or maybe it's the second dawn, and the wind and rain don't abate, but the sun lightens the air. Suddenly a stretch of silk is pulled across her little shelter and the water stops piercing her.

The storm echoes, and Singix hears her own breath in this little silk shelter. She hugs herself tight but peers out through waterlogged lashes. Someone kneels beside her, and Singix is unafraid.

The person has seven big eyes arcing across their face and forehead, each starry and bright like a different hour of the night sky between twilight and dawn. A nose like a rabbit and a mouth like someone's loving mother. Hair blue-black is like the dark predawn sky, roped with jewels and salt stone. They smile, and Singix smiles back.

They share the shelter and Singix sleeps, dreaming of stars and shivering waves and strange glowing fish. When Singix wakes, birds chatter furiously and drops of water fall heavy from the broad-leafed fruit trees and slide down vines.

The starry-eyed companion smiles with teeth of every kind,

sharp, long, blunt, chewing, and holds out their hand. Singix takes it, and the person leads her through the forest, past springs and waterfalls, past fallen trees and torn roofs. Directly to the king's manor they lead Singix, and when they reach the front gates they let go. They whisper, "Do you know my name?" while winking three of their seven eyes.

"Yes," Singix answers, and the companion vanishes.

After the ruckus of Singix's return, she solemnly tells her father the king that she sheltered with the demon of beauty.

"Es Sun," the king says, and Singix smiles. Though she's only six years old, the council of avatars gives her the epithet, naming her for her friend. Her father, who rules on behalf of the god of strength, decides that when she comes of age and marries, her consort will rule the Remnants on behalf of the demon of beauty.

That changes, of course, when Singix is engaged to the Vertex Seal.

The Ceres Remnants came to the islands many generations ago, refugees and survivors of a brutal, elaborate, far-reaching civil war couched as a war of religions. They arrived from across the ocean on strong ships filled with people, animals, seeds, and books. The archipelago of seven inhabitable islands curves around what had likely once been a supervolcano, long fallen beneath the waves, and now only its children remain. The islands are lush with forests, fruit trees, almost no fauna that threaten people except for a few venomous snakes and a spider or two. They don't even have deadly lions or a plethora of mosquitos or annoying leeches. There are flesh-eating fish in several of the springs, but they are the holy pets of the demon of family. Both clear freshwater springs and hot sulfuric springs abound, gifts from the god and demon of hierarchy, respectively. The

Remnants claim in tones of innocence that the islands were uninhabited by people, which seems unlikely, and nobody believes them, but nobody challenges them about it, either.

After several generations, the Remnants adapted completely, establishing themselves and their culture and architecture and beliefs as if they'd always been there. It is easy to forget—or ignore—that they had not. The most useful and lucrative discovery they made was the unique silkworms living on the second and fifth islands, whose silk spins quite durable and, in the right conditions, glittering. On the islands, they use the silk for anything and everything, but especially tightly woven cloth they stretch between godgrass stems or willow whips into spiral hats or painted and embroidered shades that can be stuck into elaborate hairstyles to keep the rough sun off the pale faces of their people. The shades can be slipped out of hair and used like a fan against the sticky air on those few rainy afternoons when the wind stops.

As Singix Es Sun grows, she remains curious and learns the art of silk making and painting shades. She reads every book in the vast royal library—at least the ones in the sections allowed for women and non-avatars. She is satisfied and good-natured. There is so much to observe and appreciate on her islands, it doesn't occur to her that she might go elsewhere. She earns a reputation for having an encouraging wisdom in addition to beauty, and her opinion is sought by those who need—or simply like—to feel better about themselves.

She never thinks about the great empire of Aharté. Why would she? On the islands they don't fear the empire, for it is known the strict magic of She Who Loves Silence cannot cross the water. But never let it be said the empire doesn't greatly discomfort the Remnants. The power of Aharté, while obviously they would never think it surpasses the power of their seven gods and seven demons, is too strange, too frightening, because it is so very joyless.

Only the god and demon of obedience, the most likely to agree with each other, might say the empire is all right.

Singix Es Sun is twenty when her father begins earnestly seeking a consort for her, inviting proposals from the various islands, from the cousins of those serving on his council of avatars. But it's the empire of Aharté that answers.

On the shore of the mainland, a two-day sail from the northernmost island, a great party of miran and priests arrives. They camp there at their southernmost steeple, arrayed with flags and pennants, and an envoy in a burnt-brown mask waits. It seems they wait for seven days straight, though probably several of them trade off with the mask shared between them.

When the Ceres captain allows the envoy and eight soldiers onto his flagship, the envoy speaks in crisp Ceres and immediately claims that it would be to the benefit of the islands to accept the offer of the Vertex Seal to marry into his family rather than face the inexorable momentum of the empire's conquest.

Though it is known—isn't it?—that the power of Aharté does not cross the sea, that assurance isn't necessarily enough of a reason to gamble your entire nation of islands. Especially when you have a daughter who will make an acceptable trade.

The Ceres Remnants welcome the empire onto their third island. The envoy is feasted and traipsed around, and when he leaves it is with a proclamation from the king that the Remnants will welcome a personal proposal from the Vertex Seal.

It comes in the form of a letter, which is delivered to Singix without being opened.

Even as far north as Moonshadow, I have heard of your

encounter with the demon of beauty. We do not have such beings here, but the god we do have, Aharté, I strive to meet every day, in every breath.

It is not the opening of his letter, nor the end, but part of the middle when Lyric mé Esmail His Glory attempts to woo, which is not an inclination he is naturally prone to. But Singix reads it, and considers it, and thinks this is a man she can appreciate. A partner she might be able to love, and create a better world with. A man worth the terror of leaving home never to return.

Because to her the nights she spent missing when she was six, when she met the demon of beauty and earned her unearned epithet, were inexplicable. Ephemeral, awesome, terrifying. To seek such a vibrating moment with every breath seems a thrilling way to live.

She leaves her home island with hope, a book of devotions hand-transcribed, and that first letter written by the Vertex Seal himself. It is a prayer, and a promise.

For a little bit, in the hope and fear of pre-wedding nerves, in the touch of an apostate, in the laughter of a god's mistress and friends, Singix understands what it means to breathe with god.

She would have been a wonderful queen.

20

Apostasy

Iriset has never worked so quickly in her entire life as she does that night.

Sidoné argues vehemently against the scheme, but Her Glory says, "What will happen if we reveal this? War, at best. Devastation, heartbreak, and a murdering viper able to flee in the wake of their success at worst. *Plus* war. Better to hold this secret and use the shake of confidence it will give the culprit to root them out. Investigate, do not let them think they won. There will be murder—the murder of a mere handmaiden—to use to our advantage. But we will still have bait. It is a good plan."

"You want me to die," Iriset says, but Sidoné talks over her, through gritted teeth:

"And your tool will be free and roaming and married to your brother!"

"I can't marry the Vertex Seal!" Iriset cries.

Both Amaranth and Sidoné hush her.

Iriset grits her teeth and interrupts, "Even if I do this, we would only have two days until the marriage. A craftmask to fool from a distance is one thing, but a craftmask to fool so intimately has never been done. Not since the Apostate Age! It would require *real* human architecture. Changing my face, my hair, my eyes. Not a mask that can be removed, or a single body part or inner system reworked, but an *entire* physiological transformation! I—"

"Can you?" Amaranth asks, still holding her gaze upon Sidoné.

"Yes," Iriset says because she is, after all, prideful, "*with time, but*—"

Amaranth turns, leaning over her, and says with extreme calm, "Let me take this choice from your hands, kitten. You will do as I command, or I will swear that you murdered Singix, and reveal that you are Silk. Never forget what you owe me."

Shock silences Iriset, and her heart pounds so viciously her ears ring, blocking all other thoughts and sounds.

Her Glory holds her hard, hot gaze on Iriset's, exactly like it would be death to glance away.

Sidoné speaks, but Iriset doesn't hear.

"I have no choice," Iriset says slowly. She touches her bottom lip as if surprised by the words falling from her mouth.

In that moment she believes it: She has no choice. Who would take her word over that of the Moon-Eater's Mistress? And she *is* Silk. Once the accusation is made, there would be no hiding it.

"This is madness!" Sidoné says.

"It will work," Amaranth answers. "Iriset can do this, and will, and we will hold the empire together for my brother."

"Ama—"

"Get to work, Iriset," Her Glory commands.

Iriset stares at Singix's slack face. She folds fear up, and then grief, tucking them away to deal with later, so that now she can study the task before her with a designer's eyes. In her chamber is a mask of her own face, and half of another mask made, waiting for its singular design. She can do this.

She *wants* to do this.

She wants to lie to Lyric méra Esmail, the brutal, disciplined, devoted, faithful Vertex Seal. She wants to prove this is possible. Take the place of his wife, become her in every way. Iriset can set herself as near to the Vertex Seal as it is possible to be. With nothing but her pure skill. Because she can.

No greater challenge of design will ever reveal itself to her, and if she passes it up, she'll regret it for the rest of her days—though her days would likely be greater in number. This is true apostasy being asked of her, the worst sort, and beyond even that, they'll have to conceal the murder of a woman she cares for, a woman she admires. If she's caught, nothing can save her from Lyric's brutal justice. Not even Amaranth. She'll be dead and unraveled before she can part her lips to beg mercy.

But.

What is a long life if you do not seize every chance at greatness?

Her focus narrows onto that moment, that choice, and she understands on every level of her inner and outer design that she was born and raised for exactly this.

It will be her legacy.

She says, "There is a tile in my room that is loose, four tiles from the south window, if you begin just west of the center. Beneath it is a crystal stylus, several scraps of silk. Bring me everything you find. Bring me also fresh vellum, and a—a basic design kit. I will have to make two full-body masks: one for me and one for her. And I will need as much time as you can give me."

Amaranth sends Sidoné, and Iriset gets to work.

Singix's beauty makes it easier, for she's a study in symmetry and smooth features, high square cheeks and perfect shining skin. The nose will be harder, being longer and straighter, and the hair. Iriset panics for several breaths when she realizes she doesn't have time to do anything about her knotted, curling brown hair to force it shining and smooth as obsidian; that panic whitens into numbness as she traces the ghost letters on Singix's forehead, trying to see into her thick hair. She'll do the best she can.

"We'll send for Garnet an hour before dawn," Amaranth says, kneeling beside Iriset to watch. "That is three more hours from now."

Sweating with tension, Iriset asks Amaranth to copy the ghost writing on Singix's face and hands, then keeps to her merciless pace. She strips to her loincloth when she pauses to finalize the mask of her own face, once the sketching and design of Singix's is finished. She changes the eyes to remain closed and, with the stylus, hooks the silk mask to Singix's dead face. Then she activates her work with a spark of ecstatic and the mask sucks itself against the body.

Iriset stares at her own dead face.

Amaranth gasps and reaches to touch, but doesn't quite put her finger to Singix's lips. She curses softly.

Disconcerting is the word Iriset thinks.

It's quick work to darken Singix's skin tone along her arms and neck with a simple crawling design that will gradually cover all her body, and longer work to arrange her hair not only a brighter brown but rougher in texture, curled, and then knotted. Once Iriset shows them how, Her Glory and her body-twin take over the styling. It's not perfect, and will hardly bear close inspection, but will have to do. Their performance must sell the transformation.

Amaranth dresses Singix in Iriset's discarded robe and trousers while Sidoné helps Iriset into a sleeping gown and full-skirted robe from Singix's things. Sidoné pins a veil that can fall down over her face. If they're interrupted now, it will serve to hide Iriset. Sidoné says, "You'll have to keep your mouth shut and pretend to be faint."

"I'll never get the voice right," Iriset says. "We don't have the tools to change a voice in real time—it's knowledge lost in apostatical fires." Iriset is awed and afraid as she looks at her own dead body. Her father—no, she shoves that aside. She can't worry about it now. Too much is immediately at stake. Later. Later.

"Don't say much, copy her accent, say you're insisting on speaking only mirané as you approach your wedding," Amaranth suggests softly.

Iriset nods. "And I will be grieving her, too."

Once the costumes are in place and Singix transformed, Iriset turns to herself. It's harder with her skin covered, with the wide sleeves and beaded hems, for she can't sense the eddies of flow and falling forces so easily. Ecstatic overwhelms her, lifting the hairs on her arms; rising force puts heat in her cheeks and clouds in her head. If only she had her silk glove.

Thank Silence she'd already begun this second craftmask days before. It's relatively simple—for her—to shift the design to Singix's symmetry. She says, "This will do for now, but I will need some more items to truly change my living face. I'll need chips of quartz, any kind but as flawless as possible, and raw silk. To make a more permanent mask, one that will become part of me. For my whole—my whole body."

Her Glory makes mental notes, nodding with each item. "Tomorrow."

"Wait!" Iriset thrusts out her left arm, having nearly forgotten the jade cuff tied to her internal design. "I don't have time for the ghost writing on my hands right now, but I will have to transfer this—I can, but if anybody is watching the schematics, they'll know immediately."

"Can you do it quickly? Can we wait for the last moment, when we say she—you have died?"

"Yes, quickly. And if none are paying attention it won't matter at all, but the time will be marked for Menna to see."

A star mirror with four points hangs upon the tiled wall of the bathing chamber and Iriset stands before it as she places the mask. The stitching requires careful points with her stylus, and Iriset stops breathing before she recalls herself and exhales in her eight-count. Life and rhythm are part of the point; a static mask will do no good. With the sharp tip of the crystal stylus she pricks the seam of the mask to her hairline while Amaranth carefully holds the bottom, her fingers protected by a layer of sheer silk. With each breath, Iriset pricks a new stitch, along her ear, then jaw and chin, then down the other side of her face. Her skin heats and she breathes balance until the moment comes: She closes her eyes and with two styli activates the pressure points. Ecstatic force snaps to life, answering the system of threading designed into the mask, and the silk sucks against her face.

It hurts, like the heat sting of a bee, like a fresh bruise, like the sudden ache of a fever's touch. When Iriset opens her eyes, they're still her own in the mirror: sandglass brown, faceted with a few strokes of darker brown near the pupil. But everything else about her face has changed. Gone her square Osahar jaw, gone her dark peach skin, gone her delicate cheeks and upturned nose.

Instead, a nearly perfect Singix Es Sun watches her. High, broad cheeks, long nose, perfectly flushed lips, sweeping brows that cut pure black against this pearly skin. The ghost lettering glints almost exactly right. It doesn't shine fully yet. Iriset parts her lips and her teeth are her own, her tongue her own, but who will notice a thing like that? It's the unsparing, ruthless work of real human architecture to reshape bone. This is merely a mask, shifting muscle, skin, cartilage. The rest will come later.

"Oh, Iriset," whispers Amaranth. Her face appears beside Singix's in the mirror. "Shockingly good. I...I feel very conflicted suddenly."

"You should," accuses Sidoné from across the room, but her tone is gentle.

For her eyes she's drawn a pupil and iris with a layered rose pattern of facets, based on her own eyes, and put the shading in as best she's able. It will only work if none have memorized the exact details of Singix's eyes, but only need to see what they expect: vividly brown irises, rich and varied in their sun-brown, like a field of earth that only changed with rain and drought—the shading of satisfaction or thirst.

It helps Iriset to think of it poetically, like an artist. Like Singix would. She knows in her liver that Ambassador Erxan is wrong: Doing art makes you more of an expert in it.

The pain of masking her eyes momentarily blinds her and makes her cry.

It's good, for the illusion. She lets the tears burn, dripping down her cheeks.

◆

Iriset waits beside a low divan, sitting and then standing in anxious jerking motions. Her gaze slides to the cold body of Singix Es Sun, wearing Iriset's face and her robe. It's the death of Iriset mé Isidor tonight, and Iriset finds it extremely easy to act distressed.

Her father will hear of it. Bittor. Everyone she's met. They'll all think she's *dead*. Can she still help rescue Isidor? She hadn't thought of that when she agreed. Thank the red god she's already sent the plans. Bittor will find a way to free her father without her distraction. He must. She looks at Amaranth to reach for the comfort of having had no choice. Amaranth would have blackmailed her regardless. And she knew. How did Amaranth know? Why did she keep it a secret? Had she always known about Silk or was it only a perfectly timed guess?

Then Garnet méra Bež thrusts open the door, stopping to stare first at Amaranth and then at the peaceful, dull body.

Sidoné is behind him, and slipping in with them is the Vertex Seal himself.

Iriset catches her breath.

Lyric's hair is mussed from sleep, his face unpainted, and a shadow of morning stubble darkens the skin around his mouth. He's only in loose trousers and sleeping robe.

"Oh Silence," he says quietly. The nearest to a curse he ever comes.

"Lyric," Amaranth says, surprised.

While Garnet closes the suite door quietly, Iriset clutches her fists together over her heart. This is going to be so much worse than she imagined.

"What happened?" Garnet asks.

Amaranth says, "She ate a poisoned candy—one of those there, marked with Ceres. A gift to the intended of the Vertex Seal. She ate it, at Singix's offering, and moments later was simply dead."

"Take the candies," Lyric instructs, though Sidoné already has the long box in hand and offers them to Garnet. His Glory slowly, as if moving through a sandstorm, lowers to one knee beside Singix's shoulder. "I..." he says.

"An assassination attempt," Garnet says darkly, looking at Iriset. She bows her head. But can't take her eyes off Lyric.

The Vertex Seal's face is bent in tragic lines. "My poor little arguer," he says.

"What?" Amaranth demands.

"I had—I had asked her to remain with us, with you, sister," Lyric says quietly. "She had such a certainty in her soul. A core of integrity, despite what she'd been made to be."

Amaranth glares briefly at Iriset and says, "Perhaps your future wife requires your comfort."

The last thing Iriset wants at the moment is the intense attention of the Vertex Seal. But Lyric stands, a tender grimace turning his mouth, and he comes to her. "Princess Singix, this must have affected you badly. I am so sorry for the failure of my security to keep you safe."

"I..." Iriset clears her throat and, glad for the roughness in her voice, whispers in carefully turned mirané, "I grieve for her as well, Your Glory. She saved my life."

Lyric smiles grimly and holds one hand out, palm up. It's for Iriset to place hers against his. She keeps her ghost-writing-free hands hidden within her deep sleeves and shakes her head, allowing herself to shiver openly. She silently breathes away the ecstatic pops still heating her blood. Singix was full of flow; Iriset will need to learn to center that even, rhythmic force.

"Of course," he murmurs. "You should sit, Princess. Your own handmaidens will be sent for."

"No," Iriset whispers. "I will sit, but please no more attention for me, Your Glory. Do what you must for the poor girl. Find who hurt her."

The Vertex Seal nods and drops his hand. He asks Garnet to send for the proper investigators and General Bey.

Sidoné brings Iriset water, and Iriset turns her back onto the room to sip it. She leans against the wall, eyes closed, just listening and breathing. Exhaustion threatens to numb her thoughts, but she needs to chase it back: If Amaranth sells this and wins Iriset space today to be alone, she needs to continue working for several more hours before she can risk sleep. Iriset counts the remaining items on her architectural agenda, prioritizing them: body skin color, ghost letters, hair, then finessing the edges of her mask, then beginning the work to reshape a few more muscles. She'll make a layered diagram—like a double dome that holds more weight and shape than a single—for her nose and cheeks and brow bone. The chin needs less work, but Singix's jaw is—was—less squared. Iriset is lucky that the design could be done mostly with slight additions to her bone structure and musculature, not erasures. Those latter were more painful and Iriset has never undone them before.

General Bey arrives while Iriset contemplates the possibility of inventing a new sort of mask, one that's semipermanent but can be stripped off at once. The focus helps her remain calm.

The older man's presence draws her attention again. She catches herself reaching up to pull a cloth mask she doesn't have over her eyes, and quickly tucks her hand away again.

Bey stands over Singix's body. Someone placed a blanket over her, and Garnet now flicks it aside to show the face of Iriset mé Isidor.

A slight gasp alerts Iriset to the presence of sharp-boned Beremé mé Adora, the prince of the mirané council, and maybe

Amaranth's not-so-secret lover, who told Amaranth to bring Iriset here for some unknown reason. With her is Menna mé Garai, the chief architect of the palace, likely the most dangerous person in the room now, who might see the edges of the masks.

"It was inevitable a life such as hers would lead to such an ending," Bey says in his gruff, judgmental way.

Iriset's legs tremble.

"And yet who expected her death to so perfectly serve the empire?" Amaranth says.

"Gentle Aharté," Beremé murmurs, and Menna makes a gesture with her elegant mirané-brown fingers meant to request the blessing of She Who Loves Silence.

Lyric says, "Yes. She served, in the end. The Moon-Eater's Mistress is as skilled as always at seeing the hidden value and virtue within a person's soul. I will personally preside at the unraveling ritual for Iriset mé Isidor."

At that, so tenderly spoken, Iriset cannot remain upright. She bends her knees, allowing herself to sink slowly to the floor.

"Princess," says Sidoné, moving to her side. She grips Iriset's shoulder.

"Perhaps," Amaranth says, "we may remove ourselves, and this body, if you have seen what you need to see?"

Giving in, Iriset allows Sidoné to escort her through the arched doorway into Singix's bedchamber. There's no more she can do for the scene in the sitting room. Either the ruse will work, or not. She says, "Let me sleep for two hours, no more. I need it too badly, but then I must work again, and I will need those additional things I listed. And—none of Singix's people can come in here."

Sidoné presses her lips together. Her eyes are faceted so dark brown and nearly black. Iriset murmurs, "It would be very difficult to copy your eyes."

"Good." The glare turns somewhat fond, and Sidoné touches Iriset's brow, drawing her calloused fingers gently down her face. "Sleep. I will wake you, either to your work or our mutual execution."

21

Every kind of courage

It takes Iriset seven additional hours to complete her initial design. Three of those hours are spent on her hair alone. She has to weave single-strand silk into her hair for a framework, and activate it in stages to straighten, thicken, darken, and soften the strands. Even so, there remains a gentle wave that she decides she can claim has always been present but that Singix's maids remove with hot irons and cream. For her skin she uses a crawling design related to her cascading distraction design, anchored in four places. The change burns but settles quickly, and Iriset's small birthmark against her left ribs and the mole on her neck and the scars on her wrist, right hip, and at her knees remain. Singix had a birthmark above her right knee. Nobody will know the difference.

In all her years working for the Little Cat, Silk has never undertaken such a project. The nearest to this she has come was creating body redesigns to change the gender-forward appearance of two clients to their specifications, removing a distinctive birthmark from a thief, returning about two-thirds vision to a young woman blinded in an accident, and of course investigating apostatical cancer.

Sidoné placed Seal guards with orders that the princess requested not to be disturbed by anyone, including Ambassador Erxan or any of her handmaidens. But Iriset knows no plans are foolproof, and someone might get past the Seal guards. Food is brought by Sidoné herself, along with the requested accoutrements, and an update regarding the investigation.

All evidence was removed from the front sitting room, and the box of candies traced to the mirané hall, where princes had been welcome to leave gifts. Every gift passed through an architectural web and every gift was tasted and tested to the best of the Seal guards' ability, yet this poison had gotten through. Either the murderer is extremely lucky, or the murderer is extremely powerful. Sidoné seemed relieved and admits that while a lucky enemy could be from anywhere, a powerful enemy should be easier to isolate. It's someone with access to the residential petals of the palace, who could slip poisoned candy into Singix's possession after the tests and webs. That's a narrow list.

Iriset thinks of how easily Shahd moves around the palace, leaving to put messages in the Little Cat's drops, taking care of Iriset's secrets, and she knows it doesn't narrow the list very much. They're still investigating the Ceres party themselves and making a list of everyone who disapproved of the marriage. It might have been almost anyone, and they're still out there.

Nauseated from intense focus and anxiety, Iriset eats little of what Sidoné brings. But she needs the fuel. If she faints, someone will discover her. If she stops working, she'll vomit from the stress of thinking what her father will go through, and Bittor, when they hear of her death. Her grandparents.

Despite her years of practice, nerves put a tremor she cannot afford into her hands. To counter it, she spends too long balancing her inner forces, and has barely finished applying the patches drawn in careful imitation of ghost writing to her hands when the outer door of her chambers opens and her name is gently called.

It's the voice of the Vertex Seal.

Of course he can command his way past the Seal guard or Sidoné.

"Wait, please," she begs, thrusting her tools and scraps under the low-hanging bed. She pulls on a heavy robe over her naked body and walks barefoot to the bedchamber door and opens it.

Lyric waits in the center of the sitting room, holding a tray covered in food and a squat carafe. Unlike this morning, he's fully dressed in the usual dark red priest-like robe, with his hair combed into soft curls. Still he wears no face paint or mask at all. Iriset is dead, and he holds to her recommendation.

She hugs herself. "Your Glory."

"Princess. Singix. I recognize the unusual intimacy of my presence here, alone, and if you prefer, I will leave. Or I will send for one of your attendants to chaperone. I hope, though, that you might allow me to stay. May I?"

At her signal, he sets the tray down upon a low table with a coal brazier built in. He waits for her to tuck herself onto the pillow beside it before joining her.

This room, where so much happened in the last day and night, is dark wood designed similarly to Iriset's—someone else's now—but the stucco walls have been painted a vivid, heavenly blue. It gives the room the feeling of being underwater, or perhaps in a cave made of sapphires. The ceiling is a low, shallow dome striped in blue and black. Rugs woven in spirals dot the floor, as do luscious pillows and low benches built into the northern wall beneath a long rectangle of lattice that opens over one of the inner courtyards.

It's hers now. Hers if everyone believes she's Singix of the Beautiful Twilight. The only mark of Ceres in the room is a small icon of a pregnant god reclined upon a many-petaled flower beside the door. Iriset recognizes her from conversations with Ambassador Erxan.

Tapp. The god of courage. *Between the sun and the memory of the sun*, Iriset thinks, hearing it in Singix's gentle voice.

She's going to need every form of courage, small and large.

With that in mind, Iriset meets Lyric's gaze and looks immediately away.

He says, "Sorrow has etched an even fuller beauty into your countenance, Princess."

Iriset shuts her stolen eyes as a wave of shame and anticipation flushes her cheeks. She wonders how the physiological reaction shows through her mask. Does it darken these changed cheeks with that same pretty pink glow she so admired in Singix? Her own desert-peach skin would have grown duskier with the blush. "I do not know to thank you or not," she whispers, careful with her language. Shaping the words as near to Singix's accent as she can; whispers hide all manner of vocal fluctuations.

"I need no thanks, but only for you to take care. Eat. There is a variety. I was unsure what to request for you." He doesn't gesture but keeps his hands calmly against his thighs.

The tray holds several kinds of bread, thinly sliced root vegetables and bite-sized squash dumplings, cured meat, an egg broth with tiny floating green herbs, and sweet oats. There's water, and the squat carafe. Iriset picks up a triangle of cornbread she thinks has fennel seed baked in, and tastes it.

Lyric rolls a slice of meat around a carrot and pops it into his mouth.

They eat. Iriset is finally ravenous and focuses on chewing slowly. The broth is delicious but too hot for this weather. Everything else is cold. She sips her water, and then Lyric pours two cups of golden liquor from the carafe. The cups are the size and colors of a nightjar's striped egg.

"To Iriset," Lyric says. "I am grateful for her sacrifice, and will remember her name to our children."

Iriset can't respond for the nausea that tingles in her stomach suddenly; she drinks the liquor. It's so airy and hard it seems to effervesce in her mouth and throat. Tears spring to her eyes. She gasps.

Lyric drinks and then takes her hand, the one with the empty cup. He cradles it in his and waits for her to regain herself.

"What is it?" she asks, rasping just a little.

"Honeybite."

She lifts her brows. She knows, but Singix probably did not.

"A generic word for any strong home-brewed liquor," he says. "This is the Seal guard specialty. They make it in their barracks, where only force-blades should be stored. They claim the energy from the blades sharpens the flavor." The Vertex Seal smiles slightly. "I rarely partake, because our bodies are perfectly designed by She Who Loves Silence, and I prefer not to alter her creation."

"But?" Iriset murmurs.

"But we grow imperfectly, and the effects of the world upon us sometimes need softening. A little will do no permanent damage."

Iriset licks her bottom lip and nods. Her hand remains cradled in his, and a shiver of ecstatic force tingles from her knuckles to his palm.

"Singix," he says carefully, as if she's wild and needs to be tamed.

"Your Glory," she replies, curling her fingers around the cup.

Lyric plucks the cup away and asks, "Will you allow me to teach you a balancing meditation? It might help you sleep, or at least to relax. That was a spark of ecstatic force I felt—and for it to be so bold in an untrained body suggests your inner balance is upset."

Cursing internally, Iriset hesitates. *Flow.* Singix's dominant force was flow, and of course Lyric would notice otherwise. He *does* have training from the Silent priests. And Iriset herself showed him, only a few nights ago, how to be even more aware.

"Please," she says.

The Vertex Seal shifts so that he faces her directly upon the floor pillow. He crosses his legs and asks her to do the same. It proves difficult to maintain her modesty, but the dress she wears has a full skirt and she manages. Lyric explains in simple words what he'll do and expect from her: It's exactly the meditation Iriset taught him in the Color Can Be Loud Garden.

Suddenly, she's blinking back tears.

"Princess," he says, horrified. "I apologize for—for whatever has caused you this new grief."

"Singix..." she says, about to say something about Singix. Iriset catches herself and quickly adds, layering her best soft accent into her voice, "Please, my name, you may use it. I am not grieved by you, Your Glory. Iriset—last night, only last night, told me my, ah, *dominant force* is flow, and...yours is rising, and she said...she said if I reached for you and...oh, I do not like to think she is dead." Iriset pulls away and hides her stolen face behind her stolen hands.

Her words are half-lies, but her emotions are real. Guilt

pinches her heart too sharply, thinking how recently Singix was alive, had feared her marriage and turned to Iriset for friendship and advice. The smell of bathwater against her inner thigh. And here Iriset sits, preventing the balance of justice. Her father taught her only to feel guilt for actions she would change if she could. Would she change her actions? No. But if she could have saved Singix, she would have.

Lyric quietly says, "Singix, it was Iriset herself who taught this meditation to me. I think she would like for you to know it, too. For us to find balance between us."

"Yes," she whispers. And Singix would want Iriset to be kind. She would not blame Iriset at all.

He holds his hands out, palms up, and she puts hers against his. His instructions are simple, basic, as he describes how the meditation works. Iriset's struggle to put flow dominant serves to cause enough frustration to create the illusion she's unpracticed. Lyric takes his own rising dominance and its mirror falling, matching it to her flow and ecstatic.

For a long while they breathe together, palms connected by the tug of energy.

Iriset follows his lead, letting herself go with him into balance, only occasionally breaking it as if she were a beginner.

Her body gradually relaxes. She's aware of the eddies of warm breeze sliding in through the lattice, the scent of broth fading, replaced by a rich lotion of some kind. Spicy fennel. Her bottom grows weary of the stationary position and she flexes her muscles subtly, even as her knees tighten. Ecstatic fixes some of her newly straight and soft hair to her neck. She hears Lyric's even breathing, and the ghost of his pulse through their balanced connection.

This connection to him, to his inner design, along with her

slightly aching muscles and her relaxation twist together into a key and unlock her desire again. The heat of it knots in her loins, and Iriset's eyes jerk open.

Lyric is looking at her.

He wants her, too. She can see it in the slight parting of his lips.

She pulls her hands away and breathlessly says, "I am tired."

What she wants to do is dive forward and kiss him, straddle his hips, pull aside his robe, and sink herself over his cock. *Then* they'd be balanced, inside each other.

It's most certainly not anything Singix would consider or even *think*. She turns her face away.

Lyric stands, a little awkwardly. "Princess. Singix. Thank you. Your trust has honored me."

Nodding, Iriset stands, too. She keeps her gaze lowered to his chest, focused on the crossed, embroidered edge of his robe. In two days, she'll be gone. Or she'll be dead.

He's so different with Singix than he'd been with her. Softer, kinder. And also more commanding. Iriset doesn't know if it's because of the kind of husband he wishes to be, or the kind he thinks Singix expects. That night in the garden, he had not seemed to put on a pretense, but met her, Iriset, person to person. They'd been close, despite their arguing, despite the vast differences in their needs and philosophies. Here, there's a distance between them.

A jealous piece of her thinks Lyric preferred the irreverent, arguing Iriset to his bride. Is she jealous of herself?

He says, "I'll send in your servants."

"No." Iriset reaches out and lets her fingers skim his wrist bone. "I need the rest of the night alone, please."

"Then in the morning. I am afraid even this tragedy cannot

delay further our rituals. Tomorrow is the day before our marriage, and there are many pieces of the ritual that must begin. Do you—" The Vertex Seal pauses. He doesn't continue.

"I am ready," Iriset says. It's what she must say. But she's thinking, *Fuck, the design seed.* She lets her expression crumple a little bit, showing grief only, not deep frustration woven through it.

"We will mourn her afterward."

"An unraveling," she whispers.

Lyric nods. He turns to go and Iriset surges forward with a sudden, dramatic idea.

"Wait," she begs. Her pulse pounds with sparks of ecstatic force. "Your Glory, I have one request."

"Anything," he says, surely unable to imagine that his gentle bride will ask something he can't grant.

"For Iriset, I would like to speak with her father."

Absolute shock slackens Lyric's features, and then he frowns. "To what end?"

She swallows and covers her eyes with her fingers—the only respect she can offer without a mask. "I lost my mother when I was young, and it was very difficult. The criminal must have resigned himself to his own death, but it is not worthy of us, of the Vertex Seal, to force him to learn of his daughter's death suddenly, or coldly. And with no comfort at all."

Her mirané is too good, too sophisticated for Singix, but Lyric doesn't seem to notice. Iriset wants to peek at him, to learn the path of his thoughts, but does not.

In a moment, his hands touch her wrists, lowering them from her eyes. "Mercy," he says softly.

"Yes, it is your Days of Mercy. For her service, may I give this little mercy to him?"

"If you give me a promise in return," Lyric says.

"Anything." Iriset repeats his promise, despite the risk.

The Vertex Seal holds her hands. "When we are alone, for the rest of our lives, you will not hide your eyes from your husband."

A reply sticks in her throat. She shivers and stares into the chips of moon-red and brown that make his eyes so perfectly mirané. Iriset nods, and Lyric leaves.

She remains standing in place even after the door closes, flushing, shivering, weak, and then near laughter. It's unbelievable she's survived so far. But she has. Spikes of adrenaline keep her on her feet as she stares after him, terrified and utterly triumphant.

22

Essentially

Iriset sleeps hard all night, awakening only when Anis mé Ario enters long after the sun has risen. She draws back the thin sheets and says, "Princess," then helps a groggy Iriset into a diaphanous silk robe with so much skirt she might as well be fully dressed.

As Iriset bathes and relieves herself, Anis softly explains that Her Glory has sent her to attend Singix because of Singix's request to be surrounded by mirané in the hours leading to her wedding. Her Ceres attendants are being treated to a vacation of sorts, and only the ambassador complained. Is there anything Singix would have Anis say to him in particular?

Iriset says in carefully accented mirané that Erxan should join her for a morning walk. She can't avoid him forever, after all, and better to know right away if her craftmask and disguise will pass his inspection.

Anis dresses her in what Iriset points out—hoping she gets the underclothes correct, but as Iriset acts as if she knows what she's doing, Anis has no reason to question her. The handmaiden's face is painted in bright lines of gold, white, and sky blue across her cheeks and temples, and when Iriset realizes the slight mussing under her eyes is evidence that Anis hastily mopped up tears, she turns away as if to conceal her own grief. In truth, it's wonderment. Had yet another person liked her enough in so short a time to miss her? She puts her folded hands against her mouth and waves Anis away to collect herself.

It doesn't matter. Her last old life is as over as surely as the one before it ended.

While brushing Iriset's hair, Anis says, "Princess, Sidoné asked me to let you know the meeting you requested is being arranged for later this morning. Please—please give the Little Cat the condolences of all the handmaidens."

Iriset stares at Anis, breathing through her mouth in gentle shock. "I—I shall." But she says no more, at risk of putting anything undeserving into Singix's mouth.

The handmaiden covers her eyes respectfully, and then the ambassador arrives, worried and sweating. He clasps Iriset's hands and speaks in rapid Ceres.

In her careful mirané, hushed to at least partially disguise her voice, Iriset says, "I would like to honor Iriset mé Isidor by speaking only in mirané, Uncle." The endearment she says in Ceres, knowing her pronunciation is good.

Erxan squeezes his eyes closed for a moment. When he opens them, they're watery. "Ah, Princess," he says, obliging her in mirané. "I am so upset at the loss of our little artist."

"It was awful," Iriset whispers, hugging herself for effect.

He touches her elbows gently. "There, child, you'll be well. We won't allow anyone to hurt you. Though..." He lowers his voice. "They're saying the poison was meant for her, because of her father. That you were the target is merely thin rumor. I was apprised of the truth. Those responsible for the investigation needed to freely inquire after motivations and any knowledge I might have."

Iriset nods. She blows a shaky breath. He has no reason to suspect anything. "They spoke with me for a very long time yesterday. I am frightened. But I will do my duty."

"We shall walk to the Star Steeple Garden and show these miran you are fit, and bold." He offers his wrist to her for escort. First, she gestures for Anis's help with her long cape.

As they walk along the seashell paths of the garden, Iriset remains quiet, and merely pretends delicacy if she needs to avoid any topic. She moves slowly, as if aching from the weight of duty. The culture of Ceres is her best ally in this deception, for its royal women are allowed to prioritize self-care and hide strong emotions from men. To claim they're very well and calm, but also withdraw. (A mirané woman would be expected to rage and vow revenge, to be bold and decisive in her emotions, active in pursuit of justice, and to struggle with Silence. It's exactly how Amaranth is behaving.)

During their constitutional, Erxan pauses twice to ask if she needs to return to her rooms, or to reconsider being tended to by her own servants. Iriset explains haltingly that she wishes to ready herself for her wedding in all the mirané ways. The ritual is tomorrow at noon, and today at midday she must begin the long process of physical and spiritual preparation. Iriset was briefed on what to expect, as Singix's appointed translator and companion: ritual baths, vows to Silence, fasting, and purification. None of that should affect her delicate architecture, but the design egg... Even thinking of it recalls vivid sense memories of whispering a lecture to Singix Es Sun, seducing her a word at a time. And worse, Iriset doesn't know actual details of the process of making it, or to what extent it might affect her crawling design or the layered craftmask.

When they've wandered a long enough path to be seen by plenty of miran and palace attendants, Iriset asks Erxan to escort her back to her rooms so that she can have a bite to eat before her appointment.

"I asked to speak with Iriset's father, in her honor," Iriset explains.

"Ah, Princess!" Erxan's voice alone does well to convey how appalled he is. "He is a criminal."

"I must, Uncle." Iriset reaches for Erxan's hand with both of her own though she's never seen Singix initiate physical contact with any man.

"Ah, child, you are too good. It is what your demon of beauty would do." He squeezes her hands and instead brings her to his own rooms, where there is food and drink aplenty. They share a bowl of tea and a cold fruit soup and a fish roasted in yellow leaves. All of it light and delicate, perfect for someone about to head into a day of taxing ritual.

There is a knock on the ambassador's door, and Sidoné's voice calls through that they're ready for Singix.

She reaches for Erxan's hands again, almost giddy with nerves at seeing her father like this, and relieved the ambassador has not called her out. Touching his fingers, she bows her face and says, "I will meet you again as a wife, and forever grateful." It's easy for her to feel a soft affection for him, her first true friend in the palace, who liked her—Iriset—who spoke with her smartly of art and philosophy, as if her thoughts mattered. Who reminded her of her father. And she's lying to him, so awfully.

Erxan says, in Ceres, "All virtues build your crown."

Iriset glances up at him with a sad smile, only to find Erxan frowning deeply at her hands.

A cold shudder of ecstatic force washes down her sternum, hitting her navel like a diamond. "Erxan?" she whispers.

His frown deepens, twisting the tips of the ghost writing on his forehead. "Princess, your great-grandmother's..." His eyes widen.

Staring at her left hand, she can't possibly discern what's wrong. But it has to be something with the silvery ghost-writing sigils. "I..." she begins, then swallows on a dry tongue.

"This isn't...you..." Erxan's hands tighten miserably around hers and he looks up, lost and afraid, but there is a spark of ecstatic that rushes from him to her like a blaze of wildfire.

Anger.

"No," she says quickly, grasping him back, leaning up on her knees. "Erxan, you don't understand—"

His mouth opens and he sucks in a breath for a cry. Iriset dives forward, pushing her hands at his mouth, shaking her head. "No," she says, in a burst of force. "Quiet!"

They fall back together. She lands half on top of him, clutching his mouth, desperate. What is she going to do? "Erxan, you have to understand," she hisses. "Please! Don't make me—"

He bucks wildly, shaking her off, and rolls, yells inarticulately.

Iriset reaches out, pushes her palms to the layers of cloth over his chest. Shoves hard ecstatic force and a tear of rising—like suddenly loosening a knot, familiar and easy—and Erxan's face bursts pink, his jaw seizes.

She feels it as his inner design spikes in a hard, frozen moment, and his heart stops.

He collapses back to the floor with a thud. Iriset grabs at him, choking out a cry of very real distress.

"Princess? Ambassador?" someone calls from outside, muffled by the door. "Is everything all right?"

She stares at Erxan's curled lips, his bloodshot eyes.

She killed him.

Iriset's throat aches as if she's thrown up. Her inner design bursts and roils, and she presses her fists together against her belly. She must control it, or her design fluctuations will disrupt the work she's done, expose her, ruin everything—

"Princess?"

She breathes. Tries to align herself. To push away every thought and fleeting emotion about what just happened.

Ecstatic, her dominant force. Popping, spiky, effervescent.

Flow, Singix's dominant force. Give and take, breathing.

Falling, Amaranth's. Her father's. Gravity, attraction.

Rising... Lyric's. Heat, yearning.

Ecstatic, flow, falling, rising. A rhythm and a current.

Erxan is still dead, but Iriset feels calmer—distanced. Dissociation is sometimes a gift. Iriset calls, "Help me."

The door opens, and Seal guards enter in formation with Sidoné, all with their blades free.

"He collapsed," Iriset whispers, standing on slightly shaking legs.

One Seal guard rushes out, the other kneels at Erxan's side. Sidoné comes directly to Iriset, demanding, "What did you eat?"

Shaking her head slowly, Iriset says, "Erxan ate the peach preserves and soda bread. I did not."

For a moment, Sidoné only works her mouth as if attempting to shape all kinds of words. She grasps Iriset's elbow. Frowns. Her gaze slides to the Seal guard and she shakes her head. "Go tell Amaranth what happened. She's in the Hall of Shades. Be discreet. Take a Seal guard with you."

"But my father is—"

"No, not anymore."

"But—"

Sidoné is on her feet and in Iriset's face. Coldly, she says, "No."

Iriset grasps at her robe, ready to beg. Sidoné leans in very closely, just as more guards enter, with a handful of attendants. There's noise and abrupt movement to hide Sidoné's next words: "After this, it is a risk not worth taking. Do you have any idea how thin a thread it is we're dancing along right now?"

"Yes, I do," Iriset whispers back, hands curling into fists against Sidoné's chest. "Thin as silk."

They both breathe too hard, staring rudely, their faces close enough Iriset can't quite focus. She lowers her gaze to Sidoné's angry mouth.

"That expression doesn't belong on Singix's face," Sidoné says, voice shaking. "Especially not before she enters the temple for the marriage rituals. Get rid of it and go to Amaranth."

"This is even more reason for me not to go through with the marriage."

Sidoné's frown is very grim. "I agree. But what matters is Amaranth. Go ahead and convince her."

───── • ♦ • ─────

The Moon-Eater's Mistress holds relaxed court in an alcove cut into the curved wall of the Hall of Shades, across from the magnificent Summer Sea Fountain that churns and spills water in arcs of green and blue like waves of flow and rising force. Amaranth lounges in a wide, low chair of carved wood, in the center of the rose-and-orange-tiled alcove. Long teal cushions line the edges where some of her handmaidens rest, sipping iced wine and leaning sadly against one another.

Amaranth reads beautiful religious poetry from a volume by Sarah of Heaven, one hand holding her place, the other stroking the opal scales of a lattice snake splayed in heavy coils across her thighs. Her Glory pauses when Iriset and a Seal guard approach. Her handmaidens—all three, Anis, Ziyan, and Istof—rise to their knees to greet Princess Singix. Six miran lounge about, men and women, all older than Her Glory, and one is missing an eye. Iriset would have remembered meeting her, for sure. Three of the others she's spoken with before.

"We are glad to see you have emerged," Amaranth says. "It is good you could join us, as these are people who share our misery about Iriset mé Isidor."

Iriset nods and looks back at the miran gathered. There's Hehet méra Davith, who unsettled Iriset in the mirané hall. She'd asked Sidoné about him eventually, and the body-twin made her promise to keep her distance, because he leads the biggest mirané faction opposing Beremé's appointment as the chief prince, and therefore is Amaranth's political enemy. Iriset can't avoid him if he's right next to Her Glory. And beside him is the gossip he pointed out, Dove méra Curro, and the daughter of... Iriset can't remember her name, but she was a contender for Lyric's marriage. Did Singix meet any of them? Iriset can't recall. This seems like a contentious group.

When nobody says anything further and Iriset only stares, Amaranth says, "Leave us, everyone."

One of the miran protests: "But this yard offers such a unique view of the eclipse!"

Amaranth does nothing, remains quiet and still until the miran would have had to say something to excuse their behavior. They choose to leave.

When they're alone, Iriset kneels near Amaranth and tries to decide where to begin. She shoves away thoughts of her father, and swallows demands. The Summer Sea Fountain fills the silence with trickling and a soothing pulse of flow.

Iriset stares at the lattice snake in Amaranth's lap. "Ambassador Erxan is dead," she says quietly in Singix's accent, eyes on her hands folded against her knees.

Amaranth sits up straight in a slow, continuous movement. "What happened?" she asks with equally quiet calm. "Poison?"

"I don't know," Iriset lies. "It might have been a heart attack. I'm fine."

"I was hoping for more time to focus only on the first murder before another death muddled things," Amaranth says with a strange kind of distance.

Iriset, feeling distant herself—no, untethered—looks up to find Her Glory staring past her, up at the hot blue sky. White and black circles dot Amaranth's chin in a narrow line, and her lips are black. Green shadows her eyes, with blue streaks across her temples. All the colors of Design. A silk mask is pinned into the braids crowning her head. Iriset wants one. She misses the comfort of it fluttering at her cheek, ready to be drawn across the eyes.

"Sidoné is with him. His body. And the people investigating. She'll come here when she knows more. Who are your suspects?"

"You need to be focused on other things right now," Amaranth says dismissively.

Iriset opens her mouth to argue but stops. It's true, after all. "Sidoné won't let me see my father."

"Oh, I heard about that, you fool." Amaranth snorts. "Or my brother is the fool for agreeing in the first place. It's better this way."

Seething, Iriset bows her face. From a distance, she'll seem soft, demure. Singix. "He's going to hear that I'm dead."

"That can't be helped."

"Amaranth," she grinds out, barely keeping herself still.

Her Glory's hand brushes Iriset's hair. "This is too plain for Singix, you know. This braid."

"Amaranth," Iriset repeats, twisting her fingers up in Singix's thick skirts. "At least let me send my father a message. *Please*."

Amaranth sighs. "Then you'll go to the temple, peacefully, and give yourself over to marriage preparations?"

Iriset shudders. There are so many reasons to say no. Apostasy goes against Aharté's most basic tenets, but to lie like this at the joining ceremony will make a mockery of the Holy Design itself, of the entire tradition of the marriage knots. Iriset might wonder which Lyric would judge more harshly, but then, he's already told her, hasn't he?

There is no shade to brutality.

None to apostasy, either.

That's the reason to agree. The only one Iriset ultimately needs. It was inevitable, wasn't it? From the moment Amaranth said her true name.

If Iriset, as Singix, marries Lyric, she won't only have performed the greatest act of apostasy imaginable, but will do it from the bed of the Vertex Seal.

"I will," Iriset says, condemning herself to glory.

Amaranth nods as if she expected nothing less. "Will your work hold up? The design egg is said to be made of inner design, and the priests make it by seeing through all pretense and lies."

"Do you doubt me now?" Iriset snaps, offended.

"No small amount of my reputation and power is on the line here, as well as your life, *Singix*."

Iriset grits her teeth. "I will manage."

Her Glory studies her.

In a sort of counterstrike, Iriset says, "Are you prepared to do this to your brother?"

"It is necessary," Amaranth answers immediately, which means she's already thought about it. "Not only for the pursuit of justice, but to preserve the alliance between the empire and the Ceres Remnants. If the murder was an attempt to interrupt it, we can only win by seeing it through."

"Would your brother agree?"

"Do you truly care about that? About his consent?"

Iriset pauses. She does care but isn't sure she wants Amaranth to see it too clearly. Because it isn't principle that makes her want Lyric's consent, or even fear for her own life. It's that she cares what he thinks of her. She wishes otherwise—wishes she could slice out this treacherous, caring piece of her inner design. She herself—Iriset—is dead to him, his murdered royal arguer, and Lyric wouldn't even consider granting her father mercy. Why should she give any to him?

Iriset lowers her eyes to the pulsing lattice snake. Its scales ripple and it opens its small mouth to reveal teeth like tiny ferns—harmless and soft, ruffling in the pops of ecstatic force shimmering off Iriset.

"I thought so," the Moon-Eater's Mistress says. "Now stop distracting yourself before what will be the greatest test of your skills. And write your note for the Little Cat. I will see he gets it. Only, make sure it doesn't implicate anyone, all right?"

"Yes. And—"

"There's more?" Amaranth drawls.

"I want Shahd for my attendant. I need someone I trust even if she doesn't know it."

"Fine," Her Glory says easily. "Now come here." She draws Iriset nearer. The snake shuffles deeper into Amaranth's layers. "What you've done here is truly magnificent, you know. Your beauty would distract anyone." Before Iriset responds, Amaranth kisses her on the mouth.

Ecstatic force tingles inside her, as it nearly always does when she's touched with desire. Iriset chooses not to fight it, but let the tenderness comfort her, let this kiss mark her. It very well could be the last kiss she'll have from someone who knows her name, for possibly the rest of her extremely short life.

As if hearing her thoughts, Amaranth smiles against Iriset's mouth before withdrawing. "I wanted to taste one thing before my brother," Amaranth confesses.

Iriset remembers the smell of bathwater and her similar betraying thoughts. What a place this is, to make love into such a game.

— • ♦ • —

The note she sends back to Amaranth with Anis mé Ario reads:

Your eyes, Amakis, your eyes and the clouds in the sky. You will see me again, if you look.

It's part of a Cloud King song her father used to recite, and her mother's name, and a promise she thinks only the Little Cat will understand.

— • ♦ • —

The cleansing and purification rituals for marriage are grueling for someone with nothing at all to hide. Iriset has plenty. Though a regular person could relax and meditate, Iriset is required, over nearly twenty-four entire hours, to constantly spool out the priests' designs and thin them enough to fool them into reading what she needs them to read of her true inner design without ruining either her craftmask or her crawling design.

It is exhausting.

It is *thrilling*.

There is no more space for fear or regret, anger or hope. For grief. There is only what is essential.

Iriset has never known herself as completely as she does in those hours. She bathes, she kneels, she repeats mirané chants meant to encourage the designs of the Silent priests, she does not sleep or waver. She puts on the appearance of devotion, and she bends it to her own use.

Just after dawn, when the Silent priest who accompanied her through the afternoon and night draws the tiny egg from Iriset's tongue, Iriset feels like a god herself.

The priest cups the egg in her mirané-brown palm and smiles. "Very good, Princess. We are finished."

Iriset sags, sweat tingling the small of her back. She's in a dark womb-like room in the Silent Chapel, beneath the ground and carved with force application into the glassy earth. The old red moon, when it fell, caused such heat and pressure upon impact that it fused the earth into glass in some places. This tiny chapel is made of it. An ablution pool in the shape of a four-point star in the center of the chapel is filled with black water. It smells salty, almost like blood.

"What do I do now?" she murmurs.

"It is just past dawn, child, and there are people waiting for you, that they may prepare your body for the noontime ritual. But never fear." The priest smiles, her dark eyes crinkling. "Relax, drink, eat, and feel your body. Feel the balance and maintain it if you can. But if nerves prevail, do your deep breathing and remember this space. The echo of—" She snaps. The sound snaps back three times. "The echo of Aharté."

The priest gives her a small box of sandglass, only the size of her thumbnail. The egg is inside. Iriset curls her fingers around it and presses it to her chest.

On shaky legs she leaves the small room, climbing narrow stairs cut directly into the earth. She holds on to the egg, a little awed by it. So tiny and yet so full of the essence of who she is! It's perfect, she thinks, giddy, until she remembers her father's words. *Nothing is perfect.*

Still. Whatever else, nobody can ever top this game.

As mirané attendants from Amaranth undress her and bathe her in sweet-smelling water and scrub her with rare sugars, Iriset relaxes. They rub her scalp with oil, never finding the seam of her craftmask. They slide fingers through her hair, pulling it straight, caressing her. Two of the girls sing pretty songs, teasing rounds about marriage and laughter. Iriset smiles and hums along sometimes, making the girls laugh and pinch her gently— encouragingly. The other girls ready her wedding shift and the mask she'll wear.

She's fed the airiest cheese and wafers flavored with mountain sage, and they share candied mirané fennel seeds—a wedding treat, because of the resemblance to the egg. Many foods at the feast later will have fennel seed baked, ground, and boiled in. There will be garlands of feathery fennel leaves decorating the low tables, and a sharp fennel-brewed liquor that numbs the tongue. (Centuries ago, this plant was brought to the desert from one of the conquered lands and it thrived. In the red earth of the mirané desert, the fennel flowered red, and so it was renamed. They do so like to name things after themselves.)

When Iriset has eaten enough not to grow lightheaded, she stands in a warm breeze as they dry her and rub creamy lotions into her skin. She's not painted with any geometry or design, for she's to meet her husband as simply as possible. Her hair is combed and left loose, hanging in heavy black layers past her waist. The wedding shift hangs from her shoulders, shapelessly, skimming her breasts and belly, bottom and knees, all the way to brush the tops of her feet.

The mirané handmaidens collar her neck with a silk necklace, knotted in tiny patterns of white, black, sea green, and sky blue. A cradle is woven into it, and there they place the sandglass box holding her egg.

No rings nor jewels, no lip paint nor eyeliner. Nothing in her hair but a crown of bright fennel flowers that look like fireworks. For a beauty like Singix, none of that is necessary anyway. (Iriset hopes the princess would forgive her.)

The wedding mask is a thin ceramic oval in plain mirané brown. Where it lies over her eyes, a hundred tiny, nearly invisible holes allow her a hazy vision. Its ties are skillfully laced through her hair, and with a single correct tug, the mask will easily fall away.

Iriset is made ready.

Her hands are cold.

23

Through with around toward

Those who attend will say that the wedding of the last Vertex Seal was magnificent.

They'll say the air itself hung breathlessly as Lyric méra Esmail and Singix of the Beautiful Twilight began their marriage walk exactly as the sun slipped behind the moon. The light shimmered bluish and pinkish, cooling the heat of the summer, and the two walked toward each other to the beat of a force-drum. Everyone lining their path breathed to the same rhythm.

Force-ribbons arced into the sky, bursting into stars and flowers, into the seven symbols of Ceres virtue, into mirané prayer script for blessings and unity. Everyone held banners, flowers, pennants, and water jewels that dripped like ice. The colors were riotous, the breeze heady with flow and ecstatic charges. People laughed, they called out the names of Lyric and Singix, they rang bells and made an entire cacophony.

Iriset is aware of none of that.

She walks carefully on bare feet, following the bold lines of the narrow rug spooling out before her. It leads her to Lyric.

Tension pricks under her skin and she breathes through it, keeping her pace even, telling herself some nerves are normal for any bride. She's passed every obstacle thus far, even those that she herself might have said half a year ago were impossible.

This next obstacle, though, is not one of design but of emotion. It's not a crime—it is betrayal. There are no laws against lying to someone or deceiving a partner. Iriset is unsure whether there are even specific laws against lying to the Vertex Seal.

Going through with this will be a magnificent, unbeatable coup for Silk's reputation, for human architecture, and apostasy.

All those days ago in the apostate tower, her father refused to be rescued, saying he would not become a villain in his own mind. Yet that is exactly what Iriset is doing to herself now. This kind of betrayal is the sort only a villain would choose. She knows it. She took the name and face of a woman who offered only her compassion, curiosity, love. She killed for her own gain. Now she will slip into the marriage, life, bed, heart of Lyric méra Esmail. Just because he deserves a lot for the things he's done doesn't make her actions any more pure.

With every mask to hide behind, she cannot hide from herself.

Why is it so easy, then, to take each step, to look through the hazy eyes of her mask and stare at the Vertex Seal, unflinching?

He's dressed the same as Iriset, barefoot and wearing nothing but a long white shift, a silk necklace to cradle his sandglass box and seed, and a mirané-brown ceramic mask.

His mask matches his skin perfectly.

Lyric moves meditatively: Smooth and purposeful. Tightly controlled. She remembers the confident shift of his bare muscles in the sunlight as he practiced the combat forms with his soldiers, the casual skim of his fingers down her forearm when he showed her the forms for the force-blade, and Iriset thinks he's nervous, too.

They meet, hands up, palms together, and their inner designs reach for each other: her flow and ecstatic, his rising and falling.

For a while they breathe together. It's their prerogative to draw out this moment as long as they like. When they're ready—and it happens simultaneously—they reach for each other's masks and tug the ribbon holding them in place. Both masks fall away, tumbling to the ground where they shatter exactly as they are meant to.

The tiny ceramic daggers and slivers scatter around their bare feet, and it's considered a good luck sign if there's a little bit of blood.

Lyric méra Esmail smiles at her, and her pulse leaps ecstatically. The smile reaches his eyes, and he begins the Four-Force Vow.

> *As blood beats through my body, so does my world flow through you.*
> *As flowers lift after the sun, so does my world rise with you.*
> *As epiphany sparks, so does my world charge around you.*
> *As the Holy Design yearns for its center, so does my world fall toward you.*

Iriset catches her breath. Though she knows the words, she's never felt them, nor understood them, and in this moment they shimmer in the air with a weight of their own.

Voice soft, for his ears only, Iriset offers the vow back to him.

Then Lyric turns from her, and she unlatches the silk necklace containing his design egg. He does the same for hers, and then they put on each other's. The weight is the same, but Iriset thinks Lyric's necklace is warmer than hers had been. It settles over her collarbone with a pleasant tenderness. She doesn't care if she's being overly fanciful. It doesn't matter that this wasn't meant for Iriset mé Isidor. It's hers now.

And then it's over. That's the entirety of the public ritual.

Singing breaks out, in four parts, of course, lifting, twining melodies and countermelodies, with clapping hands and sudden high-pitched cries. With their voices, the miran create a dome of forces to shiver around the couple, containing them, urging them on.

Iriset hums. The note trembles down her chest, vibrating through her bones and into her hand, leaping to Lyric. He glances at her with slight surprise, and Iriset recalls that Singix knew nothing of design-song.

She lets her note fade and squeezes his hand, fluttering her lashes nervously, as Singix was prone to. She glances down but he touches her chin, nudging it up again. Together they walk back along the ribbons to the Hall of Princes, where a feast awaits.

The throne, perched heavily over a chunk of mirané-brown moon rock, sits empty and yet somehow thrumming full of intention, and Lyric takes her to it. He accepts a small coin with four tiny spires from Garnet, who seems to appear from nowhere, ready as always. Lyric presses the coin to his thumb.

Blood appears, and this he smears on the moon rock.

Iriset brings his thumb to her mouth and kisses it.

They're seated then at a low table before the throne, upon firm pillows that can support them for hours. Today, for this single day, the Vertex Seal and his wife are displayed for any to see. Ironic, Iriset is well aware.

The cavernous Hall of Princes, striped black and white, with its vaulted double dome directly overhead, fills with noise and color as the miran pour in, extravagantly draped in colorful robes and masks of wire, gold, flowers, and even pure forcelines, or crystal.

Iriset quickly loses track of the finery and who wears what. She sips her fennel liquor and holds her husband's hand, allowing him to do most of the speaking, and she wonders what Bittor would have worn to her wedding, or her father, and she looks for Raia mér Omorose, who had been her friend, but she can't find an. Perhaps an wasn't invited to Singix's wedding—or more likely an is holding some of the elaborate designs around the hall for either security or decoration. Diaa of Moonshadow, Iriset's new mother-in-law, sweeps around as if she's the host, mostly ignoring her son and his wife on their wedding day. Nielle mé Dari is here with her small king husband, wearing a truly appalling mask of what must be intended as an ode to the Ceres virtues based on the seven separate colors and chunky style. Iriset wishes she could tease the former handmaiden.

The food is delicious, brought out in small bites and shallow cups for quick swallowing. One course is nothing but perfumes—some effervescent as hot alcohol—another course is salad entirely made of flowers crystallized with specially designed honey. They crunch and break delicately over the tongue, sweet and hardly there.

So much energy and light swirl around her, plowing the air for her attention, that it's difficult for Iriset to look at anyone directly until they are close enough to kill her. Someone wanted Singix dead and here she is, alive and well and almost entirely married. She attempts to note who is standoffish, but most everyone fawns over the Vertex Seal today, though one or two shoot Iriset a glare, probably just jealousy. She remembers them anyway. Iriset knows the Seal guards are hunting, too, and Garnet and Sidoné and very likely people Iriset has never even heard of scour the hall for weapons and tricks. She can only perch on her pillow and pretend nothing bothers her, she isn't afraid, she doesn't wonder if every mask conceals an enemy, she knows she isn't a vivid target, of course not.

Iriset is remarkably good at pretending.

Except one moment, in the middle of it all, she feels a shiver at the nape of her neck and glances behind her.

The numen stares at her, its face half hidden behind the nearby throne. Its ruby-pink eye studies her knowingly, and once she stares back, it lifts a hairless brow, then smiles and gestures as if drinking.

It knows. Somehow, it knows.

Iriset holds its gaze. With the null collar around its withered neck, it can't reach through design to reveal her. It might speak, though, or scream, and if it finds the right words, she's finished.

The numen does nothing.

Lyric caresses her knuckle and she glances back at him. His gaze slides past her to it, and before he can speak, she asks, "Is it hungry? Does it eat?"

"You are kind, Singix," he answers, with a slight censure.

She picks up her small cup of liquor and stands. Many notice, some going quiet as if expecting her to speak. But Iriset moves to the numen and offers it the drink.

The smile falls off its face as it accepts, lifting the cup in salute, and drinks every drop before setting the cup onto the edge of the step where it's chained.

Iriset leaves it there and returns to her husband's side. She wants to ask him about the creature, why he lets it suffer so, but suspects his answer will be irritating, and she doesn't wish to put shadows between them already.

Lyric is the one who softly says, "I am sorry about Erxan. You have had such a trying few days."

She nods. "Did they discover what happened?"

"Heart attack," Lyric says, "though he seemed so healthy."

Iriset glances at her cup to hide the relief and guilt she's unsure she can hide. (The Ceres party has already approached and done their best to wish the couple well, and Iriset let herself cry then, and say she would pray for his ghost. And after that, she said she belonged now to the empire.)

Before the sun sets, Lyric stands.

At his signal, designers dim the lights, except for a pink-silver moon of wire and force that floats over Lyric, pouring soft light around him. He says, "Mirané princes, friends, allies, you have our thanks, and that of the Vertex Seal, for witnessing the binding of myself to my wife. This is the first day of my happiness, our future, and the seed of an alliance between us and the Ceres Remnants. These are the Days of Mercy, and as you have sought mercy from the Vertex Seal, I ask you in return for the mercy of your good wishes, your hopes, and your accordance with Silence. Tomorrow is the Crowning Sun, and you are all invited to the ritual that shifts the angle of days from rising to falling. When you see me again, I will be re-formed by the will of Aharté into a new man."

Lyric looks down at Iriset, holding his hand to her. She takes it and lifts herself to her feet beside him. He twines their fingers together and faces the assembly again. "A joyful, strong, resilient, and complete new man."

For a moment Iriset lets herself believe what he says: that their marriage will make him better.

———— • ♦ • ————

They retire, followed only by Amaranth, Sidoné, Garnet, and Beremé. Lyric doesn't release her hand, and Iriset clings to him. Direct to his private rooms he leads her, up and up one of the palace towers, and at the door he pauses.

"Thank you," he says to their entourage. "We will manage. Unless…" He glances a question at Iriset, who lowers her head and shakes it.

Garnet steps forward and puts his hand on Lyric's neck, a thumb against his jaw. "Brother," he murmurs.

Lyric smiles. "Always."

Amaranth mirrors Garnet's gesture, only puts her hand on Iriset's neck. "Sister," she says softly—wickedly. But Lyric's hand tightens encouragingly around hers, and Iriset smiles for the Moon-Eater's Mistress.

Then Beremé, with a coyote's sharp smile, offers them a long white scarf of silk. Near a hundred jewels are sewn into it, in every possible color. "For your pillow," she says. "Each prince of the mirané council contributed a precious gem, attached by their own hand."

"Thank you," Iriset says, accepting the gift.

"Have fun," Amaranth says, teasing her brother.

Lyric raises his chin and smoothly opens the door. As he ushers Iriset inside, he says, "Good night, sister."

The last thing Iriset sees as the door slides closed is Sidoné's hard, conflicted expression.

Then she's alone with her husband.

Iriset distracts herself by studying the room. It's plain, an octagonal shape, with three more doors spread equally with the door through which they'd just entered. Each is a holy arch, the dark wood carved with intricate floral patterns. The walls are rich, sunset blue, and the vaulted ceiling is a lattice dome. Purple evening light cuts through from the west.

A brazier hollow is carved into the floor, tiled smoothly in a paler blue and waves of green that stretch toward the walls. Some cushions pile against one wall, but otherwise there are no decorations nor furniture.

Lyric points toward one arch. It has neither door nor screen, but leads to a hall angled down that coils sharply out of sight. "Through there is our private bathing room, with a long pool, a heated tub, and many mirrors. There is also a closet, with most of my clothing, and room for yours. Some has been moved, but you may see to the rest, or have a new wardrobe created." He nods to the door across from the bathing arch. "There is a more intimate sitting room, or study. It can be whatever we wish. I've used it as a library and meditation space. And through that final archway"—he indicates the door they faced—"is the bedchamber."

Nodding, Iriset walks straight for it. When she reaches it, she glances behind her at Lyric, who hasn't moved. "Are you... joining me?" Iriset carefully keeps her voice soft, accented.

"Yes, I..." Lyric comes to her. He takes her hand again.

Through the archway, stairs lead up in a soft curve. Alcoves cut into latticed windows allow in light and air. The corridor breathes with the warm evening breeze. A skull siren trills harshly nearby, and Iriset is glad of the company.

Lyric touches the small of her back as they reach the upper archway opening into their bedchamber.

Nothing but a huge round bed graces the octagonal room.

Four pillars hold up a ceiling mosaicked with shards of black, white, and blue glass, and a center sun of mirané brown like an open wound. The walls are nothing but tight lattice and four-point-star windows of thin glass. To the west the lattice is a falling pattern, like rain and meteors; to the south it depicts the eddies of flowing water, a river with curling rapids and peaceful rhythms; in the east fire reaches high, drawn by rising forces through spirals of smoke; in the north the lattice is a million tiny sparks, four- and eight-point stars, pinpricks and needles of energy between them. The balance and simplicity take Iriset's breath away. The design must be intense if it keeps out winter ice. But worth it.

She turns in a full circle, then stops abruptly. There are two doorways, arched with holy points, including the one through which they entered, and hanging against the plain wall between them is the icon of Tapp, the Ceres god of courage. It's the same one from Singix's bedroom.

"I wanted something of yours awaiting you here," Lyric says softly. Almost shyly. Iriset glances at him: His gaze is cast aside. "Everything was removed that was mine alone, so that we can remake this room together."

Touched, though it's not a gesture for her but for a dead woman, Iriset lets herself kiss him.

Just upon the cheek, near the corner of his mouth, but she presses her lips there, and he draws in a sharp breath. His hands skim briefly against her elbows before he drops them again.

Iriset goes to the bed. Low, it's piled with silk and striped linen, long cylindrical pillows and square ones in every shade of blue, two flat rectangles tasseled in vibrant red. The frame is a huge alliraptor with its long jaw resting upon the tip of its own tail. They'll sleep embraced by the river monster most beloved by Aharté.

Spreading the jeweled scarf upon the bed, Iriset listens to her heartbeat, to the flow and rising forces heating her skin.

"Would you like water or wine?" Lyric asks.

She touches the bed, wondering how to pretend to be virginal. Allow him to begin everything? When he's the one untouched?

"Water," she says.

He makes no sound, but Iriset senses his departure. She's alone in the bedroom of the Vertex Seal.

She allows herself a moment, very briefly, to laugh.

Like bubbles of ecstatic force, her laughter brightens her entire design, and Iriset smiles. This part will be ridiculous. Easy. She's wanted Lyric méra Esmail between her legs since she first saw him. There are so many reasons she shouldn't be here, married to him, lying to him, dancing on the sharp pinnacle of her apostatical expertise. But she *is* here. Every choice has already been made, for good or mostly ill.

Iriset bites her lip and unties the laces holding her long shift closed over her breast. The collar then gapes wide enough to wriggle her shoulders free and pull it down and off her body. She kicks it gently aside and sits upon the bed, entirely naked but for the silk necklace cradling Lyric's design egg.

When the Vertex Seal appears in the arch with a long-necked pitcher of water, he freezes.

For a long moment he stares, vivid red-brown eyes fixed on her. His breathing speeds up and his lips part and Iriset knows their inner designs are not yet bound, but imagines his reaction affects hers. She feels popping ecstatic force up her spine, and a pool of falling force swirls in the base of her hips, drawing flow through her blood and muscles, and that yearning rising force escapes as a sigh along her tongue.

"Lyric," she says, beckoning with one hand.

He sets the water on the floor and comes over to her, but he kneels. He puts his hands gently on her knees, sliding his palms to either side. As if to hold her knees closed. "Singix," he says, and Iriset gasps in surprise—she *forgot*, the foolish girl. Something heavy and dripping like despair chokes her. This isn't for Iriset.

Closing her eyes, she folds her hands protectively between her breasts. She turns her face away from him as tears drop down her cheeks.

"Ah, Singix," he whispers, and brushes her tears away even as he misinterprets them. "We have much to discuss, griefs and losses, and I—I want to. But first, may I... offer my design egg to you with a kiss?"

Pulling herself together hard and fast, Iriset nods. Eyes still shut, refusing to think of teasing about nostrils and orifices, she frees the sandglass box from the silk necklace she wears and holds it out blindly.

His hands are warm, cupped around hers. He does nothing, though, simply breathes with their hands joined. Iriset follows his lead with long breaths and eventually a very slight smile. She opens her eyes to find him watching her lips. "May I have mine?" she asks, thinking again of Singix. She needs to banish the thought. This is her own design egg. Hers.

Lyric blinks and then quickly removes her sandglass box from the necklace he wears. They trade. Iriset grips hers in one palm while Lyric flicks open his box and withdraws the tiny egg.

Carefully, he raises it and parts his lips. He extends his tongue a little bit, just enough to touch the egg to the tip. Wordlessly, he lifts his brow and leans up toward her.

Iriset reaches for his shoulder with her empty hand, to steady him when he kisses with warm, soft lips. Then they open their mouths at the same moment, and Lyric turns his head to touch his tongue to her upper lip, then slides it deliberately into her mouth. Iriset sucks the egg into herself, swallowing. She leans her forehead against the corner of his mouth, pulse racing, and opens her sandglass box to press her finger against her egg. It sticks there and she brings her hand up between them.

Dropping her box onto the bed, she takes his jaw gently in her two hands. She meets his gaze again, and when he opens his mouth for her, she puts her finger inside, placing the egg against his tongue. As she withdraws her finger, Lyric closes his lips around her and sucks softly. The pad of her finger skims his bottom teeth and Iriset moans.

Her skin prickles with desire, needles of force dancing out of her blood, clapping a beat in her skull, and all of it drains in a swirl to her hips and thighs and belly.

Lyric doesn't move until Iriset tugs him onto the bed beside her and leans in to kiss him. He holds her face, sliding fingers into her hair and opening his mouth. Iriset hugs his head and neck, kissing hard enough to lift herself over onto his lap. She slides across his thighs, and his erection is so extremely satisfying Iriset rubs her bottom against it before remembering in a burst of pleasure that Singix had been anxious to the point of fear, and this is not the right behavior—but she also doesn't really give a shit anymore, being entirely hot and wet herself, and nothing between them but thin linen. What's he going to complain about, anyway?

Their kiss breaks off in a heady smear, and Lyric kisses her jaw, her cheek, sighing into her hair, until Iriset puts their mouths together again and—

The eggs, traded and burrowing into each respective design, suddenly unleash their power.

Iriset's back arches and her eyes fly wide open: She stares at the red-wound ceiling glass, that mirané gash, as tendrils of forces drive through her, gathering every part of her up and twisting it, reaching out of her body—and it's like light, filling her up, shining from her, except invisible. And Lyric's design reaches back for her.

They become cries of light, a moan of Silence, when their designs bind together, transforming into one whole.

Sweating, panting, they might stop there—the ritual is finished with this kiss.

Lyric holds her tight against him; Iriset melts into his chest, her eyes pressed under his ear. "Water?" he whispers raggedly.

But Iriset is not satisfied, and perhaps Singix wouldn't have recognized the ache for exactly what it is, but she does, and she recognizes the evidence of Lyric's desire, too. So she shakes her head and pushes him back against the bed, rolling off him. She grabs at his shift, dragging it up with desperate hands. Her fingers scour his thighs and she looks frantically at his face; he's so sweetly intent, and Iriset suddenly stops, panting slightly.

"Singix," he says, gratifyingly shaky, "we can—slow, we can do what we like, now, or later."

"No," she whispers, "I want this, I want you."

"I want you, too," he answers.

Iriset can see it, can see the shivering flow tightening his belly, the rise and ecstatic of his erection. The answering sparks and heat in her make her feel like a center of falling force, everything spilling, pooling in the mouth of her hips, the small of her back. She taps at his sternum, and Lyric sits in one graceful motion. He throws off the shift and is as naked as her.

He cups her shoulder, rubs a thumb into the thin skin at the join of collarbone and muscle. Then Lyric leans in and kisses her again, open-mouthed. Iriset lets him in. She wraps her hand around his cock and his body spasms. The noise he makes against her tongue tastes like that fifth force she nearly felt in the Moon-Eater's Temple. (It feels like when she stopped Erxan's heart.)

Clamoring into his lap, Iriset kisses and bites at his lips. Lyric grabs her by the bottom, strong hands steadying her though Lyric is anything but steady himself. She reaches behind herself and nudges one of his hands so that his fingers find the wet edges of her labia. Iriset arches her back to welcome the touch, leaning down, and when Lyric slides his fingers deeper, she winds her arms around his neck, pulling her face to his in a tight embrace, and whispers, "Yes, yes, yes."

"Yes," he says back, completing the quartet, dipping fingers inside her.

Iriset decides to take her time later, lick every inch of his skin, explore the joints and tendons, the flavor of his elbows and throat-knot and inner thighs, but right now she wiggles and finds his cock again with her hand. She lifts up and does her best with the angle. "Lyric," she says.

His eyes fly open and lock onto hers.

Finally he helps, taking himself to her entrance. He trembles everywhere, returns his hands to her thighs, offering to hold her weight. Iriset presses down, and fights against the instinct to let her head fall back, her eyes close. Instead she stares at him. She puts her hand to his jaw, his mouth, and when he opens up, Iriset slides two fingers into his mouth. His tongue is just as hot and wet as her.

This is something Singix would never think to do. An act singular to Iriset, making a circuit of penetration between their bodies.

Lyric's lashes flutter as they both push in as far as they can go. His mirané-brown eyes blur in her gaze, too close, too close, becoming red sparks of ecstatic force as the flow between them rises and falls and Iriset smiles, laughs. Lyric sucks at her fingers and she pulses her hips, and it is perfect.

— • ♦ • —

Iriset mé Isidor lies in the darkness, one hand trailing off the bed to brush against the carved scales of the alliraptor's back. Her other is pinned beneath her husband's limp body. Though he sleeps, she can't even close her eyes. A thick, warm breeze slithers through the lattice walls, finding her eyelashes, her toes, every exposed hair on her body.

It's too much.

Standing carefully, Iriset leaves Lyric to pad quietly down the twist of stairs into the greeting room, and from there goes down again into their bathing room. A panel beside the entrance activates light with a touch, and the ecstatic chandelier drips in eight simple lines, filling the room with a pale glow. Iriset washes her face, then runs a warm bath in the pool sunk into the floor.

It's many hours until dawn, and she slips in without oil or perfume or bubbles, only herself and the water, cradled in the belly of the pool. The moment the water laps at her chin, her breath shudders.

She did it. She is here. She *is* the best.

So what?

Singix, whom she *loved*, is dead and unremembered. Iriset killed a *friend* with raw design.

Iriset has never bothered to pretend her work primarily

served good—she knows what her father has been, knows her ambitions were for herself, not the progress of justice. Silk might chase flight and tensile strength and healing—all manner of things that *could* improve lives, but that wasn't why she did it.

Alone in an echoing bathroom, Iriset can't help thinking Singix would be so disappointed in her. Iriset is no better than the Vertex Seal, struggling to maintain a brutal system with equal brutality. Using her genius for this kind of design proves nothing but that she is just as willing to harm a few in order for *her* legacy to stand.

Iriset grips her fists around each other, pressing them to her sternum beneath the water, where the marriage knot coils. She has to keep it together. Keep herself—everything—together.

She breathes. She trembles. Her distress (and the pulse of her pain through their marriage knot) draws Lyric to her. He kneels beside the pool in a thin robe and brushes damp hair back from her face and touches her mouth, and when she brings up her arms he drags her out onto the floor, both of them soaked.

"I'm sorry," she whispers, and he hugs her tightly.

"What for?" he asks, stunned. He strokes her hair.

Iriset shakes her head and realizes his presence alone has drawn her ecstatic sobs into a gentler rhythm.

The Vertex Seal stands and lifts her into his arms. He carries her up and up the twisting corridor and back to their bed, where he kisses her cheeks and palms, where he caresses her thighs and belly, until she begs in short, hot whispering cries for his fingers to reach inside her and his tongue to press at the hollow of her throat.

24

Euphemisms

Attendants arrive early to begin their day. Lyric climbs quietly out of bed and brushes his fingers along Iriset's cheek as her eyes flicker open. Together—everything for the following few days will be done together—they stretch and accept coffee and morning tonics. They're bathed and fed a simple breakfast. Lyric asks if she'd like to exercise and Iriset says she'll only make them both sweaty again if they're allowed. He clearly meant would she like to walk or lift weights or join him in a combat formation, and after she makes her sexual insinuation, Iriset lowers her eyes and manages to put on the appearance of shyness with her hands against her warm cheeks. Two of the attendants hide smiles.

It's the Day of the Crowning Sun, the turning point of the year, and Lyric is needed for an elaborate ritual that will last most of the day. Iriset will be at his side for its entirety. They are dressed in simple robes that match in style, though Iriset's is a brighter red than the rust color of Aharté's priests that her husband prefers. The attendant who assists her is Shahd, as she had requested, and Iriset is careful to hide her delight at a familiar face. Shahd has no reason to stand out from the others yet. Then Garnet appears with Menna mé Garai, the Architect of the Seal, and Iriset has a moment of panic she carefully hides under a patina of polite bashfulness. Garnet tells Lyric in his low rumbling voice that his mother wishes to join them for the evening meal, and Amaranth and Sidoné as well. Sidoné will have to be content with Garnet's company, the body-twin says, and Lyric deal alone with his mother and sister and wife. It's said with humor and Lyric nods as if Garnet makes such choices for him all the time.

While Garnet speaks, Menna approaches with a long box of design paint. She bows and Lyric glances at Iriset. "Today will you match my face in symbol, wife?"

She agrees, and the Architect of the Seal uses a thin brush to slide lines of black and white against their cheeks. It's a simple pattern, incorporating the basic sigils of the four forces.

The art tickles Iriset's cheek, but Menna doesn't notice the craftmask. Of course she doesn't, Iriset chides herself, struggling to keep from clenching her jaw. Menna didn't notice the craftmask three nights ago when she'd been most vulnerable; she won't now. Not even the Silent priests noticed! Iriset *is* the exquisite, soft Singix Es Sun, and nobody is looking for anything beneath her beauty.

While she's being painted, Lyric and Garnet step aside for a quiet, private conference. The larger man looms over her husband, but with an air of protectiveness that Iriset recognizes from her father's court: Garnet will die to keep Lyric from harm. It goes beyond friendship and brotherhood, beyond his assigned role as body-twin.

If her crimes are revealed, even if somehow she convinces Lyric to spare her, Garnet méra Bež will kill her for hurting his brother.

The moment of pinnacle eclipse, when the sun is a brilliant crescent of fire capping the moon, is the moment of communion, when everything that the empire is—every person alive and dead, every memory and hope for the future, every building and stone, every force-ribbon and reaching, hungry military front—comes together for the singular purpose of balanced Silence under the command of the Vertex Seal. It's the holiest moment in the year.

When the sun reaches its vertex, the ruler of the empire reseals power itself into place.

Who knows if Aharté even pays attention?

For hours before the eclipse, priests lead groups of carefully curated representatives through patterns of movements and meditation, aligning massive lines of design through the human bodies. As the sun begins its pinnacle slip, everyone falls quiet, waiting for the tiny ring of a crystal to hone their voices sharper. Shadows cast by tiny obelisks and spiral pennants bend into slices, crescent upon crescent layering as the sun passes behind the moon. A hum begins at the edges of the crowd, creeping nearer and nearer to the center at a perfectly measured pace until the sun itself arrives at its peak.

Lyric waits for the precise moment beside the throne, in the Hall of Princes, where upon the carved back of the chair is etched this line: *one claimed with blood and paired with hunger, always binding.* His is the blood, cut from his arm and cupped into a shallow bowl. He kneels before the moon rock and, when it's time, presses a handprint to the surface. Iriset watches as the blood is absorbed.

Impossible, but she sees it.

The hunger belongs to the Moon-Eater's Mistress, who wakes her god during the eclipse and feeds him from her body. When the blood and the hunger meet beneath the crown of sunlight, the entire crater embracing Moonshadow City trembles from steeple to steeple.

It breathes.

Probably that is the only truly necessary point of the ritual, the part that binds the massive design into place. But the rest of the rite is important for people, for demonstrating the significance of individuals and neighborhoods: Representatives from every part of the Holy Empire, blessed with the songs and blood of their homes, link hands and breathe, give fire and sighs, spit, and blood into the ritual. For hours it builds to the crescendo, for hours it fades, bubbling and sinking like alcohol into the lifeblood of the empire. Family feasts and neighborhood parties follow, folk drowsy with the heat and echoing chimes. No businesses open, and even the army relaxes its grip—it was a good time for the undermarket, called the Sweet Night in the Little Cat's court, because though it's the shortest night of the year, it often produces the sweetest results.

There's balance to that, too: The Crowning Sun ritual reaffirms the structures of the empire, and so of course it creates pockets of shadow in which the undermarket can thrive.

Iriset has never attended the ritual before, though she's been to several after-parties in the Saltbath precinct, both with her father's court and with her grandparents.

Watching it from the center, she can see the whole thing so very clearly.

Aside from the resealing of blood and hunger, it's a sham. A performance. Pretense. A great big mask to fit over the whole empire, like saying *She passed away* when you mean she died.

The empire is balanced? The empire eliminates outliers, the marginalized or mighty, anyone or thing that disturbs equilibrium. The empire is holy? The empire makes laws and enforces faith by burning to the earth any counterbelief, creating a One God Aharté by destroying her rivals. The empire welcomes new citizens? It drags children from parents and forces them to change their names, their clothes, and beliefs. It rewards assimilation like it's the only way to be happy.

This is why there is no room for genius or change here. No room for difference. Apostasy is the worst of crimes because it seeks power outside of the Holy Design. Maintaining these rituals—the Crowning Sun, the Days of Mercy, the Glorious Vow, all of them—reinforces the Holy Design. It literally reseals the design put in place by the Holy Syr that runs from throne to steeples and across the force-ribbons to the edges of the empire. But it also pins the design back down in everyone's minds. Makes a holy rite of erasure.

Iriset is a little impressed.

But now that she's used her apostasy to infiltrate the center of the Holy Design, she wonders if she can find a way to change the Holy Design itself—or tear it all apart. That would matter. That would be a fitting tribute to the princess whose life she's stolen.

If it's possible for intellectual exercise alone to push a person into full-out rebellion, she's nearly all the way there.

———— • ◆ • ————

Iriset is exhausted once the rituals finish, though she did little but stand or kneel at her husband's side.

They retire to their rooms to drink water and rest. Lyric holds her hand, eyes lit with passion—not for her but for his god. The empire has withstood another year, and if he can make it so, it will withstand another. Despite his misgivings.

Lyric believes her to be his partner in that endeavor now.

The more time they spend together, the stronger their binding will be. That's conventional wisdom surrounding the marriage rite, but as Iriset lies there, aware of her inner design as she never was before—aware so fundamentally that she thinks she just might be able to stop her own heart from beating if she tries or, with a twist of will, squeeze the alcohol out of her bloodstream, or stop her stomach from broadcasting its hunger—Iriset realizes that the binding is already complete. The egg did its job entirely when she and Lyric kissed, weaving their designs together so well that Iriset could go around the world this instant and still feel the shape of his pulse.

That's going to be a problem.

Only consent or death can break the marriage knot. Lyric will never agree to dissolving it without knowing the truth. There can only be death or confession, if Iriset wishes to be free. Unless, of course, she finds a way to undo it herself.

She wonders if Amaranth intends to kill her. It must be part of at least some of her plans.

Iriset closes her eyes and tries, for once, to stop thinking about problems she can't solve today.

• ♦ •

Dinner is served in an adjoining suite and Diaa of Moonshadow already waits when Iriset and Lyric arrive.

Iriset took comfort in Diaa when they first met, for Diaa made her feel welcome in the palace, with a falling energy that drew Iriset's old maternal wounds closed ever so slightly. She expects that Diaa will be just as welcoming to her son's actual wife as she inexplicably was to the nobody handmaiden daughter of the Little Cat.

How incorrect her expectations turn out to be! Diaa is rather cool toward her—toward Singix.

Blinking away her surprise when Diaa merely nods greeting, brushing her fingers to one eye in a half-respectful, slightly dismissive gesture, Iriset leans nearer to Lyric. Both to remind Diaa of her loyalties and discover if Lyric noticed.

He doesn't seem to, but touches her back, between her shoulder blades, and leads her to a low, cushioned chair around the long brazier-table. Instead of coals in the iron center of the table, chunks of ice melt, releasing the cold smell of mint leaves that were frozen into the ice. A charge of ecstatic force refreezes the drops of water where they collect in a basin.

Diaa kneels across from her and smiles slightly—but it's a smile for a stranger.

Lyric reclines across several pillows with his shoulder touching Iriset's elbow, and Diaa's gaze slides between them. "How is the bond taking?"

"Mother," Lyric says with gentle censure.

Iriset ducks her face, though she would prefer to narrow her eyes and reply with a biting observation.

"I remember the intensity and disorientation, loves," Diaa says, reaching for the narrow crystal pitcher of pear wine. She pours two small cups, then some water. "There are few who can understand your situation, and I thought"—here she sets the water cup before her son—"that you might like to speak of it before the arrival of your overwhelming sister."

The explanation seems acceptable to Lyric, who plucks the water up and sips, then says, "I feel strong, not disoriented."

Iriset nods, leaning her arm against his. She wants to kiss his hair, for it shines, waving softly around his ears, and there are small curls stuck to the back of his neck. Her pulse quickens and Lyric tilts his face up to meet her eyes with an understanding smile.

"I see," Diaa says, amused. She raises her cup of wine. "And I am glad of it. I was concerned the match would be too overtly political for the binding to reach your hearts so quickly."

"An unnecessary concern, Mother," Lyric says, command in his low tone.

She hums an unconvinced note, and Iriset murmurs, "I will be what he needs me to be, Your Glory."

"Of course, child," Diaa says, nodding at the second cup of wine.

Iriset takes it and drinks, saved from further conversation by Amaranth's arrival.

The Moon-Eater's Mistress blows in like a thunderstorm, billowing and determined. She kisses her mother's hand and sits with a groan, arms stretching above her. "What a long day this always is," she complains.

"And must be," Lyric says.

"And must be," Amaranth echoes, not quite mocking.

She looks to Iriset, who says, "I've never witnessed anything like it. The empire is truly great."

Amaranth's mouth opens as if to laugh, but instead she snaps her lips shut and snorts.

Diaa pours Amaranth a cup of wine. "When will Iriset be unraveled?"

Iriset can't stop the stiffening of her entire body.

Amaranth and Lyric stare at their mother for a moment, and Diaa purses her lips. "I quite liked her, you know."

"I have arranged with the Silent priests and Raia mér Omorose for the ritual tomorrow morning," Amaranth admits.

The Vertex Seal slowly sets his cup down, and his fingers linger against it before he draws a deep breath. "I will attend."

"The body has waited too long already," Amaranth says, almost apologetic. "And tomorrow is our only chance before... Well, there will be other unravelings to concern us after the executions and whatever mercy is or is not granted."

"I know," Lyric says.

"Poor girl," Diaa of Moonshadow murmurs.

Iriset closes her eyes, her stomach grown tight and cold. Thinking not of the ritual but of her father. Tomorrow she needs to find time to analyze the state of the anchors for her distraction array, and find out where exactly she'll be during the execution in case she can still set the trigger, and hope, hope, hope Bittor manages to save him. He must. Then Iriset can flee, too. Iriset whispers, "She died for me. Allow me to attend with you, husband."

Lyric touches her knee. "You are my wife, not my subordinate. You may go and do as you prefer."

"Has there been some progress discovering who placed the poison?" Iriset asks both her husband and Amaranth.

The latter shakes her head. "The people with access are being narrowed down and questioned, and we have a list of suspects, but nothing for you to worry about right now. Focus on the start of your marriage."

Iriset frowns and doesn't allow herself to toy with her cup. "It concerns me so greatly, Your Glory. If I can help in any way, I would like to."

"Until we catch the criminal, you can help by not getting killed."

"Ama," Lyric chides.

"Sometimes frank conversation pins the right forces in place, brother, rather than elaborate knotting around the center."

Iriset says, "It is all right, Lyric. I am fond of Her Glory's… forthright… ways. And I must, if nothing else, remain alive for you—for the empire."

"At least until you've given us a couple of heirs," teases Amaranth. But the Vertex Seal ignores his sister, frowning at Iriset as if not liking something in her words. It bothers her not to know where her misstep was.

"I noticed some people yesterday who seemed to dislike me," she says quickly, eyes downcast. "Two in particular. A young mirané woman with a plain but beautiful mask adorned with tiny gems in the shape of rain, and an older miran in almost all white, but a half-mask of copper and opals."

"Those are good details to remember," Lyric says.

"The masks are still quite a novelty, to me," she tells him, glancing up at his approving nod.

"Ager mé Aialen," Amaranth says. "The young one. Those were all diamonds."

Diaa sighs sharply. "She dislikes that it wasn't she on the wedding seat."

Lyric grimaces, and Iriset nods. Jealousy was correct—and possibly a motive for murder.

"Is she on your list?" Lyric asks his sister, who answers no.

"Ager would need an ally with better access. Maybe one of her parents, though. But I think the woman in the half-mask was Naira mé Rinore."

"Yes," Diaa agrees. "Naira had it designed to connect with her sister's mask."

Iriset has heard that name. "Does she have reason to dislike me?"

"She was vociferously against your marriage," Amaranth drawls.

"Oh Holy Silence," Diaa says dismissively. "Naira would never stoop to something so vulgar as murder. And in such a sloppy way!"

Amaranth laughs with what sounds like true delight. "An excellent defense of your old crony, Mother."

Diaa purses her lips. "May I summon our meal now, or will there be more unappetizing talk?"

"One thing, please, Your Glory." It's easy for Iriset to let her face fall into sorrow as she stares at the half-filled cup of wine before her. "Ambassador Erxan. Is he... his body...?"

"It's being treated in the Ceres traditions," Lyric says gently, touching her knuckles. He slides his fingers along hers to link them. "With help from the attendants you and he brought with you. We'll send him home properly."

"Did you determine how he died?" Diaa asks. "Non-miran are so susceptible to poison."

"Heart attack," Amaranth says. "No sign of poison, either mundane or architectural."

Iriset squeezes her eyes shut. "May I have a moment with him before he goes? There are... prayers I would make."

"Of course." Lyric lifts Iriset's hand and places it near her wine cup.

With a very slight smile, she takes his advice and drinks it. The first chance she gets, she'll corner Amaranth alone and make her explain more about this investigation. Demand names. Who to look out for, the security measures they're taking—surely they'll give her a taster or something annoying, or extra Seal guards.

"Mother?" Lyric says.

Diaa sighs and claps her hands, summoning attendants with their meal.

For the rest of the evening, Iriset quietly listens to the conversation—mostly directed by Amaranth—absorbing the talk without participating. Topics range from the usual mirané gossip to troop movements at the Bow border. The latter Lyric shies away from, claiming it's business for after the Days of Mercy, to be discussed with General Bey and his miran, not at dinner the night after his marriage. Diaa and Amaranth share a look that clearly says they'll speak of it alone later since he refuses. Lyric says if they wish to discuss martial concerns, better to spend it speculating on where the rebels in the Rivermouth district are getting their money. It can't all be traced to the undermarket, especially given the recent abrupt changes to that undermarket. Which suggests they have a patron wealthy enough to hide the losses or scheming enough to wash it. Diaa makes an offhand comment about tax credits for the barges moving through that district, which begins an involved argument about repairs to the Crimson Canyon, necessary before the autumn rains, and designing a new channel for balance in the south. Lyric is interested in a proposal from the Third School that balance might be achieved with a suspension bridge instead of a channel, if the bridge is designed precisely.

("Aren't they all designed precisely," Amaranth drawls, rolling her eyes briefly to Iriset.)

Iriset, frustrated she can't make her valuable architectural opinions known, stares hard at her pumpkinseed cake, glad there's no need to grow used to a life cloistered by ignorance in return for good sex. There are two days until her father's execution and then she'll be gone, too.

Thinking of leaving, though, makes her stomach twist.

Because her pulse beats in time with her husband's. It *feels* as though she belongs here.

When it's finally time to depart, she tries to maneuver herself alone with Amaranth, but Her Glory maneuvers against it, denying Iriset a private word, so she retires with her husband without the chance to interrogate Amaranth.

When they reach their greeting room, Iriset dismisses the waiting attendants. She can tend to her husband, she says quietly, and should while the binding sets. Her encouraging smile draws complicit smiles from the attendants.

"Do you mind if I work for a little while?" Lyric asks when they're alone.

She does mind, but supposes she can't, and nods her reassurance before drifting into the bathroom. There's no way to sneak out alone to look at her array, so she might as well take advantage of this magnificent pool for a no-crying soak.

Unfortunately, she wakes up with water in her nose, coughing painfully from having slipped under the water as she dozed. It ends her bath on a sour note, and so Iriset is cranky when she walks into the half-circle study.

The entire north end is open to the air—but no, a force-lattice spreads from the tall shelves in the east to the tiled windcatcher column in the west. Iriset gasps in surprise and interest, feeling the tender web of flow and falling that keeps the wind from sucking anything out the open wall.

Lyric sits in the embrace of a crescent desk, vellum spread before him, and several thin books and ink styli. He stares, unmoving, at the work. Iriset walks quietly past him to the open wall. Without touching the energy, she gazes out at the nighttime palace complex. Shadows shimmer over the layered domes and steeples, and overhead the stars smear together. They're so full and bright around the pale, fixed moon. She can even see the squat, night-blue Moon-Eater's Temple.

Turning to her husband, she places a hand on his bare shoulder. "What do you study so intently?"

Her eyes fall to the work: It's an elaborate diagram of four-point stars and eight-point stars settled within one another, and words put down at every point, dotted with either white, black, green, or blue to indicate their force alignment.

It's the city, marked up with arrows and lines of design in order to show not only the more powerful ribbons, but what's happening in each neighborhood or district. By the balance of areas marked more heavily with black or blue, a glance could teach you where balance itself struggles. It's magnificent.

She thinks of the multidimensional design diagram she'd been constructing for her father the day they were imprisoned. That design had been alive, and once installed would have changed, pulsed, breathed with Moonshadow City and all its security. The realization that the Vertex Seal would be served as well by such a creation puts a cold rock in her stomach.

Lyric says, "I have these made regularly, that I may compare them and learn the flow of change in my city. It's a map of forces. Some places are inherently more one force or another—the Saltbath is very grounded in falling, and pockets of rebellion always darken these black, ecstatic streaks. Streets where artists sell their wares tend to drift between flow and rising."

Iriset understands perfectly but can't admit so. Lyric continues, "I want to contemplate where to push or pull, not only with policy or my command to the army, but who I can forgive when they ask, what names I should consider for making mercy. There are so many reasons I cannot grant it to…" Lyric shakes his head. "There are ways to think about the Holy Design, and individuals, so many philosophies, and I try to make choices based on all of them together."

Iriset says, "This map is to help you understand—to feel—her Design. The view of the city from the surface of Aharté's moon."

The surprise in his gaze when it meets hers turns swiftly to excitement. "You...understand."

Iriset wants to say, *And if you truly understood, would you push it to be more efficient, more wild, more interesting and creative? Make it better?* because that is what she said the night in the Color Can Be Loud Garden. When she was herself.

But all she says is "I learn to understand *you*, husband," and takes his face in her hands.

As she leans to kiss him, she notices a scrap of vellum with very different writing on it: a scrawled note, in ink that impressed itself hard into the vellum because of the passion of the writer. It says, *No ambition in the Vertex Seal!*

Iriset pauses, lips parted to take her kiss, eyes locked on the note.

She said that to him. And he wrote it down like it mattered.

Her pulse speeds with the thrill of it, the knowledge that Lyric held her challenge dear enough to put it in the margin of his plans, where he cannot help but be interrupted by the thought, the urge, to be better.

"Iriset mé Isidor said that to me," he murmurs, pulling her onto his lap. He wraps one arm around her waist and with the other reaches to touch his finger to the curling mark that negates *ambition* in the mirané characters, changing it to *no ambition*.

She sinks into his embrace, remaining quiet. Almost without thinking she aligns her breath with his—easy while his chest presses to her back.

Lyric lets his hand fall onto her knee. "I came here to think about her."

The honesty might have gutted Singix Es Sun with betrayal, that her new husband thinks so tenderly and kindly on a dead girl, but it guts Iriset with cold clarity: No matter what he stands for as the Vertex Seal, as a man he does not give mere scraps of himself. He only gives his whole. Because he married her, he gives every part of himself to her. Even this kind of sincerity that could cut her as easily as it might comfort. He is breathtaking.

When he realizes the truth, it will be catastrophic.

He adds, "Tomorrow I will attend her unraveling. And the day after tomorrow, her father will die. They'll both be gone. A criminal and—I suspect—an apostate. I cannot stop thinking of her. I'm sorry."

Globules of sorrow drip down Iriset's body like honey on a wire. Because she's alive, she feels her death as such a contradiction. While his feelings are so plain.

Iriset only hesitates for a moment before speaking. "For her...why can you not grant mercy to her father? She made such an impression upon you."

"She did." Lyric tightens his grip around her waist. "But it is not so simple as that. If I were only a man, maybe it would be enough to let him live because she died, because she sacrificed her life for yours. But I am the Vertex Seal and my mercy is..."

Iriset waits, breathing with him.

"Complicated," he murmurs finally. "Not my own to give." Lyric buries his face in her hair, breathing deeply.

Closing her eyes against the betraying desire tingling her skin where his breath touches her scalp, Iriset changes the subject. "What does it mean? No ambition in the Vertex Seal?"

"She said if I did not strive to make the world better, I was wasting my power. She said it was better to push the empire toward peace and...thriving. But we do promote peace, and the empire does thrive. Only, people cannot accept what is necessary to thrive with it. Our laws are strict but necessary. We welcome people into a better way, and there must be a price for that. I cannot see how it could be otherwise. Rebels and cults could tear it all down if they were allowed to exist, and exceptions weaken the Holy Design. If I began to push in any one direction, the entire thing would be in danger of breaking."

"You are joining with Ceres without breaking. Without conquest, without destroying my people. We are making something new."

His arm tightens around her again. "That is what Amaranth wants. I see the power in such thinking. But I also believe Iriset mé Isidor would say our marriage maintains justice, only. Does not create it. Because do we not expect our children to be mirané? You will become one of us, not the other way. It is still conquest, even if it is peaceful."

Bitterness tinges his voice, and Iriset still doesn't know what to say.

"She was right," he whispers.

Twisting in his lap, she tries to meet his gaze, to catch the mirané-brown sparks around his irises, but Lyric stares unseeing at the words scrawled upon his vellum. He says, "I do not know how to see good in other people, how to trust in the goodness. I only let myself expect the worst. How else can I rule, how else can I bind the empire together for the benefit of the greatest number of people? People do not naturally turn toward justice."

Iriset swallows her ecstatic force, swallows the cry she wishes to make, to shake him, slap him, bite at his lips until he breaks open and is brave. She swallows it because this entire conversation has nothing to do with her lies, with this perfect craftmask. What does she know about justice and bravery, anyway? She's a prideful apostate, and never before cared about anything but herself and her family. Yet Lyric méra Esmail His Glory, the Vertex Seal, is *haunted* by that single night they argued together in the Color Can Be Loud Garden.

She haunts him.

And if she convinces him now to be brave, to strive to be better, what will happen when he learns the truth? She knows already it will be shattering. What will Lyric become when she breaks his faith?

"I'll show you something good," she whispers, desperate for it to be true. She stands from his lap, holding his hand. "If you come to bed."

With a weary smile, Lyric follows.

25

About mercy and its costs

The unraveling of Iriset mé Isidor takes place just past dawn, as soon as the Moon-Eater's Mistress joins them after awakening her god.

There's no question of Iriset staying away. Not only does she need to make certain the craftmask holds, but her sheer curiosity eclipses any other consideration. Who could resist such temptation as one's own funeral?

The simple ritual is held in the Silent Chapel, within an octagonal chamber designed for such things. The walls are plain stucco, anchored with thin silicate crystals that welcome resonance from every force. No ceiling covers them; instead the sky itself melts brighter blue overhead, and the floor is the solid rock of the crater.

Singix's body—so perfectly disguised—lies upon the earth, head aligned to the north, within the confines of a diamond of sprinkled salt. She's wrapped in strips of red cloth woven especially for death, every inch of her covered but for her face, which is painted with force-sigils.

Iriset has a rough time looking at it.

With her are Lyric, Amaranth, Sidoné, Garnet, three Silent priests, two Seal guards, Her Glory's three remaining handmaidens, Nielle, Diaa of Moonshadow, and Raia mér Omorose. Iriset wants to stand with Raia, who doesn't bother to hide the tears filling ans eyes. An kneels beside the body's shoulder and touches fingers to the wrapped flesh. "I'd like one of the echo coins," an says to nobody in particular.

As one of the priests quietly instructs Raia in the basics of the ritual so an can act for one of them, there's a quiet disturbance from outside, and another priest enters. She goes directly toward Lyric and murmurs softly to him. He nods, and a moment later Iriset's grandparents are ushered in.

Her entire body goes rigid. As they bow deeply to the Vertex Seal, touching their eyes over white cloth masks, Iriset tucks her head against Lyric's shoulder. She cannot possibly look at them, only clings to her husband, grateful she can act this way without suspicion. It takes all her concentration to mitigate the harsh expression of ecstatic shock and smooth it into slow, sorrowful flow before Lyric notices something is actually wrong.

Everything is arranged as the priest who brought in Iriset's grandparents leads out both Seal guards to keep the participant number at sixteen. Lyric gently hands Iriset to Amaranth while he takes a place among the priests, opposite Raia. Iriset is not surprised Lyric requires no instruction in the role. One priest hands around perfectly balanced force-masks for everyone to wear: The unraveling requires absolute balance of design to achieve completion.

Lyric places himself in the east, where rising force dominates. Everyone arrays themselves in the proper quad structure, like points in overlapping eight-point stars. Iriset stands with

Amaranth in the west, where falling dominates. Her grandparents are together in the north, for her grandmother has a strong ecstatic force. Next to her grandmother, her grandfather is holding a bouquet of night-blooming eris flowers. The kind Iriset used to bring him when she visited.

It never occurred to Iriset that they would—could—be here.

"Everyone born to Silence may return to it," Lyric says. He doesn't speak up, for it's a small chamber and everyone listens carefully. "Aharté confirms the patterns, her Holy Design having neither beginning nor end, but only the consummation of perfect Silence. For the point that was Iriset mé Isidor in life, and continues to be in the memories we hold, in the various echoes she marked into the pattern—those we recognize, and those we cannot—this is both end and beginning."

The words are traditional, and though Iriset has heard them before, hearing the prayer applied to herself is disconcerting to say the least. She stops listening, wondering what point there is to any of it, and she remembers, as she dislikes to remember, that this is not the first false funeral she's attended. Then, there'd been no unraveling, but only a memorial, and she cried despite the lack of precipitating death. Folk of the undermarket had sung discordant songs of sorrow and missing threads, broken patterns.

Iriset finds herself crying, unable to look at her grandparents, thinking of her mother, and of Singix herself, hidden beneath the craftmask unmourned. Every blink sparks ecstatic energy, and her tears drag falling. She sways gently and glances up, up, up to the sky, wishing to leap away into the growing brilliance of morning light.

That is the rising force.

Every force makes its presence known as the two priests,

Raia, and the Vertex Seal each place a soft coin of smoky quartz around the body.

Then they spread a basic force-web across her—Singix—it—and begin a soft humming song to strengthen the four forces.

The moment of unraveling is touched off by Raia mér Omorose, who also cries. An carefully uses a stylus to begin the vibration through the webbing. The vibration trembles in Iriset's molars, uncomfortable and intense, but brief.

What once was flesh and bone, soul and force, what once was a human being—Singix of the Beautiful Twilight, sweet, curious, anxious—dissipates into threads of force.

The craftmask dissolves a split second before Singix's true face does, but it's in a blur of unraveling, features and bone structure a smear. Relief bends Iriset's knees, but she makes herself remain upright.

Together Raia, the priests, and Lyric sing a different force-note: sharp, uplifting, descending, and warbling. They draw the forces into the quartz coins, and as the final scraps of the body pass through the resonant crystal, an echo is marked into it, a memory only.

Then it's over. Nothing remains within the salt-diamond.

Iriset reaches for Amaranth, needing just to hold on to something. And Amaranth *knows*. Nobody else here but she and Sidoné knows what is real, or what's happening to Iriset. Her Glory takes her hand and steps out of place to draw Iriset under her arm in an embrace. Amaranth is both soft and sturdy, thrumming with energy from her recent encounter with the Moon-Eater and this ritual. That first morning Iriset went with Amaranth to her holy ministrations, she thought that love was a knot of forces. This feels like a knot of forces, too, and is powerful like love, only it hurts so much.

Iriset supposes pain doesn't make it any less a part of love. Maybe love is as inherently divisive as it is engaging.

(She grows nearer to the truth every day.)

Iriset is lucky and is not required to talk to her grandparents. It would be false and unkind of her to approach them as Singix. She goes with Lyric as he speaks with the Holy Peace, the white-haired old miran who leads the Silent Chapel. The priest asks to touch their marriage threads, and Iriset offers her hand for the old woman. Lyric glances at her, surprised, then offers the same.

The Holy Peace blesses them for the strength of their binding, and makes a comment about children that doesn't concern Iriset, lost in thoughts as she is (and given the contraceptive net she personally wove into her own reproductive system). Lyric weaves their fingers together and takes her away. Though when they arrive at the gaping archway leading out of the Silent Chapel, Garnet waits there. By his expression, even Iriset knows he needs the immediate attention of the Vertex Seal.

She pauses, and Lyric holds up his free hand to halt Garnet before turning to her. She lifts her chin and smiles gently. "Even the Holy Peace believes our binding thrives, Your Glory. If you are required, I'll go with your sister for the morning."

He doesn't return her smile, but studies her eyes, his irises twitching so slightly as he glances from one eye to the other and back. "Our binding does thrive," he murmurs. "Will you join me again for the eclipse?"

"Yes."

"And after, perhaps, spend the afternoon with me?" A certain vulnerability leaks into his request.

"I would like nothing better." Iriset infuses truth into the answer and lifts herself lightly onto her toes to brush her lips against his.

Lyric catches her hands and tugs just enough to keep her near. He puts his forehead against hers. "Today is the Day of Self-Mercy, and I am notoriously bad at observing it on a personal level. Having you with me is a mercy that perhaps I can allow myself."

Reminding herself harshly that he doesn't speak such romance to her but to the woman he believes her to be, Iriset manages not to melt. She nods against him, and he slips away.

Two Seal guards remain with her, as well as Shahd. Iriset asks the girl, "Did you see where Her Glory went?"

"Her Glory is spending the day in the amphitheater." Shahd bows and gestures for Iriset to follow.

As they walk across the edge of the Crystal Desert back into the palace complex, Iriset sinks her awareness through her feet, glad her slippers are thin. She can pick up echoes of the security net like this, and slightly detour on the way to Amaranth to check on two anchors at least. Amaranth will give her answers about the execution tomorrow, even if Her Glory doesn't like to.

The security net hums softly, pinging it the way it...

Iriset stops.

She kneels suddenly, touching the warm crystal with the palm of her hand.

It's different.

It's all shifted toward falling, which is not the trajectory-bind they'd worked with before.

Someone changed the design of the Crystal Desert security. Just enough that any paths or design-pockets or keys couldn't penetrate now, not without a new map, without the new codes. If they changed it here, it will be changed throughout, and tomorrow when the army and investigator-designers activate their new measures for the executions, not only will the map Iriset sent Bittor be useless, there's no way she can redesign and re-create her distraction swiftly enough.

"Your Glory!" Shahd cries softly, bending to grasp her arm. The Seal guards have formed up around her.

"I'm... well." Iriset covers Shahd's hand with her other and stands. It must have been after Singix was murdered. *Of course* they changed the security. How dare Iriset not think sooner! "I am. It is hot so early, and I have not yet been apart so distantly from my new husband."

"We can return you to him instead, Your Glory."

"No." She insists her mouth smile for the attendant. "I must accustom myself. And I am. Please."

Shahd studies her, and Iriset does her best to tamp down on the reeling anxiety eager to express itself. Finally the mirané girl nods and holds Iriset's elbow as they continue on around the broad side of the Gallery of Shades, through an outdoor path beneath rare wooden archways curling with tiny tea roses and raspberry vines.

Iriset uses the pace of her walking to count her breaths and lock it all down. She's so fucked. Bittor will be on his own, without a distraction from her. She's already tried talking to Lyric about granting the Little Cat mercy, and he won't change his mind. Should she leave tonight? Slip out while Lyric sleeps and cut her way through to her father? Or lie in wait for the execution when they bring him out? Can she use her hands to get past the Seal guard with bursts of power the way she killed Erxan? Or wait until the execution and *then* kill someone? Lyric himself? That would be quite the distraction. But she'd be sacrificing herself to it, and her father would be furiously unforgiving.

Her stomach churns.

"Your Glory," Shahd murmurs, leaning in. "I have never seen someone take to the marriage bond so strongly that it changed the way they walk."

"Huh?" Iriset says, so confused.

"Your walk is different," Shahd continues in her quiet way.

Iriset slows down. "My walk."

"Yes. Your Glory." Shahd stops and glances briefly at Iriset's eyes. "We live and we die."

Iriset stares, stunned, at Shahd. It doesn't even occur to her to fake her way through this. Instead she tugs Shahd to the shade of a massive force-fan along the path across the Blue Between Sea and Sky Courtyard. She waves the Seal guards back. "How the fuck did you know?" she whispers so fast it's more of a hiss. "My walk? You're joking."

"Your design tools were gone. The night Iriset—you—died. I thought...and then I watched and listened, and...because I was listening, your voice was..." Shahd swallows. Again. Maybe she's going to vomit. But she says, "When Sidoné told me I was to be yours, I thought it was the reason."

"And?"

"And what?"

Iriset makes her face hard, hoping no one passes by. "What are you going to do about it?"

Shahd drops to her knees and covers her eyes. "Your Glory," she wails very softly.

"Ah, get up. Get up." Iriset drags her by the forearms.

"I won't do anything," Shahd says. "Just what I am doing. What I have done. And you'll keep protecting my family."

Shaking her head, Iriset starts them walking again. "Iriset mé Isidor is dead. She can't help you."

Shahd nods and shifts them so that she's once again holding Iriset's elbow, as if escorting her.

"Then what do you want?" Iriset presses quietly.

"Being the favored attendant of the wife of the Vertex Seal is more than I thought to achieve in the palace," she says. "And..."

"And?"

Shahd hesitates on her next step. "What you have done is..."

Iriset waits for fear, condemnation, disgust; she's not quite sure.

"Humbling," Shahd whispers, eyes lowered.

"Hmm." Iriset truly has no idea what to do other than accept this revelation for the moment. Shahd can't just have a heart attack, too. "All right. But tell me if something changes for you."

Shahd nods. "What happened back there? Are you all right?"

"I can't help save my father like this," she says bitterly.

"Can I...?" Shahd looks at the path ahead of them, eyes lowered properly. Her face is shaded from the biting sun by the ruffled cloth mask on her forehead.

If Iriset could think of anything useful, she'd send Shahd out again. But there's no time for her to rebuild her array. Or even to adjust it. What could Shahd even tell Bittor? Besides, it isn't worth the risk. And there's one more avenue Iriset can pursue right now.

Just before they enter the Seven Petals Are Not Enough Amphitheater, Iriset covers Shahd's hand with her own. After a moment, Iriset says, "Thank you."

―・◆・―

Because it's the Days of Mercy, no lecture is ongoing in the amphitheater. Instead, Amaranth has taken it over. Massive paper umbrellas have been erected and force-fans spin lazily in the air, their opalescent blades moving the warm morning breezes in eddies and spirals. Strips of linen ripple across the open roof, held in place with design and creating shade in undulating waves. Upon the lecturing stage, a line of young men and women perform acrobatics and sensual dancing while Amaranth watches from one of the low steps, surrounded by her handmaidens and extra attendants with food and cold drinks. A scattering of miran sprawl around, too, calling compliments to the dancers and conversing with Her Glory.

Iriset pauses before joining the opulence; she doesn't feel prepared to sink into the abundance here, the luxury. She's too tense, her shock too great, and her inner design tight—brittle, even.

But Istof Nefru, the non-mirané handmaiden who speaks seven languages (excluding Ceres, fortunately) and moves like a graceful river heron, notices her. "Your Glory!" she calls, lifting a long arm to wave.

Amaranth smiles. She is unpainted for the day, because of the unraveling. Her natural beauty is bold, like the sun: Everything revolves around her. "You have detached yourself from my brother, sister! Yet you wander alone with hardly any attendants! Join us."

A pillow is vacated for Iriset, and she reclines upon it as though she's an exquisite eggshell, easily shattered. Unlike the others in their sleeveless robes and masks, Iriset is weighed down by the hot, colorful finery of Ceres. "Is this"—she gestures at the dancers, the force-fans, the brunch—"how you grant yourself mercy, Your Glory?"

Though not a trace of sarcasm shows itself in her voice, Amaranth's smile tilts wryly. "I beg mercy every day from the

Moon-Eater himself, Princess. And he grants it. If there is any expert on self-mercy in the empire, it is me."

A young miran dressed in a robe striped in council white and black laughs broadly enough to show off his fine teeth. His mask is painted with interlocking octagrams across his eyes. "Grant us all such mercy, Amaranth," he says.

"I can only grant mercy to myself today, Yuya, but ask me next year on the Day of Charitable Mercy."

He touches his chest as if having received a mortal wound, but still laughs.

Another miran, a woman with rich blue lip paint and bright mirané eyes, says, "I would expect self-mercy for the Moon-Eater's Mistress to be a day free of entertaining men."

Someone applauds her, and the gathered miran argue rapidly over the definitions of men and mercy. Amaranth hands Iriset a cold glass of sweetened coffee. She sips, letting their talk wash around her, trying to allow her forces to draw out in whichever direction the crowd draws, toward ecstatic laughter or the flow of debate, all of it circling around and around Her Glory's strong falling pull. She needs to be balanced before she makes her demands, beginning with a moment alone with her sister-in-law.

But Sidoné, lounging on a step two higher than Amaranth's, says, "The very existence of the Days of Mercy proves that the regular state of the empire is a merciless one."

So easy to forget, for all that many see Sidoné as a symbol of successful assimilation, her people were very recently conquered.

The gathered miran *laugh*.

It had not been a joke.

Iriset catches Sidoné's eye, but the body-twin offers no sympathy. Her words were fact. A reminder to Iriset.

"Your Glory," Iriset whispers, leaning in. "I need to speak with you, alone."

Amaranth's mouth presses into a line of displeasure. She tugs the silk half-mask that perches upon her voluptuous curls down over her face. Diamonds and mirané-brown garnets stripe it in perfect vertical lines. "The princess and I," she says grandly as she stands, "are going for a walk."

She sweeps her robe up into one hand, displaying the expanse of her thick legs, and holds her other hand to Iriset.

Together they climb up and up the steps to the wide balustrade that circles the audience area of the amphitheater, in and out of stripes of shade. Amaranth weaves her fingers with Iriset's. The heat of the day slicks Iriset's skin with sweat and Iriset spares an admiring thought for her craftmask, pliable and perfect enough to allow for such things. Her slippers do little to keep her toes from roasting against the tiled floor. Above, Aharté's pink-silver moon is a pale sliver of next to nothing, washed in the brilliant summer light, but soon the burning sun will sink behind that moon again.

"What is wrong, hiha?" Amaranth asks. Without softness or sympathy, only a plain need to know. If she knows, she can fix it, her tone says.

Iriset drops her mouth open, only to close it.

Her Glory pushes her mask up over her face so it acts as a visor, shielding her eyes with a strip of dark shadow. "Everything is going well. You have convinced the world. You are married, making my brother relax, setting the empire into its power again with this alliance. You survived your own funeral, hiha. Enjoy something today, why don't you." She squeezes Iriset's hand. "Food, drink, and after the eclipse convince my brother the best self-mercy is lovemaking. The hard part has passed for you."

"The hard part..." Iriset says it voicelessly. Her pulse stutters.

"What is it?" Amaranth asks, sounding impatient. She stops her slow walking.

"The hard part, Amaranth," Iriset snaps, "is hardly over. Did you forget *again* that tomorrow my father will be executed in front of the empire and I will have to stand there and *watch*."

The Moon-Eater's Mistress says nothing.

Iriset glares into Amaranth's mirané-brown eyes. "Save him. Swear to me you will demand mercy for the Little Cat or I will tear off this mask and reveal to everyone what you've blackmailed me—"

Amaranth laughs.

"*Blackmailed* me into," Iriset continues through bared teeth.

"No you won't," the Moon-Eater's Mistress says. "And fix your face, Singix."

"I might. What have I got to lose?" Iriset raises her brows, but she does smooth out her expression into the nearest she can get to a sweet smile. "Less than you, Your Glory."

For another moment, Amaranth is quiet. Her glance flicks over Iriset, clinical and assessing. Then she slumps a shoulder and tilts her head, swinging voluminous curls. "Who were those people you were so afraid to speak to at the unraveling of Iriset mé Isidor this morning, kitten?"

Iriset backs up to the wall. The cool mosaic soothes the hot ecstatic pulsing in her palms. "You know who they are."

"That's right. I do. And that means I know what you still have to lose."

Closing her eyes, Iriset sees the drooping eris flowers in her grandfather's hand. She absolutely believes Amaranth mé Esmail Her Glory has it in her to kill for politics. To do more than kill. It takes Iriset's breath away.

"Did you . . . ?" Iriset catches herself and starts again, making her eyes open. "Did you do it? Did you plan all of this down to the poison itself?"

True surprise bares itself in Amaranth's expression. "I . . . do not know whether to be offended or flattered by the suggestion," she says carefully.

"You only took advantage of the situation?"

"That is what I always do."

Iriset wishes she had a cloth mask to draw over her eyes and settles for toying with the embroidered cuffs of her wide sleeves. "When it happened," she says slowly, "you said you just needed some time to salvage the situation. You have had several days. But you still don't know the culprit. Do you even want to? What is it you want from this, really, Amaranth?"

Her Glory smiles broadly. "A sister-in-law, of course. But controlling you is only a side benefit, I assure you, kitten. My reputation is on the line, and I need the marriage to go smoothly and be successful, do you understand? Expansion by real alliance is a new direction for the empire, the likes of which we haven't seen in generations. It could change so much. Everything, even, given time. But if it falls apart now, it will be generations more before there is a similar chance to show the expansive strength in one move, without massacre or genocide. This marriage will be successful, as it is the foundation for the rest of my vision for the empire."

Here is where all the ambitious knots were tied, when Aharté made these siblings. Iriset stares in what can only be described as stunned awe. And horror. "That will take years. Require *children.*"

"If you would save your father above all other things, go. Perhaps you can. Perhaps you can get to your grandparents before I do, assuming I don't have people already in place. But if you are caught, if you do not succeed perfectly, you and they will be killed along with him. I will see to it. Or... you can stay. Work with me. Be the wife of the Vertex Seal. Imagine what you can accomplish at our side."

It is so similar to what Isidor the Little Cat said to his daughter. *Change something, use your position.* Iriset's breath thins as she breathes faster. But if she agrees, her father will be dead. And despite the draw of her falling force, Amaranth cannot be trusted. Clearly she'll manipulate Iriset forever.

Amaranth continues, "Think on it, if you like. Think about mercy and its cost. What would you uphold and what would you tear down, Iriset? Those are always the only choices."

Iriset draws a ragged breath. "You are cruel."

"I am merciful."

"Not to your brother."

"My brother is the most important person to me."

"You're lying to him! This will break his heart!"

Amaranth reaches suddenly and tilts Iriset's chin up. Exposing Iriset's jugular. "You *do* care."

Iriset jerks her face free. "Your machinations have caused his inner design and my own to become one. I care about myself and so I care for him."

"Hmm," Her Glory hums. "In that case, listen to this: I might have my own visions for the future of the Vertex Seal, but I will never work against my brother. If you care for him because of your marriage knot, the reverse must be true, yes? The best thing for Lyric is to keep his wife he loves. Strengthen our family. If he finds out, it will be because of you, kitten. You are the one who will break his heart."

Hugging herself, Iriset looks away. "I'll make sure he knows of your involvement."

"Fine. Mutual blackmail works for me. But you still have more to lose."

"I might go. I might throw it all away to rescue my father."

Her Glory says, "I know you might, kitten. That is why I speak to you openly, as an equal. Do what you think is best, and so shall I, always."

With that, Amaranth puts a brilliant smile back on her face and shoos Iriset off to her husband with a tease and a laugh for any who might be watching.

That evening as the sun sets, Iriset lounges against him as Lyric reads old poems aloud. Carved ice blocks drip in the recessed brazier beside them, chilling fruit neither eat. It has been a long afternoon of ritual, of simple walking meditations meant to soothe them, Lyric's pick for self-mercy. Iriset did her best to wind down, but her best was lacking.

Every scenario she runs through in her head is highly likely to end with death—hers, certainly, and plenty of other people potentially. The only truth she knows is that her father refused to trade himself for her when he had the chance. Refused to escape. Would not sacrifice her. So Iriset can't sacrifice herself, either.

Lyric's voice thrums against her back and she stares up through the domed lattice ceiling of their room: The sky is violet-pink and Iriset holds her eyes wide to see the changes, the infinitesimal darkening of high blue, the shade-flare of a long, thin cloud, the specks of black moving in perpendicular lines as kites draw their squares against the sunset.

This could be the last sunset of her father's life. The last chance they're both looking at the same fading sky. The same half-slice of Aharté's moon.

All sunsets for the rest of time will be fundamentally different simply because the Little Cat will be dead. Every future sunset diminished. The entire world diminished. Knowing it, expecting it, watching the devastation approach is so much worse than the shock, the blunt adrenaline of murder.

She sighs. Lyric runs his hand down her arm. "Singix?"

Unpleasant anger stirs at the name. Even worse, longing. But Iriset has always been a woman of physicality. She learned to feel forces against her lips and the small of her back, didn't she? She knows Silence and balance require both the domination and surrender of one's own flesh, blood, and bones.

And so she turns and kisses the Vertex Seal, kissing him like she knows what she's doing, thoughtless to any bashful pretext. She kisses him like she could destroy him with it, save her father's life with it, or discover a new force behind his teeth.

His Glory is helpless.

She has her way with him on the floor of the greeting room, quickly pulling aside clothing as she pushes him down and cheats with a few pulls on his rising force so that he's harder faster. He gasps the wrong name and Iriset refuses to speak with voice, leaving communication to nails and tongues, heartbeat and gathering pleasure. Her own intensity rips at her delicate design and she holds it together with gritted teeth and determination. Her skin ripples, and she doesn't care. Iriset is nothing but forces; Lyric, too.

Thanks in part to the marriage knot, in part to her own skill, they come apart together.

When Lyric sprawls back onto the floor, still under her, still inside, there is a relaxed, joyful smile on his face.

Iriset shifts in his lap, feeling the stickiness between them, and squeezes her muscles around him. His smile widens. He is so beautiful, and Iriset thinks about putting a hand over his heart and stopping it.

She imagines ripping off her craftmask with his cock still inside her, holding him down as she transforms back to herself. *Look what you're fucking, Lyric méra Esmail. Are you an apostate now, too?* And then she'll draw his rising force again and again, relentlessly. She'll drag them both back to orgasms until he feels the crawling design on his own skin, until he swears under her own name, Iriset, Iriset, *Iriset*.

She sits back on his lap, head lolling as if with afterglow, but it's despair.

Lyric squeezes her hips. "Bath?"

Shaking her head, Iriset curls down against him, pressing her cheek to his chest. They're a mess, tangled clothing and sweat and come, and Iriset knows however this all ends, however she *makes* it end, it will break her heart, too.

26

The Day of Final Mercy

The Little Cat is executed on the Mercy Pavilion erected every year for the Day of Final Mercy. It's a performance, you see, an ostentatious display of power.

Every year several are sentenced to die, and every year the Vertex Seal calls mercy for one name. Rarely does the choice surprise anyone, for it's negotiated and argued quads beforehand among the mirané council. But that year, there *is* a surprise.

Two, really, since Iriset has never seen the royal griffons personally before. Only their silhouettes as they fly against the dome of the menagerie. It is said that these queens of the sky were designed by the Moon-Eater himself, from a leopard, a prairie eagle, and his own moon-red flesh.

But at the end of the Apostate Age, with the Holy Syr's blessing and the approval of the first Vertex Seal, priests of Aharté determined that whatever creatures the apostate architects had created would be left alone to live or die according to Aharté's will. Those that died would pass into legend, but those that could feed themselves could reproduce without intercession, would not be destroyed. Most of the megafauna could not manage their size without additional design, and were put down with pity; the largest feather dragons were hunted for their destructive natures; the delicate unicorns fled, too intelligent to be captured, and it is possible some live in the wilds beyond the empire; those creatures made with especially bold, terrible magic like the singing trees or spliced dogs could not reproduce at all, and when they died, their kind died with them.

The griffons, though, were perfect.

At the execution of the Little Cat are four griffons: a massive queen called Seti, her vivid mirané-brown wings broad and outswept as she perches on a heavy trellis built over the royal stage, her mass and wings shading Iriset and Lyric. Another adult female clutches her own trellis, her gorgeous wings mottled with brown, mirané brown, and black markings. With her are a pair of juvenile twins. They're all thin and elegant, with lanky legs and wide paws. Their sleek mirané-brown fur is patterned with white spots and sweeping stripes that curve around their huge slit-pupil eyes like kohl. Long tails curl over their backs, or swipe in avid interest as the griffons keep watch.

Bež, the griffon-keeper and Garnet's mother, stands at the pointed end of the half-circle stage, whip and long silk leashes at her hips and around her neck. Scars on her brow are painted bold red and she wears a headdress of feathers that's like a mask, only it does not occlude her vision at all. She smells like raw meat.

Iriset keeps glancing up at the griffon queen, annoyed that they exist. If she had called the little bobcat kitten she designed wings for a griffon, would it have been such a crime? Her constant glances must read as nerves, for Lyric touches the back of Iriset's hand and says, "You are safe, beloved."

He maintains poise easily, it seems, his faith in Bež and her control over the griffons simple and resolute. Iriset smells that musty-feather smell of the griffons, and hopes their cat-eyes are a sign of good luck for whatever Bittor does today.

Her stomach is loose and sloshy. Iriset grips the rail of the half-circle royal pavilion, gasping at the sparks of ecstatic force that pinch her palms. A force-shield so thin and perfect she'd not seen it surrounds their stage, to protect the Vertex Seal and his party. It's to be expected here, in case someone decides to toss trash or flowers, but Iriset hopes there's nothing like it around the execution pillars. All night, while her husband slept, Iriset worked: She chose one of Singix's embroidered chest pieces and wove a force-shield through the back that will act as armor. She took a pencil and two quills from Lyric's desk and imbued them with charge-designs she can activate—she's toyed with tiny prototype ecstatic blades in the past. Mostly for picking locks and thievery, but they should do for shocking Seal guards back, slicing through force-blades if she's lucky. They could cut through this shield around the pavilion, certainly. The weapons are fixed to her arms under her wide sleeves with friction-buttons.

Iriset is as ready as she knows how to be for whatever will happen. She can't be a palace-wide distraction, and since Bittor must think she's dead, he won't count on it anymore. Whatever his new plan is, if she can help, she will.

He must have a plan. He must be coming.

Iriset looks out over the crowd toward the Mercy Pavilion. It seems to have been grown overnight out of the Crystal Desert, shining in striae of pink salt and white-silver quartz, with veins of iron deposits striping violently through in forks and slices like lightning. Four pillars evenly spaced in a square rise from the smooth, flat surface of the pavilion. Each for a criminal.

People, mostly miran wearing red death masks under shaded palanquins or palm umbrellas hovering over their heads, fill the space between the Vertex Seal's stage and the pavilion. The chatter and anticipation are ecstatic in the hot air. Toward the edges, groups of non-miran gather together, just as eager.

It's not bloodthirsty of them, exactly, for these executions include no blood. It's closer to curiosity that brings them here, not to witness death but to witness the Glorious Unraveling that is how the criminals die. Such architecture is—in Iriset's opinion—human architecture, as it changes life, reworks living flesh. But officially it's only a weapon, like a force-blade. Besides, unraveling is the way the Holy Syr executed the Moon-Eater four hundred years ago, and so it is blessed by She Who Loves Silence. Even if it's human architecture, technically, no gift from Aharté can be apostasy.

Semantics and doctrine, Iriset thinks bitterly, wishing Ceres fashion allowed for a mask to hide her expression. She wishes to argue with Lyric that all these who approve of this method of execution but claim innocence of apostasy are hypocrites. She wishes she were herself, to sneer in his face that his empire is unworthy of the moral heights to which he aspires.

She wishes she could unleash her rage and grief onto something that will affect the outcome of this eclipse day.

Now she understands why people pray.

Amaranth arrives, her face striped in thick black lines, and Lyric seems surprised to see her. Garnet even makes a slight comment to Sidoné, for Her Glory has never attended the Final Mercy executions before. Sidoné merely grimaces at the griffons above. But room is made among the Seal guards, attendants, and handful of miran of high enough rank to observe from Lyric's side. Beremé mé Adora tries to maneuver herself next to

Amaranth, but Her Glory stands with Iriset and takes her other hand, making herself, along with her brother, into royal buttresses holding Iriset up.

The Moon-Eater's Mistress came for Iriset.

How dare she? Iriset carefully tugs away.

There's little fanfare to the execution, as it's a performance of justice. The moment the sun touches the eastern edge of the moon, priests stationed at each cardinal point surrounding the venue begin force-prayers, calling on the crowd to join them in summoning a balanced song. Because of where the royal stage is positioned, the Vertex Seal's party joins in with the falling principle, following Lyric's lead in a soothing melody that slides back and forth between four notes, between major and minor chords. Iriset remains quiet.

The song fades and Seal guards escort four prisoners onto the pavilion. Three men and one woman are bound with prepared linen to the crystal pillars. Isidor the Little Cat is given the position at the forefront, the tip of the death diamond.

The light of the summer sun fades into a cooler blue.

Where is Bittor? Did he not act before Isidor was on the stage because her security map was rendered useless?

Miran lower their palm fans and umbrellas to let the eclipse light reach their faces. Iriset lifts her chin. She imagines how the wavering blue sunlight catches the ghost writing on her forehead. What will her father see? Rays of rainbow light, mimicking a mask? Will it dazzle him? She is so far away, but she can see his face, see that he turns in her direction.

This is the end. Iriset feels so much it is like feeling nothing at all. All four forces crashing together so strongly they negate.

The rumble of conversation lifts, though nobody cheers or cries out either eagerly or in protest. It's not Silent, but neither is it fraught. Beremé murmurs something to Amaranth. One of the Seal guards on the royal platform coughs.

Iriset barely breathes.

Priests of Aharté, in their dark red robes and silver masks, bring out the unraveling collars, affixing them to the prisoners in pairs. Each collar is wrought of four echo coins and threads of force gathered in long, narrow webs like ladder rope. They settle over the shoulders of the criminals.

Iriset stares hard at her father, memorizing him like he's the last sunset she'll ever see. His shorn hair is slicked back as if wet, his beard shaved away. He's clean, wearing a simple robe and trousers, no shoes. They've painted something onto his forehead and chin, and maybe his hands, but she can't see well enough from her distance.

When a thrum of unexpected falling force slinks beneath Iriset's slippered feet, she's startled into glancing down. Above her the griffon queen *screams*.

Miran cry out, some flinging hands to shade their eyes as they stare back at the griffon. There's a moment of echoing silence, then Amaranth gasps and Seal guards leap into action. But Lyric stares at the same thing Iriset sees: Arcing across the sky to the southeast are filaments of light like fireworks. They burst in the air, reaching for one another, forming sky graffiti that spells out a prayer in the sacred calligraphy of Silence:

Silk is Syr
Heir of Aharté

As the filaments fall, rippling toward the crowd, they twist and flip, sparkling with black and gold ecstatic charges. Then a voice rings out across the space via design amplification:

"Yesterday rebellion dropped from the moon, but today it rises from beneath our feet!"

It's Bittor's voice.

Iriset stops breathing.

On the Mercy Pavilion, the Little Cat struggles against the pillar, shaking his head, mouth moving but she can't hear.

Another burst of light, but instead of graffiti, it's only fireworks, ecstatic color spiraling in every direction: beautiful and harmless. Distraction.

It's all a distraction. Bittor made his own. Iriset almost laughs in sheer relief.

Sudden movement and the shifting of the crowd draws Iriset's attention in the other direction: A man has leapt high, and he's running over the crowd's ambient forces like dashing over the surface of a lake. He couldn't use the map to rescue the Little Cat quietly, so he's making a spectacle.

Gasps, shock, shrieks, and the vibration of force-blades ping against Iriset's attention, but she can't look away. It's Bittor; she knows his shape and motion. She knows how he's performing this trick: tension soles, a boot-net she played with alongside Dalal, for escaping over water. Its purpose is reacting against the power imbued in the force-threads, in ambient forces, not infiltrating them! Genius!

Nobody can stop Bittor as he runs his jagged path. They can't shoot him without aiming into the crowd. She leans forward, eager. Someone grasps her elbow. The miran stare up, pointing and shying away from the ripples of force shocking out from his every step. It's their own security Bittor is bouncing off, and overhead more fireworks explode.

But Bittor suddenly veers away from the Mercy Pavilion. Away from the Little Cat. Running directly at Iriset instead.

Around her the Seal guards shift closer, into a combat-design pattern, but she can see Bittor's face, see those cat-eyes locked over her shoulder. He's focused on the Vertex Seal. His hand curls around something small. A crystal blade jutting between his thumb and index knuckle—she knows it. She made it. It will slice through the force-shield.

Bittor flings it with perfect aim, and Iriset sidesteps in front of Lyric. She snaps her fingers and charges the thick Ceres chest piece with ecstatic-flow shock. Lyric grabs her as the tiny dart slices through the stage's energy shield, hits her chest piece, and falls away.

It would have cut Lyric to the heart. Her ears are ringing as she stares at Bittor with Lyric's hands gripping her arms. She didn't even *think*.

Bittor skids to a halt, sinking—motion is what keeps the force-soles active, in this experimental form. Iriset stares at him as his twisted expression plummets to shock, and she mouths, "Bittor."

It's a soft, wounded word, his name on the perfectly symmetrical lips of Singix Es Sun. Bittor pauses, staring.

He hesitates with another dart in hand.

The Seal guards grab him.

They drag him down below the royal stage, but Iriset can't see. She's jerked away in the arms of her husband, who holds her too tightly. "Singix," Lyric says, sounding like he's begging. "What are you doing?"

"I—" Iriset twists her neck to look back for Bittor. She sees flashes of force-blades, hears the roaring of the crowd. "I couldn't..." She closes her eyes and leans her cheek into Lyric's hand before she says something incriminating in her shock. Iriset was not made for emergencies. She should be kept in a locked room with design tools and left alone. *She saved him.*

Garnet says to the Seal guards, "Take him to the execution

platform." There's scuffling and commands snapped out, and Iriset tries to tug free, to look for Bittor, but Lyric grabs her face. He's wearing a plain mirané-red death mask with sharp, squared cheeks and a hundred tiny holes as a screen over his eyes, but he tears it off and studies her like he's never seen her. For a moment Iriset almost hopes he knows who he's staring at. Iriset mé Isidor, daughter of the Little Cat.

"Singix," Amaranth says, crowding them. "You're mad. You shouldn't have, even with Iriset mé Isidor's design armor."

Iriset resents Amaranth trying to help her, but even more so her own name behind it, used as a layered threat. She shakes her head, holding Lyric's red-flecked eyes. "I had to," she murmurs.

Lyric melts toward her and touches his forehead to hers. "It was reckless to protect me like that," he says for her alone.

"I had to," she repeats. She touches his jaw tenderly. Her hand is shaking. Bittor didn't try to rescue the Little Cat, he tried to *assassinate the Vertex Seal*. Why?

"Unbelievable," Amaranth says.

Both Iriset and Lyric slide the Moon-Eater's Mistress different looks and she backs away, lips pressed in a disapproving line.

Lyric steps to the fore of the platform. A guard offers him a small coin, and Lyric presses it to the hollow of his throat. His voice is amplified across the quartz yards. "Tell me his name," he commands.

The Seal guards are shoving Bittor up onto the execution pavilion, and the crowd is almost silent, trapped in place by the danger and drama. There are no more fireworks. Any accomplices Bittor had from the Little Cat's court have faded back and slipped away. The griffon queen grips her trellis, her wings flared to shade her children. All her feathers fluff and tighten, up and down in agitation.

The answer to Lyric's command comes from a priest, standing upon the execution pavilion. "Bittor méra Tesmose, of the Saltbath precinct." The name rings across the sky.

The guards force Bittor down. Iriset chokes a protest and tucks her mouth against Lyric's bare shoulder. She peers over Lyric at the prisoners.

Bittor's face is aimed right back at the royal platform. At her.

Behind him, the Little Cat is staring, too.

Force-blades angle against Bittor's throat, pinning him on his knees. He's going to die, not unraveled but decapitated like an animal for eating. He came with fireworks and heretical words. *Silk is Syr. Yesterday rebellion dropped from the moon, but today...*

Iriset turns sharply to her husband and clutches his arm. "Mercy," she whispers.

Surprise lights Lyric's eyes and touches his fingers to her cheek. Iriset hardly knows what shows in her false-dark-brown gaze, but she is abjectly desperate. She caused Bittor to falter. He made a choice to aim for the Vertex Seal instead of the Little Cat, and she stopped him.

"The name has already been selected," Lyric murmurs. "This young man chose to die this way, at his master's side."

"Show him you are a better master. If he dies now, everything he wrote in the sky stands." Iriset is careful to modulate her words as best she can. "We have martyrs in Ceres. Do you have them here?"

Lyric studies her for what seems an age, again, but can only have been a handful of paired, rapid breaths. He glances past her, at Amaranth, then at one or two other people gathered around them. Iriset can't even imagine what they answer with their expressions; none speak.

Finally Lyric takes his death mask back from Garnet and

replaces it. He touches the coin to his throat. "Mercy is given to Bittor méra Tesmose, by the fair will of Singix Es Sun. Release him, pardoned of his crimes against the empire."

Though she doesn't know if she should, Iriset grabs his shoulder and lifts herself up to kiss his masked cheek before everyone.

Bittor is untied and shoved off the stage into the crowd.

He stands and lifts one hand up to the stage and flicks his fingers in a sign of mercy—as if he grants it to the Vertex Seal in return.

Then he's gone, somehow, vanished into the shocked, admiring miran. Iriset lets out a long, careful breath, feeling her entire body tremble with its release.

She wants to go home. Home to the old tower, her shielded study. Her spinners. Sit down. Give in to her weak knees and sink to the floor of the stage. Lean against Lyric's leg like a child or a dog.

The execution will not wait for her recovery.

Lyric calls out, "Proceed. We have had our final mercy, and four is the holiest number."

Behind her, Beremé hisses, and Garnet says, slightly appalled, "Lyric."

Amaranth snorts softly, as if entirely unsurprised.

Iriset's lips part in horror. Actual, cold horror. She and Bittor cost one of those other prisoners their own mercy.

No shade to brutality, she thinks, in layering dismay.

The shifting light flares as the sun fits almost entirely behind the moon at the eclipse crescendo. Rays of vibrant silver, too glaring to look at, are flung from the crown of the moon, and a sliver of the sun itself winks at Iriset's watery eyes.

On the Mercy Pavilion, the priests move into place, and Iriset remembers to stare out at her father.

He looks back at her. Even at this distance, she can tell. His face is a cold moon, and she imagines the chipped gray of his eyes. She grips the rail with both hands and does not know how to breathe.

The priests speak, mouths moving, and though the elaborate design Bittor shattered has not been replaced, the Glorious Unraveling commences.

Isidor the Little Cat's shoulders heave, the only sign of distress, and tears fill her vision with clear fire, but she doesn't blink. He keeps his chin high and his eyes on the stage—on her, but surely nobody else suspects he stares at anything but the Vertex Seal, or maybe the griffons.

Tears spill down her cheeks with heavy, hot trails. *Dad*, she thinks, her entire body aches to say, to call to him. But she already fucked up today. He wouldn't forgive her if she dies with him now. Even if it would feel right, righteous, rebellious, afterward she'd be dead.

Make me proud, Iriset.

Forces flare: cracking ecstatic, wavering flow, smoky rising, and sleek falling lines like rain. They aim at each prisoner, surrounding them in an orderly cocoon, pressing nearer, and the echo coins of the prisoners' collars flash, the force-ropes direct all the power, and just as it happened with the disguised body of Singix Es Sun, the Little Cat of Moonshadow unravels: flesh, blood, bone, and spirit.

The collars fall to the pavilion, empty now.

It's over.

Iriset cannot breathe: Her father is gone.

Not only dead, but unraveled to his very core.

Iriset begs leave to return to bed, being weary and emotionally compromised. It's a dreadful thing to witness, she murmurs to her husband, and she'd like to be alone.

She makes it calmly to their rooms, then allows Shahd to unwind her hair and help her into a simpler day gown. The young attendant brings a lunch sampling shortly after that, and a small cup of harsh root liquor she recommends Iriset knock back medicinally.

So it is done.

Then Iriset crawls into bed. She clutches pillows against her breast and buries her face in the silk sheets, grimacing and baring her teeth, all to keep from crying again. Her tears dried on the rail of the royal stage, and she'll give the empire no more today.

———— • ♦ • ————

A lovely chime wakes her. It's designed into the walls to allow someone in the greeting room to alert someone upstairs that a visitor has arrived.

Iriset wants only to remain in bed, but she's Singix, and so forces herself up. Down the spiral corridor she goes, barefoot and quiet, to where Shahd waits patiently alongside Anis mé Ario.

Iriset's heart pinches as she stops herself from sighing with relief just in time. Anis is not Singix's friend. "Handmaiden," she says.

Anis's tall, lanky body looks lovely in the layered robe she wears and her face is dotted with white and black like freckles. Her jade cuff hangs heavily against her bony wrist. "Your Glory," Anis says, holding out a cloisonné box that fits in the palm of her hand. "Her Glory sent this for you, a gift she thinks you should open when you are alone."

The accompanying wink suggests the gift is sexual in nature, and Shahd smiles like a knowing auntie despite her age.

"Thank you." Iriset accepts it. To be polite, she asks, "In which garden does Her Glory relax this afternoon?"

"She is bathing in the Lapis River Pool during the heat of the day, but will retire to the Color Can Be Loud Garden for visitors. You would be welcome, I am sure."

Iriset doesn't want to see Amaranth now. "Thank you," she says again.

Anis nearly speaks further, but in the end bows respectfully, briefly touching her eyelids, and departs.

Shahd looks at the cloisonné box expectantly, but Iriset cradles it to her chest. "Alone," she murmurs, and flees back upstairs.

Inside the box is a small gray coin of smoky quartz. When Iriset holds it between her thumb and forefinger, a soothing drag of falling force teases at her fingers.

It's an echo coin.

Iriset's heart clenches and she presses it to her lips. This is an echo of her father's falling force. Not truly a piece of him but a memory of it, a memento she can carry always.

Her Glory fetched it somehow from the priests on the Mercy Pavilion, by bribe or simple request, Iriset has no idea, and now it's hers.

Sometimes there are no words to express an emotion exactly, and as Iriset holds the coin, she wishes she could understand the complicated glow of admiration and anger, resentment, need, and simple attraction Amaranth mé Esmail Her Glory, the Moon-Eater's Mistress, causes her to feel.

27

We pay for what we do

A long time ago the Little Cat waited for Iriset to walk into a room before cutting a man's throat. Blood splashed her face and she twitched away. It was one of the only times she saw him kill. He didn't do it often, finding little use for murder unless it served some other scheme or purpose. But he wanted his daughter to see it, to feel it. Isidor asked her if she understood why.

She didn't, and guessed perhaps it was for shock value or to drive her away from the court, maybe because of the way the forces play together in blood differently when it's outside the body. Other guesses, she can't remember. Finally, Isidor told her it was because everyone pays for what they do. Even her, even the Little Cat. Even the Vertex Seal. Maybe even Aharté (if Aharté exists at all).

When Iriset wakes in a world in which her dad is dead, she keeps her eyes shut against the vague morning light, trying not to think as her husband touches her shoulder and rises. She reaches for a pillow to bury her face in.

The Little Cat told his daughter to make him proud. She wonders what his last words for his apostate would have been.

(They would have been the same.)

Her father is dead, and Iriset is not surprised to find she doesn't want revenge. Not against Lyric, or Amaranth. If she wanted revenge she'd have to include herself as a target. She didn't save him. She could have, she knows it. But that isn't what the Little Cat chose the last time she spoke to him.

"Make me proud," Iriset mouths silently into the pillow. "Do something. Make a mark."

That's what he said.

Do something with this position in which you have found yourself. Make a mark, or change something. Anything. The whole empire. If anyone can, you can. I've seen what you are capable of doing when you decide.

Make a mark.

When she agreed to this scheme, when she replaced Singix, Iriset did it because Amaranth insisted. She did it for pride, for her own gleeful glory.

The greatest apostasy the Holy Empire has ever seen, and it's a secret.

Now Iriset is awake, clarified, and she knows what to do. What to *change*. She's already designed an array to distract, simple and easy for a genius like her, tied into the design security of the palace complex.

Now Iriset understands it shouldn't be an array to distract, but to destroy.

What Iriset wants is to show the Vertex Seal, show everyone, they're wrong. Their power and beliefs are built on a faulty foundation. Flawed. Ungodly. Silence has a core flaw.

That's why her father is dead. Why Singix is dead and Iriset is transformed and married to the brutal king of this Silent, boring world. Unable to be what she is.

Silk is Syr, Bittor's graffiti declared.

That's good. She can answer that. *Be* the flaw.

Silk is Syr, and hiding in the heart of the empire. The heart of the Vertex Seal.

How can Aharté matter when Iriset is what and where and who she is?

The laws of Silence are already broken, so now Iriset will make them shatter.

Someone sits on the bed, and her inner design squeezes as threads of the marriage knot twine pleasantly. Lyric has returned. Anxiety, grief, anger, lust spike in her guts, but Iriset quickly smooths the turmoil into longing and sorrow. Singix's feelings. She can't afford to show her truth now, knotted with marriage to a sensitive, priest-trained Vertex Seal.

He says gently, "I brought water for you. I can feel the disturbed nature of your heart." If it had been a metaphor, it might have been romantic.

He helps her sit, and Iriset keeps her gaze on his mirané-red fingers curled around the little stone cup. She takes it. Lyric combs those fingers through her long, slippery hair. Singix's hair, that barely tangles, that probably couldn't hold the knotting style Iriset learned from her mother and grandfather. Iriset drinks and the morning light grows.

Lyric sets the cup aside and asks, "What's wrong?"

Iriset has no idea what lie to tell, and so she says, "I was thinking about never seeing my father again." It's a safe excuse, as Singix's father is far away. Iriset knows few details of their relationship, only that Singix's mother died when Singix was a child, and her father rules alone with a council of avatars and brokered this alliance with the Vertex Seal—or rather, with his sister. And Singix never expected to see him again.

Lyric needs no further explanation for her upset on the day after the execution of Isidor the Little Cat; he, too, holds the poor, dead Iriset mé Isidor near the surface of his mind. Besides, that rebel tried to assassinate him, and this new wife of his stood in the way. It was a rough afternoon for everyone. He climbs onto the bed behind Iriset as if she's shielding him again, and wraps his arms around her, pulling her between his legs. His naked body folds around her, warm and smooth, and Iriset leans back the way her body wants to. Lyric gathers her hair and pushes it over one shoulder, baring her neck. With his lips against her pulse, he says, "When my father died, it took me a long time to find all the places grief hid." His sigh trembles along her collarbone. "I've always practiced meditation, walking the labyrinth at the Silent Chapel, but after he died, I did it again and again, making myself think about him, as if I could compel the grief to squeeze itself all out quickly and never bother me again."

Iriset would like to find a way to do the same. "Did it work?" she whispers, only slightly distracted by his thighs bracketing her hips and Singix's hair falling softly against her breasts. When she looks at herself, at his skin against hers, she can't help but wonder how those crater-red forearms would complement her own—Iriset's—desert-peach Osahar skin, with its flushing and fine dark body hairs, the little line of them from her navel to groin. Singix's skin is so pale, and her body hairs barely curled, so soft against Iriset's tongue that night, and she remembers a dark pink birthmark almost like a love bite on Singix's knee that she didn't have time to give herself. Thinking of it, Iriset skims her fingers against the knob at Lyric's wrist, turning herself on and still so very sad.

"No," Lyric murmurs with humor. Iriset barely remembers what she asked. "But it did help me...put the grief somewhere. I gave it to Aharté, to Silence. Sometimes it's hard to set foot in the chapel now, if I'm having a bad day. But most of the time, the labyrinth is a reminder that grief can...gleam. A pearl of grief, small and simple and built very carefully. Set into a little earring I can wear if I like so I know where to find it, and carry it with me most of the time, but it's not overwhelming anymore."

Iriset laughs softly at his overdrawn metaphor. She knows exactly where to put her grief. "Do we have to be anywhere today?"

"There are places we could go, but nowhere we must until the eclipse," he says.

Iriset takes one of his arms that is wrapped around her waist and tugs until she has his hand. She lowers it to her belly and flattens it there, sliding his hand lower as she parts her thighs. Lyric inhales sharply and Iriset pushes his fingers past her labia. She lets her head fall back as Lyric cups his palm against her and touches a finger to the edge of her hole. Iriset raises an arm to grasp at his face and hair, arching her back to press her bottom against his inner thigh and groin, seeking the soft bulge of his cock. She hooks her leg around his knee, spreading herself against him, a wide-open offering. Lyric accepts, playing his fingers against her as Iriset hums encouragingly, pulling his thick hair and gripping his thigh with her other hand. He sucks at her neck while he dips his fingers inside again and again, drawing back out to paint wetness around in long strokes. Their bodies thrust slowly together in time with their breathing, and as he grows hard, the little movements of his tip against her spine make her gasp again and again, until she stretches her neck to kiss him open-mouthed and just as wet.

It doesn't take very long for Iriset to come in a long, rolling ripple, and Lyric doesn't stop touching her, gently pressing her clitoris until it's too much and she squirms up onto her knees. Without looking back at him, Iriset tips forward, panting with ecstatic after-bursts. She lowers to her elbows and lets her head fall. Her hair slides messily over her back. "Lyric," she whispers. She needs him to take from her, take more and more so she can excuse her desire for him, excuse the way she feels despite who he is and what he's done—what he's refused to do. (Who she really is and what she hasn't done—has been too afraid to do.)

He moves, grasping her ass and spreading her cheeks to see. Iriset knows her whole body is clenching and she wiggles impatiently. Lyric gets up, hands on her waist, and reaches down around her belly to touch and position her, and she squeaks when his fingers skim oversensitive parts. With a little laugh, he gets a hold of himself and pushes inside, all at once. Iriset's whole body jars with it, and she sighs in relief, at his rising force crashing into her. Lyric moves, and she braces herself languidly, so glad to be in rhythm like this, the push and pull, her almost-but-not-quite-smoothed-out bursts of ecstatic force fluttering upward like bubbles in ecstatic wine. Every push and every pull ties the threads of their design seeds tighter, and her nipples brush the sheets and Lyric's mouth is at the nape of her neck, lips open, breathing hard. It's not really a kiss, but that doesn't matter.

Thanks to the marriage knot, she feels his orgasm gathering, feels it with a strange, wonderful peace, a flush up her spine and heat in her cheeks. By the time Lyric comes, she's forgetting to be sad or angry or ambitious, forgetting to worry about Bittor's force-graffiti or her father's commands or murder or Amaranth's schemes or how she'll break all their hearts. Those are problems for later. Choices for later. Now, with her inner design melting into Lyric's, the only thing she wants to make is a little mercy for herself.

She'll pay for that, too, one day.

———•♦•———

During the remaining few Days of Mercy, there's no regular schedule for the Vertex Seal or his wife, no meetings or lectures, no visits into the city—none of the things Lyric and Amaranth and their people normally do. It's a holiday, after all, and the hottest time of the year. The only constant is the noontime eclipse ritual that Lyric always participates in. Iriset goes at his side.

The rest of the time, she fucks him. Her husband is very willing, and she can't help remembering the afternoon when Amaranth rolled her eyes and said Lyric's body is a temple. Oh, it is, and dedicated to worshipping the sensation of her tongue tracing lines of rising force along the underside of his cock, to the tickle-pop of ecstatic when he sucks at her ribs or hip bones, the flow flow flow of building orgasms, the falling to each other's core as they kiss until their lips are numb and their ears ringing.

After four days Iriset barely remembers what her own mouth is supposed to taste like. In between, she asks him questions about his philosophies, under cover of a wife eager to understand her new home and her new husband. (She needs to know, after all, the intricacies of what he cares about, if she's going to ruin him.)

Lyric tentatively shares with her the basic understanding of Aharté he was taught, that the purpose of the Holy Design is balance, and when someday true balance is achieved, there will be neither conflict nor suffering because all creatures will be at peace in the living Silence Aharté promised them. He admits that some days he wishes he were just a priest, responsible only for his own knot in the pattern, and coaxing those around him into a more perfect alignment. Not responsible for an entire empire.

He gives her copies of *Word of Aharté* and *The Writings of the Holy Syr* he personally transcribed and bound when he was fourteen, and shyly offers to read them with her. First *Writings*, he says, because he finds the Holy Syr to be more explicit and meandering in her thoughts than the plain commands of Aharté. "You like Aharté's wife more than Aharté?" she teases. Lyric smiles the softest smile she's ever seen, and insists he only appreciates the argumentative nature of the Holy Syr's philosophies.

Iriset asks if he ever feels hints of a true living Silence. Lyric closes his eyes and whispers to her of perfect moments when the wind or sun, or a trilling skull siren, traps his attention and he's aware of his entire body, his pulse and his thoughts, aware of voices around him, when he feels the pattern of what happened just before, and feels what will happen next. They are never urgent moments, but simple epiphanies of pure understanding. That, he thinks, is living Silence: understanding without urgency, deep experience without desire in any direction.

"Without desire?" she murmurs.

His smile tilts a bit wry. "Without desire for *change*, without ambition, or..." He touches her lips, stroking the sensitive skin, and trails his finger along her chin to her throat. "I have felt living Silence when we are together, when—when our designs are so completely unified and I feel pleasure, satisfaction, comfort, and...things I cannot even express. It feels as though everything in the world is focused on me—on us—but not because we matter more than everything else. It is because *everything* absolutely matters. Each knot in the pattern is vital to the pattern, each *is* the focus, which is an idea almost beyond our comprehension, but not beyond Aharté."

It is going to be so easy for Silk to take this faith away from him. Everything does matter, every piece of the design, and Iriset is an expert. Nothing about architecture is beyond her comprehension.

Iriset says, "Your sister feels that with the Moon-Eater."

Before Lyric can protest, Iriset continues, "She does—she calls it a moment of unity, not peace. Not Silence. But it is the same thing, I think."

Lyric kisses her again, and her heart pops ecstatically, her body arches with languid flow, she reaches for him and his design with a rise of yearning, and he sinks into her, falling, falling, falling.

She remembers, too, what she said to Amaranth that day in the Moon-Eater's Temple, that every force is also love.

———— • ♦ • ————

And then it's over. The Days of Mercy end, and life in the empire returns to its structures.

Iriset is ready to put her designs into action.

The first morning of normal time, Lyric gets up early to drink his coffee and tend his adorable herb garden on their private balcony before dressing and putting on whatever mask he'll wear for the day. Once Garnet arrives with his schedule, he's off, and Iriset is alone.

It takes an appallingly long time to ready Singix Es Sun for leaving. As Iriset selects a silk square painted with ocean waves in undulating stripes of green, she idly mentions to Shahd that although she hasn't worn masks yet, because in Ceres it was considered a sin to hide what was gifted to her by the demon of beauty, she thinks if she makes a mask herself, then no one need take on the burden for her. "Does that seem a thing the miran would approve of?" Iriset asks softly, affecting a bit of anxiety in her posture and voice.

Shahd hums, head tilted and smiling a little at Iriset's Singix act, but she gamely says, "Mask making seems a very appropriate hobby, Your Glory."

"I'll look into it," she agrees, and with that pin planted, she takes herself to find Amaranth with Shahd at her heels.

• ♦ •

It is a bit strange that the Moon-Eater's Mistress has no official office of her own, though previous Mistresses certainly have. Amaranth prefers to take meetings in a garden or the menagerie, or travel to the homes of those she'd like to persuade or investigate or intimidate. She's likely to blow in and out like a summer storm, and uses that capricious reputation to overt advantage. The only predictable part of her day is awakening the Moon-Eater.

Today Amaranth is set up in the Bright Star Obelisk Garden, according to Shahd's sources. On the way through the palace complex, Iriset keeps her chin up and her eyes ahead, for she is the wife of the Vertex Seal. It allows her to see the people who dart out of her way, the ones who pause to stare, and those who touch their eyes respectfully while others merely flick fingers to lashes almost dismissively. A pair of miran pause to bow, eyes covered, and Iriset hears one of them say, "—neglect my duties for that in my bed, too." The other hushes her, and she snorts behind his hand. "Even if she understands, I'm sure she's learning to love it."

Iriset pauses, incensed at the insult to Singix, but before she can do more than draw an angry breath, she recalls that Singix would never respond to such words. She turns her pause into a little stumble and looks away.

Maybe it was a mistake to keep Lyric secluded, she thinks, chagrined, if it played into stereotypes the miran have assigned to the Ceres Remnants. But Shahd speeds up enough to walk at her elbow and the girl says fiercely, "By the end of the day I'll make sure every Seal guard knows she was rude to their new consort."

Rude is certainly one way to put it, Iriset thinks sourly, but only murmurs her thanks.

"Your Glory," calls an unfortunately familiar voice as they step out from under a peristyle walkway into the vivid summer sunlight.

It's the leader of Beremé's rival faction. Iriset wants to curse but instead smiles blandly. She has no idea if Singix has formally met him, but surely it won't be strange if she knows the name of a prominent mirané prince. "Hehet méra Davith."

"Introduce me to this stunning woman," says Hehet's companion, whose name Iriset already knows.

The lanky Hehet bows with a hand over his eyes, and the masculine-forward miran beside him does the same, but with more of a flourish.

"Your Glory, this is The First Dove Song at Dawn méra Curro," Hehet says, "a gossip and idler. Dove, you were at the wedding feast, you know who this is."

"Her Glory of the Beautiful Twilight," Dove gushes. Clearly he was born in the same year as Lyric and Garnet. As the man stands, he lowers his eyelashes while sliding his gaze just to the side of Iriset's cheek, on her ear perhaps, somehow achieving an affect that is both flirtatious and respectful.

Iriset looks directly at him, studying the planes of his face. Singix is a foreigner, after all, as so many want to remind her, so she might as well take advantage. His eyes are too small for his nose, but their vibrant color makes up for it, and his jaw and cheeks are balanced and sharp. "Do you sit on the council, The First Dove Song at Dawn?"

"I do, and mercy, Your Glory, just Dove."

Sliding her eyes to Hehet, who boldly watches her back, Iriset asks Dove, "And did you argue for or against my marriage?"

Hehet's eyes widen, and Dove laughs nervously. "My Silence," he says. "*For*, Your Glory, I was in favor even before I heard of your beauty."

"I was too forward in asking directly," she immediately demurs.

"Her Glory can ask whatever she likes," the idler promises.

Looking at Hehet again, she tilts her face consideringly. This is a good opportunity to fix another pin of her plan, so to speak. Slowly, as if carefully picking her words, she asks, "If you are a leader of the miran, and you a gossip, one of you must know more about the man who attacked the royal platform."

Dove lights up. "Ah, yes, when you so bravely threw yourself between harm and our Vertex Seal! What a story that is, Your Glory."

"Instinct," she says, letting her gaze fall to the crushed white shells of the path.

"Proof, I might say, that your marriage is blessed by Aharté," he agrees.

"Do we need proof?" Iriset frowns as prettily as possible.

Hehet puts a lazy hand on his hip. His forehead gleams with sweat, and the same already gathers under Iriset's breasts thanks to the sweltering morning. Standing here under the sun is not good for anyone. Hehet says, "Proof is elusive in most arenas these days."

"I must have patience, then."

"Bittor méra Tesmose," Dove says, shifting as though to cut between Iriset and Hehet. "His name. He was from the Little Cat's court, but there's been no rumors regarding his whereabouts since the execution. That I've heard, at least."

"Oh." She tries to look and sound only vaguely disappointed.

"Shall I keep you informed?" Dove offers eagerly.

Iriset smiles her best Singix smile. "Thank you."

"We've just come from the Moon-Eater's Mistress," Hehet says, and something about his confiding tone makes it sound as though he wants her to think he's not a threat. "Her Glory is interviewing some miran in the Bright Star Obelisk Garden on your behalf this morning."

"My behalf?" Baffled, Iriset doesn't bother hiding it.

Dove grins. "Every good secretary in the palace of the Vertex Seal is an even better gossip."

With a growing sense of dread, Iriset makes a distressed little hum and hurries away from them, toward whatever mischief—or worse—Amaranth is plotting.

The Bright Star Obelisk Garden was once a water garden, but after the death of Safiyah the Bloody's brother Dalir, the waters were drained and the obelisk erected in his honor. The water channels were replaced by blood-red tiles and rows of pristine glass-vein succulents both small and large. In the sunlight they twinkle and glare, shining in every shade of green and yellow that glass can manage. Crescents and circles of stretched linen have been lifted high with wire stalks and placed strategically to imitate yet more succulents while shading the low benches. Rainbow bees buzz around looking for sweet ecstatic pops, and regular blue-and-yellow butterflies bob in the air. Hidden force-fans circulate a breeze so that even at the height of summer it's not terribly unpleasant.

Several of the benches and gazebos are occupied by loitering miran, and Iriset spots Amaranth's handmaidens perched on low pillows, each engaged in one of their hobbies: Istof is practicing calligraphy and Ziyan repairing a long-necked lute, while Anis embroiders on radiant orange silk. Beyond them, in the shade of a succulent-shaped umbrella, Amaranth sits on a stone bench speaking with a young mirané man Iriset doesn't know.

Iriset sweeps in, her thin slippers crunching softly on the path. Everyone covers their eyes as she passes. When she reaches Amaranth, the miran with Her Glory stands and bows deeply, both hands over his eyes.

"Singix," Amaranth says merrily. "This is Huya méra Luméri, and I believe he'll make a very good secretary for you. He knows everything there is to know about the schedules of mirané princes and various palace itineraries, and is aware of all the necessary levels of propriety. Also, he came up through the army and has some combat-design training."

Iriset stares at Amaranth for a moment, then looks to Huya. He straightens, eyes lowered. He's a thin young miran with a beard shaved in repeating waves along his jaw, and a sheer green scarf wrapped through his thick braids. The long end flutters against his temple, ready to be pulled across his eyes as a cloth mask. The only cause to argue his appointment is because Iriset wants to, not for any good reason. She can handle a lightly trained combat-designer. So she nods only a little stiffly. "Very well. Thank you for helping me, Huya. This is Shahd, and she can situate you."

"Your Glory," Huya says.

"Why don't you do that right now, Shahd?" Amaranth suggests. "I'll attend to Singix."

Once they leave, Amaranth gives Iriset a slow raptor smile. "I saw my brother."

Iriset ignores her and sits daintily beside Amaranth on the bench. "Who killed Iriset mé Isidor?" she asks, picking at her layered gown, hoping she can stop wearing these heavy chest pieces sooner rather than later. The pressure isn't bad unless it's too hot to breathe easily.

Amaranth groans. "Ah, Singix, what a question."

"Your Glory," Iriset says through clenched teeth. "It's been nearly a quad since she died. We all owe her better than this."

"We don't know," Sidoné says from behind Iriset, and Iriset startles hard.

The body-twin touches Amaranth's shoulder to brush thick curls away and glances right at Iriset. Her black eyes are tired and serious.

Iriset frowns. "That's it?"

"If we knew," Amaranth says with false drama, "the culprit would be bound and arrested, and you would certainly have heard."

It's hard not to roll her eyes. Iriset barely keeps her expression soft when she stares at Sidoné. "Suspects?"

Sidoné shakes her head. The thick red paint across her eyes and the bridge of her nose gleams in the sun. "The truth is, the evidence was never much, and there is no good trail. We have conjecture and suspects, yes, but nothing to single anyone out."

"We need more information," Amaranth drawls.

"You mean another attempt on my life."

"I do." Amaranth lifts her eyebrows as if challenging Iriset to complain about it. When she doesn't, the Moon-Eater's Mistress continues, "But I've gotten you a secretary with excellent skills, and Lyric has already requested a larger rotation of Seal guard for you."

"More security won't encourage another attack," Iriset mutters, thinking.

Amaranth laughs. "I can hardly leave you obviously vulnerable after what you've done to my brother."

Reminding herself she can't scowl with Singix's face, Iriset only turns primly away. "I'll allow Huya to make me some appointments, then, with whomever you want, Your Glory. And I want to go into the city. I'll send a message to Nielle mé Dari, who was very friendly to me." She lowers her voice to add, "Being seen out and about might create some opportunities. And I can continue to investigate myself who was eager for this alliance between the empire and the Ceres Remnants, and who resented it. Was Dove méra Curro in favor of it?"

Surprise colors Amaranth's answer: "Yes, but that's because he loves nothing more than a stirred pot."

Sidoné laughs once, but it's not very amused.

"You asked him to recommend secretaries?" Iriset says.

"I did." Amaranth looks past Iriset, in the direction from which she'd come. "You ran into him."

"And Hehet méra Davith. He doesn't like me."

Both Amaranth and Sidoné flick disagreeing looks at her. "Hehet doesn't have opinions like that," Amaranth says after a moment. "He doesn't care one way or another about anything that isn't a fact."

"Well. If you say so. Who does Hehet's faction think poisoned my candy?"

"Ama already told you," Sidoné says, leaning closer. She brings her body heat and a whiff of citrus perfume. "Hehet won't think anybody did it until there's proof."

"But Dove thinks it was a conspiracy between two princes who support the supremacy of the Four Fronts general—Lapis mé Matsimet, you remember? And that the conspirators worked with Beremé's approval." By her wrinkled nose, Amaranth clearly doesn't suspect her sharp-faced lover.

"Why would she approve?"

Sidoné says, "Beremé's faction openly disdains alliances of any kind, preferring the empire to grow as it always has. By violence. Which murder is."

Amaranth rolls her eyes. "Murder is beneath Beremé."

That does seem likely to Iriset, but so does the idea that Amaranth and Beremé are engaged in a long-term game of their own that might or might not include murder. If it was Beremé, Amaranth is protecting her. Fine.

"Lapis is a strong suspect," Sidoné says. "If the empire stops conquering new people in favor of alliance, those alliances will come with ceding of territories, and if we cede somewhere, we must do so elsewhere and her power will lessen, especially compared to her brother's. She's due home again soon, and perhaps will take the opportunity to complete what her subordinates could not."

Iriset grimaces delicately over the thought of playing bait for a long time, and anger tickles ecstatic force in her chest.

At least while she waits, she has plenty to do.

28

Graffiti

The Crimson Canyon is a lightning shape cut into the rock of Moonshadow City from the Saltbath precinct southeast into the Flower precinct, and home to hundreds of people.

Narrow stair-paths zig and zag from the crater floor down along the cliff walls, between shelf-houses, balconies, and caves, descending beneath the line of sunlight. The base of the canyon is one of the only places in the city from which Aharté's moon is never visible. Ropes have been strung across the open canyon from balcony to balcony, hanging with tiny force-lights and long wind-whistles. There's little breeze in the canyon, but when the wind penetrates, it does so with a tight roar that sends the lights bobbing and spinning, and the whistles a-scream. People swing off shelves using elaborate ropes and pulleys, or climb down hemp ladders, and others sit on balconies with their legs dangling. Those with shared histories and hardships draw together into neighborhoods, despite assimilation laws forcing them to marry outside their cultures. The empire can legislate marriage laws and reproductive taxes, but not stories. Not values. Not the unwritten markers of a stolen past.

Up in Moonshadow City, traditions and the most obvious of cultural markers must be hidden behind masks and under fashion so that they can't be easily taken away. But in the canyon, it's little trouble to identify ruddy-tan Sarians by the metal sewn into their scarves to keep ghosts away, square-faced Urs with too many horse figures woven into their hems, People of the Bow who paint on red freckles as an ancient sign of luck, and those descended from sturdy Pir tribes who bead their wealth into their clothes. There are peach-faced Osahar who remember how to pass along secrets through the knots in their hair. The only people missing from the canyon neighborhood are miran. And masks are few and far between.

This is where Bittor was born.

He was often hungry as a child, but never quite starving, and believed that kids without families were just meant to live on the edge like that. Street kids are rare in Moonshadow City because the complex infrastructures that divide and assimilate families also happen to take a lot of care of orphans. But Bittor's cat-eyes triggered various superstitions in the canyon—superstitions that kept people from taking him in, but also from turning him in or letting him starve. Because he was naturally athletic and fearless, he scampered up and down the ropes and pulleys and force-ribbons in the canyon like a sticky-fingered lizard and managed to get enough work running messages to last until he drew the attention of a post carrier who served the northern block in the Flower precinct and hated the messy-to-outsiders address system in the canyon, not to mention the perilous journey down. Her name was Tesmose mé Fira and she was afraid of heights. Bittor, at seven years, saw her shaking at the top of the stair-path and tried to help her combat some sudden-onset extreme vertigo. Bittor had never experienced vertigo and so his advice was lackluster. But his enthusiasm charmed her into ignoring his eyes and hiring him. Then she started to feed him and cleaned out a storage room in her housing petal for him to use. She registered him with the Silent priests and they gave her a stipend for her compassion. It was a solid, if not especially loving, relationship.

By the time he was fifteen, Bittor knew his way around the surface streets and alleys across the city and treated the Great Steeples and soaring petals of Moonshadow like the walls of the canyon, scaling them easily to use as excellent lookouts and even better access points. Thieving was more lucrative, and more fun, than postal delivery, and Bittor learned to appreciate good food and always having it.

He fell into a trap—literally—set by the Little Cat for enterprising thieves and was adopted again. As he studied new skills of subterfuge and sleight, Bittor blossomed. He was one of the few from the undermarket to meet the Little Cat's daughter before she officially joined the court. The first thing Iriset mé Isidor said to Bittor was "Osahar. Like me."

"How do you know?" Bittor hoped she was right. He'd never had a clue about his birth family before.

Iriset, only fourteen, poked a finger a little too sharply at his cheekbone, then jabbed at his brow, almost getting his eye. Bittor shied away. "My skin? A lot of people have skin this color. Sarians sometimes."

"Your skull." Iriset flashed him a bright grin. "We could be cousins. Also—" She tugged a thick curl of brown hair hanging over his ear. "Texture. See?"

Spinning around, Iriset offered him a look at her heavily knotted brown hair.

Bittor took it as permission to touch, so he did, but carefully.

And still, "A lot of hair feels like this. I know a mirané boy whose hair is just like ours."

Iriset rolled her eyes hard enough it rolled her whole head back as she laughed at him. "You're obviously not mirané, and besides, it's not one of those things but all those things. Texture, color, bone structure. And I have a theory that a lot of Osahar are inclined to strong ecstatic force. But if you won't believe me, that's your problem. Give me your hand."

He did believe her. And gave her his hand. He regretted it immediately when she shone a bright force-light in his eyes just to watch the slit pupils constrict, but he never pulled away.

When Bittor hears the rumor that the Little Cat's daughter was murdered in the palace of the Vertex Seal, he's in the hidden backroom of a wine shop with Dalal mé Roné and her little four-year-old son, Ooris, whose father was a mirané one-night lay and the blood bred true. They, along with the surviving members of the Little Cat's court who haven't fled, use a series of drops and old tunnels to stay in contact and reorganize with sympathizers in Saltbath. It's lunchtime and Ooris is helping the owner of this particular wine shop, Pel, roll out dough for frying—to a certain definition of helping, of course. Dalal busies herself with a design stylus, extracting the security map Iriset smuggled them from the crystal infrastructure.

Pel's brown-faced daughter bursts into the secret room, giving off nervous, jerky waves of flow. She doesn't even slide the door all the way closed before she says, "There was an assassination attempt on the Ceres princess! But Iriset mé Isidor stopped it somehow, and—and it killed her."

Bittor, on his feet with a hand on his retractable baton the moment they're interrupted, flinches. "What did you say?"

"The Little Cat's daughter—"

"Is this a rumor or a fact?" demands Dalal, also on her feet. Her son starts to cry, staring between his suddenly frightening mother and Bittor's blanching face.

The girl shakes her head. "Everyone is saying it, the bulletin graffiti, too. I didn't see it on the official scripts, but it only happened at dawn this morning."

She goes on, but Bittor doesn't hear more than a word or two through the noise of rising and falling in his skull. Suddenly he's sitting down, and he can't feel the tips of his fingers. Staring at his hands, he tries to snap—she always said, Iriset always said, snapping was ecstatic and could jump-start almost anything, especially if your dominant force was ecstatic. His fingers are too numb; he makes the motions but feels nothing.

Dalal's hands cover his, curling his fingers up, and she holds tight. They sink off the benches and onto their knees on the ground. Ooris pats Bittor's face, wiping at tears. He blinks and more fall, but he barely feels grief. It's all physiological so far, Iriset would say. His body reacting before his brain catches up.

He hears a song, a broken melody, and realizes little Ooris is trying to sing. The melody is something to focus on, and his hearing returns in a rush.

Ooris pats his face again, still singing a song Bittor recognizes. One of the old rebel songs Dalal's grandmother sang. "That's a good song," he says hoarsely.

"Mama taught me," the little mirané boy says. "Are you better?"

"No," Bittor admits, gaze lifting to Dalal. He might never be better again. But he knows what to do next.

In Moonshadow City, graffiti is used for a lot of things. Art, sure; tagging, of course. But also advertisements both simple and elaborate, and passing messages that might be official, rumored, or illicit. It's not unusual for all three kinds to be layered into a charged graffiti design. Any artist can paint a tag onto the side of a pylon or a skiff, but artisan-designers can make them come to life.

Or at least give them the illusion of motion, create a looping series of actions to tell a quick story or transform from one thing into another. These can be affixed to pylons or skiffs or any surface. But they can also hang in the air itself, drawing energy from the forces crisscrossing the city from steeple to steeple.

In the Morning Market there are always several rows of force-graffiti listing changes in prices and what fruit is available today or how many of yesterday's cactus buns are left for half price. On artisan lanes, designers compete directly, showing up the galleries across the street or sabotaging new graffiti with tiny ecstatic viruses. Graffiti posters explode in happy little fireworks, showering safe, bright confetti onto sweepstakes winners or to celebrate a wedding or the birth of a child. Often graffiti pops up satirizing this or that small king or mirané prince. The Moon-Eater's Mistress is a popular subject, and her brother but less so, and while their mother, Diaa, frequently complains that Lyric ought to outlaw the use of their persons in jokes, it isn't their specific faces used, so neither of them are interested in censorship. Amaranth rather likes it when one of her handmaidens or Beremé brings her examples. Technically, the force-flowers the palace architects designed to decorate the sky during the welcoming procession for Singix Es Sun were developed from graffiti techniques.

Graffiti is rather ubiquitous in Moonshadow City, in other words.

It's a perfect tool to disseminate information and have a bit of fun. Even when he's devastated, Bittor can't help but be drawn to plans that are a little bit fun.

The graffiti fireworks he and Dalal design for the Day of Final Mercy are a dangerous sort of fun, but Iriset always loved her apostasy, so in her honor they lean in hard. The distraction works, and he skips and steps across the network of security like it's a tight trampoline, has his force-dart ready to cut through almost any armor, except the princess meets his furious gaze and he thinks she says his name.

He falters, and everything else falls apart.

She looks at him like she knows him, and it's not one thing: not her pear-blossom skin or the anguish in her pursed lips or the shape of her skull or her sleek hair or the shocking lack of any kind of mask.

It's all those things.

Bittor doesn't *know*. But he hopes.

And when the Days of Mercy end, the fragments of the Little Cat's court are ready with baskets full of salt coins holding brand-new graffiti, to scatter around the city.

29

Unrest

The security for Singix Es Sun is tight. Besides her secretary, Huya, and her personal attendant, Shahd, Garnet assigns twice as many Seal guards as usual to orchestrate Iriset's leaving the palace to visit the home of the small king of the Ecstatic Steeple Shadow precinct.

It takes so long for it all to be arranged that Iriset assumes a little petty revenge on the part of the Moon-Eater's Mistress.

In the meantime, she plays her role to avoid suspicion. Since none of the design tools Sidoné sourced for her the night she became Singix made it back into her possession after the wedding, Iriset must start from scratch building or acquiring before she can get to the real work. So Iriset allows Huya to set up meals and tea with mirané princes, accepts future invitations to visit other small kings and enjoy various high-class entertainments in the city. She takes Shahd on long, meandering walks in between appointments as if learning the palace complex—but really remapping the security nets for herself. Though not strictly necessary as she can't use an the same way as before, Iriset wants to see Raia mér Omorose again, and commissions an aviary to be installed in the arched ceiling of her greeting chamber, populated by a small flock of skull sirens and bright green-and-yellow finches. The finches are a sharp counterpoint to the cries of the sirens, and when they sing at sunset or titter with the dawn, it's more pleasant than chimes. Raia designs a ribbon for the birds to follow out through the lattice in the spiral stairway, for fresh air and room to spread their wings, and a net of forces to catch the birds' droppings and whisk them away. Though an doesn't know they're friends, Iriset finds comfort in Raia's company. It's a struggle to keep her opinions of ans design to herself, even though they're mostly complimentary. When she reveals herself at the end of all this, she hopes Raia will be on her side.

When the time finally comes for Iriset to visit Nielle, Huya gives her a half-circle mask of sheer blue silk and silver wire, and too many Seal guards escort them to the royal skiff. The skiff is designed like most, an oblong cup perched on four skids perfectly balanced between the forces, with specialized hooks in front to latch on to the force-ribbons threaded throughout the city streets and smoothly tug the skiff along. Though many skiffs have bubble roofs of glass or flow-thinned crystal panes, this has tiny steeples to anchor a force-shield that is perfectly see-through but impervious to weather and most projectiles. Iriset leans forward to study the prime steeple in the narrow nose as best she can with only her eyes: It's flow force, to be expected, while the three balancing steeples in the back have rising and falling to either side and ecstatic in the rear for those occasionally necessary bursts of speed or sudden brakes. The driver hovers in a smaller cup attached to the skiff's nose from which they can hold and tug the force-reigns to steer and maneuver.

Iriset sits carefully on one of the cushioned benches with Shahd and Huya in front, and a Seal guard beside. The rest of the guard company slide alongside the skiff, attached to its dynamics by individual skaters. Iriset wants one. She folds her hands in her lap to keep from touching anything as the skiff shudders and pulls forward.

Life as her father's daughter had seen Iriset sheltered in many ways, despite the murder and apostasy, or because of it, and she's experienced only a fraction of what Moonshadow City has to offer. A few times she ventured out of Saltbath wedged between her protective grandparents, who took her to the Edge Market to shop for exotic seeds in the hot greenhouses. Once Bittor snuck her into the rafters of the layered dome of the Theater of Silent Delights to listen to a choir from Eastrass City perform at a charity event. Though she didn't thieve herself, sometimes she joined Dalal or Paser on jobs when they had to break into especially well-guarded buildings and the Little Cat's designers needed Silk's skills to pry apart their security nets herself. In the early morning she'd wait alone for them to complete the job in one of the all-night cafés perched along the force-lines of the Cirrus Suspension Bridge, listening to the cries of skull sirens and watching the city wake up under the moon.

On the way to Nielle's home in the Ecstatic Steeple Shadow precinct, the ribbon skiff passes through the Silent precinct with its labyrinthine streets and spiraling tower gardens, then the Lodestone precinct, which is much more perpendicular but terraced with rosette houses and shops, and Iriset has plenty to stare at, including the distant chain of island apartments hovering high off the ground in the Falling Steeple Shadow precinct. She knows they work thanks to ingenious loops of falling force, but exclaims anyway.

Despite the heat, the layered city streets are alive with pedestrians and fellow skiffs, cafés with their doors thrown open and force-fans working hard. Several times people pause to stare and Iriset waves back shyly, though by the time anyone realizes who she must be and begins to point, the skiff has already moved on.

The Ecstatic Steeple itself casts a massive shadow most times of the day, curving across its precinct with the passing of the sun. Iriset appreciates the temporary shade as they drive beneath it, resenting that they can't drop the bubble shield so that she can feel the strength of her dominant force respond to the power crackling around the steeple.

They arrive just on time at the fourth small king's manor, set off from the wide avenue behind a garden of granite boulders in red-pink-white, and miniature juniper trees shaped into perfect spheres. The home is built like two concentric star succulents, each with four elegant towers offset from one another. Very conservative. Iriset suspects that Nielle hates it.

Before exiting the skiff, Iriset turns to Shahd. "We'll be here for two hours. Is that enough time to see your mother?"

"Of course, Your Glory," Shahd says, fingers to her eyes. The attendant climbs out and hurries off, messages for undermarket drops hidden in her sleeves.

The moment Iriset alights, Nielle is there with all her enthusiasm and a ruffled pink split-skirt dress, bare arms gleaming mirané brown, and an elaborate mask of thin orange leather strips charged into place. It seems combed into her heavy updo of curls, and it cups over her upper face without touching the skin. Perfect for a hot summer day to let a breeze in between mask and face. "Your Glory!" she calls. "Welcome to Ecstatic Steeple Shadow! Come in, come in."

Before Iriset can do more than nod, Nielle offers her arm and whisks Iriset to an inner courtyard. This one is lush with tropical plants kept alive all year by carefully tended force-shields to trap moisture, heat, and light. A picnic of chilled fruit and dry pear cider is already spread out, and Nielle doesn't pause her chatter even to share the snacks. Iriset lets herself be overwhelmed, blissfully sweating among trumpet flowers the size of her head and striped pink-and-green boe leaves.

Both have long removed their masks and Iriset lifts Nielle's from the picnic blanket. She inspects it and tentatively asks, "Where did you get this? It seems suited to the weather."

"Oh, well…" Nielle grins, and Iriset is struck, just as she was when first meeting the handmaiden, that enthusiasm is all Nielle ever needs to make her unbalanced face appealing. "I made it," she confesses.

Iriset parts her lips and reverently sets the mask back down. "Amazing. How?"

"Let me show you my workshop." Nielle leaps up from her cushion and hauls Iriset after her with a giggle. The workshop is much larger than the half room Nielle used back in Amaranth's petal, and absolutely dripping with supplies. Iriset feels ecstatic in her pulse, and rising lifts her chin as she turns around, inspecting it all with excitement.

Nielle sits her down and shows her the basics, asking all sorts of questions about whether Singix can draw or is any good with colors. Then she goes on a tangent about how different cultures actually think different colors go well together, and how she thinks that Ceres prefers bold colors all mingling together because of their tropics, but the mirané people are more strict and like to make perfect matches of only two (or four) colors, and does Singix think that's because of Silence and the rules of design, or were the miran born that way and created their faith and art to match a natural visual preference?

"Is it visual preference, or emotional?" Iriset wonders, and Nielle hugs her, declaring that she knew they'd get along. Then they get down to business. First on the agenda is the mask Iriset brought.

Nielle breaks down its elements and complains at its lack of decoration or statement, though backtracks that naturally a person as breathtakingly gorgeous as Singix needn't make a statement after all. Unless she wants to.

Iriset admits she likes the plain blue mask, and that the frame and cloth combination remind her of the silk squares her people use for fans and shades and hair decorations.

"If you like it, then perhaps just some trim?"

They work for an hour in pleasant companionship, Iriset asking all sorts of questions about the tools and where Nielle acquires them, and Nielle blithely answering. Iriset mentions that this might be a fine hobby for a foreign princess to take up and in return is gifted with enough tools to nearly complete a starter set. Nielle bumps their shoulders together and says, "And I'm making this one just for you."

Glancing at the mask, Iriset lifts her brows in a question.

"You'll see," Nielle teased.

When it is time for Iriset to depart and Huya comes to fetch her, Nielle hands Iriset a small box of beginner mask-making supplies, then with a flourish presents the real gift. Nielle offers the full-face mask, looking boldly into Singix's eyes. Iriset glances at the creation.

The mask is deep green ceramic, edged at the brow in white fur. Ugly black thread is sewn across the eyeholes like slicing scars, with red glass beads rather like blood splattered around. It's appalling, nothing that suits the perfect loveliness of Singix of the Beautiful Twilight. Iriset loves it.

She says so, then promises to wear it the next time there's a gathering of small kings at the palace.

"It's Leq'ina," Nielle says, frowning.

Iriset knows the name of the Ceres demon of obedience—each of their virtues is ruled by a god and a demon—and she raises her chin. "I know," she says. "Leq'ina icons often depict him with a full mane of white hair. I will acquire a silver veil and bead it with glass and pearls to accentuate the likeness."

Nielle seems mollified. Good, because that's everything Iriset knows about the demon of obedience.

———— • ♦ • ————

Shahd waits by the skiff already, and when she helps Iriset climb up, she squeezes her hand twice to let her know the notes were delivered. Iriset hopes Bittor can do something to get her grandparents to safety, and that he can coordinate with her on the timing of her new array.

They take an alternate route back to the Crystal Desert, down along the border between Lodestone and Saltbath toward the Silent precinct. This time of year, most businesses shut down for an hour or so after noon to escape the worst heat of the day and allow force-fans to recharge. The royal skiff slides them through the larger streets without much traffic or audience.

Iriset is feeling pleased with herself, smug even, at how good she's getting at this game. Though it's frustrating that she must go through the process of gathering design tools again as Singix when she already did it as herself.

A sudden brake jerks her gently forward on the bench. She grabs for the safety handle against the side of the cabin as Shahd leans forward to inquire after the driver's reason for such an abrupt stop. But Huya snaps his fingers and uses a ring-trigger to activate the skiff's external force-shield. It crackles in a smooth web of ecstatic flow, and the Seal guard in with them puts a hand on the hilt of his force-blade. Outside, the eight other Seal guards move: Four step off the skates to realign themselves with the four still riding the sides of the skiff. They're ready to move into one of the intricate combat dances to raise power.

Nothing attacks. Iriset frowns, a little wiggle of uncertainty in her chest.

"Let's go," the Seal guard inside says. "Slow and steady, keep in a pear-blossom eight-nine form."

But the skiff doesn't move. They've just passed into the Silent precinct, driving along a broad bridge-avenue ribbon above the middle-class residential neighborhoods. Tall houses are built tightly together, some of them over shop fronts, others with small balcony gardens. Beneath the ribbon at street level, canvas shades and umbrellas are a quiet, flickering rainbow. Everything is strangely still, even the handful of children on the elaborate playground at the end of the bridge.

"Why aren't you driving?" asks Huya.

The driver, a middle-aged miran with ambiguous gender-forward features whose name Iriset didn't catch so she doesn't know what to assign them, shakes their head. "There's a disruption in the ribbon ahead, nothing for our slides to hook into. We can go back?"

"Do it," the Seal guard in charge commands. "Ilay, Asmet, tie off the skiff to those rising platforms."

In case the bridge gives out. Iriset grips the safety handle tight enough to whiten her knuckles.

Before the driver manages to reverse the force-loops, Iriset feels the ripple of a large blast of rising force, and the air in front of the skiff flashes in vivid silver-gold lines. A crawling graffiti.

The skiff backs up, but the graffiti is huge: An alliraptor lifts up from the road, opens its jaw, and silently roars, then a woman appears behind it. She crouches and pets its head. The alliraptor curls its scaly tail around her and they sit together. She kisses it, then strokes it, and the alliraptor unravels into fine threads of blood-red and mirané-red, re-forming into a spider looming over the woman.

Silk is Syr, the graffiti announces.

Oh, fuck, Iriset thinks, craning her neck to see as the graffiti hangs there, and then to either side of it, more graffiti bursts to life: *Silk lives*, one says; another says, *Moon to crater*, invoking Bittor's rebellious words from the Day of Final Mercy.

• ♦ •

Six other locations across Moonshadow City experience similar displays at the exact same moment in the early afternoon. That's seven total, a very unbalanced number meant to discomfort the illustrious Silence of the city. Nobody is hurt, it was only graffiti. (Though some youths in the Fountain precinct use the distraction to shoplift several pocketfuls of rare snail shell buttons.) But everyone is talking about it, and nobody believes it was a coincidence that Singix Es Sun was a direct witness to the largest graffiti.

When he sees Iriset, Lyric immediately cups her face in his hands and studies her carefully. "I'm restricting you to the palace for now."

Jerking back, Iriset lets herself gasp in shock and disagreement. "Why? Does it not make you seem weak to keep me hidden away? Shouldn't we show we are not afraid?"

He doesn't let go of her face as he says firmly, "I am not concerned with seeming weak or seeming strong: I'm only concerned with being so."

Iriset feels herself flushing under his palms and covers his hands with her own, slotting her fingers between his. The gentle command of his tone makes her want to shove her tongue as deep in his mouth as possible. It's a struggle not to. His affection threads inside her like thin little worms, digging at the roots of her anger. The only way to combat her very requited feelings and keep her mind sharp is to act like it's just sex.

See, Iriset is *well aware* of the problematic nature of her lust for her husband.

"Lyric," she murmurs. "You promised me I was not your subordinate."

His eyelids flinch twice in obvious surprise. He is unused to his wife challenging him at all.

Lyric drops one hand from her face but leaves the other, sliding it down to cup her jaw. "Then allow me to prioritize your safety for a quad or two so that the city army has a chance to eliminate this trouble," he says, settling his thumb against the corner of her mouth. She turns to kiss it, preferring to bite or suck, but they are standing in a cavernous entryway of the Hall of Princes.

If she were Iriset mé Isidor, she would push harder, point out the reasons she should get to do what she wants, that she can protect herself. If she were Iriset, she'd ask the Vertex Seal why, if he's so worried about her safety, he hasn't started decimating his own court until he discovers who tried to kill Singix, discovers who *managed* to kill his "little arguer." But the role she's playing doesn't allow demands, and she needs more time to prepare before she strips the disguise away. So Iriset only schools her face into sorrow, a pretty little pout if she's being honest.

"And, Singix," Lyric coaxes. "I *am* afraid."

When he uses that tone with his perfect, beautiful, undemanding foreign wife, what can she do but agree?

30

The nature of empire

Iriset takes the first few days of her restrictions to hole herself up in the study she shares with Lyric to fully redesign the distraction array into a destructive one, adding poetry to the graffiti's grand imagery, and snippets from *Word of Aharté*.

An unforeseen downside to the palace restrictions is that her personal attendant can't leave, either, so Shahd can't check the drops for messages or news about Iriset's grandparents. Shahd is immediately aware of Iriset's frustration and asks if there's anything else she can do. Her eyes shine when she looks at Iriset—ever since Iriset admitted what she's done, becoming Singix, Shahd has looked at her sometimes with this light.

It's difficult for Iriset to parse, as she can't tell if Shahd has developed a passion for her, overcome by Singix's stolen beauty—for which Iriset couldn't blame her—or if Shahd fell fully into rebellion for the romance of it. Or could she almost grasp what Iriset is truly doing? Either way, Iriset has clearly become an object of some kind of devotion. Her instincts tell her to use it.

Of course, she can't just ask Shahd directly.

Iriset opens the thin drawer of slowly accumulating beads,

buttons, wire, and crystal shards for mask making. Removing four tiny opals shaped like grains of wheat, she offers them. "You should take these, go to your family, and not come back."

Shahd leans away, hurt. "You don't want me here? You asked for me. You know I won't tell—I haven't, why would I now?"

"Because it's dangerous. Before, I was only doing what Amaranth wants and surviving and trying to save my father. But now I'm going to do what *I* want."

"To rebel? With Bittor méra Tesmose?"

Iriset blows a heavy breath, wishing she could get word from Bittor. She tucks the opals away. "Rebellion is more of a side effect of my real goal."

Shahd waits for clarification. The young woman is almost vibrating.

"I want to prove a point. The Holy Silence is incomplete. Aharté's teachings flawed. And the Vertex Seal is *wrong*. About so many things." Iriset tries to speak evenly, but when she talks about Lyric, her voice trembles. "But especially apostasy. And mercy."

"You really don't fear apostasy? Or Aharté's wrath?" Shahd's voice is quiet.

"I'm married to Aharté's wrath. What's there to fear when he's in my bed?" Iriset says viciously.

Shahd gasps—not at the tone, probably, but at the conceit.

Iriset swallows back the spike of emotion just to breathe for a moment, and glances down at her sketch, giving Shahd a respite from her gaze. "So, will you help me, Shahd?"

"*Yes*," the girl breathes.

It occurs to Iriset a bit too late that she's creating herself into another kind of god.

―――――― ◆ ――――――

As most days Iriset has to act the part of Singix for hours, and she can hardly work at night now that she's married to an attentive husband, it takes a bit of time for her to complete her initial redesign and choose the best locations for her new anchors.

Having Shahd on her side makes setting those design-anchors throughout the palace complex rather more straightforward. With an attendant, Iriset has no need to make excuses as everyone assumes she's on her way somewhere, or merely pausing to examine some strange mirané bit of architecture or a flower she's unfamiliar with and Shahd can give her the name of. In each anchor location, Iriset tucks a little shard of silicate or opal charged with an open loop inside a wall or under a tile or concealed in the roots of a succulent. The activation trigger will close all the loops at once and bring her design to life.

Shahd not only keeps watch but provides excellent distractions. When Iriset needs to plant an anchor in one of the dining rooms tucked inside the mirané hall while lunching with a trio of mirané princes on the council's foreign relations committee, Shahd spills rose wine down her robes for a momentary distraction. Because she is sweet, quiet, and mirané herself, she never receives more than a tsk or pitying glance for her clumsiness. Once, she even distracts Huya for two entire minutes so Iriset can fiddle with a tricky anchor that needs to be set near a fountain with strong natural falling and rising forces that might disrupt the charge glue.

They never try anything if Amaranth is nearby, which she often is, drawing Iriset into her circle as if to prove that there's no reason to leave, no reason to fear.

———— • ♦ • ————

There are two other major threads to her scheme, and eight days into her restrictions, she's working on one.

A nearly invisible design net, painstakingly knitted using strands pulled from the force-shield behind Lyric's desk, spreads over her worktable among the detritus of mask making. She's got her makeshift stylus poised over a thin smear of crumbled ochre that's spread over the net. Iriset stops breathing, activates the net, and touches her stylus to the ochre.

A flash of heat warms her lips, and she watches as the reddish powder shivers and tiny particles are drawn to the center, as if by a magnet. The moment the particles are grouped tightly enough that she can see the shape of them in contrast with the rest of the ochre, Iriset hooks a falling line from the design net and casts it across to the string of ecstatic pins, and then holds her breath again as her design completes.

She's looking down at a thin orange coin of reconstituted design-grade hematite the size of her little fingernail.

Iriset allows herself a smug grin—nobody does this kind of thing anymore, because it's so much delicate effort for so little reward when a licensed architect can simply buy hematite in the Descent Market. Iriset can't request hematite without answering difficult questions, but she can ask for red ochre for making her own dye combinations for painting masks. Red ochre is red because of hematite. Which Iriset has now extracted and formed into a very sleek coin.

Hematite is a perfect carrier for the disruptive dome she's building to give the numen.

Sweat itches at the nape of her neck, and Iriset sweeps the remnants of ochre into a little jar, rolls the used design net tightly, and puts it with her styli in the hidden compartment. Then she stands and stretches. A sensation draws her attention, like a string pulling from her stomach down her spine. Usually nausea climbs up, but this is a falling nausea, she thinks to herself, curious more than worried. Her body has been treating her to several kinds of queasy feelings lately, though they've tapered off.

Though she can't work naked as she used to, she isn't wearing the majority of Singix's layers, and is barefoot. Eddies of natural force tease at her lips and open palms, and up her ankles. It's soothing as so few things are these days, so she closes her eyes and opens herself up further, breathing her eight-count meditation.

Extending her fingers to catch a few more drifting force-tendrils, Iriset notices a stutter in the flow of the architecture. Blinking, she flattens her hands to the tiled wall, walking her fingers like spiders over the old design until she finds the stutter again.

The secret door opens easily under her hand when she reads the pattern of taps knotted in. Of course she hurriedly explores the narrow passage, and finds that the stairway opens into a small chamber on the level below. The room is clean, empty, with no furniture, but a beautifully mosaicked ceiling of four-petaled vivid red flowers and old sigils spelling out a very intimate love poem.

Clearly previous Vertex Seals kept lovers.

She wonders if her husband knows. If not, this could make an excellent escape route for her if it becomes necessary. A way to slip out from under the watch of her guards and secretary. Maybe even to plant her anchors at night when Lyric sleeps.

Just as Iriset returns to the study, Shahd knocks and calls in that Singix Her Glory has a visitor.

Iriset grumbles to herself but quickly tucks everything away. Out in the main room, Iriset is surprised (and slightly dismayed) to find Diaa of Moonshadow. She's spent several meals with Lyric and Amaranth's mother, and the former consort just hasn't warmed up. Diaa hasn't said anything as blatant as Menna's racist comments when she paints Iriset's face some mornings, but Iriset has the direct comparison of how warm Diaa was to Iriset that she knows Diaa doesn't care for Singix. Which makes no sense! Everything about Singix is more likable than Iriset, from her manners to looks to level of criminal engagement.

Iriset can only suppose Diaa would dislike anyone married to her son.

"Your Glory," Iriset murmurs, lowering her gaze just enough so her lashes flutter closed for a moment. Singix was always fluttering her lashes.

"Your Glory," Diaa repeats, sweeping toward her. "You're looking pale, my dear, and I know you're feeling constricted lately. We all are."

Diaa cups her arm around Iriset's shoulder. The older woman smiles sympathetically. She has her hair slicked back, and a crescent mask of stiff purple lace sits against her forehead, either end curling asymmetrically around her eyes to make sharp points against her cheeks. The color brings out the reddish flecks in her mirané-brown eyes, very like Lyric's.

"You're under restriction, too?"

"Not so much as you, no, but since that terrible business with poison and the death of the Little Cat's poor daughter, it's been more difficult than usual to bring into the palace all my favorite things. And, you might as well learn now, being the wife of the Vertex Seal ought to privilege you to bring in anything you fancy."

As Diaa speaks, she walks Iriset to the door and shoos away

Shahd and the hovering Huya. Her own attendants wait outside, as well as a Seal guard, and Iriset watches, extremely impressed, as Diaa efficiently and lightheartedly dismisses everyone in favor of only those who belong to her household because she has some delicate things to discuss with her successor.

Then Diaa of Moonshadow whisks Iriset away and sneaks her out of the palace.

Iriset is most definitely paying attention. She'd recognized quads ago that Diaa had built a specific power base for herself that allows her to go where she wishes and say what she wants, but witnessing it in action like this shows Iriset that she's really not all that subtle herself. She keeps quiet, only voicing an almost-protest once, when she realizes Diaa is taking her through a hidden passage toward a private skiff, but her heart isn't in it when she asks, "What of the rebels?"

"The graffiti?" Diaa laughs, handing her a wire half-mask to occlude everything but her mouth. "My dear Singix, there are always rebels, and always graffiti, and for now I am grateful that it isn't featuring either of my children. Besides, that Silk apostate is dead, the Little Cat is dead, so this is merely the dying gasp of a fallen tribe."

Diaa is definitely too smart to truly believe that, but Iriset will take advantage of both of them pretending it's true.

They slip free without fanfare, and Diaa takes her daughter-in-Silence to an exclusive auction in the Opal precinct, where everyone has anonymous full-face masks—Diaa provides one for Iriset—and the bids are made with small placards designed to glow when a price is raised. Diaa acquires a basket of cocoa nuts and dried berries from the Bow for a shocking price, and that's that. They stop for cordials at a fancy shop on the roof of a luxury apartment spiral, surrounded by glass windmills fracturing sunlight into rainbows. Diaa gives Iriset a silk pouch with some of the nuts and berries. Diaa leans in like they're gossiping: "The cocoa can be ground and baked, and one of my attendants is a genius at cookies; I'll bring you some. It also makes a lustrous hair dye, though not for your tone, I imagine." She pinches the ends of one of Iriset's long braids. "But I've heard you're learning mask making, and I've noticed that some masks rather smell of glue. Cocoa smells marvelous to me. And the berries always come with the cocoa—I believe the merchants think they keep the cocoa fresh. They're not useful for dye, but they add a tart sweetness to tea."

Iriset thanks her genuinely, wonders what changed Diaa's mind, hopes it's not those pesky rumors of how, ah, compatible she and Lyric are, and drinks her cordial.

They do not get caught.

Two days later General Lapis mé Matsimet returns home, and at the welcoming banquet Iriset greets the general in the ugly mask of the demon of obedience.

Lapis laughs to see it, asking if it's a hint at what Singix of the Beautiful Twilight plans for her reign as the consort of the Vertex Seal. Iriset returns the smile, wondering if it's true that Lapis would benefit from wanting Singix dead and this marriage a failure. But she only says, "Naturally."

The general has been most recently at the eastern front, where the empire presses against Huvar, but she swept south to the coast where the islands are before returning home. She knows the gods and demons of virtue and has brought letters from Singix's family for her. Though Iriset hadn't intended it,

Lapis likes her instantly, and shoos even her burly twin brother, General Bey, away, rearranging seating placards at the throne table in order to plop down beside Iriset, though as the honored guest she should be with Lyric. The Vertex Seal accepts the general's seating arrangement then with an amused, distant smile, and says he himself prefers Singix's company to all others, and thus can't argue with Lapis's desire.

Lapis wears a formal white army summer uniform, her chest covered in the mirané-brown ropes of both status and accomplishment. Instead of a mask, her mouth is tinted a darker blue that spreads past her actual lips to make her mouth seem larger. The same effect surrounds her eyes in black, giving her a dangerously eager look, like a hungry, staring corpse. There is a gruesome scar on her bare left shoulder that begins in teeth marks at the top and courses down toward her elbow in furrows of hardened, darker tissue.

"A sarly staff did that, in the Bow," Lapis says when she notes Iriset staring. "I got all my movement and muscle back, but it pulls like a motherfucker."

Iriset twitches her lip at the curse, and says softly, "I am surprised you do not paint it."

Lapis's large mouth tilts in a speculative frown. "Good idea! Aharté pink and Seal red, maybe, like a holy wound."

This banquet is held in the mirané dining hall, at a massive low table shaped like a square that, once everyone has arrived, lifts off the floor upon force-stages. People sit along both the outer and inner edges, with the most honored at the throne side in the west. White, red, black and pink bulbs of light hover in the air, the colors in honor of the imperial army and Lapis specifically, and smoky images of singing alliraptors snake between the lights, grinning happily as they hum soft, discordant melodies. (Iriset wonders if the numen is ever brought to this room, or if it eats at all.)

While Lyric rules the western table, across the square in the east Amaranth holds her own court, surrounded by miran and military elite, including the commander of the Seal guard, Iumeri Selk, a warrior with Bow-black skin who wears ibis feathers in his hair and flirts constantly with Sidoné, though both of them are too close generationally to their conquered grandparents to be allowed to marry. Sidoné told Iriset she thinks Iumeri flirts with her exactly for that reason, and when she's having a bad day she flirts back, though she'll never marry a man, not even for politics.

When wine the exact silver-pink of Aharté's moon, infused with ecstatic to make it bubble and fizz, is served, Lapis stands with perfectly balanced strength and calls, "A toast!"

Bey says, "This is a banquet in your honor, sister. Ought we not be toasting to you?"

Laughter spreads, and Lapis touches the fingers of one hand to her left eye. "Yes, I will accept a toast to my name, though it perhaps should wait until I've managed to solve all your city-born rebellions for you."

That's met with gasps and laughter both, and Bey glowers. "Your methods will not be welcome in Moonshadow, sister, for you cannot raze in a city."

"A good force-quake might dissolve all the cult graffiti," she drawls, "and remind people to whom they owe allegiance. It's never a bad idea to be bold in such a reminder."

"And how should we be certain a force-quake wouldn't disrupt the bridges and ribbons while it erases graffiti?"

The banter feels rehearsed, like the Mirror Generals intend this argument to be public, perhaps to teach the miran something, or place the foundation of an argument they'll later make. Iriset is eager to answer anyway: A good architect can pinpoint certain frequencies in flow and rising, and therefore target the stick of graffiti but not the clutch of a bridge.

Menna, the Architect of the Seal, lifts her voice and says much the same. "However," she adds, "such a thing might not be done over the entire city—a specific neighborhood or precinct only."

"That would not do, for is the graffiti not popping up in *every* precinct?" Lapis widens her blackened eyes almost comically.

"Indeed," Bey says, "though there are patterns to it, in timing and revelation. We believe the instigator is centered in the Saltbath. After the first incident, the next three were equidistant from a point near the south canyon of Saltbath."

Amaranth calls, "Isn't the Saltbath where the Little Cat was captured?"

"It is," General Bey says. "I believe, again, given the timing and the nature of the art, one of the ringleaders is likely to be Bittor méra Tesmose, granted mercy these two quads ago."

Iriset lowers her eyes immediately at hearing his name, lest any reaction be noted.

"This discord is well spread," Beremé mé Adora says. A silver-and-black mask pinches her sharp nose, dyed-leather vines crawling up between her brows to arc across her forehead in twisting spikes and spirals, spreading over her temples like buffalo horns. Her eyes are unmasked, piercing and mirané brown. "And unconnected to any known cults. Interestingly, I heard, General, that much of the graffiti depicts a non-mirané woman embracing an alliraptor."

"Embracing," Lapis says, pretending to be scandalized. The general remains standing between the seated Iriset and Lyric.

"Oh my," Iriset murmurs.

"Is it not what you witnessed, Singix?" calls Amaranth.

Lifting her face, she tells the Moon-Eater's Mistress, "It was spectacular, Your Glory. The woman sat with the creature and tamed it, and she kissed its scales and it…unraveled." Iriset says the word almost like a question, as if maybe it's the wrong choice, though she knows it is not.

Several bodies away, Diaa of Moonshadow sets her cup of wine down stiffly. "That Silk person was no Holy Syr."

"In memory it may be that she becomes more dangerous than she was alive," the Vertex Seal says. He wears no mask, and the only paint on his face is silver dots placed among the black freckles on his cheek and temple to appear like bright little shadows. If only he realized it had been that very Silk who told him he need wear no mask, who had admired his freckles.

"Apostasy," Menna declares.

Lapis raises her cup again. "To Aharté and the Glorious Vow."

Iriset dislikes the toast but does her part.

Once everyone shares a sip of wine and passes their cups to the person on their left, Hehet méra Davith says, "I noticed something curious about the copies of the graffiti presented to the council," and there are a few murmurs of protest from miran who wish the subject turned.

"Do tell," Lapis encourages.

"There is one repeated motif wherein the woman—Silk, presumably—uses what must be a design stylus to draw wings on the alliraptor as if to give it flight. In this one, the woman wears no cloth mask, but bears quite a resemblance to Iriset mé Isidor."

Iriset widens her eyes, glad there's no need to hide her surprise. How did Amaranth not think Iriset needed to know this detail? It's unbelievably frustrating that she and Bittor can't coordinate! She looks to Lyric, who does not appear surprised, but only grim.

"Even more evidence to tie the rebellion to the Little Cat and Bittor méra Tesmose," General Bey says, as if that's all that matters.

Amaranth finally speaks up again. "I wonder if any of you have seen the most recent graffiti from today, princes?"

"From the Design precinct, Your Glory?" Iumeri Selk, the Seal guard commander, asks.

"That's right," she almost purrs, and Iriset braces herself for whatever Amaranth is about to say. "It depicts Silk—very much like Iriset—together with a man, maybe Bittor méra Tesmose himself. They smile with teeth like an alliraptor, then they kiss, and a star map appears around them, then Silk devours the man. Isn't that odd?"

Most of those gathered murmur and frown, but Iriset stares down at her fizzing wine. This is a message for her. Finally! Bittor realized a way to reach out to her.

Iriset remembers that star map. She'd been playing with it because her mother had asked her father once if the Cloud Kings knew what the stars were made of, because their castles were so much nearer. Isidor couldn't answer, because he'd left his family when he was so young, but the stars became a connection between them. Iriset designed a star map out of the four forces, a pretty display that could be charged like a force-lamp and set to glow. It was intended as a gift for her father the year Iriset turned sixteen.

"Perhaps he wants everyone to know his relationship with Silk, that he is her voice in the city? That they act as one?" Amaranth muses for the entire hall.

Iriset is grateful for her full-face mask. She hides her hands under the table and grips her knees. She understands the message. The trigger for the star map had been set into a necklace of knotted yarn and hematite, and she was wearing it the first time she kissed Bittor. She'd kissed him out of grief and the desperate need to be distracted, cheered up, before she faced her father. The kiss had triggered the design. As stars burst around them, Iriset had cried harder, thinking her mother wouldn't approve of her little girl making out with a thief from the undermarket. But Bittor had reacted to the map with awe.

That day, the first time she kissed Bittor, had been the fifth anniversary of her mother's funeral. An anniversary that will come around again in eighteen days.

Beremé says, "Perhaps, General Bey, we should revisit the option of a force-quake at the next meeting of princes. Though it could disrupt travel and trade throughout Moonshadow City, it might be good for the miran, merchants, and small kings to feel personally how disruptive such civil rebellion is to the empire. If it hurts the Holy Design, it hurts all of us."

The small king married to Nielle, Sian méra Sayar, throws up his hands but before he can argue, Hehet méra Davith raises his voice to suggest Beremé is merely joking, in a rather disdainful tone.

"It might convince some of the populace to turn them in," says Iumeri Selk from beside Sidoné.

General Bey snorts. "He isn't hurting anyone, or inciting any riots, and so it is difficult to coerce cooperation."

Iriset struggles to keep the bitter smile from her lips as she remembers General Bey's methods of coercion.

Lyric says, "I have confidence in my generals, as should the princes. Together, we will settle this in the most balanced means."

His statement forces a slight silence, and then Diaa of Moonshadow asks Lapis if she's considering taking any husband, which distracts everyone into a different sort of arguing.

But not Iriset. She has a deadline now.

———— • ♦ • ————

Alone in their chambers that night, Lyric catches Iriset's hand and tugs her toward him. His jaw is tight with tension and he studies her. They're washed of paint and the sweat of the day, oiled and robed in loose linen, ready to relax into bed.

"Lyric?" she murmurs.

"You were upset at the banquet tonight." He says it as an invitation to confide.

Iriset lowers her gaze, thinking fast, and leans her forehead against his jaw. "Do you really believe this graffiti rebellion is related to me? To the poison?"

"To the—no, not at all, sweetheart." Lyric touches his fingers to her chin, lifting her face. "Though if they are linking Iriset's likeness to themselves through their art, perhaps this Bittor méra Tesmose is angered that she died under our care. That may be why he initially attacked."

"When he tried to kill you," she whispers.

"And you stepped between us," Lyric whispers back. "Perhaps you are one of his targets now."

"It's only art," she assures.

Lyric huffs softly, with humor.

Iriset goes in for the kill. "It seems there is always rebellion brewing in the Holy City."

Lyric's smile falls away. "Always?"

With a little shrug, she walks around the bed to hold a hand to a little skull siren perched on the scales of the alliraptor bed. It followed them up from the aviary downstairs. Though it cocks its head, she has no seed, and so it merely ruffles its crest and hops along the alliraptor's back. "Since I arrived, there has always been something, and treated casually enough it seems to be common."

"There are criminals everywhere," he says dismissively. "Even those nearest to us."

Swallowing, Iriset says, "But—this is rebellion. Not crimes like murders and thievery. The cult of Singers when I arrived, and this new rebellion, are a different sort of crime, are they not?"

He nods reluctantly. "Crimes against the empire, against She Who Loves Silence, not against individual people. State crimes, I suppose they might be called. But, Singix, some people chafe at laws, at community itself—they will never be satisfied with what is necessary to govern such a vast state, with such different folk within."

"It is the nature of the empire, then? It requires rebellion, for balance?" Iriset can barely keep her voice gentle, so near to herself, to what *she* would say if she were here. She likes being herself with him so much. Too much. She wants to tear into him—tell *him* he has only eighteen days left of her. *Better make the most of it, Lyric. You'll never have the likes of me again.*

Lyric opens his mouth, then stops. He sits upon the edge of the bed and puts his elbows on his knees, cupping his chin in his hands. As Iriset watches, his gaze seems to unfocus, as if he thinks so deeply his vision blurs. "It is the nature of Silence in our mortal, flawed grip," he says finally. His shoulders heave in a sigh. "Balance requires some specific acts, specific placement of regulation, both literally—physically, like the force-steeples—and spiritually. The empire was built on these acts and regulations, and if they are not maintained, the entire structure will collapse."

"What if the structure is weak in places? Or rotten in its very center?"

The Vertex Seal glances sharply at her. "What are you thinking, Singix?"

She shakes her head quickly, coming around to sit beside him. She is *not* Iriset, his royal arguer. *Not yet.* "I apologize. I meant nothing critical of you, but I am worried for you." Iriset touches the side of his leg. "Is that not my prerogative now? To worry about my husband?"

It mollifies him. He covers her hand. "The center of the empire is strong, and good, because at the center is pure Aharté, and Silence. Human beings are not pure, and in our time the miran and my ancestor Vertex Seals may have pushed too hard in one place, or in one direction, marring balance, causing harm to the structure, allowing weakness to take hold. And others latch on to those places. Extremism, some of the laws of assimilation, the occasional corruption of small kings—those such things open the doors to apostasy and rebellion. But it is the extremism, corruption, and outdated laws that should be changed, cleaned out, for the rest of the body to survive."

"Rebellion points to weaknesses in the system, but not that the system itself is weak?"

The look Lyric gives her then, thoughtful and veering toward suspicion, causes a chill falling to drain through her skin. She's said too much, analyzed too much. He says firmly, "Rebellion points to the faithless. To people who want selfishly for themselves, not for the greater good of Silence. The current protest is not suggesting Isidor Salisidor was innocent, or that the army or myself have done something wrong. What is it that this Bittor méra Tesmose is protesting with his apostatical graffiti, except Aharté's Silence itself?"

Exactly, Iriset thinks.

Though Iriset also thinks it's possible Bittor is using the graffiti to consolidate power, to regrow parts of the Little Cat's undermarket that were cut away or atrophied. Whether he believes in his message or not, he still chose rebellion. He must have crafted the graffiti to honor her. How often had Bittor listened to Silk spell intricate arguments for why human architecture should not be a crime? She's never had faith in Aharté, and didn't hide her faithlessness from her friend and lover. He's doing this for her. Centering her. She can't wait to answer him.

In eighteen days she'll be ready to shift the heart of this empire from the inside, even if only to destabilize it, to prove that it's always been unstable. Apostasy only exists if you believe in god. Lyric believes in Silence, and Bittor may believe in rebellion, but Iriset believes in herself.

In her quiet, Lyric squeezes her hand. "And, Singix, what is the alternative? The empire is not perfect. How can it be, with flawed rulers and flawed citizens? But it is better than the chaotic hell that was the Apostate Age. Someday everyone will see the goodness in balance, in Aharté's Silence. That is what I hope for, what I work for. I know it is a real thing, a goal that can be met, because I am bound to it, as is my sister. The Holy Design moves through us and with us." He lifts her hand to his chest. "You must feel it, too, when our hearts beat together?"

"I do," she whispers, a lie, because faith is not what she feels in moments like these. She feels the effects of the marriage knot, a miracle of human architecture despite what the Silent priests claim. She feels the inevitable break between them: the promise of triumph and the cold, brutal look in his eyes when he sees what she's done. When she shows him Aharté's will is not as strong as her own.

Late that night, while the Vertex Seal sleeps, Iriset slips down into their study, rifles through her accumulation of leather and beads, glue and ceramic with which to make elaborate mirané masks, finds paper and charcoal, and she begins again to draw Lyric's face.

31

Even the red moon fell from the sky

If the reminder of her husband's fanaticism teaches her anything, it's that she needs to prioritize the final piece of her plan higher: destabilizing the marriage knot. She can create her ruinous, ambitious array, she can reveal herself, her power, and set the numen free, but without dissolving or otherwise unraveling the marriage knot, there's nowhere she can run that Lyric can't follow.

And she assumes he would follow.

Iriset asks Diaa of Moonshadow a few questions under the pretense that she occasionally feels an odd twist. Diaa overreacts by interrogating Lyric himself in case there's something wrong with their marriage knot, who in turn worriedly tries to take Iriset to the Silent priests who constructed their design eggs in the first place for a deep analysis. Needing to avoid that at nearly all costs, Iriset lies her guts out to Lyric, saying she was only trying to find more in common with his mother so that they can grow closer, and honestly, the twists she occasionally feels in their marriage knot only are pulling them more irrevocably together. Obviously, she has sex with him about it.

Having dodged that dart, Iriset attempts to investigate the knot in more detail herself, but it's most prominent in her inner design when she and Lyric are near to each other and Lyric will notice if she pokes around. Iriset gives him a massage one evening, perched on his naked bottom, and runs her hands vigorously all over him. If she can distract him with friction, maybe he won't detect the little investigatory threads of force she simultaneously slips in.

That doesn't work, either, thanks to the very marriage knot itself. Who knows if Lyric has always secretly been this horny or if he's just feeding off Iriset's natural inclination, but the investigation part of the massage lasts only a few minutes before Lyric is moaning softly and nudging his ass up against Iriset's. Then she's the one thoroughly distracted by having to pretend she's never fisted a man before while she tries to get Lyric to tell her it's what he wants.

They end up in the bathroom, both it and each other wrecked, and while panting in the afterglow on the cool tiles with her ankles dangling in the warm water, Lyric melted and passed out with his hand curled over her belly, Iriset wonders if maybe she's been wrong this whole time and she should stay with Lyric forever. Do what Amaranth wants; use the position the way her father suggested; take what Lyric offers, the love and power; be happy.

But it's only a passing postcoital thought. She could never be happy in even the most holy cage.

She sits up with a spark of ecstatic, sways because she's rather melted herself, but Lyric is passed out! Scooting closer, she rolls him half over and plasters herself against him. She digs her fingers into his hair, scratches her other hand down his spine, and he only murmurs. Iriset pecks her lips against his cheek, making sharp kissing noises to send ecstatic pops into his inner design.

It's slightly awkward, and as mentioned, Iriset is droopy herself. But she manages to get a good look at the knot, at how tendrils of forces reach from his toward hers, and hers does the same toward him. If she had her old silk glove, maybe she could pinch along the whole thread, even where it goes thin and insubstantial in the air between them.

The knot design is so old, so intimate, and somehow pure. *It's magic*, Iriset thinks in a rare, sleepy concession to romance.

And it's definitely human architecture.

Without her glove and a few styli and a diagram to record the intricate lines, this is the best Iriset can do.

For more information, she's going to have to research the old-fashioned way.

The Holy Library is housed in a fat spiral tower in the north of the palace complex, with various levels accessible by the long staircases that gradually step up the outer wall. Books, scrolls, stacks of illustrations, and even diagrams and old tablets are arranged on hundreds of pillar shelves. Statues, old pre-Silence religious icons, and foreign art scatter among the collections. But all the books she wishes to view are high in the crowning level, forbidden to everyone but the most advanced Silent priests and architectural masters. Even Singix of the Beautiful Twilight can't access them without express consent of the Vertex Seal.

Fortunately for Iriset, she has unfettered access to him. Though Lyric is surprised at the request, he agrees easily. She only says, "You mentioned the Apostate Age to me, and while I know of it, I would like to better understand the dangers, the—the nuance of what you fear."

Lyric nods. "I do fear apostasy and its great temptations. And so when you delve into it, when you find the miraculous, the beautiful, remember the price we all paid for that beauty, for those miracles."

He trusts her so completely. It's a heady feeling, icing on a cake of darker, pettier delight.

Iriset's attendants and Seal guards aren't allowed to accompany her up the narrowest portion of the spiral staircase, beneath the holy arch, and into the crown. An intricate security web spreads across the entrance, and Iriset expected something of its nature. She removes the thin crystal stylus hidden in her hair and carefully unknots just enough of the web to allow her craftmask and other designs to slip through. A pulse of ecstatic alarm rushes out, but Iriset catches the pulse just in time, looping it into stasis. She breathes carefully to release the shock of near failure even as she reknits the web and allows it to mark her personal design and therefore record her entrance.

Awe makes her lightheaded this first time she wanders the tables and shelves covered in ancient texts carefully preserved with thin fields of architecture to keep time from spilling its detritus upon the delicate treasures. There are bones—entire skeletons fully articulated!—of rep-cats and river dragons, a minotaur, bones she can't begin to identify, and six different kinds of wings Iriset barely restrains herself from caressing in yearning reverence. There are horns of a strange material that seem gold dusted, but the gold clearly grew through the bone like capillaries. Overhead, filling out the ceramic dome, is a cloud whale skeleton: its eye sockets large enough for Iriset to nest in, its backbone so delicate she sees light through it.

Then there are the books. Iriset would need years to study them all. She only has *days*. But she touches every spine, as if to absorb knowledge from each, while looking for anything that might contain the kind of human architecture that led to the development of marriage knots. Anything in a language she can *read*, that is. So, mirané, Sarenpet and its older form, and any Osahar-mirané or Osahar-Sarenpet dialect. Most of the books she identifies are written in some variety of Sarenpet, thank the Moon-Eater.

For several days Iriset spends the dwindling hot hours of her afternoons in the crowning level, researching apostatical design, specifically unraveling and binding, the sort that those old architects had used to give new appendages to humans, reworking and rebinding muscle, tendon, bone, as well as the sort they had used to re-form trees into hybrid mammals or transition lungs into gills. There's almost no complete information, only stories and condemning tracts, but Iriset reads between the lines. The real problem is she can't experiment. One slipup and it's all over.

A few tracts are signed by people long erased from imperial history, known in their time for soaring ambition and wild invention: Eliri Who Touched the Sun, Fortin Rare, Ariel Osahar, and even one supposed name of the Moon-Eater. So Iriset makes notes in the margins of ancient books, talking back to these geniuses, and boldly signs her notes, too. She's giddy to think that someday somebody will find this research and know that Silk had been here.

———— • ♦ • ————

Fifteen days before the anniversary of her mother's funeral, while passing through the Winter Sunset Courtyard on her way to join Amaranth, Iriset slows down as a sickly pink-white color catches her eye.

The numen crouches in the sun, bare feet on the seashell gravel, long fingers splayed to hold it in balance while its face turns up to the bright sky. It wears those faded gray trousers, and its short robe is discarded against a glazed-brick flower box. There's no sign of the null-wire collar, except for a darkening around its throat like a raw mark, and similar at its wrists and ankles.

Four Seal guards surround it, in a twelve-pace circle.

(In the forbidden library, Iriset came across a collection of books about numena. They were small and in perfect condition, written in looping silver letters of a very old mirané dialect she could hardly understand. Iriset took one to a chair and cradled it against her lap, paging through, admiring the art and tiny words.

They were fairy stories. Tales for children about creatures made of air and light that can take any form, but usually lovely youths to steal children away, seduce princes, or sometimes cause deadly pranks. None of the stories mentioned black diamond eyes, or anything to do with why a numen might have tried to kill a Moon-Eater's Mistress a hundred years ago.)

"Numen," Iriset says, staring at it under the sun. If they let it out sometimes without the null wires, maybe she won't have to break into its prison to help it.

It snaps its head down to look at her with those black diamond-shard eyes.

Despite the disapproving hum from one of her own guards, Iriset moves nearer. "Do you like the sun?" she asks it.

The numen tilts its ugly head in a shrug.

"Have you had a picnic? Shahd, will you give me some of the grapes in your basket, and a flagon of rose wine?" Iriset holds her gaze on the numen, watching its blank expression for any sign of—well, anything.

Nothing. But it doesn't look away from her.

Ecstatic pops in her chest as she wonders what it sees. She's in one of the thin leather masks she designed herself. It braces against her forehead in undulating black and ties into her hair, then hundreds of silk strands dyed green, blue, and black fall down over her eyes, parting over her nose to be swept aside like perfectly arcing cheekbones. When she moves, the silk shivers like iridescent butterfly wings. It occludes her vision rather a lot.

Shahd makes to walk around Iriset and bravely offers the refreshment to the numen, but Iriset stops her and takes the cold flagon in her own hand, and the cup of dark grapes. She steps forward again. "Numen," she says, "do you have a name?"

"Stop, Princess," it says in a broken-glass voice.

Startled, she does, without thinking.

One of the Seal guards moves to Iriset and touches his painted eyelids. "The creature is correct, Your Glory. Allow me to bring your gift to it."

Singix has no reason to disregard the Seal guard and so Iriset submits. But when he takes the grapes and wine, Iriset pushes her mask up into her hair so that the dripping waves of silk brush her forehead and let her eyes free. She watches as the numen accepts the food and drink, carefully not allowing its skin to touch the Seal guard's mirané-brown hands. It plucks a grape and opens its thin lips to bite the dark flesh with alliraptor-like teeth.

Shahd shudders beside Iriset.

Without saying more, Iriset leaves, her small entourage hurrying after. When she arrives at Amaranth's side, she tells the small group, "The numen was loose in the Winter Sunset Courtyard, free of its collar."

A mirané prince, Elit mé Orsir, who is in her sixth decade

and staunchly pro-Silence, waves a hand from the low sofa upon which she lounges beside Amaranth. "Free of its collar, but not loose. They lay a null wire into the garden gravel, and so it is as trapped as always within that circle."

Iriset's body seizes tight. A null wire in the garden gravel.

Stop, Princess, the numen said just before she stepped into the nulled circle. She'd have lost her craftmask, the crawling design that changed her skin and hair, and been stripped bare back to her own apostatical face.

It had saved her.

Iriset barely hears the conversation next for the ringing in her ears. Shahd directs her to a cushion, arranges her gown and mask, and by then a shallow stone bowl of chilled wine is in her hand, and Amaranth is introducing her to a familiar Silent priest.

"Here is Holy Brother Seth, Princess," Amaranth says, touching her fingertips to his wrist. "Just appointed as the new Silent voice on the privilege council, perhaps soon to sacrifice even his name."

Iriset nods, careful not to bow or touch her eyelids as a woman of lesser position might. The priest is mirané, typical in hair and eyes and shape of his face, but real humor shows in his charming smile. Oh! Iriset hides her recognition, but this is the more pleasant of the two priests she met with Amaranth and the Holy Peace the night Her Glory debuted her scarf-dress. Amaranth had won. She'd gotten the priest she wanted appointed to Lyric's council. No wonder Elit mé Orsir is here, too.

"Are you well, Princess?" the priest asks.

"Shaken by her encounter with the numen, I imagine," says Elit.

"I am," Iriset murmurs, and carefully sips her wine.

"You should join my son and me for meditation soon," the older miran says. "If you balance yourself in Silence, such creatures cannot harm you."

"Thank you, prince," Iriset says demurely. "I meditate with my husband."

Elit hums in pleased approval.

Holy Brother Seth says, "The numen never seems anything but at peace to me. I do wonder if it has come to an understanding of Silence in its long confinement."

"Everything returns to Silence," Elit says, as if agreeing with him. It is a line from an old mirané prayer poem. When she says it, Elit looks at Iriset, who viscerally recalls Singix is a heathen, of course.

"Why do they bring it out?" Iriset asks Amaranth. She can't bring herself to assure the old mirané prince that Lyric's children will be raised to Aharté alone.

"I could tell you they do it because everything living deserves the sun sometimes," Her Glory says, "but it's in order for the Architect of the Seal to refresh the designs of its prison."

"How often? I wouldn't like to run into it again."

"At least every quarter of the year, unless something is damaged."

Maybe Iriset can trigger the need, hide a lock disruption inside something else.

Conversation rolls around her, ranging from the upcoming celebration of one of the empire's conquest anniversaries to fashion—during which Iriset's mask is greatly complimented and she manages to speak a little bit about its construction. Her mention of Nielle sets off several miran on gossiping about an affair between two different small kings, and they bring up the most recent Silk graffiti, but it's nothing Iriset hasn't heard before, except for a rumor the Vertex Seal is considering a temporary moratorium on advertising graffiti in general. She tells them he hasn't mentioned it to her, but it's a good idea.

The whole time, Iriset spirals, lightheaded thinking about what would have happened had she stepped over the null wire. She envisions a Seal guard reacting on instinct, cutting her down with their force-blade on the assumption she's an assassin. Or she's hauled before Lyric, stripped of her design, face burning with reaction to the violence of disruption, her skin streaked pearl pale and peach-brown as the crawling design struggles in tatters. His face, his pain, transforming into brutality. Oh, that she does not doubt.

Her mouth waters sickly, hotly. That isn't the way she needs it to happen. It needs to be her choice. Her intention.

Beside and behind her, Shahd says, "Your Glory, I think my princess is ill."

"Perhaps she is already with child," says the old mirané prince approvingly.

Iriset lifts her hand and waves it, but can't speak, for if she parts her lips she'll vomit. She imagines the hole in the apostate tower she had to crawl through to reach her father, and standing on the Mercy Pavilion herself, bound to a pillar and the collar of unraveling settled heavy on her shoulders. Without proving anything or establishing her legacy. Without showing Lyric how wrong he is. Without changing a thing. Except she killed Erxan and stole Singix's life. The things she's changed here already are terrible. Singix should be mourned, not turned into this facade. Iriset's legacy will be nothing more than *using* Singix.

Amaranth claims to be hot and starving herself—as gossip always makes her ravenous, she laughs to her fellow miran as she leads Iriset away.

"What is wrong, hiha?" Amaranth asks when it's only the two of them and Sidoné. They press near to Iriset's shoulders on either side. Seal guards and two quiet attendants, including Shahd, trail them far enough they'll not overhear the soft talk.

"Are you sick?" Sidoné asks kindly.

"*Are* you pregnant?" Amaranth asks unkindly.

Shaking her head a little too frantically, she takes a struggling breath through her nose, wishing there was cool air somewhere. That would be good for her stomach, too. "I nearly lost my craftmask."

Amaranth scoffs. "You should just stay away from the numen."

Iriset pulls her mask down to shade her eyes and cover her upset. She hates null wires, hates everything about them, and when the army put them against her skin they were so cold, and she was made into nothing.

She's shaking, every deep breath atremble.

Sidoné frowns and puts her fist upon the butt of her forceblade's handle where it hooks against her hip. The body-twin says, "How did you nearly lose your mask? What is happening? Does it deteriorate? Do you need to make a new one?"

Iriset presses her lips together to hold back a laugh. She takes another deep breath, then calmly—not really—says, "It is not deteriorating. But nothing can survive a null wire, and I nearly stepped over one. It was unmarked; there was no way for me to see it. Only luck saved me today—saved all of us today! Luck will not serve forever."

"I thought you were too much a genius mind to rely on luck," Amaranth says sharply.

Oh well, Iriset supposes now is the time. She steps even closer, tilting her face up to glare into Amaranth's eyes. "Two people have caught me already. *Two.*"

Sidoné sucks in a shocked breath, but Amaranth narrows her eyes.

Iriset continues, "It was my *genius mind* that alleviated the situation, both times."

"Ambassador Erxan," Sidoné says, plainly enough that they must have already suspected.

"And?" Amaranth demands through clenched teeth. Iriset can feel the ecstatic anger rising off her, lifting Her Glory's natural falling force into conflict with itself. Iriset is careful not to glance Shahd's way.

"It's taken care of," she says. "This charade is strong, and I am good at it, but it will break eventually. No matter your threats to my family. It will happen and wouldn't it be better to choose when?"

"My choice, sister," Amaranth says quietly.

Iriset cannot disagree aloud. Nor tell Amaranth she has fifteen days. Speaking slowly to keep her voice from trembling, Iriset says, "This marriage is secure. Your reputation is intact, and you won whatever you were playing with the Silent priests. I'm not going to have your brother's heirs, so if you want them, he needs a new wife. You have had plenty of time to arrange things so that when Singix vanishes, or dies, you can manipulate events to your favor. Tell me when and it will happen."

Her Glory snorts. "We still don't know who poisoned that candy."

"That's irrelevant now," Iriset says as the gnawing in her stomach sharpens into rising anger, too. "It's been almost three quads and nobody else has tried to kill me. You wanted another attempt so you could track the evidence better? Well, it isn't happening. If someone powerful had wanted to murder Singix to stop the marriage, we thwarted them already. Maybe they gave up, maybe they can't get to me anymore because of the extra security. Maybe they're dead!"

Sidoné looks around at the guards and attendants with a frown. She angles herself to hide Iriset and her low fury.

"Is there something you aren't telling me?" Iriset demands. "Have there been other attempts I'm not aware of? Other forms of sabotage?"

"No." Amaranth studies Iriset, peering so boldly that Iriset takes a few deep breaths, needing to calm her inner design or Lyric will come here. Lyric will want to know why his sister has upset his wife.

The thought makes her laugh, a slightly hysterical giggle that she does her best to swallow. Everything nearly rained down around her today, if the numen hadn't stopped her. Iriset cringes. She cannot let herself be accidentally discovered. The only way to survive the brutal look in Lyric's eye is to control the situation. To explode it. To be reborn as Silk, Iriset mé Isidor, on her terms. Not have this pretty identity stripped away before she's ready.

She has to wound him on purpose. He'll never change his ways without a *brutal* awakening. She knows him too well, now. Every thread of his inner design. It reaches for her, and she can't help reaching back, thanks to the cursed marriage knot. Thanks to all the toxic longing she's had for him since the moment they met.

But she can't tell his sister that.

The same sister who is frowning heavily at Iriset now. "I've never seen you so thrown, even when you were in prison, or on the pavilion watching your father die. You're shaking."

Iriset wishes for once her dominant force wasn't excited ecstatic. She could really use some inherent flow or falling right now. "Your Glory, what matters now is that the threat to this entire plan—your entire plan—is discovery, not murder. Discovery. There is only so much luck, so much genius, so many threats I can remove fast enough. I will do everything in my power not to let myself be revealed, but it's inevitable the longer I stay. You might want me forever, but that's impossible. Don't you see that?"

"You don't sound like the arrogant apostate I know," Amaranth says, intrigued and unbothered. "What changed?"

Iriset sucks air through her teeth, clenches her jaw, and lifts her chin with all the arrogance she can summon. The summer sun glares and Iriset wishes she could feed on that rising force instead of sweating. "Nothing changed except I achieve my apostatical glory, Amaranth, every time I fuck your brother."

Amaranth narrows her eyes and shoves up the leather curve of Iriset's mask. Silk strands caress Iriset's cheeks and lashes as Her Glory leans in as if she can see through to Iriset's thoughts.

"You're a mess," Sidoné says.

"I'm definitely not myself," Iriset jokes, but it comes out hollow.

And then Amaranth abruptly leans away, adopts a stance of disinterest. "I don't want to let you go. I want you to complete your transformation. Become Singix well enough you cannot *be* discovered. Not a mask, but real apostasy. I know you can."

"Why?"

"Maybe it's enough for me that my brother is easier to manipulate when he's happy."

"*Amaranth.*" Iriset doesn't know what else to say. Has she ever used Her Glory's name like this before?

"He's in love with you."

When Iriset's knees tremble, she reaches out and Sidoné

catches her elbow. She shuts her eyes and pulls free. Amaranth is the only person who's ever called Iriset a bad liar, but she only thinks so because the Moon-Eater's Mistress sees right through everything.

Amaranth says, "You're in love with him, too."

Iriset shakes her head wildly, hanging on to her whisper by a thread. "That doesn't matter. How I feel about any of you doesn't matter. I'm going to leave, so figure out what last thing you want from this puppet consort you created, and I'll try to give it to you before I go."

Her Glory watches her sadly, somehow more magnificent than she's ever been here under the bursting sun, sweat at her temples and golden paint smearing her lip. Beside her, Sidoné grips too tightly the hilt of her force-blade, unwilling to agree, unwilling to deny.

Stepping back, Iriset nods once. She steps back again. "While you're thinking about it, remember that even the red moon fell from the sky."

She turns, and before she's gone more than a few paces, to her surprise Shahd slips her hand into Iriset's, squeezes, and leads her away.

• ◆ •

"What does that mean?" Shahd asks later, while she combs oil into the ends of Iriset's stolen hair. "Even the red moon fell from the sky?"

"What do you think?" Iriset returns the question, eyes closed, doing her best to luxuriate in the lavender flower steam from her too-hot bath. The skin of her fingers and toes is wrinkled.

"Anyone can fall?"

"That's right." With her eyes once more drifting shut, Iriset says, "All design degrades over time if it isn't supported. The water clock must be refilled, the arc of rising adjusted to the season's wind or the shift of the earth due to yearly floods. Ribbons sewn up from ice damage. Everything in this world must be maintained. And everything dies. It's possible the old red moon's fix in the sky simply eroded over time thanks to a bad maintenance plan." Then Iriset smiles rather slyly, glad to feel such things again after the day she's had. "But it's more efficient if someone makes it happen."

32

The lie of love

"Singix, do you think you might be pregnant?" Lyric asks her with exceeding gentleness two mornings later.

They're curled in bed, before dawn, and his hand splays over her naked belly. Iriset was entirely asleep until he said her stolen name, and groggily hums a meaningless tune, snuggling her bottom back against him and turning her face down to kiss the arm that pillows her head. The words he spoke do not sink in.

He says them again. "Singix, do you think you might be pregnant?"

Iriset squeezes her eyes closed and groans as cutely as possible. As if she doesn't have enough problems. She can't believe her husband is listening to rumors. Or so confident in his own virility. Though, they do have an awful lot of sex. Keeping him to herself for those last Days of Mercy really stirred up the hopes and expectations of his court. But none of them know Iriset can't get pregnant.

Lyric slides his hand from her belly up between her breasts, skimming his palm over a nipple, until he carefully cups her throat. She shivers as he strokes her jaw with his thumb, pressing gently until she looks around at him. When she does, he lowers his lashes bashfully. "We have been married for three quads and you have not bled."

"Oh," she whispers. Right. She wouldn't.

"I..." Lyric licks his lips. "I would be glad."

It's Iriset's turn to lower her eyes as warmth spreads from his hand throughout her face and down her neck. "I... My cycle is irregular, and sometimes change can delay such things. Change and stress."

"You have been under tremendous stress, for which I am so sorry."

She tilts her chin to kiss him. "Stop apologizing. I will speak with your sister and perhaps consult a doctor, and... maybe."

"I mentioned the possibility to my mother. If you would like to also speak with her."

Iriset thanks him for the consideration, and doesn't say she's fairly sure she'd rather eat the scales off a lattice snake than discuss pregnancy with Diaa of Moonshadow.

She kisses Lyric on his jaw, then lingers at his neck. She breathes deeply of his early-morning sex-sweat-pillow smell. Six years ago she used a specially designed force-web to essentially hold her reproductive system in stasis unless the surgery is reversed. It took weeks of planning and exploration, and then hours to physically accomplish. Iriset is uncertain she could loosen the threads without being discovered performing human architecture even if she wanted to. But she's equally uncertain it would fool anyone if she fakes a period. Amaranth shuts herself up in the Moon-Eater's Temple for the two most intense days of her cycle, but Iriset doesn't know enough about Ceres traditions or cultural taboos to know what Singix would do. She can hardly *ask*.

She only needs to distract him, and everyone apparently, for thirteen more days.

Amaranth has invited Iriset to join her for the morning at the Moon-Eater's Temple, in a cheeky version of an apology—"I know you enjoyed yourself when you felt him come," she said with a bold wink. Because Iriset is Singix, she has no excuse not to be persuaded.

While Her Glory awakens her god, Iriset waits with Sidoné behind the partition screen. The lattice in the screen is designed with a constant labyrinthine pattern to allow the gaze to trace it slowly, carefully, for meditation, and Iriset sends her eyes along the path. She parts her lips to taste the rollicking tangle of forces with which Amaranth engages.

The force-knot Amaranth draws pulls tighter and tighter and Iriset perches on her stool, sinking inside herself to feel the weave of her inner design, of the marriage knot and its strictures. She prods at them, plucking at them with pops of breath and ecstatic snaps. If Lyric notices through the knot, she has an excellent excuse in Amaranth's worship. When the ripples of the Moon-Eater's release hit her gently, she follows them through her inner design, from the marriage knot to the quietly nauseated feeling in her guts, wondering if a version of this ritual could undo the connections linking her inner design to Lyric's. Unbind the knot without his consent. The Moon-Eater's awakening shakes her in her core, like a deep resonance. Like auditory, emotional friction, ecstatic pulled out like taffy. Not coincidentally, perhaps, Iriset used resonance to affix the design web over her uterus all those years ago, meshing the frequencies of eight crystal coins placed around her belly. It's not unlike the unraveling, which also involves...

Iriset sits up straight.

The web is gone from her reproductive system.

There's nothing woven through her inner design except the marriage knot.

Panic drains Iriset of heat and sense, and she just sits there for a moment in a nauseating twist of dual realizations: first that if the resonance of the design eggs coming together was so powerful as to undo her own excellent inner work as a mere *side effect*, then resonance *must* be the key to undoing their marriage bond without consent or death; second, she might actually be pregnant.

"Do you believe in the Moon-Eater?" Sidoné whispers.

Startled from her thinking, Iriset nearly falls off the stool. Sidoné grasps her wrist to steady her and Iriset manages to say, "What's to believe in, or not? There is something here."

The body-twin presses her lips together and nods, as if reassured. "I want you out of this, too. The entire situation is a bad one."

Iriset raises both eyebrows as high as they go. The body-twin not fully on Amaranth's side?

Sidoné meets Iriset's gaze. "I am privy to Amaranth's thoughts and motivations, but in this, she has no pure motivation. She has always been precise in her political schemes, in every plan and movement. The web she wove to arrange this marriage was breathtaking. But Amaranth herself"—Sidoné lowers her voice again, and Iriset leans nearer until her breath ruffles the fine hairs beside Iriset's ear—"does not know why she is doing *this*, pushing you, demanding we continue this charade. She claims it will be good to have you with us, with Lyric, because you're powerful as an ally. She's placing a weapon where she can wield you at will. But she's ignoring the personal cost of betraying him, and I think the real reason she risks so much with you is the Moon-Eater's influence. She feels something in here with him that cannot be replicated elsewhere. The intensity of it. She seeks danger, seeks to achieve new heights, to prove that her life outside this temple matters, too."

"Why are you telling me this?"

The body-twin squeezes Iriset's wrist, fingers digging into the flesh. "Because I see it on your face. You feel him. Whatever she touches in there, you touch it too, and I do not. If there comes a time when I cannot follow her, you must. Do you understand, Iriset mé Isidor? You must."

There's something wild in Sidoné's vivid brown eyes.

Just then Amaranth appears, a hand pushing the lattice neatly aside. "What are you whispering about, my loves?" Her mouth looks bitten, her head tilts languorously, and her other hand holds her robe closed between her breasts.

"You," Sidoné says, though Iriset would have lied.

Amaranth's smile is triumphant. She likes attention—any kind of it. Leaning down, she kisses Sidoné at the corner of her mouth, dropping open her robe. Iriset glances at her luscious hanging breasts, and beyond them at Her Glory's belly, the soft folds of mirané-brown flesh. Iriset's mouth nearly waters as she imagines putting her mouth all over that body. Does pregnancy make one even hornier than usual? Fuck.

Fluttering her lashes at Iriset, Her Glory bends from a standing position to press her palms to the cool tile floor, seeming to melt a bit, still in the throes of her comedown. Slowly, she stretches up onto her toes, with her hands still on the floor, groaning a little. Then Amaranth stands, arching her back with her hands reaching overhead, fingers splayed. "Tell me," she commands, still mostly naked. Her voice trembles deep in her chest, more of an invocation.

Iriset shakes her head slowly. She has no intention of telling Amaranth or Sidoné. If she's pregnant, she'll just take care of it. Add it to the list! "I have to go."

Before either says anything, Iriset rushes out of the temple to where Shahd awaits—and nearly runs into Diaa of Moonshadow. Seal Commander Iumeri Selk is at her side in full white uniform and armor, his white mask a brilliant contrast to his dark brown skin.

"Ah, daughter-in-Silence," Diaa calls, "is Amaranth still inside? We're looking for her. Well"—the older miran smiles with exactly the appropriate amount of flirting at Iumeri—"this one here is looking for the body-twin, more like."

"Yes," Iriset murmurs. "They're both on their way out. I'm feeling slightly nauseated, if you'll excuse me."

Diaa sends her a truly alarmed look, and Iriset recalls that Lyric said he spoke to his mother about her potential pregnancy. "My Silence, you should sit down. Iumeri, get this child some water, would you?"

"It's not terrible," Iriset insists, "but I should rest."

Amaranth appears with Sidoné just as Shahd is taking Iriset's elbow to lead her away.

"Mother, what can I do for you? Take care, hiha," Amaranth says kindly to Iriset, and though he glances longingly at Sidoné, the Seal Commander offers to escort Iriset. But Shahd quietly gets in his way and they make their escape.

———— • ♦ • ————

It wasn't a lie: Iriset is nauseated. Her insides feel like a cold marsh, and her head rings dully. But she can't afford to return to her bed and simply rest. These new potential complications are a problem for later. Now there's a silicate anchor in her pocket, ready to be pinned in place. She estimates she needs six more days to get all her groundwork laid since she can't exactly be overt about what she's doing.

Iriset hasn't visited the Color Can Be Loud Garden since the night she held that strange vigil with Lyric, before Singix died, before Iriset stole her face and gave up her own life. It feels odd to be here.

Shahd lets go of her hand and says she'll fetch ginger tea for her stomach. Iriset smiles wearily, glad for Shahd. When she returns, Shahd will make sure there aren't others in the garden to witness Iriset's actions. Maybe Shahd knows more about signs of pregnancy than Iriset and they can talk about that, too.

The Seal guards fan out to tuck into the alcoves and balconies, to peer behind the large, waxy square leaves of ilyen trees, as Iriset chooses her bench. Then the guards disperse but for one, who turns his back to her as she's requested lately.

It's so rare for her to be alone that Iriset will take the illusion of solitude, glad she can sigh without expecting a response, glad she can peer at the invisible design threads tying up the roses, touch her fingertips to the little design panel hidden in the plinth of a marble statue. Even taste the force eddies in the air without anyone to see her stick out her tongue. It will be complicated to find the right fork in which to settle her anchor here, but of course not too complicated for her.

The lilies haven't changed at all, their vibrant trumpets bending toward her extravagant design, aching for her craftmask. Iriset brushes her hand against their tonguelike leaves, picking up traces of red pollen at the tips of her fingers. The pollen jerks into ragged starbursts of ecstatic when the tiny powder touches her skin.

Iriset wipes her hands off on her skirts and sinks onto the bench. It's a cool garden, shaded with its glass lattice dome and lush trees. Force-fans create a breeze, as they do everywhere in the palace complex. The entire place is such an amazing, intricate design. Designs upon designs, really. Like a living body.

That reminds her of the pulse she used to feel, when she was only Iriset, sleeping at night with her ear pressed to the thin pillows and her palms against the tiled floor. The pulse, like breathing, that holds the palace's design together somehow. She's never had a chance to investigate, and there's no obvious cause for it in the security layers she'd been digging into. Maybe she doesn't notice the breathing as Singix because so much design constantly runs over her skin and weaves through her flesh.

She's too loud.

With a little self-deprecating smile, she considers how much she gave up, how much she took, when she became Singix. And yet, even as her shoulders droop, she thinks of Lyric sitting here beside her that night, telling her about brutality. He said her name—*Iriset*—and she knew even then.

A different Seal guard appears and taps the one with her on the shoulder. They nod and trade places. Then the new guard approaches her, and Iriset glances over, irritated. He approaches with purpose, yet there's no sign of Shahd or any other messenger. "Yes?"

He says nothing but keeps coming, and Iriset gets to her feet. "What? What are you...?" And then she laughs, for she spies a small force-wire in his hand, curling and snapping ecstatically like an eager snake. She laughs because it's too ironic, the timing.

Her amusement gives him pause.

Just enough for her to decide: He's too near for her to get the stylus in her hair, the one designed to kill, before he gets her. And if she runs, he'll whip the wire over her head and the touch of it will either kill her or ruin her craftmask, or both. So, recklessly, Iriset screams and runs *at* him, arms up around her head to ram his stomach with her right shoulder and all her weight. Like her father taught her.

The assassin does not see it coming and grunts, though he's in lacquered armor. He stumbles and drops his wire. Iriset nearly falls, but grits her teeth and stomps down on his foot. Heat slices her shoulder and arm as she jerks away, then she rears back to bring up her other leg and smash her slippered foot against his groin.

It doesn't hurt him. Iriset barely shoves his balance off.

But that's all the time it takes for the other guards to fling themselves around her and use their force-blades to cast arcs of bright design around her in a shield, and their robes harden with charges of raw power.

Sinking to her knees, Iriset shakes and gasps for breath. She lets her inner design rage. Lyric will feel the violence of this, no matter where he is.

Panting, she stares through the legs of her loyal guards as another Seal guard kicks her attacker back into the lilies, and she whimpers in regret over the poor flowers. But she's glad she didn't have to kill him herself. She'd grown complacent, worried only about discovery and destruction, not Singix's unknown enemy.

Iriset clutches the bleeding wound the assassin gave her, distantly, numbly relieved it'd been a regular knife and not something with applied force: Only her flesh is wounded, not her crawling net, nor any of her design.

If she were herself and human architecture weren't ridiculously banned, she could grit her teeth and knit flowing force through the skin with her stylus until her crawling net taught her own body to heal fast enough that there wouldn't even be a scar by morning.

A distant voice calls her guards and two jog away, and Iriset gets up to follow.

There's a body sprawled on the grass, tucked half under a sculptured juniper with blush-pink berries.

The guards are holding the space while one kneels, pushes thick black hair out of the body's face. It's sticky with blood, dragging across Shahd's slack mouth.

Iriset stops.

She hears the explanation through ringing in her ears: They think the assassin caught the girl returning with tea and slit her throat.

The Seal guard who says it isn't even telling Iriset, but reporting to the other guard. Iriset hears it, hears it like it shouldn't matter to her. She sinks to her knees and bends over her lap, lets blood and rising force rush up into her face as she presses it to her knees. Shahd shouldn't have been here. She should have been with Amaranth's handmaidens, or with her family. Not here. She was only sixteen.

Someone says, "The assassin is dead, too. Blood in his eyes, probably force-popped."

She believed in Iriset.

--- ◆ ---

Lyric arrives breathless. "Singix, are you well?" He lifts her up.

"Of course not," she snaps, smearing her blood onto his bare shoulder as she shoves him. She blinks, staring at the color of it, brighter red and bluer in undertone than the rich mirané brown of his skin. Why is blood colored as it is, she wonders, falling into a daze of fast thought, a spiral pulling her down into her own mind.

She kneels beside Shahd's body, ruining her gown in the blood. Shahd's eyes are oddly half open, her gaping neck drenched in blood that still seems to ooze, but that's just the light and the breeze. Iriset tastes blood in the back of her throat.

She's the one who said discovery was the greatest threat, not the murderer. She let her guard down, she's the one. It's her fault.

In a daze, Iriset stumbles back to her feet and before Lyric can catch her, she marches back to the dead assassin. *Force-popped* is slang for too much ecstatic force in the brain. A common accident in elder designers. She crouches and slaps him, even though he's dead. She slaps him again and again, each time driving her own ecstatic into his face and body, there has to be something she can trace: And there it is, a signature, a—

Lyric and Sidoné both grasp at her, pulling her away from the body. Her palm tingles with force and Lyric hugs her, begging her softly to stop.

But she has it. She closes her eyes, lets him drag her away, and imprints the signature, the feel and shape of it, into her memory.

The palace doctor smears her wound with stinging antiseptic and a bandage to hold the edges together until it heals of its own slow accord. Lyric wraps a fresh robe over her bloodied gown, to show anyone who sees them pass that Singix is well. He tucks her hand against his arm and walks her slowly to their tower. She's thinking furiously, because all her anchors could be used to trace this thing she found, whatever it is—a weapon, or a tangled force-loop that could be a pain device, something to shock him if he didn't obey. It can be traced, palace architects won't think so, but she can repurpose her anchors to do it—

—but then she can't use them for her graffiti. She'd have to start all over again, but she doesn't have *time* and it's very likely the blown anchors would be discovered by the investigator-designers or Seal guard. They might figure out someone is surgically altering the security groundwork, and if they put Raia or someone as talented on it, it could even be traced back to Iriset. Raia might recognize her work. Silk's work.

Iriset should do it for Shahd anyway. She should. Justice for Shahd—and Singix herself—should be more important than whatever legacy she thinks she's leaving behind. She's no good at this! People keep dying around her but she keeps trying. What hubris! Who will die for her next?

Suddenly Lyric picks her up.

Surprise has her throwing her arms around his neck, and her injured arm burns. But the Vertex Seal cradles her against his chest and pushes his face against her neck. They've just arrived in their private rooms; she didn't even notice where they were. Lyric holds her, silently, and she grips him tightly enough to bruise, aware of the pounding of his heart mirroring hers.

When the last Vertex Seal finally speaks, his words are like a ferrous pin anchoring an elaborate design into a wasteland of silicate crystal and red-moon rock:

He says, "I love you," and Iriset starts to cry.

Absolutely wretched sobs, drawn out from the awful hollow in her chest, because he loves someone who doesn't exist, because Shahd stayed for her, and her father is dead, and she killed Erxan with her bare hands, and and and so much, and it's all Lyric's fault but she loves him back! She does, she can't help it, and what is she supposed to do about that? About the people in the center of this? Stick to the plan, shake the empire to its core because that's what they deserve, that's what everyone who pretends the laws of Holy Silence matter more than lives and healing and progress and science and hope and all those other things Iriset doesn't believe in but must be better. Absolute Silence is a design flaw, and if nothing else, Iriset hates a design flaw, and once she latches on she'll never let go until she solves it or gnaws it into ugly, unanswerable pieces.

Lyric walks up the spiral stairs with her in his arms and deposits her, crying, on the bed. He vanishes and returns, pressing a cup of water to her lips, but she's too upset not to choke, so he drinks from a different cup and kisses her with the sharp taste of honeybite on his tongue.

Then he takes off his shoes and hers, and climbs into bed, wrapping her up, and he just begins to talk.

Whatever comes into his head about what's going on in the empire is what he tells her: There was recently a regime change in Huvar, and the new kings have sent extra taxes to prove they're more loyal than the last city leadership, which causes its own hassle for accountants and could be a smoke screen for something yet to come. General Lapis left Moonshadow to head back toward that territory just in case. A food shortage far in the west of the empire in what used to be the Land of God (*Ilium Va* locally, he says) caused a rift in the regional government, half of whom claim it's Aharté-blessed drought to clear out the people for a generation or so, while the other half say it's just bad farming because of the empire's assimilation laws that give the native farmers who know how to cultivate the land from hundreds of years of experience very little impetus to help the homesteaders. Several force-bridges are delayed in construction across jungle canopies in the empire-controlled Eastern Bow, probably because of their fire dragons, but also probably because of a bribery scandal that stretches from the distant construction sites all the way to the Ribbonwork precinct here. A man was arrested outside the town of Melit on suspicion of planting a bomb on behalf of a local insurgency; he claims he was in that desolate neighborhood harvesting lightning truffles, which is so ludicrous a defense he's being brought to the Holy City for a mirané trial. And that barely touches on the intricate plots and issues occurring within Moonshadow itself: this so-called Silk rebellion and whether to disrupt honest graffiti artists to curtail it; the implementation of a new tax upon artisans and whether architects count as such; constant arguing over whether to lift the second-generation marriage restrictions—just to name a few of the most pressing. Lyric keeps talking until her hitching sobs slow, and she can draw long, eight-count breaths, leaning into him and listening to his voice.

    He doesn't realize, but Iriset begins to really listen to what he's *not* saying, her brilliant mind seeking patterns, and she concludes hazily that Lyric's job is less to directly rule, and more to act exactly as his title suggests: He's the Vertex Seal, the pinnacle of the arc of justice, and from his height his most important task is determining where the attention of the throne needs to settle from moment to moment. He's a focusing steeple, drawing power and law, and from him power and law spool and spiral to hold down the weft and warp of the empire.

Iriset wants to say, "You're an architect, too," like she said to Amaranth once.

She wants to say it, to push him into so many arguments built to make both of them better. That's the lie she tells herself most often: that they're both going to be better people at the end of this, molding each other with arguments and love. Because isn't it love, this feeling when he comes into a room still discussing a scheduling mishap with Garnet, and makes his way to her just to absently touch her hair? Isn't it love when they sit across a low table during dinner with his mother and sister, and Amaranth says something outlandish, but instead of arguing with her, Lyric catches Iriset's eye for her alone to see his amusement?

It's warm, it's desperate, it fills her up to bursting. Isn't that love? It's selfish and eager and aching with guilt, but isn't it love all the same?

Or is love impossible if it begins with a lie?

Yet when she drinks her water and kisses him, when he doesn't need to talk anymore because their mouths are busy, as his lips burn down her spine and he presses his teeth to the rise of her hip, when he digs his fingers deep inside her as if to plant his gentians there, Iriset forgets she's ever lied about anything in all her life.

33

The last thread of silk

Iriset hides for two days.

Sidoné arrives the first morning with coffee to tell Iriset that the assassin was a Seal guard, but they know nothing about his suspected employer. The moment he was defeated, his Seal guard mask buzzed with ecstatic energy that flowed into his mouth and nostrils and eyes and ears, surging to disrupt his brain functions. Beremé and Garnet and Sidoné, who hates to agree with the mirané prince, agree the real culprit had been near enough to know when their plan failed, and somehow triggered the mask's shift with a very well-hidden trail of architecture. Menna tore apart the garden looking for any remaining threads or empty spaces in the palace's design to account for it, but hadn't been able to prove anything. (Thank the red god Iriset hadn't had a chance to put down her anchor in that garden yet.) Three people who wore versions of the jade cuffs to track their motions through the palace complex had been near enough, including Shahd, but they've been cleared. The truth is that most people with enough influence or motivation to wish Singix harm are not required to have their access and movements tracked like attendants and handmaidens. The Vertex Seal decreed a temporary law that everyone entering the palace complex needed to be cuffed or carrying a similar mark that would allow them to be traced. The Architect of the Seal had to bring in additional designers on a work-for-hire basis to get enough constructed, set, and tuned as quickly as possible. Iumeri Selk is working with Menna to make a list of everyone near enough to be able to trigger the death-design. It includes Amaranth, Dove méra Curro, Iumeri himself, and Diaa, many of whom Iriset had seen just prior to the attack. There are six others so far, all miran but one.

Iriset hides in the menagerie gardens with Huya pretending he's not there, too, playing up her very real grief and possible (badly timed) pregnancy to be left alone by everyone. She dedicates the first day to wallowing in self-recriminations, denies even Amaranth's offer to borrow a handmaiden, and the second day she spends studying the griffons as they soar against the glass dome of the menagerie. She watches as they catch rising force, as their wings cup around it, shaping themselves to lift or dive or gracefully circle.

She has an idea about flying—or at least about falling up.

But that night before she can start working it in, Amaranth appears in the Vertex Seal's suite and insists on a family night. Iriset somehow finds herself curled up in the large alliraptor bed with Lyric and Amaranth as well as Garnet and Sidoné, who arrive with pillows and extra blankets, pajamas and snacks, sweet tea for Lyric but honeybite for the rest of them. Iriset is coddled and comforted and not required to speak or act at all. Garnet is the first to raise his glass for Shahd, and Iriset realizes as far as he and Lyric know, Shahd is the second attendant to die in Singix's place.

Iriset knocks back the honeybite and asks for another.

She lays with her head in Lyric's lap, ear pressed to his thigh, as he and Garnet laugh over a story of the first time Amaranth returned from the Moon-Eater's Temple successful in her solo awakening. She'd kissed fourteen people, Seal guards, attendants, mirané ladies, gardeners, and the old Architect of the Seal before Sidoné calmed her down—and Amaranth insisted she had to kiss two more for a round sixteen, a holy number! Her Glory had dragged her entourage (large even then) to the Vertex Seal's office where Lyric was studying with their father and laid it all out for them. Esmail had been amused, but left it to Lyric, who could not argue that sixteen was indeed a holier number than fourteen, and so Amaranth needed to complete her design for the good of the empire. Fortunately, there with them, always, were Garnet and Sidoné, who Lyric suggested would be the best finale. The body-twins accepted their kisses, Sidoné with a laugh and Garnet only reluctant because he was shorter than Amaranth at the time and disliked being reminded of it. Later, Amaranth had teased him that it had been her kiss that bestowed upon him the growth spurt necessary for those broad muscles and proud stature.

The alliraptor bed tilts breezily beneath Iriset, and Lyric caresses her hair, laughing softly so that it vibrates through his body and into hers, and she's relaxed and not thinking at all of what extreme power everyone at that slumber party wields, the destruction they cause, or what is certainly soon to come.

When she transitions back to some semblance of her daily royal life, Iriset is not above using her volatile emotional state to spend more time alone, supposedly idle with reading and mask making, which she does do—but the focused alone time allows her to layer specialized ribbons, like the kind that pull skiffs across the city, into her graffiti. They aren't designed to pull skiffs to and fro, but to lift her high into the sky. She'll be like the griffons. Or a numen herself, a creature of power with reams of silk exploding around her like spider legs, like rays of sunlight, like wings.

When she imagines her display, it's glorious. She'll make Silk into a god.

It is kind of hilarious that of everyone in the palace complex besides the Vertex Seal himself, Iriset is the only person not required to wear a locator cuff. Lyric had originally thought to allow exceptions for Amaranth and Diaa as well, but Amaranth took one anyway, to show her support of the policy and prove she has nothing to hide. Diaa reluctantly did the same, though certainly lectured her daughter over it in private.

Since she's not being traced, Iriset manages to use the secret lover's door in the study to sneak out of her quarters late at night without anyone noticing, to plant three more anchors. There are only seven left to go. And nine days until Bittor's deadline.

───── • ♦ • ─────

Most visitors from outside have stopped coming, thanks to the annoyance of having to wear a tracking cuff. But not whirlwind-of-chaos-and-fun Nielle mé Dari. Nielle offers to make the journey regularly, seemingly delighted at the hint of danger. When Nielle comes to work with Iriset and share a meal, or visit the handmaidens who haven't "broken free," as Nielle puts it, their easy camaraderie feels like a different kind of friendship than any Iriset has experienced before, because Nielle doesn't appear to want anything from Iriset—from Singix—*but* friendship.

She definitely doesn't believe Iriset is anything but a gentle princess. It's safer that way.

They spend the afternoon of the seventh-to-last day making masks in the Blue Between Sea and Sky Courtyard, and failing to gain access to the numen. Iriset has made a mask of its face and took Nielle with her to attempt a visit under the pretense of gifting it the mask—with the null disruptor button pressed to the underside. It couldn't be arranged in time and Nielle had to return home. Iriset will ask her husband to intervene next and grant her an audience with the numen. She knows she can persuade him.

Iriset holds the mask in hand now. It's delicate ceramic and glazed not quite the exact silver-gray-pink shade of the numen's skin, but close. She glued black glass beads at the edges of the eerily round eyeholes and painted jagged black lines emanating from those eyes. The mouth is gritty and sharp with pink quartz shards. It's horrid and she likes it.

When she enters her quarters, the finches and skull sirens are in a tizzy. They hop from branch to branch of the force-aviary webbed against the dome of the greeting chamber.

Two Seal guards not of her own complement stand at the arch opening into the study.

Fear pops ecstatic charges up her back. All her tools are hidden in there.

Huya widens his eyes at Iriset, but she's watching Amaranth's handmaiden Ziyan mé Tal hum a melody up at the aviary to capture the attention of the panicked skull sirens. Iriset had no assigned handmaiden today because Nielle was with her, so Ziyan's presence means Amaranth is here.

Iriset goes quickly to the study, noticing that the Seal guards glance at each other for a split second, as if considering whether they might deny her access. Luckily, they don't try it.

Within is Lyric, surrounded by Garnet, Sidoné, and Amaranth. They're a tense quartet: Lyric is seated against the fore of the crescent desk, his posture vibratingly rigid, with Garnet slightly behind him and toward the force-wall, large arms crossed angrily over his chest; Amaranth towers in the center of the room, her hands spread not in supplication but discord, and Sidoné crouches near her, head down as if either listening to something only she can hear, or in despair.

The way they turn sharply and as one to her when she enters teaches Iriset all she needs to know: They'd been discussing Singix.

Drawing herself up, she looks at Lyric. "What happened?"

He hesitates, staring at her worriedly. "Leave us," he says to the others.

Iriset glances at her worktable: It appears undisturbed, except for some of her mask-making paraphernalia not where she left them, and there's a scatter of dark beans and dried berries... the cocoa and berries Diaa gave her when they snuck out of the palace. But nothing incriminating on display. They haven't discovered her design tools, penetrating her alarms without triggering them.

Amaranth disregards her brother's order and takes Iriset's hands. "A girl in the offices of the Architect of the Seal was found dead, with poisoned paint on her hands. It was paint meant for you, for your mask project."

"Poisoned paint?" Iriset blinks. "That is what killed Dalir méra Idris?" She says it as a question, but she knows: That Vertex Seal, the brother of Safiyah the Bloody, was murdered by the relatives of criminals he executed with an ingeniously poisoned face paint.

"It may be similar, and we're collecting everything you have already, paints and dyes." Garnet says, his voice a low rumble. "Menna will look into it, and your combat-designer."

"Huya," Iriset says absently, imagining poison spreading through peacock-green pigments, smeared on her fingers. If it's not face paint, but for her art, maybe it's a creeping poison, architectural like her crawling design that changed the color of her skin, that dyed her hair and pulled its texture smoother. What if she touched Lyric with that poison? She looks at him.

Immediately he pushes off the desk and strides to her, nudging Amaranth away. "You're scaring her."

"I'm all right," Iriset protests, reaching for his face; she stops at the last moment, a flash of Erxan's too-wide eyes and his yell under her hands. "I—I was thinking how easily I could spread such a poison to you."

He takes her hands in his own and presses them to his cheeks.

"It will have come from outside the palace," Iriset murmurs.

"I was suggesting we send you away," Garnet says. "For safety."

Iriset gasps, inadvertently gripping Lyric's face. He doesn't wince, and she drops her hands, turning to Her Glory as Amaranth says, "It's a bad idea."

Lyric steps closer behind her and covers her shoulders with his hands. "I would not like to see you go, but... I want you safe most of all."

"Might they not follow me?"

Garnet says, "I doubt it. We could spirit you away in the night, with a small group of very trusted people. Perhaps Her Glory could spare Sidoné for a time."

Sidoné surges to her feet. "We could keep you safe, away from here. Until the culprit is caught, or until…"

"That is the problem," Amaranth says. "We do not know when you could return, if you were sent away and we continued to make no progress. Whoever is behind this has hidden for quads. They have powerful friends."

"Who is more powerful than you?" Iriset asks, and Her Glory scowls.

"I can't imagine being without you for an unknown amount of time," Lyric says softly. She hears him draw breath to say more, but only silence follows.

"Lyric." Iriset twists her neck to meet his eyes briefly, then continues on to Amaranth, Garnet, and Sidoné. "I must consider such a thing closely. For what message does it send if I go away? Not only to potential enemies, but Ceres? My father will not like it."

Lyric squeezes her shoulders, but Sidoné says, "Singix," very firmly, in disapproval.

Iriset says, "I will go if I must, but perhaps you will find the culprit now? Soon? Because of new evidence from this attempt?"

"Maybe," Garnet says. "Everyone is being traced. I should go supervise now that you are here."

"Do you think the girl, the dead girl, was involved, or another casualty?"

Sidoné answers, "Menna thinks a casualty."

Iriset closes her eyes and leans back into Lyric's chest. Menna probably wishes the poison had found its way to Iriset! Or Menna is behind it all. Iriset needs to get to the paint herself, to peel apart its forces. Try to detect the signature she caught on the assassin. But she doesn't know how to get Singix there. Maybe Amaranth can smuggle her some. With a small sigh, she asks, eyes still shut, "Who could hate me so much? Who, to destroy so many lives for mine?"

Her husband slides his hands down her arms and hugs her, his cheek against her hair. "Only a monster," he murmurs.

"Or someone who does not value those other lives," Garnet says.

Lifting her head, Iriset asks, "Was the girl mirané?"

"No," says Sidoné.

She looks to Garnet, who adds darkly, "But Shahd was, though Alishe—the Seal guard killed—was not."

"Shahd was killed by the assassin, not our villain."

"I am not mirané," Iriset says.

"Nor was Iriset mé Isidor," Lyric says.

Iriset tries not to melt at hearing her real name on his lips. Does she imagine a note of longing in his voice? (Probably.)

"We already suspected a miran," Amaranth says dismissively. Disgustedly, even. "I need a drink."

That night, she begs Lyric to stop her from thinking and halfway through the buildup of a truly epic orgasm, she turns the tables: She uses a slip of silk and ties his hands and takes out her love and impatience on his body, makes him yell and squirm, and thanks to all that practice analyzing Bittor's rising force again and again, she's very good at edging and doesn't let Lyric come until she thinks he's suffered almost enough.

After he passes out, she leaves through the secret door and plants her final anchors.

The design is ready; it only needs the trigger.

Iriset slips back into the bedroom she shares with the Vertex Seal and because she is ready, in love, and on the verge of winning, she wakes her husband up. He remains groggy, but Iriset grabs clothes for him and says she wants to pray in the Silent Chapel.

He goes easily then, never hesitant to visit his god's house. They walk the labyrinth hand in hand under the stars, and when they reach the center where a shallow well cuts into the rock of the Crystal Desert, she slowly strips off her clothes. Lyric, at peace, doesn't notice at first. When he does, he sucks in a breathless gasp. Iriset spreads herself against the hard, cool ground and waits for him. In the dawn light he kneels and touches her, gently, worshipfully, and Iriset closes her eyes to imagine it's her own body, her Osahar skin and knotted brown hair, her sandglass eyes and fuller lips. Her spine that arches, her ankle hooked over his shoulder. He'll never look at her this way again, never touch her this way again. At least her insides aren't changed, the night-shaded pink and brown all Iriset, the deep places inside her he manages to reach, *her* tongue and *her* teeth glinting in the light of Aharté's moon.

On the sixth afternoon of the Scorched Sky quad, a force-bridge in the Falling Steeple Shadow precinct explodes in a tightly designed burst, scattering pages from Silk's old design pamphlets. It kills a half-quad of people, injuring more, and the lines of force that suspended the bridge flare a white so bright it gives off heat like a vicious fire. It takes architects and investigator-designers five hours to put it out.

The moment the force-light fades, name-sigils appear in the air, hanging like afterimages of light: Silk. Every sigil reads *Silk*.

After an epic meeting of the mirané council, Lyric authorizes General Bey to prepare the Holy City army for a full offensive into the Saltbath precinct and root out Bittor méra Tesmose. The army issues a statement via ribbon alarm and bulletin graffiti: *Turn against the cult of Silk and apostasy, or your homes will be leveled on the fourth day.* The message rings across Moonshadow City, radiating from ribbons and steeples, four times. Every four hours it repeats. (Iriset does not know yet, but the voice is Lyric's. Almost none of the citizens of the empire can recognize it, but he insists that it be his word, his responsibility. Menna mé Garai and Raia mér Omorose capture the echo, and the Vertex Seal doesn't shake or quail.)

When the bridge exploded there were still five days left on Bittor's timeline, but Lyric has taken them down to merely three. If anything else changes, Iriset is ready. Her array is set, she has the charged robes that will become her wings, and she is so eager, despite everything, to strip off this Singix identity and be herself again.

There is rebellion throughout the city, but soon everyone will know that real apostasy lives at the side of the Vertex Seal.

34

The assassin

Deep in the night, Iriset wakes to the urgent chimes of their private alarum.

She sits up just as Lyric jolts out of bed and grasps for trousers.

Garnet's arrival is announced by footsteps leaping up the spiral corridor from the greeting chamber below; the moment he appears, he says, "Sian méra Sayar is dead."

It's Nielle's husband, the small king of Ecstatic Steeple Shadow.

Lyric keeps dressing. "Has Beremé summoned the privilege council?"

"No."

"It's not necessary until the sun is up. I'll go to her, and have General Bey brought, and Menna. Do you know what happened?"

"He was assassinated at the fourth ascent, in his Steeple Square, while your command rang out."

"The army will have to go into Saltbath today instead of waiting for the fourth day."

Iriset draws her knees to her chest, watching her husband

and his body-twin plan. Because she's naked, she remains in the bed, wrapped in the sheet. The perfect excuse not to speak.

"It will go against the command," Garnet says.

Lyric pauses, eyes on the tiled floor. "I know that, but the murder of one of my small kings must be met with clear fury, not ambivalence."

"Yes." Garnet puts his hand on Lyric's shoulder. Compels eye contact for a moment. Then Lyric nods, and they turn to go, but Lyric suddenly spins and kneels beside the bed.

"I..." The Vertex Seal stares at her, frowning, something pressing to be said, but he doesn't say it.

She kisses him. This is the very last time, and she can't even relish it. "Go," she whispers.

Iriset huddles alone when they've departed, the sheets pulled over her head. She squeezes her eyes closed, curled in a ball, wishing she could cry.

But it's not grief nor fear that pounds clear through her blood. It's resolution.

If he'll be meeting with his mirané council, that is a perfect time for her to enact her plan. She has to start now, even if Bittor's deadline hasn't struck: The army is going to surprise the insurgents, and Iriset will trigger her graffiti and warn them.

She throws off the blankets and pulls on a robe, then goes down to ask for coffee and for the night attendant to wake Huya.

When the coffee arrives, she drinks it on Lyric's balcony with his herb garden as if he were there with her. And when Huya appears, she tells him that she's going to go into Moonshadow City to comfort her friend Nielle, whose husband is dead. At his protest, she makes it a command, and if he doesn't like it, or her Seal guards think they can't keep her safe, they need to make the Vertex Seal himself tell her she can't be friend to her friend—and then they'll all be fired.

After Huya vanishes in a flurry, Iriset dresses in Lyric's clothing. His priest-red trousers, shirt, his sleeveless red tunic. Over it she throws a layered Ceres mantle that falls from her shoulders in waves of deep blues and greens, with streaks of silver and pale cream-orange. The chest piece that flattens her breasts is simpler than most, encrusted with lines of milky glass and black embroidery.

By then the sun has arrived, and Iriset hurries into her study to gather the craftmask and the strips of silk that will hang over her shoulders like a cloak until they are charged into ecstatic power. She also needs her weaponized stylus, which she keeps stuck to the bottom of the desk if she isn't wearing it as a comb in her hair. And the resonance pill for dissolving the marriage knot.

She doesn't notice Diaa of Moonshadow awaiting her until Her Glory clears her throat.

Iriset stops cold. How did Diaa get in without permission from Huya? Except... Diaa lived in this tower when her husband was the Vertex Seal. Iriset does not let her eyes slide toward the secret door. But her blood chills in tiny ecstatic pops.

"Diaa," Iriset says, acting surprised.

The older miran lifts her brow in mutual surprise, offering no explanation of her mysterious arrival. "It is barely dawn and you already are dressed to depart?"

"My dear friend Nielle was bound in marriage to the small king murdered last night, and I go to comfort her."

"How good of you." Diaa smiles with genuine warmth. "You are sinking into your role admirably. I suspect my son already believes he could not live without you."

Iriset lowers her eyes politely.

After a moment, she looks up. Diaa studies her with a peaceful expression. "My bound-daughter"—she uses an old mirané word that means such—"are you sure you should leave the palace complex at such a time? Perhaps your friend can be sent for, and comforted in the bosom of safety here?"

"That is my thought, as well, Your Glory," Iriset says carefully, "only to go myself and bring her back. I do not think she will come alone; she will want to remain where her husband is. The marriage binding is so intense, you must remember."

Diaa hums her agreement, glancing away sorrowfully.

"I have some coffee, in the front room, if you would like. Though it may have grown tepid."

"Thank you, no." Diaa draws back her shoulders. Her mirané-brown face is painted with spiral blossoms like a pink chrysanthemum. The color makes her lovely mirané eyes seem slightly more reddish than usual.

Iriset bites her bottom lip. "I wish to gather some materials from my worktable to take to Nielle."

Diaa nods casually, and Iriset walks calmly, as if nothing is wrong, to her table. Her mask-working materials are in boxes and woven baskets, with the sheaves of parchment and pencils on the table itself. As Iriset chooses a basket, Diaa moves behind her.

Rising force lifts up her spine and Iriset freezes just as a knife touches her throat.

Diaa grips her from behind; the blade presses beneath Iriset's jaw. "You are so beautiful, Singix. It is such a pity you aren't mirané."

Iriset breathes shallowly, taking great care with her neck, as fear skitters along her flesh. "I...That is what you've come to say? Is that why you dislike me?"

"I don't dislike you, child. I simply cannot risk my son's children being born without Aharté's most important blessing."

"Not mirané," Iriset says. This has never been about politics, not the way Iriset thinks of politics. Not about alliances and empire. Or proving Lyric's devotion or Amaranth's schemes. It's only about race. Iriset, for a moment, thinks she might laugh.

"You believe I'm pregnant," she says. "Lyric told you, he said. That is why you tried again after so long."

Diaa shrugs, and Iriset imagines she feels the knife heating against her skin.

Iriset says, "But everyone—even the mirané council, even Beremé herself, and—and Lyric!—decided this marriage was good. Necessary. If Aharté blessed it, which she did, she will bless our children, too. There is nothing for you to worry about, bound-mother." As she speaks, Iriset grips the edge of the worktable before her, searching blindly for the stylus stuck to the bottom with friction-buttons.

Diaa says, "Do you believe in Aharté at all, Singix? You have other gods; you cannot argue to me any faith in She Who Loves Silence."

Ecstatic force continues to pop in Iriset's blood, and hot rising force burns up her body in a flare of panic. "And so you—you'll just murder me here?"

"Unfortunately, the investigator-designers have those berries."

"What?" Iriset's fingers pause in surprise.

"I told you they made a good tea, but you didn't drink it. Now they'll know, and you're the only person who knows I gave them to you."

"They're poisonous?" Iriset sounds appalled even to herself.

"Merely abortifacient."

Iriset does laugh now, high with disbelief.

"These used to be my rooms, Singix. There is a third door to this study, did you know? It is hidden in the architecture and leads down through the petal to a rendezvous chamber. I am unsurprised neither you nor my son are aware. He fell in love with you so very quickly."

Silk. She needs Silk's cold focus. Iriset takes a deep breath, enough that the blade presses sharply to her skin. She says, "You will break his heart."

Just then, her finger brushes against the charged comb.

Diaa says, "He will mend. And be stronger for it and marry a mirané girl."

Iriset considers screaming, but Diaa continues quickly, as if sensing it, "I've known Huya since he was a baby. His mother was one of my first attendants. Did you forget how long this palace has been *mine*? They will never suspect me. None have yet. Not even you."

"Diaa," Iriset whispers, stalling. "Please. Please let me live. Let me go." She must be careful as she unsticks the comb not to drop it, or move too fast, for Diaa has but to slice. Iriset can't save herself from a spurting artery with *any* kind of architecture. Her heart pounds so hard she wonders if Lyric can feel it—but he's so tense and stressed himself, he'll think it's his own pulse. "Please," she says as she strains, lifting her chin. She can't—quite—reach the damn thing.

"Be still. Begging is no use. You are bound; the only way to undo the marriage is your death."

With nothing to lose, Iriset hisses sharply, shoving ecstatic force out through her skin: Her hair raises, she shudders with the static charge, and Diaa gasps, and her whole body jerks in surprise. Iriset kicks back, twisting to try to free her neck. The blade cuts, but shallowly, and Iriset spins free, grabbing the stylus and brandishing it before her. It's plain pink quartz, thin enough to be delicate as a princess's hair comb, and gleams like a shard of the moon.

Diaa stares at her in shock, her hands rigid and empty: Her knife clattered to the floor. "How did you do that?"

Holding Diaa's gaze, Iriset steps forward. She lets her accent crumble, shaking it off bit by bit, word by word. "You don't know anything. Singix died in your first attempt. You poisoned her *before* her wedding, but I took her place." Iriset bares the teeth that have always been hers.

"What?" Diaa's eyes widen. Her hand lowers. "You're not... No, you're lying to save yourself."

"Do you know who I am? I made a craftmask under your daughter's command. For quads I have lived as Singix, and you didn't know. They might not suspect you, Diaa, but neither does your daughter trust you."

"Iriset mé Isidor," Diaa hisses.

Iriset shakes her head. It feels so good to speak. She burns with eager forces, vivid and popping in her blood. "I am *Silk*. I have invented new kinds of designs my entire life, given wings to flightless animals, sculpted bones, and healed apostatic cancer. There is a rebellion burning through Moonshadow City in my name. I can"—she touches the dual tines of her crystal comb to Diaa's chest, just above the collar of her layered robe—"do anything."

Iriset activates the design.

(When Iriset created her weapon, she was thinking of apostatical theory, thinking of games she played with herself and what it might take to stop a heart, harden blood, whether a crawling design could be used to destroy a face or musculature as well as it could be used to transform. She was not thinking of Erxan. She was thinking she had to live.)

The comb shatters in the surge of forces it focuses: ecstatic arrows for Diaa's heart, hooking the threads of her inner design; flow draws them in; rising and falling slam together like a pair of vicious scissors, and cuts them.

Diaa collapses.

Dead.

Just like that.

Satisfaction unfurls in Silk's mind. And tiny pricks of surprise. It worked perfectly. Too well. It's so much cleaner than the mess she made of Ambassador Erxan. Painless.

Silk stares. She almost kneels to check... something. To seek out the threads of force and taste their angles.

Then, suddenly, panic blossoms outward. Iriset's skin feels aflame, she's choking on what she's done, ecstatic force sparking behind her eyes. *We pay for what we do.*

She can't feel her hands. She steps back, away from the sprawl of Diaa's voluminous robes.

The mother of the Vertex Seal is dead.

Amaranth's mother is dead.

Iriset remembers to breathe, gasping hugely. She bends at the waist, one hand fisted against her heart, the other flat on her knee. Closing her eyes, she draws in eight breaths in an eight-count.

She didn't want this kind of revenge, but it seems she'll have it.

"Your Glory?" Huya calls from beyond the study door.

"I'm fine," Iriset calls back. "Settling myself. I'll be out to join you shortly."

Slowly, Iriset calms down—to a level of numbness in which she can function, at least. Going to the secret drawer, she pulls out the strip of silk that is the craftmask she hasn't let herself think about this whole time. With it, her basic stylus, and the resonance pill, she returns to their bedroom.

The pill is a small, rounded opal nugget the size of her thumbnail. Quickly Iriset sketches a basic four-eight-sixteen-four hold design against the gem, activates it with an atonal quartet, then swallows it.

It's large and difficult but that's the point: Once it's in her throat, Iriset removes her Ceres chest piece and parts her borrowed robe so that she can touch the tip of the stylus to her sternum. She sparks it and drives it into her skin. The blood-pain-gasp works with a low hum to match the hold design on the opal inside her, and it catches.

The forces meet under her breastbone, and Iriset's whole body thrums.

As she breathes through what will hopefully slowly, methodically, break down the marriage knot, she lifts the stylus to her left temple. With another deep breath, Iriset tears the Singix craftmask seam.

It hurts.

Like stripping skin off her face. Flaying design from muscles. The burn makes her catch her breath, but she doesn't hesitate. The craftmask peels away bit by bit, even and strong. It tugs at her eyes and loosens a few lashes and fine nose hairs, and she whimpers as it detaches from her lips, the sensitive skin bruised and new. Heat fills her skull as her muscles reclaim themselves, jaw squaring off, cheeks widening into a slight tilt, and her tendons, muscles, cartilage bending to fit where they belong. She pricks her eyes gently with the stylus, releasing the tiny nets that changed the color of her irises. Her vision blurs, as if her eyes are melting, but that, strangely, doesn't hurt.

Once she holds the used craftmask limp in her hands, she

tears it violently in two, whispering a goodbye to beloved Singix. She sets the remnants beside the newly completed craftmask on the bed, then begins the process of retracting the crawling design that will cause her skin to burn and flake away, revealing her own flawed desert-peach. She deactivates the secondary net so it will dissolve slowly over the next few hours, stripping the softness and black gleam from her hair. There's nothing she can do to make that happen faster. Or, she can, but it would be debilitating.

Sweaty and shaking, Iriset takes off the rest of her clothes. Her skin feels tight, wrinkling in places it bends the most: knuckles, elbows, knees, groin, neck. Closing her eyes, she rubs at herself, moving the transformation along. Skin puckers and flakes away. It's disgusting.

But Iriset is methodical about it, taking care with one arm, then the other, then her torso and what she can reach of her back. Her hips and legs are easier, having had more time, and the skin of one of her feet comes off almost like a glove. Iriset grimaces, equally disturbed and fascinated.

When she's as finished as she can be, she puts the trousers and tunic and slippers back on, and does her best to sweep the skin into a pile. It's translucent and clear and will continue to quickly deteriorate until it's nothing but dust.

Her breastbone hums with a deep resonance.

Trembling and exhausted, Iriset stares at what she's leaving behind.

A mask of her husband, the Vertex Seal, waiting here in the room above his mother's body. Proof of who she is and always has been. Proof of what she's done to him.

It will be a quieter devastation than her public display.

A private message for the Vertex Seal: She's not a god. Just an apostate, and maybe a bit of a monster. Like him.

If she goes now, fast, she'll have time to find Bittor and warn him. Make sure he's safe. And her grandparents. Dalal and her son. The remnants of the Little Cat's court who were her family long before she infiltrated this one. Iriset will be safe, too, slipped away into the city to be Silk out there. To keep pushing her work. To live.

Only slightly shaky, Iriset returns to the study. Diaa remains sprawled on the floor, those pink blossoms still beautiful against her skin. Iriset drops a scarf over Diaa's face, then gathers the rest of what she needs, including a long strip of orange silk to be a cloth mask for herself and her father's echo coin. Before she can change her mind, she leaves through the secret door.

Her only stop on her way out of the palace complex is the Color Can Be Loud Garden, where she kneels on the lawn beside the bed of force-hungry lilies. Iriset plants the final anchor, the trigger, with a crudely designed delay. She hooks its delay into the breathing foundation, that natural rhythm of the palace architecture. She doesn't have time to make it precise, and only knows that at this pace, the delay will deteriorate sometime in the next five hours. At that point the anchors will connect and close their loops, and her massive design will activate. Silk's spiders will climb all over everything.

Once it's done, she retucks her cloth mask and bows her head like a regular attendant, and Iriset mé Isidor leaves the palace of the Vertex Seal.

RISING

Confession is always violent.
—*Word of Aharté*

35

The mouth of chaos

Iriset's goal is the Crimson Canyon, but the northern tip is halfway across the crater from the palace.

The city moves and churns with life, though rather quick and more frantic than one would expect on a warm late-summer morning. As if a great hailstorm looms on the horizon. There are no pop-up vendors, nor the usual news graffiti advertising daily deals in such and such market square or what time a show begins in the Amphitheater of Stars. The only graffiti she sees is an innocent arch of spray-designed pink flowers so faded they must be quads old, and the remnants of some sigil declaring the rare sunstar bushes were finally blooming in the Wave-and-Moss Garden. Iriset spies evidence that a few walls have been treated with anti-graffiti force-nets, and it must be because of fear that they'll be charged penalties if rebel art appears on their buildings.

Along a curving street lined with fire-stalls and cafés, Iriset finds doors flung open and pedestrians calling to friends seated upon stools and cushions with their pipes and coffee. There aren't many smiles, but neither do the people seem overly anxious—except when an army-standard ribbon skiff slides past, gathering furtive frowns in its wake.

Then the alarum rings out from the ribbon system, and Iriset freezes in the street at the reverberation of Lyric's captured voice: *Turn against the cult of Silk and apostasy, or your homes will be leveled on the fourth day.* His voice purrs up her spine with rising force as the message repeats three more times. It seems to resonate with the hum that is obliterating their marriage knot. Iriset presses her fist over her sternum. The pill is a choking ache deep inside. She wishes it would dissolve already.

When Iriset crosses into the Saltbath precinct with its needle minarets and honeycomb streets, the design patterns shift around her like the loosening of a too-tight robe. She pauses again, touching her palm to cool red-blue-black tiles, and listens. She parts her lips to taste the eddies of Saltbath forces. This was her home in Moonshadow City, where she'd been born and lived every day of her life until this summer. She knows the flavor of the specific way that the city's design knots and weaves, and the sparks of ecstatic tingle exactly as they should—except no.

Iriset chooses a shaded alley between a silicate warehouse and the workshop where the crystals are carved and polished into usable tools or decorations. With her stylus she creates a tiny break in the wall and reaches in, tugging gently at the flow threads. Her lips are too raw from removing the craftmask to be helpful in sensing nuance of energies, but oh, how good it feels to welcome the coursing power of Moonshadow City back into her body. She leans her forehead against the tiles, absorbing every rhythm and pulse of the working design.

Though she's only been gone a season, some of the nuance has changed. The pull toward the canyon is stronger, probably from security nets and way stations forcing flow to pause, and... Iriset realizes suddenly, eyes flying open, *her father's tower is gone*. Of course it is, it was ruined and invaded, but the network of designs she wrapped it in used to be an invisible shadow shifting the patterns of forces in specific ways nobody had ever detected—and the shadow has entirely vanished.

The Little Cat's tower has been dismantled, probably physically by the army and thread-by-thread by the investigator-designers. They explored her work, analyzed it, learned from her.

Iriset shoves away from the wall and heads quickly toward the southern ribbon hub, tucked in among branching garages, across the block from a row of mechanics (including her grandmother's shop, closed up and dark). At the hub, Iriset crawls under a skiff and unpeels the flow skate from the ribbon, splicing deep enough to lay a tiny little anchor with her own knotted hair and a whisper and the tip of her stylus.

— • ♦ • —

It's around this time that Amaranth is standing over her mother's body. Every ounce of her inner design and willpower focus on maintaining a certain poise for the Seal guards and designers crowding the study.

According to Diaa's Seal guard, Diaa had been feeling poorly and remained in her rooms all morning. It was Huya, Singix's combat-designer and secretary, who discovered the woman exactly as she is now: sprawled dead on the floor of Lyric's study with no apparent injury.

Amaranth was quietly and urgently fetched (isn't it interesting that the palace sought the Moon-Eater's Mistress before the

Vertex Seal in this as in so many things!), and once the Seal guards and two investigator-designers checked the study for poison and traps (they'd found remnants of an oddly charged crystal and not been surprised by the secret door), she was allowed in with Sidoné. Huya reported that he'd swept the entire suite, and Her Glory Singix Es Sun was not present. There were some odd things in the bedroom, however.

Immediately, the body-twin left again to alert Garnet, who would bring Lyric. Amaranth dragged herself upstairs to the bedroom and discovered the evidence she most disliked to find. The kitten was not coming back.

Now Menna of the Seal crouches at Diaa's head, with one of the investigator-designers and two palace designers. They hold a stasis net around Diaa, trying to locate a cause of death. "Her heart, maybe," Menna says softly. Just what she'd said about Ambassador Erxan. She glances up at Amaranth. "Your Glory, I cannot say more without more invasive investigation. But there is no lingering design, that I can say certainly."

The investigator-designer adds, "I recognize no regular signs of design-effect. And there is no injury that I can find that would cause death. I am sorry, Your Glory."

Clenching her jaw, Amaranth nods. She can't allow herself to embrace the body as her mother's, to accept her mother is dead. Not yet, not without a plan. She'll rage in her grief, once it arrives, and she can't afford to flail now. But she can, and does, believe that Iriset mé Isidor is capable of murder methods that leave no trace for an architect trained under the Glorious Vow to find. She's done it before, after all. And Amaranth ignored the trespass.

The Moon-Eater's Mistress shudders with the effort of swallowing back fury.

Diaa must have said something, discovered something, to make Iriset act. It must have been terrible, or Iriset would not have risked so much. The daughter of the Little Cat of Moonshadow is a survivor. And she loved Lyric too much to do this without necessity. Maybe even loved Amaranth herself.

Amaranth whispers the worst curse she knows.

If there's one thing the Moon-Eater's Mistress excels at, it's controlling herself. So many believe otherwise, that she's ruled by excess desire, but they believe exactly as she wishes.

She needs to know what happened here, and why. Nothing else—*nothing*—matters more. Not yet.

Lyric enters softly between two Seal guards who startle back when they realize it's the Vertex Seal. Garnet is not with him. Amaranth looks up in time to see the moment Lyric realizes what has happened.

His entire body goes still. He doesn't even breathe as he stares at their mother. Then he draws a deep breath, holds it, and releases it. Again, and again. After the fourth calming count, the entire room is fixed on him, and he says, "What happened?" in a dangerously quiet voice. "Where is my wife?"

"She's missing," answers Huya méra Luméri. "She said she wanted to visit her friend, the wife of—"

"Find her," Lyric says, then he kneels at Diaa's shoulder. He places a hand over her eyes, another over his own heart, and murmurs a prayer. When he releases their mother, he purposefully smears the painted flowers against her cheeks. He touches the paint to his own face, smearing it there, too, against his freckles. Tears glint in his lashes when he stands and turns to Amaranth. "Are you all right?"

"Hardly," she answers humorlessly.

Lyric takes her hand, and then puts their foreheads together.

Amaranth wants to let herself crumble, to press against him and weep. It's been so long since she could be only a little sister. She wants Sidoné and Garnet to appear in the archway, then close her and her brother both up in a tight embrace. The four of them, balanced and together. Unbreakable. They can survive this together; that's how they survived Esmail's death.

But of course, their quartet has been harshly divided for quads by the lie Amaranth and Sidoné know. By Iriset herself.

It's time to tell Lyric. Send the Seal guards and architects away. Tell both him and Garnet. If Iriset has done this, she will not be found. She'll vanish into Moonshadow City, and someday Lyric will feel their marriage bond snap. They'll have no other sign of her living or dying. Holy fuck, but Lyric is going to need his family. But he might not let Amaranth help him after this. He might hate her for a while. No, he'll definitely hate her for a while. That, more than anything, sets her pulse racing. She must maintain her composure! She knows him. She knows how to bring them together in this.

Leaning away from her brother, though it tightens her chest with actual physical pain, she says, "Singix isn't coming back."

Lyric's eyes fall shut and he flattens a hand over his heart. He looks like a corpse himself, mouth tight, eyes bruised and hollow. "She has to."

"Not if—" Amaranth can't help it; she stares down at their mother's body. Oh, it hurts, and she can't fight the reality for much longer. It's like monsters slinking nearer and nearer in her peripheral vision. They'll get her soon. She can't stop it.

"Not if..." Lyric frowns at her, then at Diaa's body. "You think Diaa did something to her? You think our mother..."

Amaranth doesn't know what to say first. Shock chokes her. What if—

What—

Could that be why? Diaa hadn't discovered Iriset's secret, but Diaa had *tried to assassinate Singix.*

All the pieces kaleidoscope together, slotting where they belong.

Amaranth's breath shudders out of her.

(She hasn't known from the beginning, after all.)

"Mother..." Amaranth says, and then hisses her frustration and pain. It makes her teeth cold. "She hated this marriage, but I thought I'd—I'd won her over. I thought...she wouldn't do this...She..."

"I can find Singix," Lyric says, and without giving Amaranth a chance for more confession, he shoves out of the study.

——— • ♦ • ———

As Lyric méra Esmail His Glory is halfway across the Silent precinct on the trail of his runaway wife, the entire palace complex lights up in brilliant design.

Silk is here.
Silk lives.

36

Bittor

It begins with a slight shudder of rising force in the Color Can Be Loud Garden, as the delay loop Iriset placed expires with an ecstatic spark, releasing the trigger.

Swift on the heels of the shudder is another and another, from the nearest anchors in the Seven Petals Is Not Enough Amphitheater and the menagerie, then a cascade of pop-shivers spreading across the entire palace complex from the Moon-Eater's Temple to the Silent Chapel.

Most architects notice, though they shrug it off as a hitch someone caused with some sort of update or maybe it has to do with the hundreds of extra force-cuffs. Raia mér Omorose stands in surprise: An knows the security webs very well, and this should not happen. Menna of the Seal also is aware something is wrong, though she's less able to pinpoint that it's the security webs.

Of course, everyone with working eyes sees it when the aforementioned security net begins to glow. Normally the net remains invisible without a specific design frame set over various sections to allow for updates and manipulations (frames

Silk doesn't need, *scoff scoff,* because once she marks a few linchpins, she can mentally construct the rest of the design out).

The net flares silver, in undulating pulses of flow and rising, and the ground beneath the mirané feet sparkles in long threads. People leap onto chairs as if they've seen a skink or they perform silly tiptoe dances to get away, or a few crouch to touch—those are either architects or children or fools. Yes, there's already some screaming from the ones most likely to faint during the next stage.

While everybody reacts to the floor or lawn or gravel as though it's suddenly turned to lava, little pink sparks of ecstatic travel the threads, moving too fast to catch, and they grow eight legs to wave around and suddenly the lovely silver net is a lovely silver web covered in creepy crawling spiders!

That isn't the worst, though. Where the threads meet and crisscross, the spider-sparks shoot up bolts of rising force that crash together hundreds of paces in the air, swirling over the dome of the mirané hall. There they form a single massive, elegant mother spider.

All this happens in merely the time it takes Raia to throw anself out of ans workroom and onto a petal balcony two doors over.

An cranes ans neck to look up at the gargantuan (beautiful) spider. Raia has never seen anything like it—the power it must consume! The complex directions that had been completely hidden! How...!

Now the screams really let loose, and in a very subtle, genius trick the likes of which Silk should be known for, the natural rising force and terrorized ecstatic of the screams themselves feed the churning design.

The giant spider steps over the palace with its long, silver-pink articulated legs, each ending in toes with delicate claws that were dainty on the adorable little spinners Iriset kept in her workroom. On this spider, each toe could squish a couple of miran if they stand near each other.

But the spider's made of forces, not mass, so it squishes nobody. The few unlucky enough or so slow that they come in direct contact experience a dramatic frenzy of their internal forces and collapse. They'll (probably) be fine after a nap or a thorough inner balancing.

The spider moves gracefully, smoother than an arc of wine poured by a talented attendant. It makes no sound but hums with forces, and skull sirens shriek, flocking toward it in a terrible mess. Lattice snakes ruffle their feather-teeth toward it, the rainbow bees fly a tad too high for their own good, and the rep-cats duck into shadows. The less said about the state of the griffons in the menagerie, the better.

Where the spider goes, it leaves behind gorgeous woven sigils that shimmer the same silver-pink as the spider (as Aharté's moon in the sky).

Can you guess what they read?

Silk is here.

Silk lives. Silk is Syr.

The spider is so large, and so bright, it's visible against the afternoon sky from the four precincts at the edges of the Crystal Desert: Morning Market, Descent Market, Silent, and Design. Thousands of citizens of Moonshadow City see Iriset's glorious design, but not Lyric, who races toward his wife.

———— • ♦ • ————

Iriset doesn't see it, either, though she was supposed to be flying high with the mama spider, arms outstretched, glorious in the robes of the Vertex Seal. Instead she's at the bottom of the Crimson Canyon.

In her physical condition she's lucky she made it this many miles as it is, and chooses one of the two paths down into the depths of the canyon with shallower stairs, though it takes longer to reach the bottom. As she descends, the light fades into long shadows thanks to the angle of the afternoon sun, but there are force-lights tied across the narrowest parts of the canyon walls and gas lamps burning at the end of curving poles. The best thing about the canyon is everyone ignores her and vice versa. It's easy to fade into the flickering shadows with their warm gas-flame color, like dropping into another world.

On the lowest level of permanent residence, a wide terrace carved into the cliff, Iriset slips past the temporary stalls and tents, through a raucous crowd clearly unconcerned with the city army. They should be. The combat-designers could drop percussion bells down here, or trance ribbons, and everyone would be out. But that's not her current problem so she keeps going until she reaches the northernmost tip of the canyon, then climbs one of the ladders down to the sand-and-mud-caked floor. She wipes her palms on her robe skirt and walks along the barren bottom.

There are no homes or stalls or even lean-tos here, but several cave mouths hidden beneath the layers of overhangs. One is the entrance to an elaborate warren of undermarket hideaways. Nobody lives in them—though they often fill with squatters during the winter—because when the Lapis River overflow pours through the canyon during the spring and sometimes autumn, the hideaways flood first.

Iriset ducks under a low shelf into a cave. She remains bent in half, sliding her hand along the rough rock in an awkward shuffle until she suddenly is free to stand in a pocket cavern. It's black as night, and there's nothing with which to make light, so she continues using her hand to feel for the second jagged hole in the eastern wall. She squeezes through and around a sharp turn, then comes into a room that buzzes with latent force.

Iriset claps and an echo of ecstatic answers, showing her the diamond etched beside the entrance. She places her hand over it, taps a code with her fingers into the hidden design panel, and the forces answer: A thread of bluish light flickers to life just above her eye level. It streaks around the artificially smooth walls of the cave, illuminating a diamond-pattern netting across the ceiling. Iriset glances at the stones spread in what is supposed to seem haphazard fashion, and carefully picks up two granite chunks shot through with lines of quartz. She leans them together against the wall where a similar vein of quartz crawls up the red rock. When they are aligned just right, the quartz veins pulse with ecstatic force, which begin a cascade effect, lighting the diamond net in a pattern to reveal hidden sigils.

It's a map that Iriset helped her father and one of his cryptographers create before she ever took the name Silk, and Bittor has not forgotten—the location of the Little Cat's surviving court is marked with the sigil for Silk.

———— • ♦ • ————

Three hours before sunset, Iriset arrives at a wine shop at the southeast edge of Saltbath. Thin glass bottles are bricked along the porch roof like glinting teeth, and in its shade small tables stand on short feet, surrounded by flat cushions and customers sharing rose wine and juniper mead. Iriset walks past them and into the dim stucco foyer. Two women lean upon the counter, both in sleeveless robes with long lines of black tattoos streaking their forearms and dotted with leaves and berries in vivid purple and blue. (Tattoos are controversial for being a permanent alteration of the body, but not technically considered apostasy.) Iriset spares a brief regret for the lovely ghost writing on Singix's hands that used to decorate her forehead and back into her hair, with all the names of her ancestors. These two are likely a branch of Bes people, the only people Iriset is aware of who tattoo for pleasure or art, though their high brown foreheads suggest more of a Sarian lineage. By that same high brown forehead on both of them, plus the shape of their upper lips and their feminine-forward physicality and style, Iriset guesses they are mother and daughter.

She places her hands on the counter and says, "I am here to see Bittor."

Though the younger woman scowls in a pretense of ignorance, the older peers at Iriset. "Are you?"

Iriset pushes back her hood. "I do not know you, honorie, but he will wish to see me."

"Your name?"

"Mama, it's Silk," the younger whispers. "The graffiti—or, at least she looks like..."

"Yes," Iriset says. She leans in to rudely look into their eyes. "But I've been out of touch too long to know his new codes. Since the Little Cat was taken. Tell him to come here or let me through. It is urgent."

"Prove you're not army."

Withdrawing her stylus, Iriset says, "Let me repair that cut on your arm."

The woman lifts her eyebrow and Iriset picks out a thread

from the hem of Lyric's very fine tunic. It isn't silk, but should work as easily to knit flesh. She loops some between her fingers in an infinite knot, then presses it to the woman's warm brown skin. With the stylus she pricks the points of a simple star polygon pattern, and then draws on the woman's inner forces of flow and falling to fuel the design. The woman hisses in surprise, and possibly some pain, though it's more hot than sharp. As Iriset works, the silk thread sinks in, tightening the skin, and in a brief echo of sympathetic magic, it basically teaches the flesh to sew itself back together.

"Human architecture," the daughter says quietly, either in awe or in fear.

"Fast, too," her mother says, pressing at her healing wound. She jerks her chin and the daughter dashes out of the shop. "I'm Pel," the mother says to Iriset. "Drink?"

"Thank you."

"There's a stool if you'd like to come into the back."

Iriset accepts the hospitality and the cup of rose wine. It's cloudy, cut with rice liquor, and it sits hard on her tongue but slips down like a trickle of smooth fire. She touches her eyelids with thumb and forefinger in appreciation.

Pel sips at her own cup and studies Iriset. "You're probably better for him dead."

"Not personally," Iriset answers, taking no offense. "And not if I miraculously revive. But you should go visit friends in another precinct."

"You bringing the army behind you after all?"

"No, Bittor's done that himself, with the assassination of Sian méra Sayar last night. I'm here to warn him. To help."

The old woman's crooked front teeth gleam when she grimaces, and Iriset thinks, as she often has, that there's no need for anyone to have crooked anything. Superstition and stubbornness hold human architecture as apostasy. But this time, she thinks of Lyric, too, and his belief in Aharté's Holy Design. His insistence that humans are already designed as intended, even when born with disabilities that apostasy could mend. There are things Iriset knows she can't fix, but perhaps only because she's never given it great study. (She's never given much study to any kind of healing or developmental design beyond traumatic injury or apostatical cancers, and doesn't realize that in three hundred years of the Apostate Age, the question of what human design could and couldn't, or should and shouldn't, attempt was varied, passionate, and rife with not only conflict but disaster. There are no easy answers, only individual circumstances and a whole lot of arrogance.)

Thinking of Lyric even fleetingly makes the opal pill in Iriset's chest ache and the resonance hiccup. She has to swallow carefully and breathe obviously deep. The disintegration of the marriage knot has to be working, but she can't focus on it too clearly or it will solidify again. Maybe. Her whole body feels like it's recovering from sunburn.

"I don't think Bittor killed him, hiha," Pel says.

The endearment clenches a fist around Iriset's throat, and all she can say is "Huh?"

Pel looks darkly amused. "The small king. I am not aware of any plans to kill him, especially since he was in the neighboring precinct. But I don't know all that Bittor plans."

Iriset finishes the wine in her cup in one long go. It parts strangely around the opal she swallowed. She briefly meets Pel's gaze before politely settling her eyes on the older woman's lips. "The Vertex Seal thinks he did."

"Then he might as well have."

Before Iriset can respond to that brittle pessimism, Pel continues, "You're Isidor's daughter, aren't you?"

Iriset nods.

"I remember you on the street with your grandfather. You never came into my shop, though, not a good little girl like you." Pel snorts. "Except you're also Silk. That was well done."

"The Little Cat was good at keeping his life compartmentalized," she says lightly. Iriset learned the same trick from him very well.

"I was with Bittor when we heard that Iriset mé Isidor died."

"So?" Iriset feels her cheeks flush. She's disliking the sense of interrogation.

"So nothing in particular."

"Will he come fast?"

"Probably."

Iriset clenches her jaw. Her scalp itches and she wants to scratch away any of the last of Singix's skin. Tentatively she touches her hair. The crawling design is working hard, but it's a weird, tangled mix of sleek and rougher brown. She drops her hand into her lap and glances down. Peach-brown, maybe a little paler than usual, with rougher knuckles but her fingertips as smooth as ever.

"He's consolidated what's left of the Little Cat's people as best he can, using the graffiti as a rallying cry. But not for much besides chaos." Pel sounds frustrated.

Iriset doesn't know how to explain that this chaos *is* meaning. The protest art, the protest itself, has meaning. Disruption is all that matters when ruining a design. The design breaks whether that disruption comes from a well-thought-out plan or the wrong person sneezed and spilled a bit too much ecstatic into the threads.

Someone bursts into the front of the shop, and Pel heads out to take care of it, Iriset just behind.

A man with hair tied in the Sarian way gestures wildly, saying, "A spider! Right over the ribbon hub. It's huge graffiti, and it's weaving something!"

The man waves and runs off, and the few customers and a pale-faced server from the patio go after. Pel glances over her shoulder at Iriset. "You?"

"Me." Grim satisfaction presses Iriset's mouth into a smile. "If it's there, that means the palace array is live, too. Graffiti the likes of which you've never seen, a beautiful big spider right over the Silent Chapel. Silk lives."

"Just to match what Bittor and Dalal have been making?"

"Partly, but also to prove Silk does live, and not out here. If the army wants to root out apostasy, they have to do it to the palace of the Vertex Seal, too."

"They'll never."

"Which will only prove their hypocrisy, prove Aharté's Silence isn't perfect, isn't even sustainable. It's so easy to disrupt, and the longer we can disrupt it, the more people will see."

"Maybe even miran," Pel says thoughtfully.

"Lyric méra Esmail certainly. I was supposed to be there for the array, to show myself to all of them, but I had to come here. This way at least Lyric will know there is no Silence in his life that cannot be undone because of how deeply I disrupted every aspect of it already. Fuck Aharté—Silk is the one who can redesign the whole empire."

Someone behind them claps slowly. Iriset and Pel both spin.

"Silk is Syr," Bittor says, standing backlit in the glow from the shop door.

"Bittor." Iriset's Bittor, alive and whole, those stocky

shoulders corded with muscle, his forearms wrapped with knife-cuffs, his hair a mess around his square face, his scarred nose, and his mouth opening to shape her name.

"Iriset," he says, so rough with emotion it seems to shake the room. His robe is worn green linen and hangs heavy like it's paneled with armor on the underside. Bittor tears his cloth mask away from his face, tugging it off-kilter so the whole twisted cloth slides off his brown hair and slumps onto his shoulder. He doesn't seem to notice, for he stares at Iriset with his glinting cat-eyes, pupils long and wide.

His hands twitch against his thighs, and Iriset flings herself into his arms.

Bittor catches her, stepping back from the strength of the embrace, and lifts her off her toes. Iriset breathes so deeply, as if she can erase her memories of the past season with his smell alone. She buries her face under his ear while Bittor's arms tighten beyond the strength of her oversensitive body, and she's stuck, unbreathing, for a moment. A tremor passes from him to her—ecstatic force popping between them, dominant in him just as in her. She digs her fingers into his hair. Just like hers. Thick, rough, strong enough for knotting.

"Holy moon," he says, voice shaking, and releases her enough she slides down to her feet again. He grabs her head, cupping it, and smooths his thumbs along her cheeks. It aches, for her facial skin is the most tender. But she doesn't stop him. His eyes flicker over her face, fast and desperate, and the smile slowly spreading across his mouth is like wildflowers blossoming across the desert. For the first time in so long, Iriset feels joy—a fleeting dart of it, childlike and familiar and uplifting. "I knew it," he adds.

"How?" she whispers. "How did you know?"

"All the things," he says with that soft smile. "But mostly, Singix of the Beautiful Twilight said my name, and the most incredible, the most insane reason why that could be so was because it wasn't Singix, it was *you*."

Iriset involuntarily laughs like a sob, feeling warm rain falling force ground her in this, in her oldest friend, in being known. Bittor knows her so well that he knows exactly what audacious, wild genius she is capable of, and not just as an if, a possibility, but he believes in it. In her. Even if she's pretty sure he just called her crazy, too.

Then he kisses her, and she's kissing him back, his taste hitting her like a rising-falling back draft. (She won't think about how she doesn't know Bittor nearly as well, not his heart; she spent all her time with him on his body and reactions, on what he was in relation to her. She never thought about who he was when she wasn't around. Does she think of anyone outside of her own personal design?

Lyric. It's Lyric she knows. Lyric she studied on every level and felt—feels—in her chest, bound to with a seed of immanent Silence. She had to know him to survive, and Singix, she had to learn Singix, too. In life and death, and if she ever thinks about this, it might finally occur to Iriset that it's possible she doesn't have the objectivity to say she's right about anything. Even apostasy.)

The press of Bittor's lips is gentle, more like a reminder than passion, and he kisses her sore forehead and cheek and her closed eyelids, then hugs her again.

"Are my grandparents safe?" she asks.

Bittor grimaces. "I practically had to kidnap them, but yes."

Nodding in relief, she starts to ask more, but Pel's daughter bursts into the wine shop, panting. "The army is already coming!"

"Everyone out, go home," Pel commands the few remaining customers stubbornly drinking on the patio.

"We're supposed to have two more days," Bittor says.

Iriset leans back. "It's because Sian mé Sayar is dead."

"I didn't kill him," Bittor says with genuine shock.

Iriset stares, thoughts awhirl. She never heard anyone in the palace say Bittor did it—Lyric assumed. *The murder of one of my small kings must be met with clear fury*, he said. If someone else killed Nielle's husband, there would be evidence, surely. Lyric wouldn't raze a precinct based on a guess or a possible frame.

But Beremé would, if it suited her game. And General Bey, too, Iriset is certain, and could even have done the frame-up himself. If Lyric asked for evidence, between the two of them they could provide it.

"It doesn't matter," Pel says. "They believe you did."

"Or decided you did," Iriset adds. Iriset's pulse rocks inside her, a hard, constant tide growing stronger and stronger. Closer and closer. As if Iriset doesn't act, she might shake apart.

(Forgive her for not realizing what it is—her skin is raw, her senses overwhelmed with force-flavors, she's afraid and elated both, desperate and numb and so many things that shield her from what, exactly, is growing stronger and stronger. Closer and closer.)

"We have to do something," Bittor says, glancing out through the shop toward the twilit street. "I do. I started this."

"Did you?" Iriset asks incredulously.

"Instead of rescuing your father. After you died, I just wanted to make them pay, I wanted them to see what they'd done."

"They know. The Vertex Seal and his sister, they know now. But you're right, we should do more."

"Spread word for people to hide?" Pel suggests. "Cooperation? Don't give the army a reason to lash out?"

Bittor shakes his head, his cat-eyes glinting. "People will be hurt tonight, even if they all open their doors. Even if they don't fight back, but only watch."

Iriset grasps his face and mirrors his gesture from earlier, stroking her thumbs under his eyes. "Bittor, do you want to make another graffiti?"

"What kind?" he asks, as Pel's daughter cries, "*Yes!*"

"The Little Cat told me to survive, not save him. He told me to make him proud by making a mark, changing something. That's what you've already been doing, and that's what my giant spider is for. But listen: It doesn't have to be all at once." Iriset sweeps her gaze between the three of them. "Little things, and bigger things, all adding up to a real shift in the city. That's how you redesign anything, but especially something as complicated as the array for an entire empire. Unknot here and there, until the design is unstable enough to collapse on its own. Rebuild from there."

Bittor shuts his eyes and leans down. "Something simple, then? Small graffiti and tricks that the army themselves will trigger as they pass?"

"Yes." She kisses his forehead. Allows her breath to skitter into his hair and ignores the frantic pacing of her heart, the hard opal humming in her chest, breaking down the very last vestiges of Singix Es Sun inside her.

"Can you do that? On the go?" Pel asks. "Dalal couldn't."

"Please. She's good, but she's not an eighth of the architect I am." Iriset sticks her nose high, smirking. Bittor laughs and squeezes her shoulders. It's like he can't stop touching her to make certain she's real.

"All right. What do you need?" Pel asks. "We've got a lot, and even some design tools in the attic."

Just then the precinct alarum rings out, a single warning note.

They all startle. Pel's daughter rushes to the door through the quiet shop. She flings it open as a yell from the street penetrates, but otherwise it's only the alarum.

"Lisan, run to Fiern, tell him to spread word with you that everyone is to cooperate," Pel says. "I'll follow and find Dalal. Tell her to join you...?" She looks at Iriset.

"She should keep her son safe, but we'll be along one of the bulletin threads if she needs to look."

Pel's daughter speeds out and Pel dives through a lattice door into the back room. Iriset and Bittor follow, and Iriset makes a list of anything that can help while Pel pulls down a ladder and hurries up into the attic. Iriset grabs a basket to begin stuffing it all in. The alarum rings harshly, even this deep in the building. Through the rear, there's a window into an alley, and the daylight is nearly gone.

A loud noise from the street has Iriset and Bittor twisting to glance out, but Pel's voice calls down, "I have a bunch of rock salt in big chunks, is that all right?"

"The smaller the better!" Iriset calls back. "Needles would be good, too, and thread. Silk if you have it."

"Iriset." Bittor grasps her arm, turning her to face him. He stands with his back to the door into the wine shop, caught in shadows. She peers through the gloom at the night-vision glint of his strange, lovely cat-eyes. "Once, the Little Cat's daughter asked me what some rebels were rebelling for. I told her you rebel *against* something. But I was wrong. It is *for*—"

Someone shoves open the lattice door into the close quarters and Bittor grunts, jerking forward against Iriset. His eyes catch hers, pupils narrowing to slits, and his hands loosen, slipping down to her elbows where he grips again, and his lashes flutter.

In the sudden blue-silver light, Iriset notices every detail as Bittor's lips tighten back over his teeth and his nostrils flare, as the tiny muscles across his face spasm. Bittor grunts again, weaker. She doesn't understand until his chin drops and her gaze follows it, down to the tip of a force-blade jutting out of his chest. Its metal flickers blue-silver, casting that light up.

A snap of ecstatic force zings toward Iriset, shocking, but then the blade sucks backward and blood splatters down Bittor's robe; his knees bend and he pitches forward.

Iriset doesn't watch him fall.

Standing where Bittor used to be, with a vibrating force-blade in hand, is Lyric.

37

Husband and wife

Sometimes Silence snaps into place, a balance of perfect equality, tense and elegant and powerful in shape, in note, in purity.

The first time Iriset experiences such a moment is there in the back room of a wine shop, with her lifelong friend dead at her feet and her husband staring at her over the body.

Their eyes lock and their hearts beat in unison—while time passes around them, they're still. The entire world threads through the lines of force that dance between them, within them. Iriset's only rational thought is realizing that tide of desperation had not originated in her: It had been Lyric. He'd been coming for her, desperate to find her, and traced the path of his inner design directly to her despite the deterioration of the marriage knot.

Then, *Bittor is dead.*

Bittor

is

She can't look away from her husband.

dead

Lyric stares as if seeing through a void into another world. As the force-blade lowers, his left hand rises to touch the shining lacquer plate armor over his chest, over his heart.

His face cracks open then, and he says with raw ache, "You're alive."

"Lyric," she whispers. This is what she's dreaded. This face, this moment. And Bittor—

"No," Lyric commands, and the hard mask of a Silent priest, of a Vertex Seal making an impossible, brutal choice, resumes itself against the lines of his face, his hard-pressed lips, and turns his beloved freckles into a splatter of ashes. There's paint smeared against them, delicate pink like his mother had—

"The army is here, you aren't safe," he says, reaching for her. He takes her wrist—

Iriset gasps as the opal in her chest shatters. Her breastbone aches with empty resonance, then nothing, then she's choking but Lyric drags her over Bittor's slumped body. She stumbles, her hand a rigid claw where he touches her. Lyric doesn't look back but keeps moving across the shop and outside. She twists as he pulls at her, desperate for a final glimpse of Bittor's sprawl of hair, his—

Lyric does not let go.

Even when they reach the street and Iriset drops wretchedly to her knees to hack and vomit up the pieces of the opal. She's racked with pain but dangles from that wrist bruising by the weight of Lyric's grip.

He says nothing as she spits. As she wipes her mouth with a shaking left hand. Her hair falls around her face, mostly Osahar brown and tangled, thick waves muffling the shriek of the precinct alarum and the pounding of an army approaching.

"Get up," Lyric says, and she does, pulling against him.

Lyric drags her onward.

People cluster in hushed conversation and others rush about closing cafés and barring doors, others flinging doors wide open and lining their families in the yard for faster compliance. Some stand and watch them run past. Lyric's hand is a manacle around Iriset's wrist. She has no idea where he's leading her, she can't quite track their turns or feel the tendrils of force to know; this is her neighborhood, she should recognize a corner by the storefronts alone, or the flavor of the ribbon embedded under the street mud.

But there's nothing. No force-lights glow along the ribbons or at street corners; arched doorways and curving windows shine not at all. The sun has set and Iriset staggers, realizing the Saltbath has been nulled. No—if that were true, bridges would collapse, and besides, there's no collar or null wire large enough. The army's combat-designers must have put down their stakes and cut the precinct off with a counter-design. Not a null, but some design to interrupt the charge in force-lights. Probably a massively coordinated disrupter, which is how individual force-lights, or fans, or many daily designs are turned off, with a small wedge that slides down to slice through the flow tying the design together. There must be several key joints in the neighborhood's energy net that, if disrupted, can shut down the light in the entire Saltbath. Iriset immediately thinks of three places to begin.

She thinks about it because she can't think about Bittor dead—

The blood drying on her chin—

She can't think that Lyric hates her—hates her yet still drags her through the streets to safety—or imprisonment. *No*, she can't go back.

"Where are you—" she tries.

Lyric ignores her, slowing to a brisk walk. She thinks they're going east, but can't reach for the energy of any of the Four Steeples that anchor the city to tell her which she's headed toward. Ecstatic Steeple Shadow is nearest to Saltbath, but she can't—

They turn onto a curving street of squat petal apartments like desert roses, and here folk who've wandered to their balconies or across the fourth-story bridgeways have old-fashioned drip candles and speak in muttering worry to neighbors below. Iriset notices their shadows in flashes as Lyric leads her on and on. Toward the palace, surely, but then he tears right, north maybe, for some reason. Suddenly she hears the clatter of a hundred boots, and sharp commands. Force-flares shoot into the sky and catch in a lighting grid a block over. The army.

Iriset scrambles to stay with Lyric, her hand tingling and cold past where he grips her wrist. Her chest is hot and cold, hot and cold, and hurting with every beat of her heart. Bittor—Bittor, he is—

People are everywhere then, in the streets pushing and crying out, yelling for answers.

She has to keep it together. Somehow.

Around a corner they run into a line of soldiers in their beacon-white uniforms, lacquered armor glinting in the smaller light-grid this branch set over their progress. The army is searching the houses to either side of this narrow street, with a row of lookouts standing alert. Lyric, never a criminal, jerks to a stop and turns away so fast it's obviously suspicious. There's a yell and they're pursued.

Iriset has no idea why Lyric doesn't stand his ground, announce himself. He has Silk! Bittor is dead! Only maybe he doesn't realize it; Lyric never once looked away from her face to the man he'd skewered, crumpled on the floor between them.

Just as she opens her mouth to yell at him, she feels a zing of force-pressure, so fast and subtle she'd never notice it if the air were as alive with force as it should be, if her body weren't so raw.

Iriset rams herself into Lyric's shoulder, knocking them both to the side just as a force-dart flashes past where Lyric's body would have been. He catches himself, meets her huge sandglass eyes with shock, and lets go of her to stand up. Iriset hugs her stomach and pants as Lyric turns to the quartet of soldiers nearly upon them.

In the dark she doesn't see what he does, but his force-blade goes dull just before Lyric charges.

The soldiers aren't expecting it, and that gives him enough advantage to take the first one out with one punch to the solar plexus. The man doubles over and Lyric hits him with the pommel right in the temple and is on the next soldier before the first hits the ground. Lyric jumps, catches the next with his elbow, and jerks the man down, using the momentum to swing his legs around and kick a third with enough power he staggers back.

Iriset's mouth hangs open as she watches the Vertex Seal wipe the street with the four soldiers, using his whole body, a dull force-blade, and concentrated surges of force. All she can think of is Garnet saying *He's modest* about Lyric's fighting skills. He doesn't kill any of them, but in moments they're either collapsed or hunched and moaning.

Lyric comes back for her, breathing hard but nothing more, and takes her wrist again without saying a thing.

An explosion blows several streets away, and Lyric lifts his face to the sky, marks something, and pulls her on. Someone didn't get the warning to cooperate, to watch. They're fighting back. But Pel's daughter might still be running out here, too. And Pel is—will find Dalal. They—

Iriset sucks in a huge breath and tries valiantly to pull her thoughts together. It was stupid instinct to save Lyric from the dart, stupid. It won't make a difference to him. And she should've run when Lyric fought those soldiers! She needs to get away, he'll turn her in, he'll imprison her or just decide to save everyone the trouble and cut her down himself. That might get his reputation back, if he personally cuts away the stain of Silk from his house.

They duck through a line of frozen ribbon skiffs, head down a dark alley and away from the lamps and force-lights that hover over the army.

Lyric stops suddenly at the base of a tower supporting a bridge. She looks up at the sweeping arcs of suspension cables designed to channel water to the massive vines curling around it, lending the architecture strength and force. Its broad leaves are curled for the night, and the whole thing is only a graceful black shape against the sky, blotting out Aharté's bulbous half-moon. The Winged Obsidian Bridge, at the edge of Saltbath. This base tower doesn't only support the bridge but is crowned with a hub high enough to collect errant force-winds, and in addition to the suspension cables, it connects in one direction to a spiraling cone of apartments and, in another, a honeycomb of shops.

The crack of a force-blade snaps at her attention and she looks as Lyric uses it to slice through the design locking the mechanical entrance, before pulling her inside. Iriset grasps in the dark to touch the wall, feeling forces zing, but there's no light except for the mild crackle of Lyric's sword. He shoves the door closed again, but can't lock it.

Slowly, he turns.

The bluish light reflects in Lyric's eyes as he looks at her, then he releases her wrist suddenly with a suck of breath, as if she's poison.

Yelling from outside jolts them back into action. Lyric lurches to the locker beside the door and, with a grunt, shoves it over to collapse with a screech across the broken door. For whatever reason, he's keeping her from the army, and Iriset doesn't want to be trapped in here alone with him, but she can deal. She's had worse!

Iriset almost laughs in gasping hysteria. She's so cold! She wraps her arms around herself, rubbing her hands on her bare arms. She has nothing but the clothes on her body—Lyric's clothes! And her father's echo coin.

No, shock. This is shock. She isn't cold.

Outside, another explosion hits, near enough its concussion wake causes a zing of ecstatic force through the lines underground. The mechanics room fills with tiny flashes of pink lightning. For a second Lyric's face is clear: drawn in harsh, raw lines as if she's not the only one who ripped a mask off today.

She doesn't want to see it.

What the fuck is she going to do? She has no idea where to begin. All her good intentions, dead with Bittor. Even if she gets away from Lyric, survives the night, then what? She's no leader. She didn't even find out where he hid her grandparents.

Red god, Bittor is *dead*.

The pink concussion lightning vanishes again. Their only light now is the force-blade. They should turn it off if they don't want to draw attention. She can't bring herself to say it. Maybe they should get caught. Maybe it would be better to look General Bey in the face and sneer and tell him how right he was all along.

She could kill Lyric.

The thought makes her chest ache, in the hollow spaces where that marriage-killing resonance was. That would break the knot. Consent or death. He can fight her, but she can stop his heart. That would certainly change things. They'd say Silk unraveled the Vertex Seal the way the Holy Syr unraveled the Moon-Eater. She should.

"Iriset," Lyric says, barely any intonation. Just a word. The settling of a question.

She shudders, glancing down at the floor she can barely see. She can't bring herself to look up at him so she looks around. The small room has exposed design nets and crystalline pegs, for easy access to the bridge's architecture. In the center, a small square worktable sits empty, and little storage drawers line its legs. Iriset wonders if she can find a spare stylus somewhere.

"Iriset."

She's wanted him to say her name for so very long.

And he just killed Bittor. With his own hand.

After she killed his mother, with hers.

Yelling swells outside, then passes, as if a mob or fast battle swarms by, and neither speaks until they're alone again. Tension spits and tickles up her arms, and Iriset asks, still not looking, "Why did you bring me here?"

He takes a step closer to her. From the corner of her eye, she can tell he won't stop staring. "I have questions."

"Questions?" It's almost a shriek. Nausea twines up from her stomach, wetting her mouth, and she presses her tongue to her teeth and clenches her jaw, breathing harshly through her nose until it passes.

"I need you to answer them, before I decide what to do."

Iriset goggles at him. He wants to *think about things*. The army is outside raiding houses and shops to find a rebel who is already *dead* and Singix is dead, too, and obviously Iriset took her place and is his wife, what else could he possibly think happened? He fought his own army to get her away, and—

"Amaranth knew," Lyric says, still in that nothing-tone. He sets his force-blade naked onto a high shelf in order that it might continue to cast its spare light.

Iriset doesn't even consider protecting Her Glory. She cuts her eyes up to Lyric's and says meanly, "It was Amaranth's idea."

"That is...easy to believe," he whispers, and puts his hand out toward the wall as if he needs support.

Holy moon, Bittor had cursed softly. Oh holy moon. She still can't believe all that's happened. Last night she had days to stick to her plan, last night her husband made her holy inside his arms. Today she stripped off quads of work and Lyric hunted her down and killed Bittor without even knowing what he did. Making Bittor a casualty. Collateral damage! Where were all Lyric's philosophy and inner turmoil and *questions* before he stabbed Bittor through the chest, hmm?

Anger has a nice rising force, heating Iriset up from her shock.

"We mourned together." Lyric says it so softly, with such gentle sorrow, that Iriset falters. Her anger defuses but she doesn't want it to. She tries to seethe it back while Lyric knocks his forehead against the stucco. "We—Singix, you, you and I mourned her—you!—together. But Singix died that night in her rooms. She's been dead for quads. I married a—"

He stops.

Iriset pushes herself up onto the worktable and perches there, shoulders locked and her hands tight on the edge. If she doesn't sit here and hold on, she'll hit him, or worse. She'll tear at his hair and claw at his freckles and shove a blast of ecstatic energy into him and then he'll never have to angst about the right things to do ever again! She clenches her eyes shut, trying desperately not to think about anything. Survive. Survive. Blood roars in her ears and she counts her breaths in eight beats: in-one-two, hold-three-four, out-five-six, hold-seven-eight; in-one-two, hold-three-four, out-five-six, hold-seven-eight.

Gradually she realizes Lyric is doing it, too. The space between them is enormous, despite how she could cross it in two long strides.

Iriset stutters her breath on purpose.

Lyric looks at her, and she feels it blaze so strongly upon her that she finally looks, too. In the darkness and thin blue light, his eyes are black, and the curve of his cheek a strange, uncomfortable purple. He still hasn't asked any real questions.

Fine.

"Why did you come after me?" she demands.

Incredulous, he says, "You're my wife. I'll always come after you."

It sounds more dire than it would've two days before.

"I thought you were in danger," he adds with a hollow laugh. "I thought you needed me."

She understands what that means and it hurts: He rushed to rescue his sweet Singix and found an old argumentative apostate instead. Iriset brought Lyric directly to Bittor. She didn't think it through. She thought she had, but the resonance pill wasn't fast enough, or strong enough; it couldn't shake the connection from his side. It's her fault Bittor is dead.

"Iriset—"

Like a tension-release valve, Iriset says, "I killed your mother."

"No." Lyric shakes his head once, harshly.

"Diaa was going to kill me," Iriset goes on. "She *did* kill Singix, and when we made her think she killed the wrong person, she tried again. It was always your mother trying to assassinate your wife. Diaa of Moonshadow did not want her grandchildren tainted with non-mirané blood." Iriset allows the bitterness she feels to flood her tone. "So I killed her."

"I killed your father." He says it like it's a reason for something.

And Bittor, she thinks but doesn't say. And Bittor. She can't say his name or she'll scream.

They stare at each other, each unable to break the contact, as if between them this intense balance of horror and revelation is all that keeps them upright. Iriset feels his upset as sure as her own, and she wants to hurt him, and also to hug him. Hold him so tight he suffocates, or she does.

Lyric sighs jaggedly. "Amaranth knew. And so Sidoné must. Who else?"

"Shahd," she says, because that hurts, too. "And Erxan realized."

He sucks in a furious breath and holds his hand in front of his eyes to shield himself from her. "Why?"

"Why did he know?"

"Why did you do it—why did Amaranth do it?"

Iriset makes herself shrug. She won't think of those intense, terrifying hours when Amaranth commanded her to become Singix, after she'd tasted the woman's skin and pleasure, for fuck's sake. The terror and the *thrill* of it. The best and worst thing Iriset has ever done. (Yet.) "She said it was to catch the murderer and maintain her reputation because she brought Singix here. She did not want to let the world see that an assassin could murder the wife of the Vertex Seal in his own house. I think she wanted your wife to be someone she could control."

"And the price was to allow an apostate to run rampant!

Holding court in the heart of Silence! You—you are a human architect, and you defeated every defense in the palace. We didn't even suspect." Lyric makes a frustrated sound, a growl and a whimper. "How could Amaranth not see how much worse this is?"

"She made a choice and it was done," Iriset says. "She is not so narrow-minded about the tools she uses for *her* brutality."

Lyric's lips part, and Iriset thinks he might curse, but instead he remains quiet. His mouth droops, not into a frown but into a soft sorrow that breaks Iriset's thin control. Exactly that quiet devastation she expected. She turns away, too, sinking off the worktable to kneel on the floor. Her fingers tighten on the table's edge, keeping her from melting entirely.

In the dark egg of the mechanics room, their hard breaths slowly align again. There's nothing either can do about it.

When Iriset is able, she pushes again to her feet. "Go put a stop to this destruction," she says, her back to him. "Bittor is dead already. The wholesale ruin of the Saltbath will not do more good than that."

"Dead? What happened?"

"He was killed by the Vertex Seal himself, with a force-blade to the chest—quite the victory, don't you think?" When she hears no immediate reaction, she adds with exceeding bitterness, "Anyone who says Lyric méra Esmail His Glory lets others dirty their hands for him will have to shut up for a while."

"You were with him. You left the palace and went right to him," Lyric says slowly. "Because you know him...Sweet Silence, you begged mercy for him. I didn't know. I didn't know anything, did I?"

There's not much she can say to that. Quiet falls again, and Iriset stares at the wall while she tries not to care about Lyric's feelings. She always knew this would be terrible, even if she did it on purpose. Out of habit, and also to make herself feel better, a little, she allows herself to wonder what Singix would do. Apologize, explain herself, take care of him. Because she loves him.

The best Iriset can do is to say, "Garnet is probably desperate to find you."

Lyric grunts agreement.

Deciding not to beg him to spare her, knowing full well how Lyric considers mercy, she simply ignores the possibility that he's planning how to best incapacitate her and drag her back to the palace to stand for her apostasy. She puts on a strong expression, glad she has her back to him. "You should go. Your wife doesn't need to be rescued. Bittor is dead and the Silk rebellion won't last without him. I certainly am not capable or interested in leading revolution no matter how much you all deserve it. I think I've done enough damage already." She adds the last with appropriate relish. She knows the stories of today will ripple in every direction. Everyone in the empire will hear about Silk alive in the home of the Vertex Seal. No matter what they say or do, it cannot be erased. It will be a rallying cry. A loose knot. Iriset can tug on it later, at her leisure.

He doesn't speak.

Iriset makes her way carefully through the darkness to the narrow ladder that leads up into the bridge's inner workings. She grips the bars and climbs, blindly, past two hubs and into a curving petal where there's a knot of rising and flow for whatever reason—Iriset knows next to nothing about bridge stabilization. But she presses her palms to the wall and finds a hatch.

It pops open with a tug of ecstatic, and she climbs out onto the petal's curl. This isn't meant as a balcony, but it suits her as a place to sit and attempt not to shake apart.

From her perch upon that small petal (positioned both to collect errant threads of flow in the air and to encourage said flow in the necessary direction for the tower's integrity), Iriset can see across the dark, sparking Saltbath.

Fires flicker, and alert-sparks burst in the sky, drifting on thin wings for a while before sputtering out and disintegrating as they crash. In several spots the army's light arrays still glow, shifting slowly as the soldiers move. The wavering quality of the firelight and the explosive ecstatic charges put the night into a dream-space. Or nightmare-space, rather. Darkness, bursts of strange lights, yelling, and the occasional arc of force-weaponry jutting up from an alley. There's a bonfire in a square four streets away, and tall plants crowning some lofted apartments burn. Thin towers are nothing more than shadows, and the winding streets shimmer, shadows on shadows punctuated by the occasional streak of fire.

Iriset has no idea what she should do next. She's so tired.

But flee, she supposes. Collect her stash and her grandparents and leave Moonshadow, go north toward the Cloud Kings. At least for now. Hunker down, collect herself. She needs space to remember who she is, especially after she's been someone else for so long.

There are stars in the sky, scattered silver, except directly above where the gibbous moon blots them out, its dark side a ghostly black-gray shadow she can hardly see. She curls her hands around each other and presses them between her breasts. The wind blows, smelling of smoke and force-echo, ringing with alarum and tears.

Later, Iriset is numb, hungry, and too tired to even close her eyes. It's still dark, still nighttime, but the noises have died down, the force-bursts becoming more rare. She suspects maybe an hour remains before the morning will slick light across the sky.

And that's when Lyric climbs out of the hatch to join her.

She holds herself motionless, not looking.

He settles beside her on the small petal balcony, unarmed, and without the layer of lacquered armor. The pale linen of his shirt nearly glows in the cool darkness. He sits with his knees drawn up, leaning back. There's very little space for them both, but they're careful not to touch.

"It was always you," he says quietly.

"Always me," she whispers like an echo. "But I did change. I took her potential and made it a part of mine, and so I became something new. Someone new."

"But who." It's not quite a question.

"There were so many times I wanted to argue with you."

"But...she...would not have."

"Eventually, in a few years, maybe. I..." Iriset doesn't finish.

Lyric takes a deep breath and lets it hiss out slowly. He leans away, looking up at the stars. She can see his profile in her peripheral vision. *Oh holy moon* she wants to touch those freckles; she knows where they are exactly, even in this spare nighttime.

Iriset keeps her eyes on the cityscape before her, on the hazy layers of shadows.

He says, "I fell in love with you the night in the garden."

Her lips part in barely a gasp.

"Then you died," Lyric continues. "I was...aghast at how I felt. Ruined, shocked, changed by things I had no right to feel for Iriset mé Isidor, especially when I was mourning hand in hand with my wife. I wasn't supposed to feel changed by one night in a garden."

She wants to beg him to stop. She doesn't even want to breathe. *Have mercy on me, Lyric méra Esmail.*

"And slowly, or not so slowly, I suppose," he murmurs, "I fell in love with you again. Do you think it means bodies don't matter? That we fall in love with spirit and inner design?"

The pause lasts just long enough Iriset realizes he expects an answer. Ever the priest, questioning the world. She breaks up her pain by analyzing the architecture around her; he turns to philosophy. Iriset's chest hurts. She's quiet.

He continues, "I thought, and was relieved actually, that perhaps I hadn't known what being in love was, I'd only felt a strong connection to Iriset, but it wasn't love. This was love, this new relationship. It had always been my wife changing me, our inner designs forging a new bond together." Lyric laughs then, small and sad. "I was such a fool."

"You're not a fool," Iriset whispers, her voice feeling like tiny claws in her throat. She clutches at her own legs, digging fingers into her trousers. His trousers.

"It was always you," he concludes.

She almost—almost—looks at him. "That night in the garden I knew you were no fool. I wanted to kiss you even when your mouth was shaping my father's death."

"Imagine if you had."

"Maybe everything would be worse."

They breathe in unison together, thinking and staring out at the city.

Lyric says, "That night, I decided to be ambitious."

"I know. I saw it on your..." She stops.

But he remembers. "There is a new cast to every conversation."

Iriset winces.

"You have to go back with me," he says firmly.

"I don't think so. I won't go to prison, or to my execution. And you can't explain my presence, Singix's absence, without admitting the graffiti was right. Silk was in your bed all along, and now she's resurrected. If that's really what you want, then—"

"We have to be divorced."

It hurts.

And he says it like a plain fact. "The ritual requires a few hours, and both of us," he continues. "And so you must go back with me."

"Or you could push me off this balcony," Iriset says viciously.

"Don't think I haven't considered it," he answers in the same.

They both catch their breath then, and go quiet.

A sliver of hope crystallizes through her heart, like a hardening vein, that Lyric doesn't want to kill her. He might wish any number of things upon her, hate her, cast her out, but he doesn't want her dead.

Maybe such knowledge will be enough, and she can survive this.

She says, "I will find a way to unbind us. I am the greatest human architect in a hundred years."

"That is not something I would brag about right now, were I you."

"I have done surgery upon myself before, changed and unchanged my body—both inside and, as you have witnessed, my face and skin and hair. Can you even imagine that I cannot invent a way to unwind the threads of our inner designs on my own?" Iriset strives to push arrogance into her voice, whatever it takes to convince him and turn him away.

"I will not give you permission to perform apostasy," he answers with matching scorn.

"I don't need your permission! One day you will simply feel it, know it's done."

Lyric turns to her. "One day! No. I need this finished now. No lingering effects, nothing to cling to."

"Don't worry, Your Glory, soon you'll be free of me."

"Free of you?" He laughs an empty laugh. "Impossible."

Iriset wants to skim her fingers against the skin on the back of his hand. Just a brief touch, anything: Iriset touching her husband while they both know her name.

"Go back to the palace with me," he says quietly. "Go with me, submit to the unbinding ritual, swear you will not perform apostasy, and I... will let you go. So long as it is out of Moonshadow City, never to be seen again, I will let you go."

Pulling her hand back into her own lap, Iriset murmurs, "You cannot think I will give up my work. Not after knowing me as you do."

"Not even if I beg you?" he whispers.

Iriset hisses air in through her teeth, utterly surprised.

Lyric presses his advantage. "It is wrong, can't you see? Unbalanced. The science of it pushes humans past our limits, into the territory of gods. You can't control yourself if you go down that path."

"I certainly can—I control myself better the more I learn of design, Lyric, even human design."

"Look what you were willing to do! The arrogance of apostasy doesn't allow you to stop or mediate between pride and necessity."

"If more of us practiced, we could mitigate one another—just as with any architecture or technology. And it does so much good in the world." Iriset knocks her skull back against the tower.

"You stole a woman's life, and you lied, you killed and manipulated and—and when I think about what else you might've done with the access you had, it takes my breath away. I know you are not evil, Iriset, or you could have done immeasurable harm while you were—while I was—" He shakes his head. "Human architecture is not worth what it makes you."

Iriset sighs. "You'll never convince me of that. I've seen what it can do, how it can save."

"But the consequences! This city was brought to its knees when apostasy held sway, thousands died, and people still die of apostatical cancers today because of what those apostates did hundreds of years ago. Didn't... didn't your own mother die of it?"

"I saved her," Iriset whispers breathlessly. She's never, not once, spoken it aloud before.

"What?"

She leans closer to him, glaring into his mirané eyes. "You will never convince me that human architecture is wrong or not worth it, because yes, *yes*, my mother was dying of apostatical cancer, but *I saved her.*"

His lips part; he doesn't look away.

"I was only ten years old, but I saved her." Now, hours after this nightmare began, tears finally arrive to soothe Iriset's eyes. "Nothing you argue will change my mind, because my mother would have died, but because of human architecture, instead she is alive."

In the taut silence that follows, Iriset hears her pulse

thrumming, a rhythm in her skull again, and recognizes it this time: It's Lyric's heartbeat joining hers, through the weave of their inner designs.

"She had to leave," Iriset says, shaking a little with the urgency of explanation. "Because of your laws. I saved her, and lost her anyway, or she and I and who knows how many others I barely touched would've been taken and unraveled without a thought of *mercy*. But my mother is out there in the world, alive, and that is better than the alternative. My world is *better* because of apostasy. And I will never forswear it; otherwise it would be like forswearing her."

"Iriset," Lyric whispers, and something in his expression shifts, from anger to—to wonder, perhaps. Or it might be fear. They're so close, wonder and terror.

Behind him a line of silver light fattens on the horizon, displaying the sharp edge of the crater. The dawn puts an aura of holiness around him, glinting against his black curls, and Iriset thinks she'll remember him exactly so for the rest of her life.

She says, "Maybe Aharté is wrong. Maybe she doesn't even exist."

Then the Vertex Seal takes her hands, gently tugging her around to face him. Their crossed legs touch at the knees and he begins the balancing meditation they'd mastered together. Ecstatic, flow, falling, rising, curling through them via the circle of their hands, arms, and hearts. The light strengthens and so she can see his freckles, the pinch of weariness at the corners of his upturned eyes, and the glint of bright red among all the mirané-brown flecks in his irises. Like an array of rose petals in the Garden for Four Winds where first they met.

Lyric lets go her right hand and touches her cheek, then her mouth, his gaze tracing the path of his fingers. Iriset can't help comparing her own face to the perfect, symmetrical beauty of Singix Es Sun. Her jaw tightens and she looks down, but Lyric puts two fingers under her chin and lifts it again. "I am married to an unapologetic apostate."

"And I to an ardent priest," she says, trying to find any shred of humor.

"Mercy," he whispers, and it sounds like a curse.

38

Sunderer

Iriset goes back to the palace. Just not with Lyric.

It's the shock, maybe. Or one more knot in a string of bad decision-making. But there's something she simply must do.

Here is what happens.

———— • ♦ • ————

Lyric leaves her as the sun rises, and she remains alone with her face turned toward the east. Smoke fills the morning air, gusting at her where she perches like a ruffled griffon. The wail of emergency alarms lifts to mingle with the songs of late-summer larks and shrill skull sirens.

Iriset is hungry, but has no food. She's exhausted and sad. So she climbs down the tower and scours the mechanics room, finding a small hemp bag, a broken stylus that will suit for now, a nearly gone spool of design thread, and a handful of random crystals and salt rocks. She uses the thread to redesign a scrap of linen into paper currency like is used in the outer regions.

Before leaving, she uses a small stick of charcoal to rub ash onto her fingers and paint it across her cheekbones in crosshatches to confuse the eye regarding her facial structure. Just in case anyone looks too closely and wonders why she resembles the Silk graffiti. Then she makes her way through the only-somewhat-trashed Saltbath toward Morning Market. It's easy, because the city army has been abruptly recalled, and in addition to residents, emergency teams and units sent from the design schools and a wave of Silent priests are arriving to tend to fires and broken bones and spiritual ailments. (And to cover up or unravel bright new spider graffiti both designed and plainly painted across the streets and towers. The people won't stop murmuring hopefully about Silk until all the spiders are gone.)

The moment she's in the Morning Market, she buys a spiced pork pie and devours it too quickly. It takes several hours to make her way across the city to the Violet Break, one of the crevasses in the crater's edge that catacombs had been built into. (It glows at sunset because of some veins of amethyst.) The Little Cat had a stash there that Iriset can access. Jewels, traveling supplies, false papers, a few weapons she hardly knows how to use, and some crude craftmasks. Clothing.

Though it's midday by the time Iriset arrives, there always are visitors to the catacombs. She knows where she's going, as most mourners do, and the weariness and sorrow are easy to read on her ash-masked face. Shade cools the catacombs, and water drips deep within, resounding prettily in the narrow caverns. The few people with her murmur and hold hands, place palms to the force-diamonds etched into the walls to mark memorials. There are rough-cut caverns covered in rows of tiny cubbies for echo coins, and it's at the end of such a cavern where Iriset opens a secret door very like the one beneath the shelf in the Crimson Canyon. A force-shield surrounds her, blurring light and shadows so that she'll be invisible if nobody stares directly.

The cache is in her hand when she stops.

With it she can walk out the crater gates and go anywhere. Any of the towns or territories of the empire, or beyond to Ceres where at least she can speak the language. Or to the Cloud Kings where probably her mother went twelve years ago.

Leave Moonshadow City behind forever.

But.

There's a memory of someone who helped her, for no reason, and she wants to know why. (The miran don't say that curiosity kills cats and their kittens, but they definitely should.)

So Iriset goes back to the palace.

Presumably by now it's easy to believe she can sneak in with only a broken stylus, wearing the burnt orange of most palace attendants, and using the plumbing design to her advantage.

Not to mention the security nets are in total disarray as palace architects feverishly attempt to untangle the remnants of the massive spider design. It's gone, at least, her vivid graffiti. No more big, beautiful mother spider hunched over the Silent Chapel, no more tiny little spark spiders crawling up and down the glimmering web. Iriset wishes she could have seen it.

But places where palace architects attempted to dismantle it before it finished its course show craters in the walls, scorch marks on the hall of miran itself. A mess of broken tiles here, a smear of mud dried across a sidewalk there prove the chaos Iriset made, the panic and fear and awe her graffiti array caused. It can't soon be forgotten.

She carries her stash in a simple bag slung over one shoulder, such as any non-mirané attendant might have. The cloth mask she wears over newly knotted hair pulls across her face, casting the complex in a comforting pale orange.

It surprises her to see red, pink, and black moons of forcelight hanging in the corridors and courtyards, and dotting the edges of the layered, spiral petals of the palace. Those colors together mean someone important died, and everyone will mourn. Tragic death is the only time three colors alone are used, an odd number that can never be balanced. Sudden, violent loss is unbalanced, the miran believe. Iriset is impressed how quickly they got the moons up. Her opinion of the palace architects minus Raia is not high.

She assumes the mourning moons are for Diaa, though she does not pause to listen to kitchen gossip or the murmurings of gathered miran. Everyone is subdued. Diaa of Moonshadow had been more well-liked by every level of the palace than Iriset thought. Little did they know, she thinks, glad her stolen cloth mask hides her expression. She keeps her head and eyes down, and can't imagine the Vertex Seal has announced anything about Singix yet. He should have returned to consult with Amaranth how best to do so. He might be furious with his sister, but he's not stupid.

Fortunately, there's no meeting of the princes' council and she slips into the mirané hall and strides across its vast chamber without note, heading for the hidden arch opposite the one that leads to the office of the Vertex Seal.

(She glances toward it, not truly considering going to him, but wishing she could let herself consider it.)

The other hidden arch leads through a narrow, dim corridor, and then to a staircase cut in a tight spiral down into the bedrock.

Several design nets span the way, which she bends around herself easily, and at the bottom is a null door. Iriset skims her palm along the outer frame until she finds the design panel, then uses her broken stylus quickly to dismantle the lock. It should set off an alarum in the office of the Architect of the Seal, but she engages a delay to slow the notification, to earn herself a few minutes.

The door slides open, the light behind her piercing into darkness, revealing the numen.

Iriset jams her stylus into the arched doorframe, ruining the null. She's able to pull out a few threads and knot them into a dim light. Then she steps inside.

A smell like after a severe lightning storm pervades, dank and dangerously electric. But everything is clean, pristinely so, and Iriset wonders if numena shed skin or hair or relieve themselves at all.

It crouches in the center, on its haunches, long pinkish-white arms hanging to either side with the knuckles turned under. Lank hair drags around its face and neck, falling like an old stained-and-tattered silk veil. When it sees her, the numen grins, showing jagged black teeth like a shark.

Iriset kneels beside it. She nudges its chin up with her closed fist, and like before, the drained pink skin shimmers silvery where there's contact. It does not resist, its vivid black diamond-shard eyes locked onto hers. It seems curious, not hostile.

Quickly she unknots the lock with her stylus. The numen gasps hard as the collar falls away, and shoves at it with one foot, then raises its hands to Iriset: Both are chained with null wires. It really would have been easier to use the hematite.

"Thank you for keeping my secret," Iriset says, eyes down, as she works on the shackles. So near to the creature, she smells the lightning scent coming from it. The wires take another long moment to untwist and break, and Iriset swings her bag off her shoulder to tuck them inside it, just in case.

Then, as the numen rubs its raw wrists, she backs away to the door.

It stands slowly, head bowed, as if drawn up by the shoulders. Those shoulders heave as it takes a long breath, seeming to grow taller, and as Iriset stares, she feels forces sliding toward it like it draws them in as it draws in air. Her skin tingles and her inner design pops.

Color flushes its skin; silver, peach, and black lines appear where arteries and veins bulge in its flesh. Its hair thickens, lifting into long waves of silver-white, and the numen smiles as it tears threadbare trousers off itself, and the ragged vest, until it's naked, with a human-looking penis. Muscles cord along the starving, bony lines of its hips and ribs, thighs and chest. It lifts its face finally and its eyes are as sharp a black as ever, but the whites have cleared of tawny yellow-pink illness. When it smiles, Iriset watches with an uncomfortable fascination as its black teeth become a perfect white-ivory and blunted into human teeth except for two on either side that retain too much of a point.

By the time its teeth finish re-forming, it's wearing slim black trousers and boots, as well as a black robe with red stitching. Iriset understands instinctively that the numen crafted the costume out of pure force, just as it changed its body at will.

She can hardly breathe.

The stories are true: Numen are pure design. They're not flesh, but force. Except, something formed of more than energy has been trapped within the null wire. Iriset opens her mouth to ask—she can't resist asking—but the numen is before her suddenly, and grabs her wrists in cold, long-fingered hands.

It says a word, the same word it said the first night they met in the mirané hall. Now the word does not slither between too-large, too-sharp teeth, but is whole and firm, and obviously Old Sarenpet. She almost recognizes it.

"I don't understand," Iriset says, straining slightly against its grip, though not with her full strength. She doesn't want to be free, she only *wants* to want to be free.

"Sunderer," it says in mirané.

"I freed you, yes. I—I sundered your bindings."

The numen smiles and strokes a finger against the inner skin of both her wrists.

In that moment, Iriset experiences a thing there are not quite words for any longer. And the word they used to have (rivation) would have been meaningless to Iriset or anyone. A feeling, a sensation, of coming apart while remaining intact. It is an exact process the numen instigates within her. An ancient process. Seeming apostatical, but in truth so far from that as to be its opposite. Sacred.

The numen peels the threads of force within Iriset open to even smaller elements and, in that action, creates new energy.

(When it happens to you, it feels like love.

Warmth, urgency, longing, belonging. Love.

It feels like congress with the Moon-Eater.)

Sweat beads on Iriset's skin, released from the inner heat of creation. She's herself, she knows herself, but a tangible flavor hovers in her awareness, gathering in her pulse, and she almost grasps what the numen has done. "What?" she asks.

"You are a sunderer," it says. "You can make force."

"Make force? No, forces *exist*, they can be bound, knotted, woven, given direction, or paused, but not created or destroyed—only Aharté creates force."

The numen snorts. "Aharté."

Well, Iriset does agree with that sentiment.

"We have to go, numen, before we are discovered. You're free." Now Iriset tugs. She wants to keep arguing, but here and now is not the place nor time. "Let's go."

It tilts its head. "Yes, but first I must complete my mission."

"You can't kill the Moon-Eater's Mistress!" Iriset says. "The one you came for is long gone."

"I do not wish to kill anyone."

The numen has no accent whatsoever, she realizes. It speaks exactly like she does. "Why did you try before? That is why you were imprisoned for a hundred years."

"Miscommunication." It shrugs as casually as a child hiding stolen candy.

She stares, disbelieving. Maybe it's trying to be funny.

"Come on." Iriset tugs again, and it releases one of her hands, keeping a tight grip on the other. Fine. Iriset moves out of the room with the numen on her heels. "I can get us out of the palace, through the plumbing design, then we can talk, then we can—we can do whatever we want."

"My mission." It moves up the stairs effortlessly, as if it weighs nothing, has not been bound and weakened for a hundred years. At the first security net, the numen pushes around her, and before Iriset can use her stylus to bend the net, it plucks at the threads with its bare hand until they shiver out of the way.

Iriset pauses. It can use its hands as she used her silk glove, to directly affect the forces. Oh holy moon, she has a thousand questions. But one first: "What is your mission?"

"To free the Moon-Eater from *his* prison."

The ramifications of that simple phrase rock Iriset back on her feet.

The numen steps into her space, bending over her so all she sees or senses is it. It says, "I need a sunderer, or else I need four equally strong architects, each dominant in one of the four forces. You are a sunderer, you can do it with me and no others. It will take hardly any time at all, and then we will flee, anywhere you like. I can take you, I can make you safe and teach you anything there is to know."

Parting her lips to taste the forces that float off it with every blink and every shift of its mouth, Iriset murmurs, "We'll never make it. I was lucky to get here to you without being recognized or caught."

The numen's sudden grin dissolves between one breath and the next, and Iriset stands in the narrow spiral stairs with hulking Garnet méra Bež.

She squeaks and leans back, but Garnet catches her elbows, laughing softly at her. That's no laugh Garnet has ever made, full of wry amusement and a little wicked.

"Oh holy moon," she says again, like she's saying *I have seen the face of god.*

And it is certainly not Garnet smiling lopsided, with a lot of teeth. But the illusion is physically perfect. (Iriset knows why: It's not, in fact, an illusion. The numen has become Garnet. Even to his voice.)

"Coming?" it says, one heavy brow lifting to tease.

"Wait. I want to see the prison, but I'm not promising to help you free the Moon-Eater."

It smiles again, rather predatory. "You will, when you see."

Though she's uncertain about, well, *everything* in that moment, Iriset goes. (She will always go, can never resist such a temptation. How else did all this happen?)

With Garnet as her escort, nobody stops them, though they pass many, including a harried Raia mér Omorose.

Iriset pulls her cloth mask over her face and keeps her eyes down, bubbling with nervous laughter—amazed laughter. Whatever else happens, she's crossing the palace of the Vertex Seal with a shape-shifter, a legendary numen, and in the Moon-Eater's Temple she'll shortly understand something nobody else in the world understands.

As they cross the quartz yards, Iriset concentrates on not tripping on any of the tangled security threads. But the numen looks up at the silver-pink moon, and it waves. Iriset hisses at it to be more circumspect, and it continues stomping heavily, which is not exactly the way Garnet walks. They make directly for the Moon-Eater's Temple.

The Silent priest standing guard doesn't shift at all beneath his full black veil when Garnet and an anonymous palace servant enter. Inside the alcove the candelabras are lit, and the latticed door leading into the sanctuary gapes open. The numen doesn't even ping the security nets.

Beyond, several miran kneel before the granite altar, holding hands as they murmur a brief song of balance.

It's cool inside. The dark blue honeycomb arches lift so high in the starry dome, glinting along their angles with soft forcelight. Amaranth's privacy screen has been folded away.

"Finish your prayer and leave us," Garnet—the numen—says. Its voice cuts through the peaceful silence. (Garnet's voice, perfect.)

One miran flinches, but the rest remain bowed and murmuring their song.

Iriset touches the numen's back, urging patience, for even though Garnet is the Vertex Seal's first attendant and body-twin, he doesn't have usual business here. It sighs quietly and seems to settle into the large body, even relaxing slightly against her hand. She taps a force-rhythm gently with her forefinger, lingering in flow to encourage this patience, and the numen tilts its head to shoot her a wry look more familiar than Garnet usually would be with her.

She wonders if this is how Ambassador Erxan felt when he saw through the Singix mask—unsettled and unbelieving, even knowing the truth.

When the miran finish their song, they bow to the altar and one another, slipping out. One nods a greeting and says Garnet's name. Another, an older woman, asks, "Does the Vertex Seal wish to honor his wife and mother with the Moon-Eater? I expected him to haunt the Silent Chapel."

"His wife?" Iriset says thoughtlessly.

The mirané woman flicks her a dismissive glance. "He would not mourn her according to Ceres traditions, naturally."

Iriset drops her head and quickly flattens her hand over both eyes, under her veil. She leans into the numen as the world tilts beneath her, out of balance.

Lyric returned to the palace and killed her. Did he say Silk did it? Is that how he will control what he can of the narrative?

"Naturally," the numen says in Garnet's voice. "There will be balance in mourning, as in all things."

The miran agrees, or must; Iriset doesn't exactly see what they do except that they file past and out of the sanctuary.

When they're alone, Iriset finds herself breathing her eight-count rhythm as she approaches the altar. To lock down her grief. To move past it, to—to just focus on what is before her. The altar.

Even knowing the teeth never belonged to a god but some ancient dead monster, she remains reluctant to disturb them. The numen, however, sweeps the teeth off the altar in one strong gesture: They crash down with a cracking clatter, chipping on the tiled floor. Iriset presses her lips together, fighting the urge to chide it.

"Look," the numen says.

"At what?"

"The lines of force creating this prison."

"I can't see force with my bare eyes."

Its responding frown suits Garnet's features better than the numen's previous smiles. "Do you have your stylus?"

Removing it from the front of her robe jacket, she holds it up.

"Help me draw a basic design diamond—say, sixteen paces from point to point."

"We have nothing to mark the forces with."

The numen picks up a fossil molar. It holds it in one hand, and Iriset feels again the drawing forces for a brief moment before the molar simply crystallizes. Then it shatters into four nearly equal chunks. Each falls to the floor, and the numen smiles.

Iriset decides not to analyze how that transformation occurred right now and gathers them in the left skirt of her robe. Together, she and the numen begin their work.

39

Always binding

Maybe it is Holy Design that keeps pushing Raia mér Omorose toward the threads that Iriset personally interferes with, or perhaps an is simply like her—not quite a natural sunderer, but with the instincts to learn. And so an is drawn toward the same kinds of design problems as Iriset.

The point is, Raia notices the blip of force as the security nets guarding the spiral stairs to the numen's prison bend strangely. It's practically a miracle for an to notice, given the state of the nets and how many of them are currently bent in ways they ought not be. An has a design cube set up in ans office that alerts an to any strange knots or disruptions in the palace's complicated layers of design. The cube merely senses the blips, and then Raia must open ans floor to reveal the palace complex design map, engage with it, and hunt through four hundred years of architectural signatures, redesigns, new petals, and domes, plus the constantly rotating security threads to locate the blip. Often it comes from the office of the Architect of the Seal, and sometimes an attendant merely has broken their thread cuff. But every once in a while there's no immediate explanation.

This time, an already has the floor open, as an has spent the past thirteen hours mapping out the worst of the mess Silk created and sending memos to various teams of architects for where they should direct their efforts and how this fix is causing a cascading effect of its own to re-tangle what's already been straightened.

Raia is studying the section near the Silent Chapel when an has a feeling and glances toward the mirané hall. The blip near the numen's prison is new and Raia is on ans feet immediately.

With a security alert in hand, an hurries to the mirané hall, ready to slap the alert against the palace wall where it will set off immediate alarm. An doesn't wish to upset anyone prematurely, and so an will check on the nets anself first. It could be one of those cascading effects, after all.

As an nudges at one of the doors in the entrance arch, it opens swiftly and Garnet méra Bež emerges, followed by an attendant in palace orange, with her veil pulled across her eyes. Raia considers asking Garnet to wait, but the man looks on serious business, so an merely touches ans eyelids and lets the body-twin pass.

Then an slips inside and dashes across the wide-open hall, aware of ans footsteps echoing again and again off the high layered domes.

When an arrives at the hidden arch, Raia activates the panel at the top of the staircase and checks the security nets. They each appear intact, without tampering. An frowns and pushes ans palace key into place, then taps ans personal identification pattern into the threads, unlocking the nets. Nothing appears out of place, but something caused ans design cube to ping, so an had better check on the numen.

Like Iriset, Raia is uncomfortable with the imprisonment of the numen, and like Iriset, an wishes to have a real conversation with the creature, not only about itself but about what it has seen in its long life. Raia brought this up with Menna, the Architect of the Seal, making an official request, and Menna patronizingly explained that Raia has a few years of promotions ahead of an before such would be allowed.

Raia thinks, as an descends the spiral stairs, that perhaps now is ans opportunity to ask a single question or two.

But the numen's prison door is open, and the numen gone.

For a moment, Raia stands still, staring, trying to comprehend. An thought someone had broken in, but not dreamed someone would be stupid enough to free the creature.

It has to have been another numen—who else could have slipped past all the security netting without leaving a signature or even a scrap of design behind? Nobody Raia has heard of. Unless it's true that Silk is alive. (An hopes that Silk is alive.)

Instead of slapping the security alert to the wall, an runs back up the spiral stairs and directly across to the opposite hidden arch that leads out of the mirané hall and to the private corridor behind the office of the Vertex Seal. Raia dashes out, sliding to a stop at the back entrance just as Garnet méra Bež appears, speaking to the Vertex Seal.

Raia's mind streaks white in panic and an forgets what an had been about to say.

"Raia mér Omorose," Garnet intones, grasping the hilt of his force-blade. "What?"

"Ah, Your Glory, ah…" Raia swallows, makes an abortive gesture to bow and touch ans eyelids to the Vertex Seal, and instead just blurts, "I just saw Garnet—you!—leaving the mirané hall by the front entrance with an attendant. But you are here and… the numen is gone."

Lyric says, "Amaranth," like a prayer, and turns, running.

The Moon-Eater's Mistress is, at that moment, standing in the center of the Bright Star Obelisk Garden under the setting sun, staring at the needle obelisk that Safiyah the Bloody erected for her murdered brother. It's brilliant white granite with veins of black and chips of crystal that glint against the sky. At the base, a moat lined in burnt-red tiles trickles with water, and straight channels lead away in the four directions. As if blood surrounds it and streaks away every day and every night. Black succulents called Sorrow's Ecstasy dot the sand between the channels, each section colored after a different force. Blue, white, green, black. Amaranth stands in the black section, the hot particles of sand sliding into her sandals.

Her handmaidens are quiet around her, and Sidoné waits with her force-blade out, though only because Amaranth yelled in pure fury an hour ago, and Sidoné has yet to sheathe her weapon.

Amaranth has been calm for a while, but it's a cold calm, and she's unsure if she should try to soothe Sidoné because she senses a storm gathering inside her that soon will shatter this numbness.

She'd been so wrong.

Her (traitorous!) mother dead, and Iriset gone.

Lyric came to her this morning, in dirty robes and a terrible hardness to his face. Already she grieved for Diaa and for Iriset running away instead of coming to her. But Amaranth assumed Iriset had to be alive, for that girl was a slippery survivor. She'd prepared a flustered story for everyone, about Singix having fled in panic, thinking she could trust nobody after Diaa showed her betrayal. The giant spider hadn't helped, terrifying as it had been, of course, poor princess.

Then her brother strode into her chamber, where she reclined in distressed thought. Her handmaidens scattered at the expression on the Vertex Seal's face. He walked close and dragged Amaranth to her feet with unexpected fury. "I spoke with Iriset," he said, and within the words were layers of hurt and anger so pure, Amaranth understood he would never forgive her.

Their confrontation did not last long, because Lyric needed to take charge of the palace complex, of the entire city, and he commanded her to keep her mouth shut until he was finished cleaning up her apostatical mess.

She obeyed, keeping her mouth shut, and came to this garden to show the palace how loudly she can weep for her mother.

But all she could summon was fury. Mostly at herself, and Iriset. And her damned *mother*.

Numb and cold, she studies the needle obelisk meditatively. It is, after all, a monument to a brother's love. She's draped in pink, red, and black silk, as is everyone in royal mourning. Her hair tumbles free down her back, heavier somehow than when crusted and wound with jewels and silver wire. She pressed black handprints over her eyes, fingers splayed up like massive lashes, or horns, or the legs of a spider.

(Amaranth did see Iriset's spider, and she didn't go inside or avoid stepping on the tiny sparks. She'd followed it to the Silent Chapel and knelt under it, and when her handmaidens stopped begging her to get to safety, one brought her a blanket and pillows. Amaranth lay back and stared at the underbelly of the thing, at the shimmering, rainbow threads of forces. It seemed to be made of starlight, and the same pink-silver as the moon. Her Glory cried silently and could hardly believe the genius who designed the brilliant thing had been hers, but she'd lost her.)

Now Amaranth's meditation focuses on the things people do in response to loss. A day ago she'd have sworn she knows Lyric well enough to predict, but his noontime official declaration that Singix Es Sun was killed by the apostate Silk had shocked her—though it's a bold move, it steals the possibility of nuance from them as they continue their political relations with Ceres, and ruins a few of the threads of plans she's already set into motion. They should be planning together, all four of them. Garnet won't look Sidoné in the eye, either.

Amaranth feels bizarre, unsettled, and can't figure out why. In the empty moments between her furies, she expected grief, numbness, but not to be disconcerted. Not to be dizzy.

There are not many things Amaranth doesn't know about herself. She's intimately familiar with her body and its desires, her ambitions in particular. What she's never realized is how attuned she is to the Moon-Eater. Of course if you ask her, she'll insist her inner design is practically bound in marriage to his, but in truth she thinks her moment alone with him at his altar is the most they share, and when she leaves his temple she's only herself. She's always rather wished it were more. A romance, perhaps. Evocative and pure.

So Amaranth can't identify the strange feeling gathering in her belly as she stares at the needle obelisk. It's probably just stress unraveling in a sick little spiral right where her center of force rests, high in the bowl of her hips.

But when a commotion at the eastern garden gate draws her attention and her brother bursts into her presence for the second time that day, scattering Seal guards around him, and with Garnet alert at his heels, Amaranth suddenly knows something is wrong in the Moon-Eater's Temple.

"Thank Aharté," Lyric says, coming to her and taking her elbows. "You're all right."

Sidoné says, "What happened?"

Garnet answers, "The numen is free, and we feared—"

"Because it tried to kill the Moon-Eater's Mistress when

it was captured before," Lyric says, softer, panting now as his adrenaline pops and cools.

But Amaranth's eyes widen. "It's in the temple," she says, and pushes free to lead the way.

• ♦ •

Sweat slicks down Iriset's spine as she holds the final thread of their design diamond down with the broken stylus and places the fourth chunk of transformed crystal. The weight draws the threads, and she holds her breath, lips parted, as she moves the stylus to jab its tip atop the crystal, pulling the threads up through the center to knot them there.

The entire diamond flares to life, glowing pure silver.

Iriset laughs and looks up at the numen. It no longer wears Garnet's face, but its own vibrant silver-gray skin and hair and diamond-shard eyes.

"Now what?" she asks.

It points at the altar. "Look."

Iriset, in only her split linen shirt and loincloth, having discarded robe, trousers, and boots to revert back to her prodigal barbarian Silk self, carefully picks her way on her toes to the altar, avoiding the many silver threads of force. At the altar, she simply... climbs atop.

She lies down, spreading her arms with her palms flat to either side of her face, cheek pressed to the warm, polished granite.

The numen hops into the air and hovers there, slipping along currents of force to float over her. It mirrors her pose from an arm's length above. Its hair spills down around its face like a pretty fountain. The strands tickle Iriset's shoulders.

(Imagine the spectacle that soon will greet Lyric, Amaranth, and their body-twins upon entry a few moments later: Iriset spread upon the altar instead of the teeth, half naked and sweating. And the numen hovering over her like a pale salamander god!)

(But first!)

The numen says, "You can look now, without your eyes."

Iriset draws a long breath and looks with her skin and ears, listening to the flow of her blood, the spark of her pulse, the hope heating her cheeks, and the core of her forces pulling everything to a center. She feels her inner design and pushes that awareness through her palms into the altar, through her cheek into the altar, through her thighs and knees and toes and belly, every part of her body that presses to the granite. Like listening to something in the corner of the room, directing attention; that's the only trick of it.

Threads of force wrap the altar, thrumming against the design diamond she and the numen drew, linked, and weighted with crystal.

Their diamond highlights the forces already present, and the complex design that binds the altar, the temple itself, and all the empire. Iriset chases the design, deeper and deeper, realizing how massive the design is: It spreads throughout the empire.

Iriset falls—not physically, but outwardly, through herself and into nothing but a realm of interplaying forces. She's nothing but forces: She senses the spread of the empire's Design. Every obelisk and steeple that lines out from this center pins the threads in place, balancing perfectly east and west, north and south. This is why the empire requires equal frontiers: anything more or less in any direction and this Holy Design in the center will falter, unbalanced. Because the empire is a prison. Built and maintained for one reason: to bind the Moon-Eater.

The whole of it is too complicated to parse or understand, it's only to be glanced at by a mind like hers, human and fettered to flesh. Each layer interconnects, and the design is multidimensional, vivid, and breathing. Through space...and time.

The empire is a being, like Iriset is a being. Not merely design, but alive.

The pulse she's heard throughout the palace complex *is* the breath of a great being bound in the very center of the crater, somehow powering the balanced architecture of the entire empire.

It is said that the Holy Syr unraveled the Moon-Eater, but the truth is that the Moon-Eater was pulled thin enough to be woven into a new design. The design of the empire itself.

The numen reaches down and places its hand flat against her back, between shoulder blades, and gives her a nudge.

As Iriset spins through the threads of force, she meets what fuels it: a give-and-take between the core of forces directly beneath that altar and that high hanging moon.

It's a cycle of rising and falling forces, urged on by neverending flow, and snapped to life constantly, again and again. By the Moon-Eater's Mistress. Amaranth puts her ecstatic spark into this massive machine every day, to rebind and fuel prison—Iriset even called Amaranth an architect once!—and Lyric holds the throne, balancing her efforts with his solid presence against the red moon rock, his blood to bind it.

one claimed with blood and paired with hunger, always binding

There always are two, there have to be: Vertex Seal to bind, and the Moon-Eater's Mistress to energize. Both. (But where are the third and the fourth? There must be, must be, but where? *When?*)

The empire is prison and imprisoned.

Iriset senses the tension holding the Moon-Eater down, and he aches to be free.

Iriset opens her eyes. They're teary and hot. The lashes of her right eye brush the surface of the altar, her left stares through a veil of the numen's silvery hair toward the blue-tiled wall. "He is so angry," she murmurs, awed and angry herself. Growing angrier with every breath.

She came to the palace of the Vertex Seal to free someone. Her father rejected the effort and the numen toyed with it, but this, the Moon-Eater? He wants it.

Maybe this is the real reason she was here all along. To unleash herself and unleash this old red god, too.

He is the god of apostasy, after all.

Just then, the sanctuary doors slide violently open and Lyric méra Esmail runs in, empty-handed. Behind him come Amaranth, Sidoné, Garnet, and Raia mér Omorose. Seal guards pour inside, too, forming an offensive grid around the edge of the sanctuary.

"Stop!" Lyric cries.

Iriset pushes up and swings around in a fluid motion, dizzy, while the numen disperses into light, bursting like a rainbow, and coalesces again outside the design diamond. When it re-forms, it's shaped like itself, bright white-silver-pink, and grinning at the Vertex Seal.

But he has no eyes for it. Lyric stares at Iriset instead. "What are you doing here?"

The airy panic in his voice draws her to her feet. Oh, she's so angry with all the world.

"A Lyric to Bridge the Silence," says the numen, invoking Lyric's ridiculous full given name.

"Iriset," says Raia mér Omorose, trembling. An wraps ans arms around anself.

Her eyes dart to the architect. "Hello, Raia," she says dangerously.

Amaranth steps onto the first force-thread, and the diamond

wavers. Her eyes are on the altar. "This is mine. You should not have come here without me."

"What is going on?" demands Sidoné.

Iriset moves fast, jumping back onto the altar. "Listen," she says, arms flung out and fingers splayed. "I have seen the Moon-Eater—Amaranth, he is alive! He is the furious, pulsing heart of the empire."

"Aharté is the—" begins Lyric, but he stops, staring at his wife, at the frenzy in her sandglass eyes. Their hearts beat desperately together, still—always—connected. He feels her wrath, she feels his dread.

Then the numen is mirané, its hair turned black and waved, its skin the rust-red of the fallen moon. It wears a priest's robe, but silver-pink like Aharté's moon. "This is the Holy Design at work, if you like to think of the world that way—and I know you do," it says. "Here before me is a rising-dominant, a falling-dominant, a flow-dominant, an ecstatic-dominant, and my sunderer! Everything I could need. We are meant to do this, together."

"Do what?" Garnet and Amaranth ask with the same breath.

"Free the Moon-Eater!"

"No." Lyric makes his word a command.

Iriset meets his eyes. "Your Glory, the Moon-Eater is imprisoned here, he is trapped and suffering to keep the empire whole. That is the purpose of Amaranth's ritual, that is the balance between blood and hunger—the binding! It's the answer to the cruel riddle of your throne."

Amaranth sets her fists on her hips. "Imprisoned? You cannot just appear here, with wild theories." Her voice wavers, though, curious and concerned.

"You've felt him, Your Glory," Iriset says seductively. "I know you have, and you have felt him respond to you. Alive."

"Aharté set this throne," Lyric says. "She Who Loves Silence and the Holy Syr created the empire in its glorious form. If what you say has even a shred of truth, it is as Aharté wills. We are hers."

"At what cost?" Iriset snaps.

Garnet shifts his weight and glances at one of the Seal guards who holds a force-dart bow.

"Cost?" asks Lyric. "You know better than any how much I count cost. What would the cost of your choice be?"

Iriset stops. She knows. She's sensed the entirety of the design, and if the design burns, the destruction will ripple throughout everything. Roads, ribbons, buildings, bridges, shaken and shattered, security and glass domes, force-fans and waterways. Everything that relies upon architecture will be vulnerable and might simply break.

What a change that would be. Even her father and Bittor might feel the reverberations backward through time.

"A sundering," says the numen. "Righteous and necessary."

"Brutal," Iriset cries. She can destroy the empire. She *can*. More than rage blossoms in her chest, more than grief: It is her very unholy pride. Because she can, she *must*. Then she says the ancient word the numen taught her. "*Sunderer.*"

With the flick of his finger, Garnet signals the Seal guard, and it loosens the force-dart at her.

Iriset shudders at the impact just below her heart, blinking in surprise.

Lyric cries out.

———— • ♦ • ————

Blood seeps around the flickering dart and Iriset feels an ache, a weight, more than she feels pain. She brings her hands under the dart's tail, cupping it almost gently. She can't breathe; ecstatic force explodes in her skull, sparkling in her vision. Inside her, that thing from before trembles: She is coming apart, the prison is coming apart but remains the same. It is warm, vibrant, glowing.

The numen stills. It has waited a long, long time to free the Moon-Eater. "Do it, sunderer," the numen hisses.

Lyric dashes for Iriset, reaching, while Iriset reaches inside herself, through herself, for that vibrant power—the one that feels like love.

She falls to her knees, and Lyric catches her. The numen puts its arms around them both for the moment of rivation.

The air pops, hollowing out the ears of every human present, and a brilliant explosion of forces pushes everyone back.

The forces shove out and out (and back and through), cracking the dome of the temple. Dark blue tiles fall like heavy rain, and in the silence after, the altar is empty.

The numen, the apostate, and the last Vertex Seal are gone.

40

The craftmask

High within the spreading petal of the woman's hall, Amaranth mé Esmail Her Glory, the Moon-Eater's Mistress, lifts a patch of silk cloth from her vanity.

She found it upon her brother's bed. Alongside the torn mask of Singix Es Sun. Amaranth took all the pieces, for she suspected what the full craftmask might be.

Now, before dawn, with rays of pale light casting silver stars and diamonds onto her floor as it pushes through the latticed windows, she picks up the silk, her heart roaring with anticipation.

If she's right, the empire will be spread at her feet. If she's right, perhaps there is a way forward from yesterday's devastation.

She stills her breathing, forces her body quiet, and stands before the wide mirror between her wardrobes. With hands that do not tremble, she lifts it until the silk falls down her face.

Pressing the edge to her hairline, she smooths the silk against her skin.

Heat floods her cheeks, spiking through her eyes and bones, scouring her lips and nose like sand.

Amaranth hisses softly as the pain fades, and looks up.

In the mirror, her brother's face stares back at her.

The story continues in...

Book TWO of the Moon Heresies

ACKNOWLEDGMENTS

There have been pieces of this book in my head since 1996 when I was caught up in an anti-American protest just outside the US Naval base at Yokosuka, Japan, where I lived with my family. I was fifteen and it was the first time I wondered if maybe America is the bad guy. There have been many other realizations in the years since, and many shifts and complications to my way of thinking about power, imperialism, the world and my place within it, and how to fight for justice. But since that day, I've never looked back.

I have to thank my family first, for encouraging me and fighting with and against me. It all helps. Thank you, Dad, for taking us with you around the world, despite my opinions about militarization and occupation—not that I'd formed them at the time. I have a great imagination, but I have no idea who I'd be if we never moved back to Japan. So it's your fault! Thank you!

A thousand thanks to my agent, Laura Rennert, who continues to champion my work even when I say, "Here's this complicated and probably unmarketable idea I don't know if I can pull off."

Thanks to the whole team at Orbit for a great experience as we work together on this book. Your welcome has been overwhelming. Especially thanks to Angelica Chong, my editor, for pushing me to find better ways to tell the story (any lag in pacing is a place I didn't listen to her). Thanks for gently and firmly suggesting we needed to cut forty thousand words but also asking for more sex. Every time I go through the manuscript I'm impressed with your insight.

Thank you, Alys, Dhonielle, Zoraida, and Natalie, for New Orleans and the Wolfpack and Sailor Moon cocktails and telling it like it is and letting me disagree with you. I wrote the hottest scene in this book while you were all there, working and casually talking about careers and eye cream as I was trying not to blush.

Thank you, Justina, for your early read, when you said, "This one next. This one! But first fix this list of things."

Thank you, Tara Hudson, for letting me ramble to you about this book on a long walk years and years ago, and for acting like I made sense. I hope you like it!

Thank you, Natalie, love of my life, who was there with me that day in 1996 and has shared all my fights for thirty years.

extras

orbit

meet the author

Natalie C. Parker

TESSA GRATTON is the *New York Times* bestselling author of adult and YA SFF novels and short stories that have been translated into twenty-two languages; two have been nominated for the Otherwise Award and several have been Junior Library Guild Selections. Though she has lived all over the world, she currently resides at the edge of the Kansas prairie with her wife.

Find out more about Tessa Gratton and other Orbit authors by registering for the free monthly newsletter at orbitbooks.net.

if you enjoyed
THE MERCY MAKERS
look out for
SIX WILD CROWNS
Queens of Elben: Book One
by
Holly Race

From a major new voice in epic fantasy, Six Wild Crowns *is a breathtaking epic fantasy of dragons, courtly intrigue, sapphic yearning, and the wives of Henry VIII as you've never seen them before.*

Tradition demands that the king of Elben must marry six queens and magically bind each of them to one of the island's palaces or the kingdom will fall.

Clever, ambitious Boleyn is determined to be her beloved Henry's favorite queen. She relishes the games at court and the political rivalries with his other wives. And if she must incite a war to win Henry over? So be it.

extras

Seymour is her opposite: a reluctant queen, originally sent to court as spy and assassin but now trapped in a loveless marriage.

But when she and Boleyn become the unlikeliest of things—friends and allies—the balance of power begins to shift. Together they discover an ancient, rotting magic at Elben's heart—magic that their king will do anything to protect. Now the only hope of survival rests on Boleyn and Seymour uniting all the rival queens... before Henry can stop them.

CHAPTER ONE

Boleyn

Her wedding dress is the colour of the massacre of Pilvreen. A scarlet so vivid it had to be dyed three times in the spice of the Wyrtang tree, imported all the way from the distant land of Avahuc. A red so deep it must be stored in the petals of the Thefor flower, lest its vermillion fade. The fabric still smells of the blossom now, ambrosial, like a fine wine.

She had the seamstresses cut the bodice low on the shoulders, so it looks as though it could be pulled down her frame with one strong tug. The tailors avoided each other's gaze as they pinned the silk and measured the trim, but she didn't care. She is determined to make the most of her long neck and the dips above her clavicles, the places the king likes to kiss when they're alone and, sometimes, scandalously, when they're not.

They tried to fleece her on the train. "I want it to flow down the aisle," she had told the seamstress. The seamstress claimed she had measured the length of High Hall's sanctuary, and presented her with a receipt for thirty yards of velvet, but she knew, as soon as she saw that figure, that the woman had guessed at the length. That, or she was deliberately disobeying her. She had measured it herself, after the king proposed. The Royal Sanctuary is forty yards long, so she made the seamstress buy an extra twenty. Let the train flow out of the door, so they have to keep it open. So anyone passing by can see the two of them, and see how much the king loves her.

Even here, in the queen's chambers of the largest building in Elben, the train can barely be contained. Elben's monarchs are always married at High Hall – the one palace in the kingdom that is the king's alone, unshared with any of his consorts. She has been here a handful of times, and even then she was only permitted in the lower levels – the halls and galleries reserved for lesser nobility. To be here, on the third level, to now have her own wing of the palace, is a sign of how very far she has climbed.

Her sister fusses around her hair.

"Boleyn," she says, "You must have it up. I'll fetch my maid – she can braid it very beautifully."

"No."

"It's not right to keep it down."

"I said no, Mary."

Henry loves her hair loose. It reminds him of that first hunt, when her hood snagged in a branch and was torn off, and she kept riding anyway. The hunt where she caught not just the finest stag on her father's estate, but also the king's eye.

Mary chews her lip but relents, stepping back to let Boleyn's maid finish brushing the dark locks. The girl fetches a bottle of oil and rubs a little on her fingers before smoothing them over Boleyn's hair, paying particular attention to the ends. The smell fills the chamber – marjoram and something warmer – clove, perhaps. Sweet with a sting. The scents seep into the ancient beams that arch over her, carved with whorled figurines and roses. They even flavour the fire.

She thinks: this is the smell of my wedding day. I will remember this scent for the rest of my life. Suddenly, Boleyn feels as though she can't breathe. The room is stuffy, too full of bodies.

extras

"Make them all leave," she tells Mary, and a moment later the maids fussing around her train and polishing the coronet are shepherded out. Boleyn goes to the window and inhales the draught. From here she can see the wild gardens and fishing lakes of High Hall and, beyond them, the distant Holtwode that blankets most of Boleyn's future territory. She cannot spy the coast, or the towers of Brynd, but if she looks hard enough she thinks she sees, on the horizon, the bruising flicker of the bordweal: the god-given cocoon that protects the island from its enemies. Her chest loosens. She is going to be part of that cocoon. Part of Elben's saviour, part of its legacy.

Mary returns, gentler.

"Don't be nervous," she says. "The king adores you."

"Of course he does."

Mary tugs Boleyn's hair. "Shall I let George and the others in?"

"No. Let it be just us, for a moment longer."

"All right, Your Majesty."

"*Berevia, mun ceripucun.*"

Thank you, my pretty maid. The allusion to the Capetian queen's nickname for the sisters when they served under her makes Mary laugh. They both used to bridle at the pejorative implied in *maid*, for *pucun* can mean both *virgin* and *servant*.

Mary leans over Boleyn, so her head is resting on her sister's, and they stare into Boleyn's mirror together. Two pale faces stare back — one full-cheeked and framed with gold; the other all shadows. One all honeysuckle sweetness; the other cedar wood and smoke.

Boleyn runs her hands over the crystals on her bodice, each one worth more than her entire dowry would have been had she married a man who required one. Silently, Mary fetches the coronet from its pillow and settles it on her head. It's heavy for such a slender object, but Boleyn's dark hair offsets the silver. Boleyn watches her sister, dressed in her widow's black, in the mirror, and even though Boleyn is so, so happy and so, so in love, a sadness creeps across her. Mary has been her companion since childhood. The sun to her moon. Soon Boleyn will be swept up in her royal duties, and

extras

no matter how much favour she bestows upon Mary and her children, a growing distance is inevitable.

"Well, I suppose I'll never be as beautiful as Queen Howard," Boleyn says to fill the void.

"You don't need to be," Mary replies, smoothing the hair that has rucked up beneath the coronet.

Mary's right. Boleyn has her hair, her neck, and her mind, and Henry fell in love with all three. The rest of her – thin lips, thin body, skin that never seems to hold any colour – will never be considered beautiful on this island. But she doesn't need to be the most beautiful Queen to hold the king's attention. Haven't the last few months proved that?

A servant peers round the door. "My lady, it's nearly time."

"Are the ambassadors waiting?"

"They are all here."

"Let them come in."

The servant opens the door fully to reveal a packed antechamber, full of courtiers who have travelled to the centre of Elben to pay their respects to the newest queen. Mary busies herself with Boleyn's train, pulling and heaving at the fabric to show off its length. Their family is waiting eagerly. Dearest brother George, bouncing on his tiptoes as he talks to his spouses, Rochford and Mark, and their parents, more reserved. Their mother smooths her dress, which is far finer than the gowns she's used to wearing back at home, and their father puts an arm on her waist, muttering reassurances.

Boleyn ignores her family for now, instead paying attention to the five veiled women before her. Each one accompanies a gift – some small and wrapped in finely embroidered silk, and one so large it is carried by four servants. They curtsey in unison. Boleyn could so easily have been one of them. Before her engagement, she matched their rank – the almosts, the good but not the best. The ladies-in-waiting. *In waiting*.

Boleyn has never been good at waiting.

The first lady, dressed in the silver tulle of Queen Howard, offers Boleyn her queen's gift and steps back, her hands coming to rest

extras

over her stomach. The tulle doesn't suit this woman, and the poor thing knows it. She would have been better served in the subtler linen of Queen Parr, whose fashion would flatter this lady's curves. Howard's style is unforgiving.

"Oh, queen to be, I bring you a gift from Queen Howard of the Palace of Plythe. She wishes you great joy in your marriage to our king."

Boleyn has been drilled in the correct reply. "I, Boleyn, soon to be consort of the Castle Brynd, thank Queen Howard for her gift and her wish, and hope to be a proper sister to her hereafter."

The lady-in-waiting curtseys again and Boleyn passes the gift to Mary, who opens it on her behalf. Inside is a lute, with strings made from the vocal cords of the whales that patrol the river below the Palace of Plythe. Boleyn is impressed. Everything she's heard about Queen Howard is that she's an unthinking, flighty woman. The lute is frivolous but far from thoughtless.

The other ladies-in-waiting take their turns to step forward, offer their queen's good wishes and a gift – a book of healing herbs from Queen Parr, the cover made from iridescent dragon leather; a jewel-encrusted headdress from the ailing Queen Blount of the Palace of Hyde; and, in the crate borne by servants, a dragon with a coat of silver from Queen Cleves. No annoying little lap dragon, this, but a guard dragon about the size of a greyhound. Boleyn thanks them all, and reckons she sounds very noble doing so.

Last comes the chosen ambassador of Queen Aragon, the first of Henry's queens, married mere weeks after his ascension to the throne, twenty-four years ago. Aragon dresses all her ladies in heavy fabrics, the kind the Boleyns use as curtains. This lady looks as though she is buckling beneath the weight of her gown. If she'd only stand straight, she would tower over Boleyn, but her shoulders are curved in a constant apology. Boleyn can't get a good look at the face beneath the veil, but when the woman curtseys, one hand resting over the other in her lap, she notices how the pale pink of her fingernails stands out against the tan of her skin. The lady isn't holding a gift.